Praise for New World Monkeys

"An imaginative first novel by Nancy Mauro that's more entertaining than couples' therapy."
    —*New York Times Book Review*

"[A] trippy, hilarious debut."
    —*MORE* magazine

"*New World Monkeys* belongs to a distinct subgenre that we don't see too often anymore: Educated-Women's Lit. . . . Closely resembles the works of Alison Lurie, Diane Johnson, and Alice Adams."
    —Carolyn See, *Washington Post*

"Nancy Mauro's darkly comedic debut novel quickly veers from one eccentric plot twist to another, making for a fascinating and compelling read."
    —Very Short List

"A debut novel that cannily and artfully shows the wild side of human nature. . . . With narration that sounds at times like the work of Zadie Smith, *New World Monkeys* weaves a funny and macabre tale."
    —*Bookpage*

"Debut novelist Mauro perfectly balances humor and soulfulness in this poisonously funny, torchlight eerie, psychologically astute tale of archaic instincts, deviance, and violence. A provocative tale of evolutionary short-circuits and the wildness that flows beneath civilization's flimsy veneer."

—*Booklist* (starred review)

"Unabashedly eccentric . . . fun, funny, and touching—a great summer book."

—*Publishers Weekly* (starred review)

"A onetime advertising executive herself, [Mauro] offers a knowingly damning portrait of Duncan's profession—her delineation of people slipping into a kind of subhuman, pre-rational state is chilling. It's also frequently very funny and strangely moving. . . . A brave and accomplished debut: weird, disturbing, and intensely engaging."

—*Kirkus Reviews* (starred review)

"The language of this book is beautiful, a mix between magical realism and a narrative that focuses on the minutiae of the senses as the characters struggle to come to terms with conflicts and resolutions. . . . There are several stories at play here. Each one is mysterious and magical, awaiting the reader's myriad interpretations."

—MostlyFiction.com

NEW
WORLD
MONKEYS

A NOVEL

NANCY MAURO

THREE RIVERS PRESS

NEW YORK

Copyright © 2009 by Nancy Mauro

All rights reserved.
Published in the United States by Three Rivers Press, an imprint of the
Crown Publishing Group, a division of Random House, Inc., New York.
www.crownpublishing.com

THREE RIVERS PRESS and the Tugboat design are registered trademarks of
Random House, Inc.

Originally published in hardcover in the United States by Shaye Areheart Books,
an imprint of the Crown Publishing Group, a division of Random House, Inc.,
New York, in 2009.

Library of Congress Cataloging-in-Publication Data
Mauro, Nancy, 1973–
New world monkeys : a novel / Nancy Mauro. —1st ed.
1. Married people—Fiction. 2. Roadkill—Fiction. 3. Small cities—Fiction. I. Title.
PS3613.A88322N48 2009
813'.6—dc22   2010277706

ISBN 978-0-307-46142-1

Printed in the United States of America

Design by *Lynne Amft*

The author wishes to acknowledge the support of the Canada Council for the Arts and
the Ontario Arts Council.

Canada Council   Conseil des Arts
for the Arts   du Canada

ONTARIO ARTS COUNCIL
CONSEIL DES ARTS DE L'ONTARIO

10 9 8 7 6 5 4 3 2 1

First Paperback Edition

For my parents,
Rita and Raffaele Mauro

Monkeys are superior to men in this:
when a monkey looks into a mirror, he sees a monkey.

—Malcolm de Chazal

CHAPTER 1

Of the Spine in General

Later, when Duncan teases apart the moments before the accident, splits the seconds with atomic precision, he'll take some satisfaction in telling Lily that his instincts were good. First, a gearing-down to slow the vehicle without jamming up the brakes. Second, a swerve toward the ditch but not into the ditch. And while there was no way to avoid the blow—the thing had launched itself from the bush—he'd done his best to clip it with the driver's side rather than take it head-on.

What they won't talk about is the way Lily's arm shunted across his chest in an attempt to grab the wheel. To steer their destiny in the space before impact. He'll later recall this moment as something stretched and precipitous over which he was suspended, eggbeater legs and arms akimbo. Where life didn't so much flash before the eyes as shear away to reveal the truth; the reality of the peculiar, three-handed tangle on the steering wheel.

Once the car bucks and rears and comes to a stop, Duncan and Lily look at each other without speaking. This is his cue to take action. Lift his hands and respond to the shape of her face in the darkness, adjust her glasses, assure her they're alive. Of course they're alive, how could they be otherwise? Dying now, barely in their thirties, would just be indulgent. And if there's one thing they've been able to avoid this past handful of years together it's indulgence. Instead Duncan turns away from his wife to look at the intact airbag panels and tells himself that there's nothing he could have done differently. It was an act of animal terror. This thing that charged from the shrubs—and remains lodged under the bumper—came at the vehicle with a suicide will.

Next to him Lily moves. She cracks the passenger door open and the car fills with dim light and a pinging sound. Duncan blinks, knows he has to open his own door, get out there and see exactly what it is that's crushed under the hood. In the snapshot of headlight he'd seen something the approximate size and shape of a snowblower. Only, with a shagged hide. And tusks. His thoughts move to Jurassic possibilities, to woolly and prehistoric museum pieces. It could still be alive. If it survived the ice age, isn't there a chance the thing is still alive? An even better chance that it's angry?

He engages his tongue to say to Lily, *Stay in the car*, the way a husband should. But as he unlaces himself from the belt and turns he finds her seat empty. The passenger door wide open. His pulse starts to natter away in his head like a little hand drum. A shape moves in front of the vehicle. Duncan leans against the wheel, his chest tender from the lash of the belt.

Lily is out there in front of the car, her hand held up to shield against the headlights, her nostrils curled in disgust.

Drive enough highway road and you begin to divide the animal kingdom into new phylum, organizing creatures by the amount of carnage ruptured and splayed as you pass over them. Duncan remembers road trips as a child where his father could identify any beast by the strum it made against the transmission. *That was a blacktail prairie dog,* he'd say as they felt the knuckling against the Ford's muffler. *Born last spring, third in the litter, a tick infestation in the right ear.* In the backseat Duncan would rise to his haunches to verify the receding mounds.

It was his father who would later teach him to drive the stretch of I-94 outside St. Paul. *Duncan,* he'd say, straightening the wheel under the boy's fingers. *On the highway you don't swerve for nothing—you go through.* His father guided that Thunderbird over the entire phylum Chordata with ease, without even a glance at the rearview mirror. He was the sort of man who trusted that the miles of highway ahead would work feather and fleece out from the tread of the tires.

Those were the old days of snarling engines, however, when man was King of the Road and large beasts remained screened behind the trees where they belonged. Who would have believed that the slender leg of a deer could punch a hole through a windshield with the accuracy of a pool cue? That hitting a moose was like plowing into a one-ton stilt-walker?

All of these things, accidents. But the thing that's come at them tonight came with true criminal intent. Against his father's time-honored advice Duncan had swerved and tried to take most of the blow on the driver's side. Later, when Lily is clucking at the Saab, its hood crushed like a boxer's nose, he'll insist they were lucky. *It was trying to grease all three of us,* he'll say.

————————

The beast is quilled hide stretched over a humped spine. Something best used to scrape soot from chimney flues. Its stout hindquarters are wrapped around the tire while its forelegs stretch out from under the grille. The side of skull that hasn't collapsed under the bumper evokes the skull of a pig. But a pig transmogrified, reverted to ancestral proportions, a fossil in loose fur. Each side of its long snout is decorated with a curled fang, and the one good eye, shut in sudden death, has lashes thick as a hairbrush. Duncan can hear the patter of either blood or transmission fluid on the road.

Lily crouches near the tire. "It's a wild boar," she says without a hint of astonishment in her voice. As though collisions with feral swine are common enough along the Hudson.

Duncan looks up and down the country highway. "That's impossible." He watches the nature channel. Knows a bit about which creatures are indigenous to North Africa versus upstate New York.

At his feet his wife is positioned too close to the animal. Should he yank her away by the shoulder? At least place himself between her and the car? What if the thing's rabid? It's a possibility; there's a rim of lather around the snout. Although that might just be the foam of death. But what if it's not dead? What if it rouses itself, untangles that broken body from the all-season radials in order to charge them one last time? You hear about things like this happening. Lily is definitely too close.

But Duncan doesn't move. Doesn't risk putting a hand on her shoulder lest she brush him off.

In this moment, the moment in which he chooses not to act, the creature opens its eye. It's an eye filled with milky fury and as it scrolls down the length of snout, the pig's front quarters start to twitch and heave.

"Christ, Lily. Get the fuck back." He steps out of the high beam himself as the boar lifts a cloven hoof and begins to paw at the road, attempting to free itself from the weight of the vehicle. Lily tips herself back and gets to her feet. She moves quick, comes to stand behind him in the darkness. He can hear her breath like hard flaps.

"Where did it come from?"

And then, the antiphonal response. The animal's mouth falls open, releasing both a pool of fluid Duncan knows has nothing to do with the transmission and a sound that will certainly make him rethink ham. It's the screech of speedway racing, he thinks. The ululation of bush women, the yowl of coyotes tearing into a sack of kittens—

He starts to share this idea with his wife, to repeat these three clever metaphors, but he realizes she's no longer standing behind him.

"Lily?"

The trunk slams and a moment later she reappears in the shaft of headlight holding a tire iron. More specifically, she holds the tire iron out to Duncan.

"Finish him off."

"What?"

"Cell phone's dead. We can't just leave it on the road."

"I can't kill it."

Lily looks between him and the carnage, creating an arc of irony in the air.

Here's Duncan, then. Thirty-two and cobbled together from what he was handed, improved by bottled water and corporate slow pitch, a weekly exfoliating cleanser he stocks in the bathroom cabinet without shame. A strong thatch of hair still. Blue eyes muffled and comfortable like old shirts that will no longer snap on the line and nothing in those eyes that you'd call dispassionate. For these reasons, or despite these reasons, he cannot bring himself to take the tire iron from his wife. There are eight good seconds—he can count them—in which she stands offering it to him and he stands looking north where the highway unfurls like a wet tongue toward the house waiting for them in Osterhagen. And he knows he'll always think that Lily has short-changed him; that given two more seconds, simply nudging the total to ten, he might have made another choice. But the buzzer sounds at eight and when he looks back at the tire iron, Lily herself brings it down with a batter's crack against the base of the animal's skull.

CHAPTER 2

The Spleen

So that he won't spot them quivering, she slides her hands between her thighs the rest of the way. As they pull up alongside the old house Lily uses her sneaker to pin the tire iron to the car mat, the same way one might put a foot to the scruff of a dog who's done a terrible thing. She's never killed a creature before. Nothing with a spinal cord and flesh, an animal that protested. Mercy or not, she thinks, her hands are now the hands of a killer.

At the end of the drive, the house stands like a great, armless thing. Of the few times she's seen the place, its cantilevered gables and over-hanging eaves put her in mind of a bucktoothed mouth. All shingles and brickwork and somewhat too narrow for the sprawl of country lot sur-rounding it. Up above the house the old moon has been chewed down to the rind. Still bright enough, though, to illuminate a yard of boxwood trees, the triple-pitched roof, a crown of spires. Some of the Victorians left along the river valley are tipped with a weathervane cock, or an iron pineapple of welcome. This house, though, is undecorated.

How to walk past the front end of the car without looking? Lily wants to bend and inspect but knows this action will appear incriminating. Dun-can will tell her there's no use in wincing at damage in the moonlight. He's already unlatched her bicycle from the rack and is starting on their bags. Lily's got a few seconds here to sneak a look, make out what she can of the ruined grille. Duncan might be able to act as if his continuous motion will unbend metal, but she needs a moment to agonize freely. She slides along the fender, is about to lean over the hood when she's interrupted by a sound. A noise from above like a wet sheet snapped by two pairs of hands. It focuses her attention away from the vehicle and into the sky. A column of fog roils just over the trees. Edging back toward the passenger door she can make out a stream of bats, backlit over the boxwoods and spit up as if by some centrifugal force. The urge to cover her head is impossible to resist.

A million fucking bats. The words, although hyperbolic, are on her tongue. Probably closer to *hundreds of fucking bats.* Lily shrinks under the cradle of her arms, chin in the bracket of her clavicles, and watches as the colony passes over the trees.

"Do you see it?" she calls back to Duncan. "We've got bats now."

With a preternatural sense of geometry, the swarm flattens itself into a single plane, performing the same wheel-and-swoop maneuvers as a flock of birds. Yes, same as birds. Same as the human wave at a stadium.

"Are you getting this, Duncan?"

But he's pulling their belongings from the backseat. His only reply a groan as each bag hits the ground.

Which is probably just as well. She takes her hands away from her head; really, after a wild boar, the danger posed by bats is negligible. Lily turns back to the house instead, to gaping porch and front door. To the prospect of their summer.

While he was dragging the hog into the ditch, Duncan had an idea. Instead of stopping at the house in Osterhagen, he'd continue north alongside the railroad tracks. Drop Lily off at the side of the road somewhere and then disappear under the peaked ceilings of the central Catskills. Become a mountain man. Eat things he'd caught and skinned himself.

Instead he sorts through a bundle of keys, trying to match the appropriate one to the lock in the door. Lily is still muttering something about bats, about the collective flapping of wings. *And, Jesus, what if they're roosting in the attic?*

The only answer he gives is to get the door open. Get them in, get them on to the next disaster. First is the cloying smell of a sealed house. And then, as he enters the foyer, the sound of the floorboards. Articulated moans and protests. Duncan's hand goes to the wall immediately to the right of the door; his fingers tracing and tapping for the light switch. Behind he hears Lily approach, her nostrils working to identify the fusty odor. Molasses and smoke.

No light switch.

He can see a staircase leading up from the foyer, but the landing is lost in a scrim of darkness. He plays with the idea of driving the car to the front door, angling the headlights to illuminate the entrance. Then remembers the grille, the one headlight sunk and askew in its socket. He starts patting the wall to the left of the door instead. Lily moves past him into the hall. Duncan's beginning to think he should have worked out the details of the summer a bit more. The house had only recently fallen through a latticework of inheritance laws to land on Lily's branch of the genealogical tree. And while they'd made the odd day trip, sometimes with Lily's parents down from Albany, it now seems he hadn't fully considered the snags and realities of the hundred-mile drive he's agreed to undertake on Thursday nights to join her here. And then repeat on Sundays to get home. In the city, where he was always nose to screen, rustic and historic weekends sounded good. He'd envisioned "upstate" as the antioxidant to neutralize the free radical anguish of his office life. Now he wonders, with a certain amount of terror, how he will uphold his end of the bargain.

The lights go on. Lily is down the hall, glasses perched high on her nose. She stands for a moment with her hand on the switch, letting him know she's accomplished what he could not. He looks up to the light source, a chandelier of glass lamps and brackets, sprigs of metal daisies. The hallway itself is like a great paneled throat with lofted ceilings pinched tight by crown moldings so that he has to turn sideways to pass through with their bags.

At the foot of the stairs, Duncan drops their belongings to the floor and stretches his shoulders. It's that wild boar, he thinks. It's the long drive with its ruinous ending that's made him feel peevish and crabbed. It would be simple just to foist the blame on her, repack his bag, and follow the thruway back to the city. But he's got to trust that things will look different in the morning. After all, it was his own steady hand that blocked off a summer of Fridays from his office calendar, believing this division of the week might just be salvation for a man who couldn't decide what he wanted more: to escape his work or to escape his wife.

As if to reassure, Lily comes back down the hall, snapping on lights. Around him, the house flickers and hums.

"It's perfect," he says, touching a blistered spot of wallpaper.

Lily shuts the front door. "You would say that."

After poking through each of the open rooms on the second floor, she chooses the bedroom at the end of the hall. The mattress here is soft enough, although when she sits there's a musical response from its arrangement of coils. Around door frames and moldings, wallpaper flakes away and reveals older designs below. Lily tugs a strip under the dormer window. Several generations of paper come away like onionskins in a light, drywall dust. She blows the powder from her fingers, imagines she could peel right down to the stud boning if she tried.

Duncan carries his bag in and puts it next to the bed. She feels a contraction in her chest as if her ribs are steepling together. The room is too close for the sudden imposition of his body.

"So we set up camp here?" He looks down at her on the mattress. Something odd comes over his face; he's illuminated by perspiration. Lily is embarrassed by her splayed position on the bed and by him above. Hard to believe she once desired only this, only nightfall and him. The weight of this man on top of her. Duncan's eyes are strange, blinking, fixed on her mouth. It annoys her, this uncharacteristic watchfulness. She wants to tell him to wipe his sweaty forehead and quit it. Instead she taps his bag with her sneaker and tries to distract his gaze.

"It's too hot to sleep together."

She has a mustache. His wife. Not just a silkiness above her lip but a tuft of hair that grows thicker toward the corners of her mouth. It seems impossible that he has missed it until now. How much time has passed since they've been up close? Face-to-face? Lily reclines on the bed, an arm span away from him, her head cocked up to the light, and he thinks, the woman I married has a mustache. Where had it come from? Lily's imperfection startles him, makes him feel as though he's found a stranger in the bedroom, a tarantula in the folds of the linen closet. He recoils, but does so on the inside; a trick involving the contraction of the diaphragm and a scratch between the eyebrows to hide astonishment.

But why should he recoil from his wife? When you sleep beside someone, fuck her for years and years (five years, she made him wait until they were married), you have to expect some turn at unpleasantness. Like that sprinkling of pimples on her ass last year. He didn't get spooked. Just told her and she took care of it and eventually they dried up and disappeared. So what is it about her upper lip that fills him with a sudden sense of futility? That she would allow this—or worse, be unaware of it—somehow undercuts all that he admires about Lily. And the fact that he can't bring himself to tell her makes the gap between them all the more evident.

He can't speak. Has he not spent a thousand nights with this woman? With his head docked in her lap and her fingers in his hair? She had a pretty laugh, that Lily, and a soft touch. But now she's watching him with her forehead clinched in irritation and he thinks, surely there was a time when they were happy with each other? A time when the pace of their dealings was characterized by patient energy, a simple matter of telling one another what worked, what had to go? For instance, she used to hold the bathroom door open with one foot while sitting on the toilet. *I got my Beaver Canoe, Duncan!* She'd announce with great relief, *You can relax now.* As if he was worried. Duncan, lying in bed one morning and certainly unworried (but annoyed by her fond appellation), had said, *Lily, don't call it that.* Something about an amphibious rodent paddling its way out from between her thighs. And she had listened because back then they believed in an institute of free exchange.

Now things are different. Now he watches the dreadful motion of the swag above her lip. "You need to find your own room," she says and kicks his bags with one foot.

CHAPTER 3

The Skull as a Whole

The Osterhagen Loaning Library has a hedged cloister for smokers, a fountain spouting water from a cherub's rosebud genitals, and a hobbyist's collection of books on Gothic architecture.

Lily's guts clench as she realizes how thin the reference section is; anything scholarly has been stacked away here in the musty rear of the building, where she can feel a definite spike in barometric pressure. The humidity is like the same rolling sheet they'd left behind in the city. They've only been in Osterhagen twelve hours and already she's picking at seams, bracing herself against a summer of village life. It doesn't augur well. And she hasn't forgotten the terrible thing that charged them in the night. Twelve hours and already a tragedy in their wake.

The village, situated on a neat little rise, looks down over the Hudson and the rail line that skirts the eastern bank. The river is just a mile wide here and tidal, pulsing in an incongruous upstream direction twice a day with the incoming Atlantic. It was the library, though, that had caught Lily's attention on a weekend trip and became emblematic of the change of scenery she believed she needed. The building itself, one of the many in town to be officially recognized by the Dutchess County Historical Society, was structured in the Second Empire style, with its mansard roof and cupola poked through for light. In the lobby, a magnificent corkboard stands like a plumed bird holding the recent history of Osterhagen in its feathers. Here the shelves are lumpy with popular fiction, paperbacks tricked out in sensational frocks. So many well-thumbed covers, dog-ears left in place, it seems, for the convenience of the next reader. Lily lifts her arm and muffles a sneeze in the crook of her elbow. Around her, the worktables are taken up by teenage girls and the elderly, reminding her that this isn't a place for academic research. She longs for the consortium system of the city's academic libraries, the chain of escalators threading together the stacks, the click and chatter of microfiche reels. Here instead, the occasional sound of a throat clearing, a newspaper creased in half.

A reference desk flanks the lobby and is staffed by a pair of librarians tucked together, whispering. Lily thumbs through a rack of paperbacks. Last night they had just left the boar in the ditch. She should tell some- one about it. At the reference desk the two older women appear to have noticed her; Lily feels four eyes skirt over her hair and clothing, the bicycle helmet under her arm. It makes her uneasy, this small-town curiosity. She moves back into the shelter of the stacks.

Uncomfortable thoughts compete for his attention this morning. While Duncan is meant to be hunched over his work in the sunroom—his labor of the past hour—his mind instead drifts to the dark surprises of last night. Shouldn't crushing a wild boar under the front axle of your car warrant some conversation? Some speculation? But they just dragged it to the ditch and that was that. Not another word about it this morning before she left for the library. There's something unsavory about the way thoughts of Lily's upper lip mingle with the image of her bringing the tire iron down across the animal's skull. Her speed and accuracy are troublesome, he thinks. Unmentionable. What he should do is call a park ranger, or a guy with a truck, but of course there's no number handy. As for the grille of the Saab, well, he doesn't want to think about it. He can't even bring himself to go out and have a look. The car was brand-new. Brand-newish; a hand-me- down from Lily's parents. The day her father gave it over, Duncan watched him stroke the fender as though it were a mistress he was being made to abandon. The man was going to go ape-shit when he found out. Duncan might as well have been discovered giving his mother-in-law a good down-field punt.

In the sunroom, he leans back from the table that serves as his desk and rearranges the office supplies he's pilfered from the agency: thesaurus and lamp, a writer's stash of notepads and rollerball pens. He twists paper clips into elaborate calipers. This business with Lily, the tire iron and the mustache—it's like she's launching a personal assault against him. He has avoided her Institute wine and cheese parties, those interminable sessions of intellectual parlance on Museum Mile. He hasn't seen any of her colleagues lately, but this mustache business can't be something all the Ph.D. students are doing? All the female historians? This is Lily letting herself go. This morning she's getting ready to cycle to the library and she's telling Duncan something about the garbage bin smelling of wet dog and he's thinking, what the fuck is that growing around your lip? But he doesn't ask, doesn't give voice to his concern. He lets her ride off like a granola lesbian instead.

Duncan stares at the desk lamp and thinks, okay, she *was* raised by Catholics. But they're the colonizing kind, the crusading sort. The type to pay attention to the details of aesthetics. And her mother was so elegant, bashing those tennis balls around the clay court last month. All that keen upper-arm strength.

He scribbles some clotted ink from the tip of a pen. This is no time to be brained by pigs and whiskers. He's meant to stay focused on damage control this morning. His latest assignment is to write his way out of some-one else's flub. His boss at the agency, Hawke, was axed last month, leaving Duncan the senior man in a creative department that's keeling starboard.

The reason for Hawke getting the chop was officially unclear, but widely regarded as an accumulation of strikes against him: a salary that had reached its zenith, a squabble with the suits, the internal realignment of that classic advertising iron triangle, CEO, CCO, CFO. *Adweek* gave it a square inch of editorial space, the agency citing "creative differences." Hawke, with uncharacteristic prudence, declined to comment.

But the browbeaten knew the truth. A sudden death was never entirely inscrutable but usually deserved. Of course the probationers quaked—*Am I next?*—more mantra than question. Still, the day after lynching day, the creative department rang with fibrous excitement disguised as commiseration. Art directors and copywriters emerged from their Quonset huts to sniff the wreckage, to rub flanks against cubicle partitions, scratch at heads that were flattened from years of flagellation with rolled newspapers. If the terror of dismissal was pure, then the relief of spotting someone else's boxed articles in the hallway was exhilarating.

These were his people. And when among them, Duncan refused to lampoon. *Satire is dead,* he told Lily once while she sat in his office and compared the scattered industry of his coworkers to the roaches of the Apocalypse.

You mean metaphor is dead, she'd said.

Sure, sometimes he spots it; the twigging antennae, the rush to dark corners when the Brass drops by to check the progress of the latest Hamburger Helper commercial. He sees it in the resilient shell of an art director who must, without committing a felonious act with a letter opener, explain to the client why the Hamburger Helper Hand cannot bend down its gloved fingers to create a hang-loose sign. *It's logistically impossible to do that with only four fingers.* Sure, Duncan understands the capacity for parody, but he resists sharing this with Lily. Instead he tells her, in a voice that's not entirely free of self-pitying inflection, *You try spending your days creating commercials that most people want to avoid.*

The thing with Hawke was a grand gesture. Forget the firing of the proletariat, the recession-time dismissal of coffee-fetchers, the pink slipping of senior creatives whose work hadn't placed high enough at Cannes to justify their bar tab at the beachfront award ceremony. This thing with

Hawke was big. It was the fragging of the chief himself, the executive creative director. And it was a reminder from above that advertising was still commerce before it was art.

To his Downstairs people, those in the department, those still on payroll now that the desire for blood had been slaked, the truth was un-contestable. The last project Hawke had his hands on went yellow-belly up. The campaign idea for the generic-looking denim jean company, Stand and Be Counted, was a trap from the beginning. The product had no cult appeal. The jeans were designed without back pocket embroidery, dis-tressed indigo wash, or burnished copper riveting. They were made cheaply in Filipino sweatshops and the modest price tag ensured no starlet (thong panties splaying ass cheeks and looping high over a low-rider waistband) was ever photographed wearing them. They were flare-legged denim with an interesting name but little else to recommend them.

In short, they were perfect. A hungry sculptor's chunk of Beijing White. It was a pip in Duncan's mouth, something rolled between the tongue and teeth. The right solution would be like giving the Man in the Hathaway Shirt his eye patch. Hawke had taken the project for himself, waved back offers of help. Duncan understood; to make something where there was nothing—create a desire within a vacuum of space—this was the kind of thing you jerked off to alone.

"We're taking a collection." Leetower, one of the young art direc-tors, held up a paper coffee filter full of coins. "Hawke's severance. He's marching toward massacre, friend."

"Make it a fifty-fifty draw and I'm in." Duncan felt his pockets for change.

"They were bringing in his lunch and I smelled patchouli, Duncan. I saw a Gibson Hummingbird leaning up against his desk."

"Well, even Rome fell."

"You know what this means?" Leetower's left eye was twitching. "He's using hippies in the ads. Beatniks."

"What have you seen?"

"Kooch snuck in while he was in the can. It's worse than we imagined. Tie-dye, paisley headbands. Dylan before electric. Hawke's synthesizing lysergic acid diethylamide in there."

"How's this all connect to flared jeans?" Duncan asked. "Because hippies wore them?"

"In one of his scripts he has fifty models in bell-bottoms cramming into a VW bus."

Duncan shook his head. "Retro's been played out."

"Residual trails, brother. What is he, like forty?"

This wasn't cruelty, just the dialect of the industry. Duncan couldn't despise Hawke; the man had given him his first job. But as he shut his own office door he understood there was an inherent pleasure in watching a colleague misstep, a gentle perversity in nudging that colleague toward his own demise.

In the library cloisters, Lily walks in on the two women from the reference desk as they ravage a chicken carcass with a plastic fork and knife. They look up, startled and feline. On their cheeks, petals of grease.

"You're new." One of the women, a ginger tabby, lifts her fork in greeting. "We noticed you right away."

Lily nods, pushes a cigarette between her lips in place of a smile. She holds fast to the belief that a smile should not necessarily require one in return. This is her mother's influence, she knows. Lily can count the number of times she's seen the woman twist the corners of her lips from their usual flat line.

"Yes," she says. "Up from the city."

"We know. You've opened Oster Haus for the summer." Ginger's companion, a cinder-haired Persian, toggles at a drumstick until it gives a small sigh and comes loose from the body. "Would you like some roast chicken?"

Lily shakes her head. She has to keep a cringe from snaking out between her shoulder blades. She looks at the cigarette smoldering in the fork of her fingers and realizes it's been ages since she took any pleasure in food.

"You're suffering from the heat, aren't you?" Persian watches her over the drumstick. "You'll have to forgive us, we've come out of a wet and backward season. Supposed to be the muggiest June the county's seen in years."

Ginger sighs and forks up a load of coleslaw. "Humidity is just the start of our sorrows. It feels to me that we're going to have some trouble with tent caterpillars this year. Probably get a bad run of deer ticks on the golf course."

Persian jars a thumb at her colleague. "A prognosticator."

"It's a difficult burden, this foresight," Ginger agrees, unruffled. "I'll tell you this, keep an eye on the species of mushrooms you collect around Oster Haus."

"She's hardly going to collect mushrooms. Young people aren't interested in that." Persian untucks her napkin bib and wipes at her chin. "Mind you, if you like history, there's plenty around that house."

Lily shrugs. "Like any old place, I guess."

"Most of it's uncheery, though."

"Well, the house just came over to our side recently."

"Yes, but there was all that bad business years ago," the old woman continues. "With the housekeeper."

"No, it was the nursemaid." Ginger leans in conspiratorially. "Seems we had our very own Lindbergh baby—before the Lindberghs did."

"Who would that have been? Your great-grandfather?"

Finally, Lily thinks. The sweet spot of the interview. "It was my grandfather," she says. Like everything else sprouting from her Teutonic ancestry, she believes the story of her grandfather's abduction by the nanny evolved beyond family folklore just to serve as a cautionary tale.

"But it was hardly tragic," she adds. "They found him the next day."

"Of course they did." Ginger nods at her. "Otherwise, you wouldn't be standing here, would you?"

Thankfully the cigarette is down to a glinting stub. Lily takes the opportunity to move away from the women, to exhale and extinguish the ember underfoot. She doesn't like this turn to familiarity. Or the conjecturing that follows. Once the conversation loses its historical quality it begins to feel speculative about her own life. A comment on bloodline, the errors of the father that are repeated by the son—this sort of transparency, it's just not in her nature.

Persian catches her withdrawal. "Please don't think we're gloomy." She gives Lily a gray and brittle smile of patience. "But these stories never seem to stay buried long."

CHAPTER 4

Plasma or Liquor *Sanguinis*

Oster Haus is a papery old bone, either too frail or too forsaken to rig with air-conditioning, and by the second morning of their stay the heat inside the plastered walls has accumulated. Once Lily leaves for the library Duncan moves from room to room, drawing drapes against sunshine. The parlor, the sunroom, the smoking room, each of extravagant size, but humbled now by the osteoporosis of architecture. Floors sag and fuss underfoot, throwing up the smell of mildew and potatoes. The house had returned to his wife's family a few years earlier, dogged and gamboling, sliding sideways into their lives after the death of a Floridian uncle left Lily's parents holding the deed. The structure itself, primed for torching, dilapidated beyond its Queen Anne elegance, stands in Dutchess County, six miles south of Tivoli. It's a historical home (attested to by the bronze plaque at the front door), with three fireplaces and knob and tube wiring. A place lonely for visitors and, thus far, unvisited by fire.

Duncan might be considered an impostor here, gaining admittance to the family seat through the lax caste system of the contemporary North American marriage. But according to his schedule, he's no more than a weekend guest at the historical Oster Haus in the ostentatiously named town of Osterhagen. So he says nothing of the neglect that lurks around him. How chimney flues and dumbwaiter shafts rattle, unprovoked.

The house sits in a corner pocket of grass surrounded by a tidy barley acreage that's harvested by the town each fall. The land falls short of the river by half a mile and in exchange for the annual reaping and regular maintenance, partial ownership of it had been ceded over to the county years ago. *It's just a bottom-feeder crop,* the woman from the Historical Society told him over the phone. *Animal feed, I think.* There was trepidation in her voice, a wariness that made Duncan feel as though he and Lily had agreed to foster a particularly troubled ward of the state for the summer.

Still, there was a rustic pleasure in the idea of residing close to a crop of anything and for the first time in ages he could conjure an image of himself outside the office. His weekend self, strolling in ratty wool sweaters and gumboots, a pointer dog at heel, a fragrant pipe snug in his mouth. His serious demeanor would win him the respectful nod and quiet acceptance of the locals. The mornings, Duncan envisioned as a return to the first and happiest years of his marriage when he and Lily would remain unreachable until noon, crowded together in bed using the ballpoint pen meant for crosswords to initial and claim various sections of one another's bodies. The afternoons, then, would be turned over to work. He'd take long rambles with the dog or trace the river by kayak, contemplating the new television campaign that would make Stand and Be Counted—and by extension, himself—a true contender.

If there was one thing he'd learned from his decade in the industry, it was that the creative process was trying. Fraught with real agony. But there was also tremendous satisfaction in scoring the arc of a concept, capturing his own thoughts in flight and scrutinizing their shape. He would hold the entire ball of it in his head so that when he sat down at the typewriter he'd just be left with the enjoyable business of translating it to paper. (There was a typewriter in this fantasy, the tactile pleasure of keys and carriage.) In the house Lily, who had yet to take a summer off for vacationing, would pour him coffee from an ancient percolator and perch on the arm of his chair. Carefully pluck brambles from his sweater while he worked out concepts. What he wanted was an idea with legs. Something that would pinch the nostrils of his career and blow lustily down its dry throat.

Although, in reframing this fantasy now, he'd definitely scratch the typewriter prop. It was a contrivance of the profession that had been done to death. Also, he'd have to rethink Lily. Even in fantasy it was a stretch to have her picking brambles from his sweater.

The dog, in any case, would curl up by the fire.

In truth Duncan understood early on this dream would live and die only in his imagination. At ninety degrees it's hardly the season for wool and rubber. Also the taste of pipe tobacco makes him gag, and those long-legged, golden ideas have yet to materialize. Lily is here, however. Initially her thought was to come up alone. It has not escaped his attention that the one summer she's decided to spend away from the city is also the one she planned on spending without him.

Still, the estate is a picture and, as Duncan scans the fringe of butterscotch ripple from the kitchen window, he realizes he hasn't been this close to nature in years. There's a settled peace to an agricultural lifestyle that doesn't exist in his corporate world. It would be good to work with the hands instead of the head. Imagine if the day was just a matter of gassing up the swather and driving her in neat runnels across the field. In an agrarian life a man is at the mercy of only one thing: weather. In cities people criticize you for being mediocre or alcoholic, undecorated or on a losing streak. But who would dare criticize a man for submitting to the hand of fate when he toiled against epic wind funnels and prairie fires and flash floods? Who would expect grand acts from a man who was busy sump-pumping his field?

Lily decided to spend the summer in Osterhagen in order to end the hunting and gathering and give flesh to her dissertation. Really, she should be traveling by now. Her adviser at the university had recommended she spend at least a year tracking her topic from Western Europe to the Middle East. But she doesn't have the spirit for that kind of enterprise at the moment. For one summer it would be enough just to look up from the garble of French and German texts and lantern slides and not see another Peruvian sweater or batik blouse or scarf-looped neck from the Institute rising over her. Lily, herself now trapped for a third year in the impact of the pointed arch in Gothic architecture, needs one summer without the hovering, waxen faces of academics, their heads evolved beyond the need for a body. Somewhere along the way, all doctoral students acquire the pallor of sour milk, a twitch and eccentricity proportionate to the obscurity of their academic program. Just last week she watched a Cambodian student of eleventh-century Hispano-Moresque ivory carvings pound the shit out of a vending machine. She doesn't fully understand this tendency toward becoming curious and consumed. Though the university *is* flypaper for the susceptible mind. Full of String theorists and Bolsheviks and AM radio prophets obsessing over the hypothetical stretch effect of black holes on the human body. Not the danger of black holes. But the theory of danger. She's seen it in her own dissertation adviser, that gleam of madness when the woman's lectures turn to Byzantine iconography.

In the Osterhagen library Lily stands among the popular fiction thinking she has spanked the broadside of enough vending machines to know that at some point educational institutes are irrelevant to her own life. Who's taking out the garbage, who's signing the doorman's Christmas check—these are the basic requisites of man that need to be sorted first.

She passes under the library's cupola roof and notices where the flux of seasons has stained the joints of the domed structure. Would she have made a better engineer than historian? She could take a parallax view of the situation: get the cathedral standing, after that you can make it beautiful. But at a time when she was searching for a direction to give her life, the innovation of the pointed arch popped something open inside her. Like a tracheotomy with the barrel of a Bic pen. In builder's terms, the tension of a pointed arch allowed for taller windows and doorways, less wall, more light to enter the church—it was bullshit what people associated with Gothic, it was really a period of great light, the piercing of dark and brooding structures.

But beyond this? The art of it? Lately it feels that critical analysis is a luxury. First man gets water and food and shelter. Only then does he remember he has no clue how he got here. He starts asking existential questions that'll never get answered. And it frightens Lily to think that she just doesn't care.

By late afternoon the house pushes him outdoors away from work and onto the buffer of seed lawn. With the lacing of modern irrigation systems, the land has been divided and subdivided away from the river so that a neighboring field of stubble separates the property from the Amtrak line and the banks of the Hudson. Behind the house a vegetable patch has grown fallow but holds the lapping barley at bay.

Duncan stands on the lawn and reaches for a fist of the grain that has shot chest high. He gives it a tug and feels the resistance of the ground sucking back on the roots. That's the tenacity of the soil, he thinks, impressed by the industry of the land. Yes, it would be much easier to back machinery out of a barn than to try capturing the nuances of flare-legged denim. If only his job were a matter of baling a windrow of hay or haggling over the price of feed. He takes his phone out of his pocket and dials Leetower.

"I'm staring at amber waves of grain," he tells the art director.

"I'm staring at a dead midget."

"You mean dead dwarf. Not funny."

"Bad news, Duncan. One of the Laundry Elves is dead. The Tide shoot is cancelled."

"What?"

"Cardiac arrest. Apparently midgets don't live that long. Their hearts have to work too hard—like Great Danes."

"One of the dwarves died?"

"You'd probably get seven years out of a Great Dane. Which is like, what, forty-nine human years?" Leetower sighs heavily. "We got fleeced on the midget, Duncan."

"I can't believe this. Which one?"

"The one in the green velvet suit."

"Fuck, I loved that guy." Duncan skims his hand along the awn of the grain.

"How's the Kiss of Death campaign coming?"

"Great. I'm frenching it into submission."

"Sorry, man. See you Monday."

Duncan walks away from the cultivated field, his pastoral fantasy suddenly bruised, unsteady. He had cast the three original Laundry Elves himself six years ago for his award-winning Tide Laundry Capsule launch. Dwarves as allegorical representations of the concentrated power of detergent capsules. He drew from the childhood fable of the shoemaker. From *Snap, Crackle,* and *Pop.* Laundry Elves became the tumbling, frolicking icons of laundry detergent in North American households. Duncan had handpicked the men from the Ukraine State Circus School and saved them from a life of post-communist oppression. It was true he'd been moved off the account—the junior team needed a shot at flexing their talent—but he still felt personally involved.

Duncan moves back toward the rear of the house. The garden is a patch of pebbles and dust screened from the neighboring property on the east by a rotting hedge. What he's looking for out here is a little orderly distraction. A gentleman's garden he can plow and harrow. He stands with his hands in the pockets of his shorts, and surveys the garden. What'll he need to round his weekends? A shovel or spade, some fifty feet of hose, a bag of fertilizer. And something hardy to plant. Pumpkins and squash, masculine gourds, potatoes he can persuade from the ground. There's got to be enough summer left for a tuberous root. It would be nice to move from denim to soil now and then. Yes, he thinks. It's time to *make* something. He decides to buy a shovel.

CHAPTER 5

Of the Hand

The old library cats circle and pounce while Lily is in midflight through the lobby. "We caught you," Ginger says, creeping around the side of the bulletin board. Though the old floorboards have yawned apart over the years like a wide-toothed comb, they are deceptively silent under the woman's feet. *The better to startle you with,* Lily thinks.

"I told you she hadn't left." Persian blows aggressively into a tissue and then wipes at her nostrils. "It's only five now."

Lily backs up against the great corkboard. There's a flutter of postings, the rattle of thumbtacks in a tin.

"Will you come to the meeting tomorrow?" Ginger is breathless, shuffles a stack of paper from one arm to the other. "It's more a gathering for Skinner, really. Cheer the old man up."

Lily presses her bike helmet to her chest. "Skinner?"

"Truth is he brought it all on himself." Persian's voice is taut with recrimination. "You should have seen the way he spoiled that thing."

"He's a bachelor. We all have to make allowances." Ginger hands Lily a sheet of paper from her stack. "The Sovereign belongs to him."

In Lily's hand is a flyer emblazoned with a photo of the same feral hog she and Duncan killed less than forty-eight hours ago. Accompanying it is a plea to local residents: *Help Us Find Our Sovereign of the Deep Wood.*

"It's been gone over a week now. Skinner found the latch snapped right off his fence."

Persian shakes her head. "I never agreed with feeding an animal off the kitchen table."

"He's raised that thing since it was a piglet. Pets are like family."

Lily can hear the polite gap in their commentary as they turn to her for input. But she finds herself staggering and inarticulate under the weight of this information.

"A wild boar?"

"Wild?" Persian sneers. "Better looked after than most kids in the county."

Is the twitch in her cheek an illusory spasm? The wagging of her spotted conscience? Lily dumps the bike helmet over her head, attempts to disguise the bead-and-reel pattern of sweat collecting along her hairline.

"You'll come tomorrow at seven, then?" Ginger gets ready to press another leaflet on her. "We'll have refreshments."

Lily can feel the first trickle of perspiration sliding down her temple. "Where is it?" she hears herself ask.

"We'll be right here."

"And you might bring your husband." Persian sighs. "Save two old ladies from rolling the Welcome Wagon out to Oster Haus."

This is how it happens, Lily thinks with a foundering heart. With one sentence, one grainy photograph, suddenly the pig is hapless, domestic. Beloved.

Lily comes home that afternoon with news that they have killed the town mascot. She drops the flyer on his desk, a picture of the wild boar in better days (a silk capelet draped over the shoulder haunches) and the words *Sovereign of the Deep Wood* in Franklin Gothic font.

"Jesus," Duncan says. "I hardly recognize it with the cape."

"Did you call anyone?"

"Me?" He touches his chest. "I thought you were going to."

She turns away from him and heads for the door.

Duncan stares after her for a minute before getting up and following her out. He's thinking of the things she doesn't do when she comes home from the library. Wifely tasks she has long since given up performing. Like tossing her book bag aside and calling out, *Honey, let's fuck!* She doesn't do that anymore.

"What kind of shit luck is it to kill a mascot?" Out on the driveway he watches as Lily unlocks the car and slides behind the wheel. "What are you doing?"

"They're obviously looking for it, Duncan." She stares at him for a moment as if focusing her inexplicable anger into the cubic space of his head.

Duncan stands as his wife noses the Saab into the lean-to at the side of the house. He hears the kiss of metal and wood as she buries the ruined front grille against the plywood shell. There's an annoyance gathering in his shoulders that feels like cheap wool against the skin as Lily makes a tight, three-point turn in a car that she never drives. Then he remembers the moment before the collision, her attempt to grab the wheel away, and he thinks, she's just been allowing me to drive it all this time. Something in her expert handling of the vehicle says, *Let's not kid ourselves, the Saab is really mine. Always has been.*

Lily kills the engine. Because of the tight fit, she has to crawl over the gear shift to climb out the passenger side. Duncan briefly entertains the thought of locking her in—if only it were possible—and observing her for a few days, watching as she descends through various states of anger all the way down to remorse and dependence.

Maybe he should try. What's the worst that could happen?

She slams the door and comes to stand at the butt of the vehicle. "I don't understand. You were sitting inside with the phone all day."

He drives his hands into the pockets of his shorts. "And you were at the library." He notices a heavy grease stain across the front of her pants. "That *is* where you were?"

Lily frowns. "Right, the library." She waves a hand as if brushing away a fog of mosquitoes. "Summer school's on. Seems everyone failed the tenth grade last year."

It's probably grease from the bike chain on her pants. Duncan wonders how he's going to get it out, tries to recall the efficacy of baking powder and lemon juice on grease. Maybe if he uses a commercial stain remover before putting it into the wash?

"The day just slipped." He touches his pockets for a cigarette. "Let's leave it at that." First a morning of toil with nothing to show, then the bad news about the Laundry Elf. After that, he just couldn't bring himself to check the car in sunlight. Suspected there might still be gristle and bone in that front grille, the snatch of hackle that rises in anger at the back of the neck.

"Obviously the pig slipped your mind, too." Lily presses a fingertip to her hairline. "They're having a *get-together* for the farmer. Telling them now is out of the question."

"Because they'll think we conspired against the mascot?" He laughs. "Bad for the family name, right?"

Lily slides her eyes across him as though he were on fire. "It was a pet, Duncan. Besides, you're not the one staying here all summer."

He takes a step back. "I assume this means we're not going to be driving?"

"You can leave for the city after dark tomorrow."

Duncan lifts his foot and presses a flip-flop against the back bumper. "We should have gone to town for help the other night."

"Shoulda, woulda."

Is it the mustache that's made her so shrewd? Could that little scrap of hair be controlling her like a second brain?

"I'm just saying, maybe there was a chance."

"Duncan, you smashed its skull in half."

He swallows. "Hey, you're the one who finished him off."

She turns to him now, a surge lifting her to her toes. Like he'd just lashed her with a downed power line. But he knows what she's doing. He pulls back his shoulders, offers military resistance. Lily's attacks are deliberate and heat-seeking and he refuses to shrink beneath them. She is inexorable when it comes to laying blame. When in fact—and it's quite possible, he's starting to believe—she took some pleasure in bashing the shit out of the pig, the Sovereign of the Deep Wood. He wouldn't be surprised. She didn't even flinch, didn't even wait for him to refuse before bringing that tire iron down.

It's her, not me, he understands with a new, mute pleasure. All these years I've been trying to warm my hands over a kettle of cold water.

When she speaks her voice catches the barbed end of a trill. "Who the hell else was going to do it?"

In her bedroom, Lily flattens her cheek against the door. There's a riot going on in her gut, a primal demand that she apologize immediately, that she go to his room and say, *Look, I know that I'm an absolute horror, Duncan. My words are regrettable. I don't know why this is happening. It's cruel and I'm sorry.*

She touches the doorknob. Such an easy moment in theory, one foot in front of the other until she reaches him. To sit on his bed and say these things so that he'll know she's not a complete lunatic. So he'll know that somewhere in there, she's still Lily. Surely they're not the first couple to fight? In fact, they've had words in the past, they know how to apologize to one other. It is simple kindness and humility—an arm around the shoulder, a kiss on the forehead. That's all it would take from her to allow them to go on happily ignoring each other for the rest of the summer.

And then she'll lose her mind. She lets go of the doorknob. Whatever instinct she has to apologize must be snuffed out tonight. Even the deepest apology will just be a veneer. The words she really wants to say are the kind that contain unbearable pathos, that can only be delivered as a pleading whine—*What's gone wrong with us?*

Truth is, even before she became the pig killer, she was missing that lovely quality of vulnerability that might have kept Duncan on her side. Made him sympathetic through her mistakes, those crude blurts and haughty spells of shyness she hasn't been able to shake since girlhood. She steps away from the door, tells her gut to hush. An apology is a statement, but all she has for Duncan is a question. And tonight she's not ready for the answer.

They met shortly after their own century gave itself up to the twenty-first. When they finally began to date, he understood immediately how simple, how desirable it would be to assign their futures the same trajectory. He was a miserable slob, she was clean and smart, her hair glossy. He had contracted scabies. She was everything he considered himself unworthy of, but desired anyway. And in a few months she would be his wife.

She was waiting in arrivals for him and all he could do was unzip her jacket and slide his arms in and around her. It was easy to believe they had been bound this way as children. For the last hour of his flight he'd flexed her around in his mind like a doll with hinged joints. He put Lily through gymnastic trials, dressed her in the silk *ao dai* tunic that he'd brought back for her. Then, just as quickly, he undressed her. He fell to his knees, his mouth open against her beautiful, white thigh. She was so private, so cautious, he had come to believe the only way he would ever know this woman was through the skin of his lips.

It had taken him two hours in Vietnam to realize he was too old and too sober for the month-long Contiki tour he'd signed up for. Lily hadn't wanted to go—the ravaged scrap of land wasn't her thing—but she supported his interest. He was a bit of a war buff and had always admired the resilient country, hankered to write about the slim-hipped race. Duncan thought of Vietnam as the first war of his childhood. Remembered how his father and some of the neighborhood men, other rail workers mostly, could spend hours on the lawn discussing what they'd caught on the news between shifts. He'd told Lily that for reasons rather nostalgic the country had seized his imagination. He had loved this, how free and easy he could be with his thoughts around her. No one else had ever encouraged him to have an interior life, let alone listened attentively to the details. The things he would have gotten whipped for in Minnesota, Lily found artistic and worthy. He could reveal his passions—be run by them from time to time—and she would understand.

In the beginning he thought this was the reason they worked so well together. She was the historian lining up facts, and he was the writer filling the blanks in between. When other women would have crowed at a month-long absence, Lily planted within him the idea of getting an article out of his trip. In the end what had prevented him from doing this was the tour itself, its boozy orientation and the third-world ruts in the road between Hanoi and Saigon. He could barely hold a pen to paper. He excised the ready availability of alcohol and Australian girls in string bikinis from every phone call he made to Lily. While these things provided him with voyeuristic entertainment during the bus ride south, what he really wanted was to be with her, to hear her pretty laugh. Even while he was carousing around Saigon, or riding the waves at China Beach, or vomiting a gasoline stream of rice wine into the Perfume River in Hue, already he was conscious of doing these things for her, of turning experience into stories that might amuse. As he crawled through the historic Cu Chi tunnels, following the tight, sarong-sheathed ass ahead of him, his biggest desire was that when he returned, Lily would still want to be his wife.

In the airport he scratched a red welt on his arm and sunk his head between her neck and shoulder. He stuck some of her hair in his mouth.

"So, what have you learned?" Lily asked.

"I've learned that an overzealous customs agent can change your life in a matter of hours."

"Do you still want to write articles?"

"My notes got napalmed at Immigration. Do you know you're the first person to ever pick me up at JFK?"

"Well then," she pulled back, spread open the palm of his hand, and kissed him there, "it must be love."

CHAPTER 6

Organs of Special Sense: The Tongue

In the morning, Lily discovers she has a mustache. Jesus, she thinks, backing away from the mirror. How long since she had a close-up look? She kicks open the bathroom door to let the shower fog ease out and can hear Duncan plunking away in the kitchen below. Flipping the toilet lid down and taking a seat, she pulls the bath towel around her in a tight swaddle. It's clear there's been a breach of trust, her body has sprouted hair in formal protest, asserting its will through her follicle shafts. How long has it been this way? Lily's heard of bamboo that can grow twenty-four inches a day, of flesh-eating viruses that claim limbs faster than surgeons can cut away the offense. Maybe the mustache also falls into that category of phenomena, she thinks, stroking the lush patch. It feels like pussy willow. Of course, she's had to take the occasional tweezers to her upper lip in the past. And while she can't actually remember the last time that was, how can she not have noticed the dark growth under her nose?

Lily unwinds from the towel and stands looking at her naked body in the mirror, something she hardly does anymore. She can't bear the schism; inside she's scarlet and alkaline, outside she's all ridiculous anatomy. This hand, that thigh. The corrugated flare below the ass. She possesses neither impressive heft nor the enviable ribs and twigs of the half starved. Rather, she floats in between with clicking kneecaps and curves that are nothing more than nods to curves. Buttons sit flat over cleavage. Duncan used to

look at her with an intensity in his cocked eyebrows that was almost fright-
ening. It thrilled her to be watched that way, as though she could light up
everything that was fierce and carnivorous within him. But it's been ages
since he's even strayed a toe to her side of the bed. Can she blame him?
What about her is ravishing, exactly?

Surely he's seen the mustache. He's been in her face and in the house
for days, shuffling around; why hasn't he said anything? Even yesterday,
while she railed on about the dead boar, he just looked at her with complete apathy. Lily takes off her glasses and presses her face against the mirror. She feels her anger over the boar percolating again. He practically
forced her to kill it. She was holding out the tire iron—it was obvious that
someone had to put the squealing horror out of its misery—and he refused to step in, disrupt the flow of his own drama. But wasn't that classic
Duncan? Always floating around the peripheries of emergency. Here was a
man who felt at home in the audience with a megaphone. She's never forgotten how he wanted to write a movie about her parents, *The Missionary
and the Mogul. The Nun and the Nabob.* She had to snuff that project out.
And now here he is again, forcing Lily to play the part of the executioner.

In the mirror she tries spying some Renaissance curve, a Grace perhaps with bundled muscle under rice paper wrappings. Instead she sees the
shallow depth of field, the flat unfolding of the thirteenth century. *Lily,*
her mother would say, *a man wants a feminine woman to bear his children, a
kind hand. A helpmate.* It's not exactly a turn-on, she knows, watching your
wife bludgeon a wild boar to death with a tire iron.

A waft from the kitchen then. She pulls on a T-shirt, pokes her head
through, and sniffs. It's a familiar smell. Bacon. "He's frying bacon," she tells
the churlish face in the mirror. Once the connection is secure in her head,
the odor becomes offensive, triggers a gurgle in her belly, a finger easing
open a hair-clogged drain. He is taunting her. Lily feels a suction reversal,
and leans into the sink. Bile and orange juice tear a path up into her mouth.

She's suddenly glad she didn't apologize last night. And come to think
of it, why not keep the mustache?

He had spent years trying to be like Hawke and then the past month trying to be anything but. Duncan understands the logic behind the man's retro-sixties campaign. Those wide, swinging cuffs carried the misguided optimism and hash-stained freight of the entire counterculture movement. But the hippie was a hack idea, stale, something best dragged into the poor quarters and promptly shot.

What he didn't foresee was that Hawke's departure would leave him the unofficial heir to the creative director's struggling efforts. Duncan waited to be taken aside, to feel the warm breath of the Brass on him: *We think you're the guy to turn this ship around. The one to resurrect dinosaurs.* After all, look at what he'd done for laundry detergent. Until Duncan's repositioning of Tide, the client's strategy read: *Gets Your Whites Whiter.* Until Duncan, strategic planners insisted a product could be both *new* and *improved.* It was his campaign that had moved the needle on laundry detergent. Won him his gold One Show Pencils and earned him an early reputation as the go-to guy. Man to save sinking ships.

But reassurance from the Brass never came. Instead in the weeks that followed Hawke's dismissal he was moved from packaged goods to the seriously listing denim account. And now, after a month of false starts, he still doesn't have a single viable idea to mount and hump and enjoy. As Duncan walks around the garden, he realizes what he's doing wrong. He should be writing what he knows. Let's see: He's got a finger on the pulse of waning marriages. And getting grease stains out of trousers. And facial hair, the female variety. Yes sir, that's his specialty. It's obvious. He should be writing for a woman's journal. *Good Fucking Housekeeping.* That's what the universe is trying to tell him.

Okay, stop it, he tells himself. Just calm the fuck down.

He's come out to the garden this morning to turn a little soil for inspiration. Rationalizes that this past half hour of manual labor in frying-pan heat (really just making gentle surface wounds to freshen the desiccated soil) might in fact help him muscle out a few concepts to bring back to the office tomorrow. He needs a place to start and some serious traction.

Duncan uses a spade to expand the tiny garden plot where he will soon plant his tubers. Sweet potatoes, yams, shallots, sunchokes. He slices into the grass and feels some remorse, like he's scalping the lawn to make room for more garden. He peels away a layer of grass, revealing brown soil below, and sinks his spade into the earth. There's a feeble underground clunk. The spade stops short; he's hit a rock. Duncan bends and loosens it from the loam then shovels it onto the grass; it's the size of a generous fillet of beef and as flat as a skipping stone. He is immediately suspicious— it's too well proportioned to be indigenous. He nudges it with the spade as if it might dance for him or crawl away. The stone has the smooth contour of a beach pebble, a weary thing worn away by tides. He crouches and scrapes off the dirt. Then, turning it over in his hand, he sees someone has carved an inscription across its backside:

T I N K E R ,   1 9 0 2

Duncan drops the stone as if it has spoken to him. The inscription is not crudely rendered, but engraved with a tool. He kneels then and picks up Tinker with both hands. Maybe it's the sky clouding over or the raven settling on the clothesline that makes him turn. He looks at the house.

His wife is missing. Her bicycle is still chained to the porch rail this morning so Duncan can only conclude that she's been swallowed up by the house. Fallen through some soggy flooring, slipped behind a revolving bookshelf.

"Hey, Lily?"

The question goes unanswered through the kitchen, the bathroom, up the staircase and past the open bedroom doors. Her name feels odd in his mouth, fleshy, the pocket of air between the *li* and *ly* catching between his tongue and molars. How long has it been since he's said it out loud? Lily. A name, he realizes, he is not comfortable speaking.

Duncan stands in the hallway. Holding the rock in both hands, he begins to feel both heat and annoyance spreading across his shoulders again. It's part of the fabulous absence of harmony between them. Here he is, chasing her down. The one time he has something to show that might appeal to the historian in her, and she's chosen to disappear.

Yo, bitch?

He doesn't say it out loud, just mutters it in his head, wanting to retard the slow burn of irritation he's experiencing. Although *bitch* is one of those words that rockets easily off the tongue, doesn't get caught in the recesses of his soft palate. Lily is unrelenting, isn't she? Her rejoinders come at him with the velocity of hubcaps whisking off speeding cars. He thinks again how she couldn't give him just one bloody minute to gather his wits and kill the hog himself the other night. Yes, *bitch* seems to fit. And when he hears a shuffling sound from the cedar closet beside him, he wonders if he might have just said it out loud after all.

He opens the closet door and finds her sitting cross-legged in the dark, wearing her usual khakis. Duncan is angry, suddenly filled with the suspicion that she has been hiding in this closet—and every closet in the house—under every stairwell, behind armchairs and drapery folds, waiting to catch the vocalized bits of his thoughts. Lily is a household spy, squirreled away, desperate to catch evidence as unforgivable as *bitch*. She's waiting with restrained pleasure for an excuse to pack up and ride off on her bicycle. To shift the failure of five years onto his shoulders.

She twists her hair like a length of rope and turns her eyes up toward him. The end of her nose is red as if she's been crying. Does she know what he's capable of thinking about her? Duncan's indignation begins to deflate. A quick leaking hiss.

"I found it in the garden," he says, and turns the rock over in his hands.

She reaches out of the closet and takes it. It is an interest piece, a solid thought, an item free of emotional implication, and her reaching for it as simple as the transfer of a relic from one historian to another. Her finger traces the inscription, *Tinker, 1902.* Duncan is about to step back and gently close the door when he sees her touch the floor beside her. They look at each other for a moment. He understands this motion, the invitation in it, and so he bends down, squeezes into the space beside her. Their folded legs touch. Lily leans forward, slips her fingers under the cedar door, and draws it shut.

"What's this remind you of?" she asks in the darkness.

"The crypt," he says. "On Stanton."

Her laugh is a small, involuntary burst.

"We barely got an hour of sunlight in that apartment."

"We were translucent."

"We slept well."

Duncan touches the wooden door, imagines it absorbing the mingled high notes of their laughter, allowing only a bass-heavy grunt to escape into the outside world.

"Are you okay, Lily?"

He feels her leg rest against his. "It's complicated."

"Maybe you should come home."

She doesn't answer. Her knee begins to bob anxiously.

"We can come up on the weekends together."

"I can't—" She stops, swerves. He can hear the smack in her throat as she swallows. "Why don't you stay? For the meeting tonight?"

Duncan breathes sharply, the inhaled current making a slicing sound as it parts into the two lanes of his nostrils. "This accident with the pig, Lily. Let it go."

Her jittering leg falls still. "Duncan, please stay."

———————

"The blown-ball method is ancient history in most places," Skinner says, flicking an errant peppercorn from the tufting of his deviled egg. "What's taken over is those computers that call out the bingo for you."

Duncan nods. He's watching his wife across the room as she attempts to shirk off the pair of old women who've attached themselves like remoras. On the way over tonight, they'd decided it would be best to divide and conquer. To split the obligatory introductions and handshakes as a way of speeding up the evening and minimizing any chance for error.

"Thing's called a random number generator. Ever hear of it?"

Duncan turns back to the old man. He has a red sty in his eye that is visible with certain turns of the head. "You mean, like a lottery machine?"

"Instead of numbers bobbing around in a cage there's this computer that chooses them. Pops them up on a screen so you don't need people to call bingo anymore."

Normally, Duncan would have to probe these Luddite tendencies. But how to be impertinent to an old man whose pig he's killed?

"I guess," he offers weakly, "you still need people for some things."

"Well, it don't matter to me." Skinner's red eye roves over the small crowd gathered in the library reading room. "I'll probably be dead before the thing catches on in Osterhagen." He coughs and spits into his empty glass. Duncan tries not to look.

"You drive over?"

"We walked."

"Walked? You a Jew?"

Duncan arranges his face. "It's just a nice night," he says, as if answering a benign question.

The huddle of river folk surrounding Lily puts Duncan in mind of his family back in St. Paul, an inherently parochial bunch washed soft by the cycle of seasons, planed free of sharp corners, tugged back into place to dry. Here in the country, nature is oversentimentalized. He thinks of the stone he turned up in the garden, the carefully etched headstone for a pet. Or worse, the feral hog festooned with a cape.

Lily is receiving a similar type of attention. He can sense her discomfort at being led between the yard sale collection of chairs, introduced as the rightful heir of Oster Haus when all she often desires is to sail under the radar. He should have headed back to the city an hour ago, but he couldn't just let her come here alone.

"You ever learn to hog-tie, son?"

Duncan shakes his head, notices how Skinner's eye keeps returning to Lily. She's accepting a glass of punch from a man with a thinly knotted ponytail.

"My boy's out at the ranch now, while I'm here. From Poughkeepsie but he knows his way round a boar from when we lived in Augusta. Which was before I gave up hunting. Out on the back trails—behind the power station—is where you'd likely spot them. This was fair sport, so no guns. But we'd take dogs, generally. Two per man—one was a bayer—kind of dog trained to bark a hog up against an embankment or tree or whatever. The other's job was to take nips at it, keep it occupied enough for us guys to come from behind. Once you got practiced enough, you grab up the hind legs and there you go. Hog-tie. When things go right, the pig doesn't even know what hit it."

Must have been in better days, Duncan thinks. Skinner's cheeks are a lace of veins over sunken bones and blown red by the force of a phlegmy and persistent hack. He's a small man, hair shorn down to a quarter inch of silver bristle over the ears. But in these remains, a semblance of structural power, a man brought down to basic mechanics. Down to cable rope and wire.

"Mind you, lost some of my favorite dogs that way," he says. "To the tusks. But like I said, it was fair game. Nowadays the dogs wear those Kevlar vests. You ever eat dog?"

"I don't think so."

"I did. Once when I was serving in Korea. I done some other things at the time too. That your wife?"

Lily has turned and is watching him from across the room, giving him a look that, in a nautical situation, might read *boat in distress*. He nods and says, "Yes, it is."

"Keep your eye on her," Skinner says, shifting over to the food table.

"Though none of 'em are much better than swine, anyway. I went through two myself before I got Sovereign of the Deep Wood. And I've had him longer than both of those put together."

There is a minor incident at the punch bowl, an upset glass of pink liquid that has the old library women clucking and futzing about with napkins. Lily takes advantage of this moment of distraction to move across the room toward him. Duncan watches as she approaches, feels a tricky hit of pride; she really is beautiful. Even more beautiful when cornered and anxious. When she reaches his side she takes his hand as naturally as she once did.

"You're tired, I'll bet," she says with an earnest delivery.

"Early day tomorrow." He squeezes her hand. "You don't mind if we leave early, do you?"

"Of course not." She returns the pressure of his hairy paw.

Duncan smiles wistfully, as if vocation has indentured him to an on-call life forever at odds with social pleasures. To those watching, he and Lily are pleased at the prospect of retiring together, walking home in the moist evening balm. Outside the small ring of truth, they must look like standard issue, a catalog couple with more love than grievance.

Beside them Skinner leafs through a tray of hors d'oeuvres. "Doesn't anyone know I'm a vegetarian?" He peels away bread skins to assess sandwich fillings.

"Let's get out of here," Lily says under her breath. Her hand is still in his, she makes no move to twist free. Duncan looks down at their twined fingers. Why is his pulse coming as a soft, messy thump in the gut? Is it the thought of the long drive back to the city, the empty house waiting to swallow her up?

Skinner backs away from the food tray while folding a deconstructed canapé into his mouth. He comes to stand between Duncan and Lily so that their hands must fall apart out of courtesy. The old man chews with circular intensity.

"My son figures the latch on that fence was busted from the inside, you know." There are bits of crust littering his shirtfront but he makes no move to brush them away. "Busted from the inside means the pig pushed his way out." While he's still anchored between them, the zagging course of the red sty suggests his sights are on a wider audience. Duncan feels a trigger of electricity down the notched rail of his spine. Could the old guy suspect?

"One thing I know," Skinner continues with the plangent, rattling voice of the lung-sick, "is that an animal does not run away when it's treated good."

There's a gentle oscillation among the crowd. Heads turn in the direction of their threesome. Despite his wizened stature, Skinner commands energy from the room. He suddenly pushes past Duncan and Lily as though inspired and weaves between the gathered chairs. "Let me tell you what I told my son. And this concerns anyone who gives a rat's ass about this town."

Slowly, shoulders are squared toward the man. Teaspoon chimes of silver and porcelain are stilled as he stops between two chairs and turns. "I told him, that boar did not run away. He was stolen. There is a thief among us."

Duncan feels his wife's arm press against his but he doesn't dare look at her. Their hands, which moments ago were clutched together, now drag at the end of limp arms. Skinner regards his audience with a left eye that is blue iris and red menace.

"Why steal a pig, hey? My boy asked the same thing—and those who know Emmett know he don't ask what he don't need to know. But the reason is this: there's no ballsier move than to kill a town's pride. You go ahead and rob Wakefield's, you hurt only Wakefield. Maybe a couple of those Japs who run the place in winter. But you steal the Sovereign of the Deep Wood and what do you get?" The orator pauses, measures the radius of his net as it settles over his people.

"You get someone spitting in the face of tradition, is what."

There's something persuasive about this rhetoric, Duncan thinks. Perhaps because the content is so far removed from his own daily concerns. It's the vague yet charismatic monologue of a general inciting his boys to riot. How long has it been since Duncan himself was under any administrative rule? When Hawke was chopped, the rabble-rousing went with him.

"This is the beginning of the ruin of our town," Skinner says. "You don't need me to tell you what comes next, do you?" Scattered about the reading room, concerned Osterhagenians—mostly gray and aged—nod and wait for the visceral call to action.

Lily reaches up and presses two fingers against Duncan's arm. He finally looks at her. Her glasses have slid down her nose, she watches the old man over the frames. He thinks of her proximity in the dark closet, the touch of her leg, those words, *please stay.*

"What do you propose to do about it? If you are called upon to save your town, will you answer?" Skinner cajoles them now, a proper general leading a congress of young men to sure death. Lily's fingers remain on Duncan's arm, not only to form two points of connection between them, he knows, but to separate them from the rest of the room.

He leans into her ear. "Come back with me tonight."

Lily keeps focused on Skinner, doesn't answer.

"You shouldn't be here alone," he tries again.

She turns to look at him then. "Where should I be?"

"The city. The apartment. School."

Her fingers come away from his arm. "No," she says quietly. "Everything is here."

He tries to stay calm under the belting swoops of Skinner's discourse but Lily has shifted away, lowered her head. Mindful of the room's scrutiny he reaches for her, keeping the motion as offhand as possible. "Look at me," he says.

She obeys. Her face is soft if only for the benefit of the crowd.

"You're getting mixed up here."

She stands within his arm, so silent and intense that for a long moment even the old man's harangue is flattened under the pressure of her stare. Then she lifts to her toes and puts her lips to his ear.

"Be mixed up with me." Her voice is an unfamiliar fever. "I'm staying."

Skinner's warbling tenor expands again to fill the entire room, to plant the seeds of reckoning in unsuspecting hearts. Duncan clears his throat, looks away from Lily and finds the old man glaring at him.

"What will you do for your town?" Skinner speaks with enough force to burst a capillary in his clear eye. Pecks of saliva stand out on his chin. "How far will you go when asked?"

Duncan hears a dangerous measure of madness and accountability in this question. Or does the real danger lie in Lily's declaration? She's going to take it standing, he thinks. And now he's left to decide. Just how far is he willing to go?

CHAPTER 7

Pigment

"Brass-on-secretary sex." Leetower crouches by the sofa, his knees making a sound like popped bubble wrap.

"No, that's Brass-on-Filipina-cleaning-staff sex. Look at the shape."

"Kooch is right." Anne bends over the camel-color cushion, scratches at the edge of the stain with a fingernail. "I can see the head of Imelda Marcos in there."

Duncan stands in the doorway to his own office on Monday morning. First thing that irritates him is the sight of the stout junior writer, Kooch, sitting at *his* desk. In *his* swivel chair. He's holding an old framed photo of Lily close to his face.

Duncan's second irritant is the deep maroon heart in the center of the sofa cushion.

"That was not there Thursday."

Anne looks up. "You're back."

"See the shit that happens when you take Fridays off, Duncan?" Kooch cranks the chair horizontally until it complains under his weight.

Anne, a senior account director, flicks an acrylic nail at Leetower's ear and points to the cushion. "Flip it over, houseboy."

Duncan walks in. With his office occupied, he's forced to lean against his desk. He watches Leetower take the cushion by the edges and turn it upside down.

"We've got a dead midget on our hands, Duncan. I heard you heard?" Anne hoists her pot-roast rump on the sofa. "Ravi's starting casting to-morrow."

"We already went through this shit, Anne."

"Six years ago. Surely there are new midgets by now?"

"The best dwarves are from the State Circus School."

"There's no money for Ukrainians, Duncan. Local casting only. Be-sides, you're off the account." Anne stops and looks at Leetower beside her. "Please tell me that's your halitosis."

"I think it's the stain."

"How's Stand and Be Counted coming along?"

"Fine."

"Good." Anne points to Leetower and Kooch. "The boys are on it with you now that Tide's on hold. And in absence of a creative director, may I be the one to remind you, no hippie shit."

"Thanks. Put it in the brief in case we forget."

"Seriously," she says. "Hippies have got to be the biggest sixties cliché, no?"

Leetower and Kooch look at each other and shrug. "We were born in the eighties."

Anne stands up. "Your mothers should have lifted furniture."

Lily is meant to be writing a treatise on the principle of luminosity in Gothic architecture, but is forced to set up shop in a dark carrel between the women's bathroom and a shelf of nonfiction. The window tables have been claimed this afternoon by teenage girls, heads bent to the task of applying varnish to their nails and punching text messages into their cell phones. Private school, Lily thinks, walking past the tables of kilts scrolled up way past regulation.

She sits down in her corner by the ladies' and thinks that to get through this dissertation, to become a Doctor of Philosophy in the History of Art and Archaeology she must eat, sleep, and breathe the pointed arch. She recalls the passionate tone of her dissertation adviser encouraging her: *Champion the acute angle, Lily! Celebrate this Arabic innovation, this great gift of the hapless heretics.* But as she touches a palm to her cheek to measure for the feverish sweat of the obsessed, it seems that for her, sustainable passion isn't so easily come by.

Physically, the arch of the French Gothic era exerted less lateral thrust than its predecessor (the round arch of the Romanesque). This allowed for more window and less wall, more light in the cathedral and less lithic darkness—here Lily could lord over colleagues studying the Romanesque. What did the round arch do but hold up the crude, dark churches of the unenlightened? Places for people who worshiped from fear, who burnt and bled their offerings—*The first systematic combination of the pointed arch and the ribbed vault in the Abbey Church of Saint-Denis ushered a revolution of both building style and theology.*

Lily scribbles this note, although she doesn't quite trust the pinpoint accuracy of the statement. Knows that history is the luxury of hindsight; people entering the Early Gothic Period didn't know they were entering the Early Gothic Period.

I, however, happen to know I am entering a Shit-Eating Period. She adds this to her previous note as two girls come out of the bathroom. Lily hears them first; the snigger and huff that precedes all teenagers, which she remembers from her school days at St. Agatha's. She looks up as the girls pass. They're the strong-jawed sort, the kind who hide behind sweeps of hair and charcoal eyes. Lily recalls plucking her own brows into similar experimental crescents. Their bodies, however, are a different matter. She has heard theories, knows what estrogen in drinking water can do to teenagers these days. She certainly doesn't remember these high-rigged breasts and grasshopper legs from her own adolescence.

Lily chews on a piece of hair. Truth is, she's probably just a revisionist. She thinks back to the last five years of her own history. Her life with Duncan. As a biographer, can she isolate the inciting event, the moment that sent the small huddle of husband and wife plummeting? Could she plot it on a graph: *The Progressive Decay of Married Life?* It's impossible. On several occasions she has tried to drum up the urgency to set things straight—for herself at least—to discern what sin she has committed to turn her husband away, and how far she should go to bring him back. Thinking his sleep and his absence were smooth walls against which she could test her long-ing and sadness, she waited until Duncan slept or left for work to finger through photographs and sniff his shirts. Here was a birthday card, a dried flower, a postcard from the weekend in Montauk when he had taught her to swim. Imagine that—she was a woman who had never learned to swim! For three long summer days he held her in the turbulent sea, teaching her to kick and breathe and simply float. At night, in the safety of their cottage, she confessed she had never learned before because she had never trusted anyone before.

But did she feel nostalgic for this now? For the cup of his hand under her neck, at the small of her back, keeping her weightless and safe above sea level? Look into your heart for a songbird, Lily. Into the belly for the pang of love. Duncan's face might be the only face she has ever loved, but is it enough? Is it realistic? The stretches without him are never long enough. This reason too, she can give for a summer in the country; an ab-sent Duncan, a present Duncan. Which will she like better in the end?

In the margin of her page, she has drawn an anatomically correct heart. She's about to shade in the valves when the restroom door opens again. Lily looks up, expecting another kilt. Instead, a squat and blocky man slips out of the women's bathroom and eases the door shut behind him. He nods at Lily, gives her a thumbs-up. Walks away.

Every idea, garbage.

On Tuesday morning, Duncan uses his arm as an all-purpose wiper blade to clear his desk of yesterday's ideas for Stand and Be Counted. The framed photo of Lily that Kooch had been studying falls into the sullage with the rest of his desktop trash. Duncan fishes it out. Lily in her silk *ao dai,* avoiding the camera lens by a shy ten degrees. She had posed for the photo with her hair pulled tight, purposefully demure. This was just after his trip to Vietnam. She came out of her bedroom with mincing steps, bowing deeply and draped in the violet silk that he had bought her. She was trying not to laugh—he remembers the moment in digital detail—her suppressed laughter and then suddenly his entire existence was bifurcated. It was a terrible juxtaposition: behind him was this life that he'd carefully fashioned from scratch, and ahead of him was the woman for whom he'd toss it all away without a second thought. It *was* terrible. But it was also beautiful. How strange that she, who moved into his arms as lithe and seeking as a child, would require such ferocious contemplation. She was soft, occupied such little space, how could he have known that she had the power to decimate him? That he would help her do it? Looking back, he realizes it was the end of their friendship and the beginning of her reign.

For five years this photograph has held agency on the right-hand corner of his desk. Now Duncan opens the top drawer of his file cabinet and transfers Lily there. Right next to his expense account file. These five years have definitely made him slow-witted; he didn't even make much of a fuss when he was moved off Tide. Felt he had it coming. But he is ready, finally, to widen the scope of the blame. For instance, why not fault Lily for a portion of his career whiteout? Point to the detrimental effects of marriage to an über-critic. Yes. He rolls the file cabinet shut. No doubt he's learned the value of self-editing with Lily around. And a tough lesson about inviting her opinion.

The last time he'd prepared work to show Hawke, he made the mistake of giving Lily his scripts, handing over his raison d'être, seeking perhaps some human compassion. Certainly not an academic analysis. She just thumbed through the deck as if it were an income tax report. *Christ, Duncan. How many more product testimonials do we need anyway?* She shook her head and let the stack of papers drop to the coffee table. *What about compelling drama? What about realism? Your scripts are about as organic as corn-dogs.* Why did he think he could expect enthusiasm from her? This was their division: Lily was a student, while he was a student of life.

He remembers when she finally settled on the pointed arch as her dissertation topic. She had launched the idea at him over dinner, the table her lectern. Duncan hardly recognized her that night. The thought was uncharitable, but he felt there was something suspect about her waxing on Gothic innovation, how she hit the consonants hard when speaking of the arch's Middle Eastern genesis. Could she have cultured this idea just to thwart his claim on creativity? Every word seemed to announce a challenge. Lily and her ache to be eccentric, he thought. There was nothing soft left in her.

"Still no word on the boar. Though I suppose no news is good news." The library cats murmur and click while they sort books near Lily's computer terminal. "What about homecoming? Has anyone asked the question?"

"That's right, he's the season starter," Persian says. "They have him run out across the field, don't they?"

"Skinner won't leave his house again—in case the pig finds his way back. Says even Emmett couldn't get him back in the pen."

"I brought him out a casserole last night."

"You know that the poor hog has no lower canines?" Ginger leans on the book trolley. "That's why his upper tusks grew so long."

"Leave it to the male species to compensate."

"Imagine foraging without lower canines."

Lily feels the twitch returning to her cheek, she can't bear it. "Anyone consider," she says, without looking up from her monitor, "that maybe the boar went back to the wild? Where it belongs?"

Ginger cat looks over at Lily with either unmitigated pleasure or sheer anxiety. Since the meeting on Sunday they've been trying to fold her into their banter and have found endless tasks to place themselves in Lily's path. Although, now that the older women have got her, they seem unsure

of their follow-up. They look at each other, something itchy in their exchange. There's an empty chair at the reference desk. Ginger is quicker on
the draw, reaches it first, plants her hands on the backrest. She ignores Persian's loud exhalations and drags it up alongside the computer station.

"Your husband is quite lovely," she says, sitting and calmly crossing
her legs. Lily understands her movements, thinks she's part of a generation
of women—she'd include her own mother in this—who can compose
themselves instantly from a handful of loose bits. "Very handsome."

"Thank you."

"How are you finding everything at Oster Haus?"

Lily fixes on her computer screen. "Quiet. Musty."

"Well, that's nothing new. The place has been empty for ages." Persian is gruff, impatient with pleasantries. "Where'd your side of the family resettle again?"

"Albany," Lily supplies.

"Your great-grandfather started up the sawmill." The old woman
stacks a tattered pile of westerns onto the trolley. "Luis Oster. Came from
the Palatine immigrants in Herkimer—out on the Mohawk."

"*Very* German. He even brought over a wife from the Rhineland."

"Well, the house is *very* American," Lily says and pretends to copy
down information from the computer screen.

"Oh, don't do that, honey—you can print off the screen at the reference desk."

"Gutsy old guy. Fired McKim, Mead and White and built the house
himself. It's a shame they all up and left."

Ginger plucks a thread from her trousers. "I suppose *you* can't understand a mother not wanting to return to a place where her child was abducted," she says sharply to Persian. "And by the nursemaid, of all people."

This bit of family nonsense had never sat well with Lily. Even as a
youngster, her precocious sense of subversion would have her rally for the
maid. What disappointment she felt at the pastoral ending. What typical
denouement that her grandfather was found asleep under a haystack.

"An unlucky house," Persian clucks. "Although the first place for fifty miles to have electrical lighting."

"Built as the Victorian slid into the Belle Époque."

"Pile of kindling." Lily doesn't suffer from nostalgia where architecture's concerned.

"The county owns most of that land," Persian says. "It seems to me they do what they can."

Ginger pulls her cardigan tight across her chest as if to guard against the century-old felony. "Anyway, everyone thinks it's lovely to have a nice girl like you returned to her estate." She taps Lily's knee. "Although the old mill's been turned into a restaurant."

"And hotel. Called the Old Sawmill. They do an excellent lamb shank."

"That's your opinion, please."

"With a cinnamon and fig reduction." Persian smacks her lips. "Cooked in a funny clay pot."

"You do like your Arabic food." Ginger turns away. "I'm not much for the Middle East myself—you know what I think about anyone who puts their women behind veils."

Lily looks from the computer. There was one question that lingered after hearing her grandfather's tale. None of her childhood storytellers had the answer. "Do you know what happened to the nanny?"

"The nanny?"

"The nursemaid," Ginger says to her colleague. "She disappeared, didn't she? Down the river?"

Persian folds her arms. "They never found Tinker. Not a thing."

CHAPTER 8

The Lower Extremeties

His is the only civilian vehicle racing north along the West Side Highway tonight. Strands of taxicabs whisk apart to accommodate his efficient slips between lanes; they are like comrades, sending him along from one hand to another. It's only later, as he drives past the George Washington Bridge under its wrap of reconstructive foil, that he's reminded of his slight contravention of responsibility. Four days in the city and the injured Saab is yet to be examined. It must be that patch of mustache stuck in his peripheral thought that's distracting him. He can't tell this to Lily, of course. Instead he'll have to claim that the exhausting process of rental cars and estimates and the sly handiwork of unvetted mechanics had just been too much to bear. When a campaign is as critical as Stand and Be Counted, he'll say, everything else must become soluble and compromised.

What a douse of cold water this bristled bit of Lily's lip is turning out to be. It appears he's spent days, ages, an entire life span not making eye contact with his wife. Otherwise, wouldn't his gaze have wandered down to her lip sooner?

He was working under the assumption that rural air could dissolve their hostilities and trigger a physical interest in one another. What Duncan would give to be curious about her breasts once more! He would push his head out the Victorian windows and breathe in chestfuls of that sweet country elixir if he felt any stirring, any inquisitive movement for what went on below her clothing. With small-town pleasure he'd chase her across the warped flooring until his fingers closed on the hem of her dress. Until he could unravel her naked. Take her in the rank hallway with the shame and force of a ranch hand lured in for lemonade. He'd tie a cow-bell around her neck and make her graze the carpet on all fours, drop grasshoppers into her pubic hair while she slept, fuck her with a cucum-ber he'd grown himself. For some reason he believed the river valley held a certain dirty kink that had escaped their condominium life. That had evaporated into the stratosphere of cathedral ceilings and elevator cars sliding up and down the side of their building. Lily and Duncan, rolling out of opposite sides of the same bed, twenty minutes of precisely timed difference between their awakenings to avoid a collision in the bathroom. And to avoid each other, the hatred of morning conversation, their lips—mustached and otherwise—grown weary of the good-bye kiss.

But what's going to change in the country? Upstate, doors close just as easily. Her bicycle shuttles her to the Osterhagen Loaning Library, any noise from the rusted crank shaft drowned out by tractors lowing in the field. The fallacy is revealed: in the country it's even easier to avoid one another. Shamefully easy, in fact, to fall asleep in separate bedrooms. He's driving toward her but he won't be able to say the words that could spike some life into their mutual indifference. This is his story, a tight circle that begins and ends with dully antagonistic thoughts of Lily.

————————

She's waiting for him. Braced in the entrance to the sunroom, her face is a lunar eclipse. She lets him pass so that he can dump his work on the table and set his computer under the lamp. Duncan feels a flirtatious misbehavior in his heart valves, a palpitation or detonation, he's not sure which. She's leaving. She got up the courage and she's going, he thinks. Still wearing those fucking khakis, although the grease stain has somehow faded a bit.

He lowers himself into a chair and turns to her. "Okay."

He doesn't know why he says this, or what it means exactly beyond his willingness to comply and to acknowledge the nullification of an agreement made years ago, when they were just babies, for fuck's sake.

"Who do you think Tinker was?" she asks.

"What?"

"In the garden." Now she fidgets around the perimeter of the room, pulling an elastic band through her hair. "You thought Tinker was a pet?"

Despite his annoyance, Duncan is nodding. He knows because he can feel his head bobbing in the affirmative. He wonders, it's not over, then? If it's not over, will it be soon? Are you trying to drive me into protracted madness?

"I thought it was a pet too." She reaches for her shoulder bag that's hooked to the coat stand in the hall. "Except, guess what I found?"

He pulls himself up straight. *How the fuck should I know?* He thinks this, but when he actually opens his mouth he says, "What?"

She pulls an envelope from her bag and comes over to the desk, moving his computer to one side of the round table. "I did a little research on this place." She slides a photograph out of the envelope. Duncan plants his feet on the ground while she drops the picture in front of him. She says, "Oster Haus, nineteen hundred, commissioned by Luis Oster, Dutchess County, New York State."

It's a portrait of their house in its youth. He recognizes the architectural details, the lead panel windows and gingerbread trim still crisp and intact. In spite of himself he picks up the photograph, handles it by browned edges. A group is gathered on the grass in front of the house.

Lily draws a finger across the sepia lawn, bringing his attention to the handwritten inscription across the bottom, scrawled right over women's skirts, over a blanket: *Family picnic, 1900.* Each face appears to have turned toward the camera, somnolent and off-guard. As if unaware that the photographer had arrived, assembled the camera box on its rickety legs, disappeared under the black cloak. A look of suspicion ruffles collars, fans the plumes on hats. He scans for Lily's features among her river folk kin. But the only thing uniting them, perhaps, is a trifling sense of irritation.

"Look at their names, Duncan." Lily leans over his shoulder so that they're nearly touching, and he can feel a radiant heat from her armpits and neck. One of her breasts skims his shoulder blade. In a voice that barely disguises her excitement, Lily reads the inscription at the bottom of the photo panel. "Mr. and Mrs. Luis Oster, Mrs. Lena Oster-Freitag, Reverend Masterson, Mr. and Mrs. Wallace Wexler." Duncan senses her feverish presentation is nearing its zenith, so he waits while her finger (nearly shaking) points to one side of the picture. "You'll notice here, Duncan"—how many times has she said his name?—"there are two more people standing to the side."

And indeed there are. Almost out of the frame, a little boy and a woman. "She's holding her hand up to block the sun." Lily makes a circle around the pair.

"Okay," Duncan says. "Who are they?"

"My grandfather—Luis Junior—and Nanny Tinker." Lily stands back, hands on hips of dirty pants.

Duncan suspects that his confusion and inability to follow Lily's postulate stems from either his lack of anthropological training or his lack of attention at family dinners. He sits there, pressing his lips together and flaring his nostrils.

"Jesus Christ, Duncan! The goddamn nanny is buried in the backyard."

He's skeptical but digs anyway. If only to watch, with curious regard, the soft-core humiliation of her body bent on all fours, burrowing manually through the dirt.

Her face has taken on a new sheen. The slack around her mouth tightened, replaced by possibility, fueled by mystery, and he doesn't dare voice his skepticism. His job, while Lily shreds through the soil without an ounce of archaeological refinement, is to spade the grass, peel it away from the earth, and expand the garden plot. He watches the way her shoulders contract below her short-sleeved shirt, and feels a sting of pity for her enthusiasm, for her bookish pursuits, her universe of dead artifacts.

"Duncan." Delivered along the edge of impatience. How long has he been staring off like that? She's leaning into two feet of soil. He drops the spade and bends down beside her, smelling in her a season. A tissue tucked away in a winter pocket. Lily is trying to pull a thick root from the ground. He places his hands on either side of hers and they pull. The conspiracy of their bodies reaching into the earth, the touch of hips above the hole, the crossing of forearms, helps to ease the tendril from the ground. They sit back in the grass. It's not a root.

It's a bone.

Unlike ad people, babysitters rarely meet violent ends. So none of Duncan's creative machinations have prepared him for a murdered nanny.

"The possibility of a murdered nanny," Lily corrects him. "Everyone's so complicit in your world."

"It's not complicity, it's just what angry townsfolk do."

"If they lynched the nanny, why would they give her a headstone? You don't carve an epitaph like that when you kill someone."

"Maybe she was good with the kid. Before she abducted him."

"No." Lily moves around the table. Night has fallen quick and hard. They linger in the kitchen, their arms and legs taut, foreheads and upper lips glistening. "I bet she got caught in the thresher. That kind of thing happened all the time during the Industrial Revolution."

"Right. And dumping bodies in the garden—was that also a hallmark of the mechanical age?"

Lily leans her weight against a chair.

"Maybe we should call the police," Duncan suggests, considering the femur that's locked in the cellar.

"We can't call the police. This is the most exciting thing that's ever happened to us."

And she's right. He understands it when she sighs, signifying that all the boredom of the universe is being held back at the moment by this private mystery. By a fine yard of floss. He looks at her. She's covered in dirt. It's crescented beneath her fingernails, streaked in her hair, across her forehead.

"You look subterranean, Lily."

She almost smiles. "Thank you."

This is his opportunity. "Why don't you let me wash those?" He nods at her pants. "You've had them on for a week."

Lily glances at herself in a cursory way. Then she slowly undoes her pants. Her hands, fingers unbuttoning and pushing, move with a complete lack of self-awareness, without lust or suggestion, as though she is alone in the room, undressing for bed and he, watching from the window. Lily pushes them over her hips and stands with the pant legs around her ankles. Duncan is surprised by her body and the things he's forgotten— the lengthy whiteness of it, the lean muscled thighs. He reaches out and slaps her ass.

Smack, like that. He doesn't know what impulse he's following here; it's delivered a little too hard and much too late to be playful. Lily's mouth twists in surprise, maybe pain, and all words are eclipsed by the sound of her skin, of his hand belting across her flesh. Duncan is immobile, can only watch as the imprint of his palm rises up from her ass.

The evening is suddenly stripped of its aspirations, it sinks back to the kitchen plane with a bump and a skid. She looks at him and says, "What the hell was that for?"

"I'm sorry." He wants to explain, but as she puts a hand out to touch the welt, Duncan has to resist a serious urge to slap the other cheek. What is wrong with him? Has he just assaulted his wife? She doesn't move, doesn't bend to pick up her pants, just stares at him. He feels movement against the left side of his zipper. Lily looks down toward his crotch, as if instructed by his subconscious. Christ, he thinks, what bad timing. They stand in the night kitchen, trapped in a song loop, in a double helix, in the

instant where simple math turns to calculus. He wants her and he wants
to slap her and he wants to run away from her at the same time. Lily bends
then and picks up the pants. She steps forward. He hunches over and swears
he can feel the heat of her warming up the metal of his zipper fly. She
moves toward him, her mouth open, tongue bunched up against lower
teeth. His lips fall slack, he can already taste her breath. She holds the
trousers out to him, then turns and leaves the room.

CHAPTER 9

The Epidermal Layer

In the morning her mustache is gone. This is something he notices right away. Even as she's racing across the backyard toward him, waving her arms. "Hey! What are you doing?"

It's like baby's skin under there with the fringe gone, Duncan thinks. He can see her clean and shapely mouth forming the words *hey* and *what* and *are you doing* into a question. Can see the twitch of lip over teeth as she bounds across the grass, papers flying from her schoolbag. Duncan stands in the garden holding the shovel, assessing the pit, trying to choose a spot to start.

"Good morning."

"You can't dig without me." Nearly out of breath. "You weren't going to dig without me?"

"No." He jams the shovel into the dirt and turns the soil.

"Are you going to wait? Until I get home?"

"Take the day off," he says.

She hesitates. "I can't."

"Right. You're on a schedule."

"Come on, Duncan. Promise."

He woke up after only a handful of hours of sleep, thinking about the kitchen. The sound of her skin flapping around it like something large and ensnared. He sat himself down in front of the computer, wanting to scratch up some new ideas, but found he couldn't concentrate on jeans with those great, winged thoughts of his wife set loose up there.

"I'll promise too—we'll both swear," she says. "No one digs alone."

This morning he asked himself whether this weekend commute was just a charade. Something they could participate in now in order to exonerate themselves later, assure family and friends that every stone had been turned. But he couldn't sit still long enough to find the answer. He feared hearing the sound and feeling her skin under his palm. There was the uncharted mathematics of the span and length of his hands traveling over her open thigh.

And now the mustache is gone. He notices it. And she's brushed her hair around her shoulders. A pink bra strap has slipped down her arm, out of her short-sleeved blouse. Is she really going to the library? How can he be sure? His attention is drawn to her pink bra, and, logically, to her breasts. To the handfuls he used to cup and slurp. To the dark nipples punching through white skin. But something tells him it's too late. They have made resolves, exchanged indelible phrases like a currency. From this position, Duncan believes, any sentimentality should be forced down to the grass, twisted into submission. He's a man, a quick grapple and down it should all go. Duncan will be safe in the garden, alone with the nanny who is simply bleached bone. It's his garden, after all. It's the shovel he bought for his own botanical pursuits. He doesn't want to promise her anything.

"Okay," he says. "Okay, I'll wait."

Lily arrives at the library in a gruesome funk. Why has she insisted on coming here this morning when there is, in all likelihood, a woman buried in their backyard? Nothing in the Osterhagen Loaning Library could possibly be of more interest. But the truth is messy. Duncan asked her to take the day off and even though she wanted to she could not bring herself to consent. There was a weakness in *yes,* shale sliced along the horizontal, and the word lodged in her mouth.

Lily climbs off the bike and shackles it to a tree. For months now she's been carrying around a suspicion that Duncan is afraid to be alone with her. A fear that he remains bound by only some ancient courtesy. And that this long-weekend business is his way of staving off the decision that has to be made about their marriage. He had caught her off-guard this morning. His invitation had flustered her and she'd ridden away like a screwball, stubborn and inscrutable.

As she walks toward the building she pulls her shoulders out of their cyclist's hunch. Lily thinks of the schoolgirls, their embellished swaggers and tightly braided abdominals. In comparison she is sag and flesh tone, the pilled acrylic of sweaters, a single gym sock balled onto itself. She has to wonder what significance her body held for Duncan that he would have stepped outside his own character last night and slapped her like that. He hadn't wanted her body—there was nothing frisky in his action. It was a motion that lacked both genesis and evolution. She swears her ass still holds the shape of his hand. Lily looks down at herself. There's an odd vigor in her belly, radiating up toward each breast. She feels a measure of twine cording all three points together, traveling through all points. She folds her arms across her nipples, hides the evidence.

"I need to get out of the city for the summer," Lily had said near the end of May. They were idle at a stoplight. Across the intersection a cyclist had just been knocked off his bike by a bus. "I was thinking of going upstate. To the house."

The cyclist was on his side, moving but still clamped to his bike by the pedals. "You're going to be late this morning," Duncan said. A small crowd flowering around the man both shielded him from subsequent knocks and prevented the bus from sliding away into traffic.

"Not that I'm saying it'll be much better in Osterhagen. Heat is heat. But the library is quiet. And Bard isn't far away."

The cyclist was trying to unlock his pedal clamps and disengage from the aluminum skeleton. Duncan watched the driver of the bus make his way through the crowd, tugging at bare elbows and T-shirts until a path cleared. He stood over the fallen man; Duncan could see his jaw turning a series of words over and over.

"The house should probably be condemned," Lily said, raising her window. "But there it is."

Duncan leaned his head out of the car to catch the bus driver's words. "That's the angriest human being I've ever seen."

Later, standing in Anne McPherson's office, he'd thought, My wife is leaving me.

"I know this is managerial bullying, Duncan, but what can I do? You think I don't see how everyone's distancing themselves? The account's ruined; they're calling it Stand and Be Slaughtered." Anne, a mercurial account director, began her pitch by shoving aside policy and lighting a cigarette right at her desk. "There's no energy left around here, no more belief. Hawke gets turfed and all we want to know is who's getting his parking spot. Memories have become vague and unreliable. Who liked this idea? Who counseled for this campaign? Who against? I don't have a single AE who remembers being in a tissue session. Hell, I don't remember being in a tissue session."

Is Lily leaving me? Duncan wondered. Or does she want me to go with her? She was dexterous this way. Meaning, with her, could be ambiguous and irresolute. And his interpretation of it, he'd come to realize, was often nothing more than a barometer of his own heart.

"Duncan, they're coming to you because you can fix this." A tidy funnel of smoke whisking out each of Anne's nostrils. "Hawke always breaststroked against the current. This time around they want a partner. Not a fighter."

"A yes man?" He two-stepped on her sisal rug.

Anne dropped her cigarette through the foam crown of a cappuccino. "What you did for laundry, Duncan, you can do for denim."

There before him had been a choice of snares: the summer with his wife or the summer on this miscarriage of an account. He suspected that Lily wanted to be alone up there, practicing the bitter idioms of marital woes: *he never did, he never could, he never would*. As though he were past tense. Something acquired, inhaled, then crushed into reusable fiber. But he wasn't about to just roll over and die that easily. He could leave the city with her for a while, leave the crowded sky of the eastern seaboard. The uncharged waters, the thin Atlantic, brackish, a rum and Coke sloshing up against the breakwater. They'd go someplace where things had round edges. A marshy substance in the air muffling what one could smell, what one could see. Cicadas crooning about the night, poplars grasping knuckles across the stretch of road. They would go to the river valley where stray oats and spores mushroomed in the cracks of wood siding, cedar planking, between fingers and toes.

The pervert is back. Like evolution, Lily thinks, while removing the volume of de Tocqueville's *Democracy in America*. He has crawled out of the bathroom and climbed his way up to the stacks. She pulls out the copy of *Democracy* because it's the only book among the hardcovers that leaves a chunk wide enough to spy through.

Lily crouches to watch; the man sits at a table, his chair tipped on its hind legs. He's positioned back to back with one of the young girls at the study carrels so that he's leaning into her, his crown nearly touching her ponytail.

Without looking at her he says, "Why don't you roll down your panties for me?"

The girl doesn't turn, doesn't respond. She's decorating a textbook with a highlighting pen. Lily, however, feels herself react as she might to a swallow of bad milk, the sensation of dairy flecks left on the tongue.

The pervert clears his throat. "Go ahead. Roll them right under your skirt."

Lily watches the girl's jaw work away at a tough nougat of gum. She brings a fingernail to her cheek and carefully scrapes around fresh acne sores. Lily recalls her own years at St. Agatha of Catania as loping and feral. Anything but innocent. It was a place where, within a week of arrival, a convent girl would be taught to speak in a pitch just below the hearing range of the nuns.

The man looks straight ahead, waits, ostensibly, for some sort of rejoinder. He keeps balanced on the two chair legs. As he waits, Lily takes a good look at the unfortunate girth of his thighs. They give him a pitiful sense of sluggishness. Overall, she'd say he's too chubby to be a pervert. She's always imagined them a race of rattish men, narrow and bucktoothed. Although his wet comb approximates the image; hair flat and scissored into rectilinear precision. Lily looks between the girl and the man, trying to decide whom she would like to win. Where does her sympathy lie?

When she can no longer bear to remain concealed between the stacks of nonfiction, Lily comes around the corner, approaches the carrels, and rests the edge of *Democracy* on the pervert's table.

"She can't hear you."

He looks at her. He hiccups, drops his chair down to all fours.

"What?"

"She's wearing earphones." Lily motions to the girl, whose head and foot are synchronized by either music or a nervous twitch. They both turn to watch as she inflates her gum into a bubble and holds it between her lips. Lily knows he is taking in the girl's pocked cheek. Something like distaste milks his eye.

"Christ," he says and looks back at Lily. "For a second there I thought I was losing my touch." Then he smiles, bares a mouthful of Chiclets and pearls.

"This is the thing," Lloyd says as he shakes out a smoke. "The world's lost every last bit of grace. In its mad rush it's become a giant, voyeuristic carnival, right? Get on the computer and there you have it, all the graphic shit you want. Pictures, video, live feed—and if that's not enough, you got forums to chat about it. Like growing a fucking orchid. A million people out there offering an opinion on sunlight and humidity. Dying to let you know you're not alone. So you've got your furries and forniphiliacs, your trannies and frotteurs, your Japanese buruseras. There's peeps, necrophiliacs, zoophiles—a list the length of my foot. Point is, whatever your hobby, you've got instant how-to access, right? A planet full of deviants ready to dish on gag balls and pony collars and the right amount of torque to apply to surgical tubing. And there's even diagrams! You do much surfing? There's diagrams for everything.

"Somewhere in this shuffle, we lost our imagination, okay? The power of visualization undervalued. Really, I'm an advocate for a gentler, simpler time. Before the gizmo age, best a kid had was a smudged magazine or two. What boy didn't wait under the neighbor's window to catch her undressing? One day she might forget that inch of blind and you'd get her unhooking her bra—that's natural curiosity, am I right? Mind you, the reality isn't so pretty. No way. Any woman over fifty unhooking a bra and it's Look Out Below!"

Lily thumbs her lighter until it gives up a weak flame. "Is that your real name?"

"What?"

"Lloyd? Sounds made up."

He gets a shot of smoke in the eye and squints at her through it. "You're an uptight broad, aren't you? I can tell."

Lily turns away, looks around the shade of the empty library cloisters, the arcade of shrubs stunted to the height of a man's shoulders. In the center of the garden, the terra-cotta putto spouts a weak drizzle from his privates into a fountain.

"What's your story, anyway?" he asks.

"My story?" She sits down on the edge of the fountain and pulls a stray hair from her tongue. Okay, the man is troubled—this is clear—but she was, for some reason, touched by his failure with the girl in the stacks. And he had cigarettes. *Smoking is such a stock tic,* he'd said, extending the crushed packet to her. *Go on, I don't bite. You're not my type, anyway.*

"I'm working on a paper," she offers finally, assessing the danger of his confidence. "And living up here for the summer." But the words lack energy and must be persuaded from her. One week in Osterhagen and she's already shrinking in her skin. A week since the charge of the wild boar that left them grabbing a hoof each and dragging it to the ditch, draping it with loose boughs. She's still feeling sick about it, more so now that she knows its celebrity status. Of course she can't express this guilt to Duncan. These details of her conscience are lost on him.

"And you were impressed with my technique in the stacks? Unimpressed?" Lloyd gestures to the building.

"Yes."

"Which is it? A critical analysis, please."

"The heart was there," Lily says and pinches the cigarette to death against the lip of the fountain. "But your approach could use some work. You know, I saw you the other day. Coming out of the women's bathroom." She remembers his thumbs-up—as though she had been sitting there to field prospects for him or to keep watch.

"An old trick." He nods. "This might surprise you, Lily, but I've been a deviant my entire life." Lloyd stands up, paces a bit. "I change locations, for sure. Same way a man of the earth approaches his hundred acres. You leave the ground idle one season and it'll turn up lush wheat the next. Haven't come around the Osterhagen library since the late nineties. And, Christ, the place is crawling!" He looks through the gate toward the main building, licking his lips as though they were trimmed with honey. "Bad school girls in uniform. Just like MTV."

Lily smirks. "You think they're bad because they roll up their skirts?"

Lloyd stops his shuffle. "You underestimate me. But whatever, I understand." He tucks his cigarettes into a shirt pocket. "It's summer, right?"

"Barely the cusp of June."

"School's out for the good kids. So who gets stuck behind in summer school?"

The question's rhetorical, she doesn't answer.

"Bad girls—that's who. Bad girls just begging for it."

"Girls like teenage boys."

Lloyd looks around the courtyard, holds up his fat hands. "Do you see any teenage boys? There are no teenage boys at Our Lady of the Apparition, okay? I'm just going to have to do." He lowers his voice. "Look, I'm not saying I'm the best out there. There are guys who could perv me under the table, I admit. But if you don't have a skill to improve, what do you have?"

Lily fakes a yawn. "My husband says all dialogue should lead somewhere."

Lloyd pats his back pockets now, takes out a stick of gum. "Husband? Really?"

"One and only."

"I would have guessed *girlfriend*."

She stands, flattens the creases across her thighs a bit too violently.

"Sometimes I get a sense, is all." He waves the butt of his palm. "Christ, you got some story to tell me, huh?"

She looks at him, tries to make sense of his shrewd eyes and baby fat and the blotch of sweat the size of a tortilla beneath each arm.

"I don't even know you."

"Hey, this isn't Butch Cassidy and Sundance, okay? This isn't a lifelong friendship—just tell me your shit if it makes you feel better."

"What makes you think I've got shit?" Lily tries to uncrank the machine of her jaw.

"You're uptight. Don't get offended, but you're going to explode." Lloyd glances back toward the cloister gate. One of the circulation desk workers walks out of the building, lighting a cigarette. She nods at Lily, turns an eye over the lumped edge of Lloyd.

"I'm supposed to trust you?" For some reason, Lily flashes on the bone that has been secreted in the cellar.

"Oh, no, you can't trust me. I am the scorpion."

CHAPTER 10

Os Innominatum (Nameless Bone)

He wills her home through the afternoon, drawing long strides around the sunroom, imposing pace and measure on her return. It's because he really wants to dig. Duncan rubs at his eyes; the heat in the house reminds him of hotboxing in his '82 Datsun. Outside, a hoot that he thinks sounds like an owl, a bark that he knows for sure is a dog.

This is about slapping your ass, Lily. He sits in front of his computer, starts pecking into the dialogue slug of a TV template. *I'm not saying that I liked it, but I'm not going to say that I didn't like it. Maybe I'm a spanker at heart, maybe I've started swinging from the trees.*

When had Lily changed? In the first days he knew her she seemed so alone—as though she'd sprung to earth fully formed or had somehow raised herself. He found the idea incredibly attractive; here was a shadowless creature that he'd discovered for himself. Once she gave herself to him, the idea became complete. She was smart in a way that he wasn't, he was creative in a way that she could never be. He had come down the hard road of experience and she roosted under his knowledge. What looked like a charmed life from without was really a great, churning machine of mutual awe. It was not so long ago that they could go entire days with the blinds drawn against everything.

These days, however, he suspects if he opened her chest he'd find the hum of a carburetor, a twin-valve engine. The night after his talk with

Anne he'd confided in Lily, hoping that she would accept the intimate offering of his vulnerability. "They're setting me up for failure," he'd said. If he was sacked now, the futility of his career would become apparent. Five years of writing snappy headlines, bones without dangling meat, left Duncan with the impression he'd been living against his fate.

"They're clearing out Hawke's regime," he told her.

"Of which you are a decorated officer."

"I should have left five years ago when I was hot."

Lily was reading the paper, her face firmly in the arts section. "So what, you feared the unknown?"

"They're calling the account Stand and Be Slaughtered. And now it's mine. Basically, this is the kiss of death."

Lily hadn't exactly laughed, but he detected an explicit mirth in her voice that called to mind shaking all his loose coins into Leetower's coffee filter collection. He immediately regretted confessing these fears to her.

" 'Kiss of death' suggests betrayal, Duncan." She looked at him over a folded corner of paper. "Who exactly is your horse-faced Judas?"

He hadn't answered, he'd said too much. Although he suspected Lily knew exactly who the culprit was: it had been five years since he'd hit gold. Between then and now a breadth of years and nothing.

There's just no way, he thinks, standing in front of the cold fireplace. The Lily he has now can't be the same one he started with. Which begs the question: Which is his real wife? He'd like to think that it's the one he married, but there *is* evidence to suggest the contrary. Her behavior around the Crusaders, for instance. As it happened, Lily did not raise herself. In fact, the idea of her parents fascinated Duncan; her father a coffee importer, her mother a Catholic missionary. They met under the shade of an Ecuadorian banana tree and joined forces to strip the natives of both coffee bean and soul. Independently, each had a justifiable ambition: profit and Jesus. Who could lay blame on either? It was Corporate America and Lily stood to inherit not only a great bundle of cash, but also life everlasting. Her parents were iconic apart. But together they were a marching contradiction. Duncan saw the potential in this situation and even sketched an outline for a screenplay. Lily hadn't liked the idea. Not at all. Around the wealthy zealots, she toughened, became android leather. Wore things with buttoned collars.

Duncan thinks about the femur in the garden. Sure, Osterhagen's a quirky little village, but maybe he'd been too quick with his theory of a nanny-lynching brigade. Most likely it was one of Lily's ancestors. What undeniable satisfaction it would bring him to drive up to Albany one weekend with news of human remains in the garden. *Some families spawn lines of gifted musicians, or athletes,* he'll tell her nabob of a father while feathering his own cap. *By the way, have you seen your daughter swing a tire iron? She's an absolute savant.*

The Crusaders had never liked him. Thought him a Turk or some-thing urban and unsavory for whose sadistic pleasure they had convent-educated their only child. On his part, he was hard-pressed to find a kind word to describe their parenting skills. While Lily hadn't been neglected exactly, she'd had a less-than-perfect childhood. The Crusaders held fast to some sort of doctrine that children should be neither seen nor heard. Hadn't their interest in Lily only begun once she'd reached adulthood? Once she'd gained the courage to make the sort of decisions that could be easily criticized?

For her part, Lily denied wanting a country life with a tennis pro and terraced gardens. But he watched her face after a weekend upstate. He thought that walking back into their apartment, swish as it was, she was struck by all that she'd given up settling for the son of a railyard worker from St. Paul.

Anyway, he wasn't tied to his roots the way she was. He had come to the East Coast believing it to have obverse properties of Minnesota, a well-turned muscle that would hammer everything provincial out of him. And clocking these years at the agency meant he was now an advertising man. Hawke had once even come into his office and perched on the cor-ner of his desk.

Duncan, no matter what shit goes down here, he said, ruffling his raven-feather hair, *I've got your back, buddy.*

Same here, the protégé had replied those several months ago, still secure within the radius of Hawke's favor.

Now he looks at the blinking screen of his laptop where concepts swim about the pixels. He'd like to recover that keen spur but feels hamfisted and crude. Can't get his fingers under that sheet of glass.

———————

Saturday night, when the air has cooled significant degrees, they continue their exhumation. Their Friday evening attempt had come up empty. Lily had *insisted* they channel linear troughs north toward the barley field. Duncan felt they should instead dig concentrically, radiating out from the site of the femur. The garden was supposed to have been his project, though he was being shouldered into the peripheries. Here was Lily digging her own history, here was Duncan providing cheap labor. After an hour of nothing he decided it was easier to avoid a quibble by calling it quits.

Tonight they're employing Duncan's method and are rewarded almost immediately with an articulated little piece they suspect is from the top of the vertebral column. It looks like a thick wishbone with a grooved spanner connecting the bottom of its arch. Duncan has seen whale vertebrae washed up in Montauk, amplified in size, but bearing the similar wing-nut design and hollowed passage for the spine. Alone, the function of the notched bone had been unclear to him. But stack two of these together and suddenly the interlocking shape of the spinal column emerges. In unearthing one of these vertebrae in the garden, Duncan finds himself wondering about what came before it and what comes after.

They can hear the faint whiz of the Amtrak beyond the fields toward the river. It makes them conscious of the private nature of their project and, should anyone come up the drive—Skinner, the universal aunties of the library, an absent neighbor popping in for a spot check—should anyone poke around to the back of the house, they've prepared a statement.

We are avid horticulturalists. We are charmed by growing things. Please just leave us alone. Duncan might even raise his shovel with a nuance of threat. The thought sort of excites him. He's never played the kook before.

Lily doesn't even wear gloves now that she's abandoned her trench system. Her excitement is like the hushed middle section of a fireworks display. She holds a flashlight on the hole with one hand and pulls back soil with the other. Duncan continues with the spadework, sweats a pleasant grassy smell into the night air.

"I've found fault with my Osterhagen lynch-mob theory," he says, conscious that they haven't exchanged much tonight beyond the gentle grunt of acknowledgment as one finds a stone, one overturns a root.

Lily sits back on the grass to wipe the paste of soil and perspiration from her forehead.

"A public lynching takes some organization," he continues. "Whelping the hounds, tuning pitchforks, inciting riot—you heard the old man last week. Plenty of time there for a dissident faction to form, right?"

"What am I agreeing to?" Lily says.

"Bleeding heart liberals always leave some record of their objection. Someone in town would have leaked the truth about a witch hunt."

"Right, and I didn't find anything else at the library."

"You have to admit, your family, they're kind of private people." Duncan leans on the shovel, injects a little cross-examination into his voice. "Not the sort to follow a leader like Skinner. I'm thinking this was an inside job. Your relative, the Bavarian count or whoever he was."

Lily looks up at him. "You're kidding me."

"No. Your great-grandfather."

"You think he murdered the nanny?" Something about the way she locutes each syllable tells him she's neither buying nor pleased with his supposition.

"I'm not saying he wielded the ax. But commissioned, maybe." He knows he's taunting, but he feels the need to elicit some sort of response from her.

"So, you're saying I'm a descendant of savages?"

Duncan shrugs. "We're all born naked, wet, and hungry."

Her smile suggests something razored into place below the nose. He has to fight back a terrible itch to nudge her with the shovel—*hey, remember when you used to think I was funny?*

"It wasn't such a problem when the savages gave us that down payment."

"It's no problem, Lily. But think about it, why else would the nanny be buried in the garden? And in pieces? If it was an accident, wouldn't they have made some effort to put her in order?"

"My great-grandfather did not kill the nanny."

They go back to digging. Him flipping soil into mounds and Lily raking her fingers through for any fine details. He continues to watch her; something about the way she squats and digs into the soil reminds him of those Cu Chi tunnels he visited in Vietnam, what it must have been like to excavate miles of underground passages by hand.

"You're like the Viet Cong down there."

She doesn't even look up. "Having those flashbacks again?"

Duncan leans on his shovel. Lily *is* sort of like the Viet Cong burrowing through layers of silt, like a small mammal chattering a hole through the planet. Of course, if she had agreed to come with him that summer she'd know what he was talking about. How both rudimentary and efficient those passages were for the North Vietnamese Army, providing an escape route into the Saigon River and allowing the underground ferrying of soldiers and supplies. How sly Charlie could remain hidden away underground, while several feet above, the Skinners of the world crouched at the mouth of the hole, weighing the temptation to charge and pump the creatures from their den against the risk of casualty: their own men greased, the sniffer dogs lit up.

"It's a hit," Lily says and stops her foraging. She wipes oily dirt from an ochre surface just now visible through her fingers. She uses one leg to brace herself against the lip of the shallow hole and starts to pull. Duncan crouches beside her but doesn't help as she tugs something from the grave. Her face changes as she works.

He watches her profile as she brings two bones up into stray light from the back porch. "The pelvis." Her voice sticks in her throat with an awe he has never heard before. He thinks she might cry.

Duncan doesn't want to touch. Doesn't want to handle another woman's privates. Lily sways back on her heels in the way of a person who's just received some tragic news. She cradles the two halves of bone, their scalloped bowls punched through like knotted pine. He does recognize something about her—yes, the mouth and the eyes—he remembers this flared beauty. This Lily.

CHAPTER 11

Sympathetic Nerve

On the way to lunch on Tuesday, they pause at the front end of the car, united by a common sympathy for ruined metal. Duncan can't help thinking that given a woman's bruised face or a bad dent, he knows which one he'd wince at first.

"Wild pigs, aren't they more of a Southern plague?" Leetower kneels by the damaged nose.

Duncan leans casually on the hood. "After we hit the thing, it got back up and charged us. I had to waste it with a tire iron."

"Jesus, that's cool."

The fabulist shrugs. "Also, the park ranger said it had rabies. So."

"I'd rather hit a hobo." Kooch flecks some chipped paint from the bumper. "They bounce, but they don't come back for you."

"It's true," Leetower says to Duncan. "I've been in his car when it's happened."

"You guys got anything on Stand and Be Counted?" Duncan tries to keep the hope out of his voice. He has been itching with anxiety.

The boys are silent.

"What's going on with Tide?"

"Casting for the third Laundry Elf started today."

"Local?"

"Domestic midget search." Leetower slides up on the intact side of Duncan's hood. "No budget for anything else."

"Fucking Anne. She never learns."

"What's the deal with casting in the Ukraine?" Kooch asks.

"Chernobyl meltdown in eighty-six."

"Anne knows that place is a gold mine of birth defects." Leetower sighs. "The next generation out of the gate got the full biological effect— like napalm babies."

"The Vietnamese that cleans our office is a napalm baby," Kooch tells them.

"I thought she was Filipina."

"Nah, I was shitting you." He smiles. "She's Vietnamese. I told her Pops was an American GI so she'd show me her tits."

Leetower knocks on the hood. "The mystery of the stain, solved."

"Hold on. I'm not alone in the Asian fetish." Kooch turns to Duncan. "I just noticed that picture of your wife."

"What picture?"

"On your desk. Where you had her all dressed up like a chink?"

Duncan feels the skin tighten over his cheeks. "We've really got to work on your inside voice, Kooch."

"No, I want to thank you." He's pulling a folded piece of paper out of his pocket. "You inspired me, Chief. My dad's retirement party's next week, bunch of vets are getting together."

Leetower shakes his head. "Not another subscription to *Interracial Spanking*?"

Kooch ignores him. "The guys want me to do a speech. But I'm aiming to go with a narrative."

"That's real ambitious for an illiterate fuck."

"Okay. This is about his first tour in '68, right after Tet." Kooch clears his throat.

When he first went to Nam, Stanford—that's his name—Stan said
to himself, "This is gonna be a piece of piss." The hard line of his
jaw was enough to make the slants cross the street when they saw him
coming. He had a quick fuse and a proclivity for small women; a sweet
tooth easily indulged in that Southeast Asian armpit. The females,
when willing, were all paperclip frames hung with floral print silks
and gloves. Unwilling, their voices were shrill, nearly optic. Once, a
village of farm women surrounded him and a couple boys, trying to
stall their inspection for hidden munitions. Like being swarmed by a
flock of sparrows; he had to waste a few to get his point across, shake
them off his pant leg.

Kooch folds the page back up. "It's not done yet."

"Your mother's dead, right?" Leetower slides off the hood.

Duncan stares at Kooch. His mouth is dry. There are several seconds
that his mind slides off its central axis, free of inertia, untouched by traction. There in the parking garage, Duncan is as primed for the arrival of
enlightenment as one can ever be prepared for an event precipitated by
nothing.

"You're a son of a bitch," he says to Kooch. "But I think I love you."

The corkboard in the lobby, community administered and partially ravaged, stands defenseless long enough for Lily to remove a sign-up sheet
posted by concerned Osterhagenians. The party assembling on Wednesday will search around Bard College for the Sovereign of the Deep
Wood. Today is Wednesday. Lily folds the sheet carefully and walks toward the stacks. She tries telling herself that besides the handful that
gathered last week, the boar is of limited interest to anyone. She's done a
little research, knows that in ecological terms, feral swine are an invasive
species, environmental hazards. Even the forests of folklore were studded

with pigs who terrorized pilgrims and charged cattle. But despite what she's read, it's evident that people love the thing; the beast's ugly snout is posted on every bulletin board in the library.

Lily finds herself scanning the stacks for Lloyd. While she knows encouraging a friendship with a pervert is not the brightest idea, she can't help but be drawn by his mastery of logic. Putting aside the content, she's left admiring his ability to reason through his deviancy and deliver the defense with conviction. She's heard a lot of horseshit in her time, but there's something curious about the way Lloyd crafts his portions. Horseshit folded into small paper boats.

She finds him in the reference section, halfway along the aisle, squatting between two sets of encyclopedias. He's removed a couple volumes and peers through the gap left behind, the same technique she employed with de Tocqueville last week. Lily backtracks around the shelf and watches as he balances nervously on his haunches. It's the position of an industrious squirrel tossed a bag of nuts. How and where will one carry off such a grand treasure? She's taken by his tenure. This is the kind of passion she needs to whip up herself if she wants to get on with the business of the pointed arch.

She moves slowly down the aisle so as not to startle him, the search party flyer still in her hand. And it strikes her then that Lloyd, with his many foibles, is the perfect confidant. They could trade culpabilities like precious stones.

She lowers herself on the carpet a few feet away. "What do you got?"

"No one," he tells her, squinting between the books as though sighting ships through a periscope. "Just testing the setup."

"For?"

"My great moment."

"Let me guess. You're the poster boy for meticulous felony?"

He turns, runs an eye over her. "You know something?" A curious twist of his lips. "Don't get too excited by this, but you're just about pretty enough to molest."

Lily has a sudden memory of being woken one night by a fire alarm in their building. She remembers how her instinct to evacuate had to fight hard against the desire to sleep through the clamor. The same feeling now with Lloyd, a clear warning and conflicting choices.

She changes her mind. Lloyd cannot be taken into her confidence. Their mutual confessions will never be of a similar nature. Hers are brusque and uncomfortable, divulged only so that she may receive some degree of clemency, while Lloyd's provide him pleasure. He takes them out of their silk pouch only to hold them up to the light.

"They'd order in a load of Latino-American ground fighters," Duncan is telling Anne. "Because unlike their all-American compatriots—big, hulking farmboys from the Midwest—these guys were slender, narrow-boned, and could slip down those Viet Cong tunnels and shafts like ferrets. They'd get smoked, most of them. The VC booby-trapped miles of those tunnels; think metal spikes under a false floor of leaves."

"Vietnam. The dark side of the sixties."

"Right. We asked ourselves, what else was going on at the time?"

Anne sits with her legs crossed, chain-smoking on his couch. "The draft was going on. Kooch's father went over."

"Only after he was caught by Canadian Mounties." Duncan scratches his head impatiently. "But also, Anne, I've been to Vietnam."

"Yes. You and the little missus."

Duncan nods. "That's why I feel I've got the edge on it. Historically." No need to mention that he went alone.

"Where do the jeans come in?"

"We put our girl soldier in the depths of the Cu Chi tunnels—"

"Women didn't serve as soldiers."

"Creative anachronism. We call them Grunt Girls."

Anne looks at the ceiling. "Yeah, okay—reminds me of the Gorilla Girls." Smoke wads up into a cloud above her head. "Could be a joint promotion in there somewhere."

"I'm thinking, photojournalism, khaki-colored TV footage. Our Grunt Girl's on her hands and knees, strapped to an M-16, and behind her, a Viet Cong soldier literally has her by the flared pant leg." Duncan sits on his desk. "The tag line is: *History Repeating*."

Anne is nodding slowly. "Double entendre, keep going."

"The flare leg is a commentary on war."

"Oh yeah? America lost the war because of bell-bottom jeans?"

"Well, call it the acuity of hindsight." He picks up his stapler, checks the cartridge load. "We *were* ill-equipped."

"This is a touchy subject, Duncan, and you want to make a mockery out of it? Never mind that the little shits buying these jeans are eighteen. What's Vietnam to them?"

"They'll get it, they grew up between Iraq and Iraq." Duncan shoves the stapler in his computer bag for the weekend. "Look, with *History Repeating* we position ourselves as the socially aware denim."

"Great." Anne lights a new cigarette. "So we're saying America's depraved and destined to repeat the greatest blunders of all time—war and bell-bottoms."

"No, we play it from the other side, Anne. Everyone promises you how much better their product's going to make your life, right?"

"Everyone overpromises."

"All we can say for sure is: Conflict is here to stay. But Stand and Be Counted is going to be here through it all."

"Jesus, Duncan. That's cheery."

"It's truthful, Anne. You're telling me you still believe in peace in our time?" Duncan has to cringe at his own Chamberlain-Costello appropriation. He stands up. "Look, anyone can sell jeans. But no one is selling what people really want—shrewdness, provocation, skepticism. Give them that and the jeans will sell themselves."

She takes a long, thoughtful drag on her smoke. "Maybe a portion of the proceeds could go to rebuilding mud hut villages or something."

"Let's table that until next quarter."

Anne is quiet for a moment. Duncan allows her time to take on the idea in her own way. It's always the same with account people, you give them the baby and then watch them handle the squirming sack. Anne needs a minute to sort out the arrangement of her hands before she can comfortably raise the thing to her chest and figure out if she can sell it—stinking diaper and all—to Upstairs.

"Well, we would be portraying an experience. Without moralizing," she says.

"And the very honesty of the portrait *will be* social commentary." He's running and gunning here. Glances at his own hands, notices they're engaged in some rolling form of persuasion, and is reminded of Skinner's speech last week. How the old man's inflamed left eye and vigilante politics seemed so at home in the Osterhagen Loaning Library.

"I don't want satire, though." Anne pushes herself to the edge of the sofa. "Too often honesty drifts toward its ribald cousin."

Nice, Duncan says to himself, *she's taking it.*

"I'm erring on the side of harsh commentary."

"So, if Stand and Be Counted had a voice, what would it say?"

"Yes, your ass does look fat."

She laughs. "Excellent. It's the polar opposite of what Hawke did with this brand."

"Well, when you're stuck, pull a one-eighty." Duncan leans against his desk.

"We'd have to be really brave to carry it off. But you're right. No one in the market is doing this—'History will repeat, but we'll be here to see it through.' "

And we have liftoff. Up against the chest and sucking at the tit.

"Exactly," Duncan says, nodding.

"Like a light at the end of the tunnel."

"Sure." He's not sure what he's agreeing to precisely, but it feels right, the soul is there, even if the concept itself needs to be fleshed out. Anne stands up.

"I might love it, Duncan. I really might." But he can see that she already does. "The idea's sick, but I expect nothing less from you."

She walks to his window, trailing ash across the carpet. "Look, I won't blow smoke up your ass on this one—it's got to move merch or we're all dead—but this is a big idea. Maybe too big given the current climate. I mean, no one wants to be reminded about mass blunders. People are going to hate you."

"So I'll take Veterans Day off."

"You should get Leetower to art-direct this. Make sure he and Kooch work their asses off; they're lazy shits who don't know how good they have it. Don't be afraid to punish them, Duncan. You're the new Dutch uncle. With Hawke gone it's the only way they'll embrace your regime."

He doesn't respond but he knows Anne is right. He himself had flourished under the fear of disappointing the great man, felt Hawke's criticism as sharply as the punch of a lawn dart. In a way, tyranny helped raise him from the crumb-size cubicles, taught him to take other people's shit streaks and bat them out of the park.

Yes. He would show the boys how it was done.

CHAPTER 12

Muscles of the Face

"Me, I was born a peeper. Shot from the womb with nose against the glass, you could say. People are much more fascinating when they think they're alone, Lily. Really. They shit, they piss, they cry; it's life thrown into high relief." Lloyd scratches the wattle under his chin.

"Voyeurism is not for the impatient," he continues, sitting down beside her along the rim of the fountain. "You go through the trouble of pulling yourself up to a second-story window but your worries are just beginning. You've still got to sift through a lot of sock darning and flossing and putting away of the dishes before you get a nude. Although, for me, it's not just about the naked flesh, you know? My tastes are more complex than that. There is something heartbreaking about the human condition. And the peeps, we're the ones who're privy to it.

"Once I was looking in on a house party—a Christmas party in the historic district by the mill? I was in the shrubs watching this woman in the kitchen. She was nice-looking, in her forties, but the lines around her face were starting to dig in. You know the age? She wasn't wearing a ring. She had this blond hair that had been pinned up and she was wearing pearls. A classic beauty, but the lines, the face, the no-ring business, she was a tragic figure immediately. She was alone, standing still, stood a second too long and I had this feeling—call it intuition—that she was out of place here.

"I watched her reach across the counter to pour herself a drink, but by accident she knocked an empty wineglass to the floor. It shattered. Now there were all these festivities going on, a bunch of people in the living room and lots of noise. So no one came when the glass broke. I watched the woman bend and scoop up the broken pieces of glass. She unfolded a fancy napkin, it was the size of a bib, and scooped the shards right in. Then she twisted the corners of the napkin together, made a bundle of the broken glass, and put it in her purse. It was a small purse, beaded-like, and it was bulging by the time she stuffed the pieces in there. Then she picked up the bottle of wine and, easy as all shit, poured herself a glass.

"I found myself watching her hands. She had long sleeves but I could see something had slid down her wrist. It was a hospital bracelet; bright yellow and white, couldn't miss it. These two little things, the glass and the bracelet—one leading to the other—happened in the span of maybe forty seconds. But they made a complete story. I knew who she was then. That day I'd read an article in the paper about a woman who'd escaped the long-term-care facility in Poughkeepsie. Acute schizophrenic. Burned down her co-op in a popcorn grease fire. I realized all this because she thought no one was watching. You can never know a person when they think you're watching."

"Did you do anything?"

"Who?" he asks, snapping from his monologue. "Did I go around and knock on the door or something?"

"Or call the hospital."

"She was beyond help, Lily."

"She was sick."

"Sometimes they say *popcorn grease* in the paper, but they really mean *meth lab*. Besides, they fished her body out of the river near Saugerties the next day."

Lily looks into his porcine eyes. "You are Satan."

"Yes, but my duties are largely ceremonial." He smiles his rummage sale of teeth. "Anyway, why must you judge me, Lily? Why must I either be good or bad, fit in one shoe box or the other?"

In a way, she can't contest him on this point. It's a mistake to believe that others have led the same life as her; one in which each word is panned through a fine-screen mesh.

"I'll tell you something," he continues. "I do love the peeping. Although lately—and this'll help explain what I was doing yesterday behind the encyclopedias—I've developed an interest in frotteurism. You know what that is?"

"Enlighten me."

"'Atta girl." He shifts closer on the lip of the fountain.

Lily inches away.

"It's the urge to touch or rub against a nonconsenter."

Lily nods and looks at the dry fountain cherub. She wonders why the angel's weak little stream of urine gets powered off at exactly five o'clock each day even though the library is open late most evenings. "I thought you were more of a dirty talker."

"Well, that's all a prelude to the frott stuff," Lloyd says. "Like vocal exercises. The rubbing and touching stuff—you can only pull that shit off once per location. Maybe only once in Osterhagen, right? Afterwards I'm going to have to beat a path to Rhinebeck or Hudson. How many chances am I going to get to stick it to some schoolgirl? The townsfolk will be cutting new eyeholes in their cloaks."

After absorbing the content of last week's pig meeting, Lily knows he's probably right. "You're actually going to try this?"

"Sure, once I'm ready to split. But I haven't even been to the botanical gardens yet."

Lily shakes her head. "Wouldn't you be more comfortable someplace crowded? In the city? In subways?"

Lloyd blows a laser-fine line of smoke. "I know about subways," he snaps. "Where's your head? The city's fucking overrun with perverts."

"I'm just saying. It would be safer. Once you actually launch."

He ignores her, gets up, paces the empty cloisters holding his cigarette like a ballpoint pen. "Okay, the dirty talk has got its own charm, for sure. The gig—as I like to call her—takes her sweet time processing what's happened to her. But when it finally registers, and this is the part I like best, she almost always attempts a recovery. Smooths on a neutral face like nothing's happened. I love this. This is what's so *beautiful* about society, Lily. All you ladies trained to be polite and kind. So when I tell a girl to squat so I can sniff her ass you wouldn't believe how hard the face works to adjust. It's like a flipped kayak trying to right itself. Reads like constipation on the face but is restorative to my soul. I fester on that wound."

Lily pushes her glasses up her nose. "I was hoping for a less precise conversation."

"See, Lily. That's why I'd never gig on you. Not once has your expression cracked. You're just sitting there watching me behind those librarian glasses and not once have you cracked. You're a hard son of a bitch. Pardon my language. But all that energy to keep such a stoic expression, you could run a small city off it."

"This isn't energy," she says. "This is how I look."

"Always? When you're working? When you're fucking? Boy, I'll bet you're a barrel of laughs."

The comment pinches, it does. And she finds herself wondering if Duncan shares this opinion. She bends one knee over the other and thinks, Am I boring? Or am I just a brilliant actor?

Lloyd stretches his arms above his head and walks back toward her. "Lily, why are you always here? Remind me."

She sighs, checks her watch. Duncan should be home in a couple hours. It's true that she's been waiting all week to get back into the garden. Still, she's surprised—and not unpleasantly so—to find herself anticipating his arrival.

"You're going to be a doctor, but not a real doctor, right?"

She switches the crossing of her legs. "I'm trying to pinpoint a moment. If that's what you want to call it."

"Excellent." He settles back down beside her. "Which one exactly?"

"I crawled through fifty feet of the Cu Chi tunnels," Duncan says. "Although they'd been enlarged so fat-fuck tourists could get through. The Viet Cong managed to dig hundreds of miles of underground passage by hand. And the only evidence? These hidden entrances as small and inconceivable as foxholes."

"What you're telling me, there's just so much material here." Anne shakes her head and sifts through a few marker renderings that he had Leetower do up.

"Right. The crafty Viet Cong squatting in a tunnel full of their own shit waiting for nightfall, the quick burn of napalm."

"I'm thinking we should get someone in on the strategy."

"What?"

"To consult. Just to cover our ass."

Duncan feels a tightening in his shoulders. "A consultant? You mean a planner?" He knows what comes next: a familiar winching sensation as the slack between him and Anne is taken up and they're both pressed to stand loyal to their nameplate duties.

"Like a details guy. To go over scripts and make sure we're socially compliant."

"No."

"Historically accurate."

"Forget it."

"Duncan—"

"Christ, it's getting late."

Anne gathers up the drawings for him. "Well, I'll say it again, this is all good stuff, Duncan." Apparently her animal sense has kicked in and she knows enough to back down. She trails him out of the office to the elevator. "Given our previous disaster with Stand and Be Counted, our strategy is to wallpaper that boardroom with ideas."

"I'm going up the West Side," he says, knowing there's not enough time tonight to explain that *wallpapering* is not a strategy. "You want me to drop you off anywhere?"

"Thanks, but there's a Quarter Pounder with bacon I've got to puke up." Anne starts off down the hall and then stops. "One more thing. I'll throw this in now because there will be no way around it later. The client wants you to work their skinny-fit jeans into the concept too. Tapered down to the ankle. Very mod. That's not going to be a problem, is it?"

Duncan looks at her, reminds himself what he has forgotten: the true enemy is always embedded. "Anne, our entire strategy comes out of the flared cut of the product. I'd say it's very problematic."

"Well, you've got three long days to figure it out, Chief."

Lily mashes her cigarette and holds the snip of smolder in her fingers. "I'm looking at the spatial conquests resulting from the Romanesque style giving way to the Gothic."

"Goths," Lloyd says nodding. "Okay, I'm with you."

"The barrel vault—the Romanesque ceiling vault, for instance? In the early churches these round arches could only span a square space. Quite primitive, really." She uses her toe to trace the shape of the archaic vault in the gravel. "So churches always had narrow naves and aisles that had to be supported by lithic piers and columns. Places were dark as hell. But in came the pointed arch and the ribbed vault—literally a stone ribbing along the seam of a vault, like a ceiling structure with a support mechanism built right in. Finally, man was using his brain." Lily crouches, scratches the shape of a four-part rib vault alongside her gravel toe imprint. "Cathedral ceilings could soar now, the span of naves and aisles doubled."

She stops, looks up. Lloyd yawns into the net of his fingers.

"Sorry, babe, you're boring me to tears."

She shakes her head and stands, turns away from him. It's really time that she gets home.

"Tell me something dirty about your life, Lily."

"Fuck off," she says and scratches her cheek.

"See, you even say that without a muscle twitch." Lloyd sighs and stands. "You and I should go on the road, sharking. You're all poker face."

"You're all talk."

He crushes his cigarette under his heel and walks around her. His head reaches just to her shoulder. "Jesus, you're a tall drink of water. Okay, let's do this: you give me the scoop and in exchange I'll do something for you. That's how this friendship thing works, correct?"

"We're friends now?"

"Don't get too attached. I'd sell you up the river in a heartbeat."

Lily smirks. She believes him.

"There you go!" He juts his finger at her. "Quick, how would you describe your teenage years?"

"Religious."

"Priests and confessionals?"

"Convent school."

Lloyd opens his mouth, his finger drops. "Lily?" his voice nearly crumbles. "Do you—are you still in possession of kneesocks?"

"I don't deal in the present tense."

"Fair enough. The convent shit's more titillating anyway. Let's get back to that."

"Hold on," she says. "You never said. What do I get out of this?"

"Oh." Lloyd puts his hands on his hips. "You're in for a treat. You and I are going on a little field trip."

At six-thirty that night, Duncan connects to the Saw Mill Parkway with an impaired sense of aerodynamics (due to the pug-nosed state of the Saab) but also with an overriding self-confidence that only a big idea can generate. Of course, leave it to Anne and her typical account-whore behavior to complicate a simple premise like *History Repeating* with a non sequitur like skinny-leg jeans. Well, he'll find a way to work around it.

Because unlike the Laundry Elves campaign, this is his chance to create compelling drama in the form of a TV commercial. It's also a chance at another gold Pencil.

Good thing Lily isn't the only one who can crack open a book. Because he's going to have to do research. By the time he traveled to Vietnam, the country had grown a lush cover of foliage over its scars. By the time he toured the rooms of the Reunification Palace in Saigon, it had been converted into a museum. He has a picture of himself standing in front of the stormer tanks that took down the palace gates in '75. There's something wrong with the photo, though, that makes him stack it at the back of the pile. It's his grin or his T-shirt logo; the great white swoosh of one or the other, or both.

If anything, the forced inclusion of the skinny-fit jeans is a reminder that his nascent idea requires protection. He will not discuss it with any of the Brass traditionalists who roost and fuck in the upper reaches of the agency, refusing to acknowledge the malleable new borders of media. Who says a national denim campaign can't provide commentary on the human condition under strife? Also, he will not discuss it with Lily. He looks at the clock in the dash. She's probably waiting for him to excavate. It's odd, but in the city he kept forgetting about the bones, the dead nanny in the loam. In fact, he'd considered lingering around the office tonight, getting in well after Lily had turned in. These are impulses he can't explain. Not to Lily, not even to himself. What kind of man admits the keen sense of self he feels at work becomes all but obscured by the time he hits the deer-strewn Taconic?

CHAPTER 13

Sweat Glands

When he pulls up to the house he finds Lily sitting on a folding lawn chair in the driveway. She's wearing a pair of cutoff jeans and is fogging her thighs with a can of insect repellent. Duncan gives the horn a weak squeeze in greeting. It produces a sound much like that of a stomach digesting. Lily jumps up, follows the car to the lean-to. Duncan winces; she's going to nail him for being late. And it doesn't help that he still hasn't brought the Saab in for servicing.

He hardly has time to cut the engine and Lily's there, pressed in the narrow strip between wall and car, spray can still in hand. "He got our number," she says as he opens his door. "I don't know how—it's not even listed."

"What?" Duncan edges out of the driver's side, they are nose to nose. Lily pushes back her hair, flustered and impatient.

"He wanted to talk to you." She backs up, allowing the door to close behind him. "I thought it was about the pig."

"Lily, calm down. Who wants to talk to me?" Duncan has to guide her back out of the lean-to and into the yard.

"Skinner—the old man. We've been summoned. Well, you've been summoned. Tonight." She tosses the insect repellent into the grass.

"What for?"

"I don't know."

"Well, did you tell him I wasn't around?"

"I don't want him to know you're not here." Her voice riles into so-pranic peaks. "We need to go over—what if they found the pig?"

Duncan is glad that she's not angry with him. Feels a clean, white flash of relief that lasts a few moments before he realizes what she's really saying. One of the last things he wants to do tonight is listen to Skinner's lung-busting hack.

"I knew I shouldn't have left you here." He turns, sets the lock on the Saab. "But you wanted to be mixed up, right?"

"That's why I'm not letting you go alone," Lily says. "If the townies are taking you down, I'm going down with you."

He looks at her, so serious in the evening light. "Thank you," he says gruffly though touched by her words. "But we don't have to go anywhere we don't want to go."

"It's not an invitation. If we don't go to them, you know they'll come here."

Duncan's exhausted from his drive. His shirt is moist under one arm and he can feel a pimple pulsing beside his nostril. "Fine. Let them come."

"Duncan."

"Or better yet, let me go there, explain the whole thing." He turns, starts walking down the drive.

"No, wait," she says, following him. "We'll go together and deny it all."

"Lily, I don't care what these people think." He stops, looks at her. Could this embroilment be her way of avoiding the truth, of dismissing the real problem between them? "You can come back to the city on Sunday."

"No! I cannot just go back to the city, Duncan." She crosses her arms over her breasts. "What about Tinker—the bones?"

He doesn't answer, doesn't tell her he'd forgotten. This Lily reminds him of an outdoor child, wild and feral. His mouth swells. He would like to fish her from the long grass and bring her inside.

"Where is this meeting, anyway?" he says finally.

"I wrote it down."

"Fine. Let's do it."

The cannon is mounted on a grassy strip of lawn between a tar-paper shack and an aluminum barn, its muzzle angled toward a yawning gap in the treeline and the ribbon of Hudson beyond.

"Here's what you need to know about firing a ten-pound Parrott rifle without blasting a hole through yourself." Skinner slaps the side of the cannon, turns his red clotted eye on the men gathered around him. "Owing to some unfortunate accidents with cast-iron pieces, this particular piece of ordnance enjoyed a bad reputation among many artillerymen."

Lily is, maybe unsurprisingly, the only woman in the farmyard. Her presence clearly compromises the Masonic atmosphere, but what was she supposed to do? Let Duncan come here alone? Between the two of them, she's the only one thinking straight about the wild boar. She watches as Skinner marches Duncan into the "second" position at the mouth of the cannon and hands him a corkscrew-ended rod he calls a wormer.

"Your job's to scrape out any leftover bits of embers before we load in fresh ammo." The old man's voice is a whistle from a reed pond. "You getting this? Otherwise, you'll push in fresh gunpowder and blow yourself sky high."

That they have not been discovered—that instead, the locals are conscripting her husband into some sort of military reenactment—does little to lighten Lily's mood or loosen the sensation of a gunpoint summoning. Duncan's face is hard under cumulative stubble, but she can still read his disbelief. He's been singled out for an elaborate hazing ritual involving exploding ordnance. Drove two hours to escape the lunatic fringe in the city only to be greeted by its rural counterpart.

If there is some significance to the firing, Skinner has yet to explain it, though Lily is sure it has somehow been instigated by their presence in

Osterhagen. In addition to the dozen or so onlookers, a small group of men—Duncan included—has been chosen to actually participate in the firing. While the old man demonstrates how to plunge the cannon tube clean Lily looks around. She recognizes two people from the library gathering last week. Wakefield, who owns the hardware store, and the sickly Armenian with the ponytail who'd dribbled a trail of cranberry punch down the front of his denim shirt. There's a fifth making up the active band around the flaking piece of artillery. Dressed in a pair of gumboots and green gunner's cap is a pint-size twist of a man who can only be Skinner's son from Poughkeepsie. Ancient in his own right and with a grizzled head, he has the same bulbous eyes that turn wolfishly on Lily now and then as his father explains how to use a tube of fulminated mercury to ignite gunpowder.

"The Model 1861 has a bore diameter of two-point-nine inches, effective range of nineteen hundred yards, and weighs eight hundred ninety pounds. One of the most accurate and economical artillery pieces during the Civil War. But cast iron is brittle—which you'll see for yourselves, there's lotsa pressure in the breech when you fire it off. That's why it's reinforced with wrought iron." Skinner knuckles his fist against the metal barrel skirting. " 'Course, they still occasionally blow up."

A chuckle rises from the villagers. Lily shudders, looks around. In the darkened lot the men are all slouch and peaked ball caps, lumps of flannel trained on Skinner's scratch track of a voice.

"Wet sponge, Emmett!"

Skinner's son, occupying the "first" position, dips the sponge end of his rod into a bucket of water and then drives it up into the tube. Lily senses there's something moist and loathsome about him. The sort of creature found under bridges, awaiting the crossing of the billy goats. Even the thought of Lloyd cycling through his comprehensive collection of perversions isn't nearly as offensive. Also, she can't ignore the fact that he's staring at her while pumping the sponge rod aggressively in and out of the shaft.

She takes a step to the left, hoping to move out of his sight line. But those eyes trail her, two poached eggs sliding sideways in their cups.

"The Parrott system here was the workhorse rifle of the artillery for the first years of the war. They kept them rolling out even after bringing around ordnance rifles." The old man watches his son tap the rod against the barrel mouth. "Seems to me if it was good enough for the Battle of Bull Run, it's good enough for our purposes tonight."

"Which are what, exactly?" Duncan interrupts. "If you don't mind my asking."

Lily watches Skinner turn sharply on her husband. He stands just under Duncan's nostrils. The old man has the unwarranted bravery of a toy dog, she thinks, and the same propensity to bite.

"Ten o'clock cannon is a warning to whoever got our boar," he says. "Go ahead and set your watch by us. Every twenty-two hundred hours. Now get ready to load."

Wakefield, blunt-thumbed and severe despite a waft of frosty hair, comes forward with a blackened sackcloth (which Lily assumes to be gunpowder) and loads it into the cannon muzzle. Emmett tamps it to the back of the tube with the ram end of the rod.

"I'm gonna sight the piece," Skinner calls with emphasis in the direction of the trees. He kneels at the breech end of the cannon and peers along its nozzle as though to locate a Confederate battery hidden in the bush.

Lily glances at her husband. He looks soldierly in the dusk, his wormer rod the spear of classic battle. She remembers the night they arrived, how he'd stood frozen on the road staring at the boar while it thrashed under the front wheel. How she'd held out the tire iron to him but knew, already, that the extension of her arm was just reflex. That she had already executed the action herself. Something alone and instinctive within her had already carried out the deed without him.

"How's this going to bring back the pig?" She hears her voice for the first time.

Skinner looks up at her. He pushes back from the cannon and brushes his hands against the obliques of his thighs. "You ever come under cannon fire?" he asks. "Eleven thousand Union soldiers did not just fall at Appomattox under natural circumstances."

Lily and Duncan glance at one another, seeking interpretation. Maybe they're being toyed with, but how much do these people know?

The old man steps toward her, zippering his hunting vest tight across the aquatic rumblings of his chest. "You might be king of the hill living in that fancy old house. But when there's an 1861 Parrott rifle trained on your front porch, you're going to think twice before you take that which does not belong to you."

It's impossible to know the depth of this indictment. Lily thinks of her conversations with Lloyd, his appreciation of her stoic demeanor, and wishes for a bit of that unflappability to settle over her heart right now.

"Prick and prime," Skinner tells his artillerymen.

While Wakefield fusses with a lanyard and the small tube of mercury, the Armenian finally steps to action. It's his job to insert a metal pin into a tiny airshaft at the rear of the cannon and pierce the sack of gunpowder. Of all the men gathered, Lily is least afraid of him. He's a pound shy of swimming in his chambray shirt and she's almost certain she could outrun him.

When Skinner finally calls "Ready!" Duncan is bent over, tying his shoelace. The rest of the artillerymen take a step toward the rear of the weapon. They angle their bodies away from the direction of the charge and flatten the palms of their hands over the ears closest to the cannon. There is a strum across Lily's spine. Duncan straightens up and looks around. He holds his post at the mouth of the cannon but looks bewildered, a man lost midstep in an aerobics class. She has a vision trimmed with gunpowder grit, her husband with a ballistic path straight through his belly.

"Jesus Christ, Duncan," she calls. "Get out of the way."

Skinner tips his pruned head in disgust. "I believe he wants to be blown into next Wednesday." There's a swish of nylon vest as he raises his hand to halt the proceedings.

Duncan, suddenly aware that he's holding things up, spears the wormer rod into the ground and jogs over to the side of the cannon. Lily can tell by the way he puts a hand through his hair that he's both shamed and impatient. She hears the coughs and brays of the outdoorsmen surrounding her. Sensing the potential for a casualty, flannel and work boots draw closer in the darkness.

"What do you boys think?" Skinner turns to his pod. There's an audible trill from his lungs, his voice a harmonica played underwater. "Will Old Parrott be a widow maker once again?"

A weak holler from the crowd. Emmett lofts his sponge rod over his head. The Armenian fiddles with his snarled ponytail. A motion lamp on the barn is triggered, bathing the entire scene in staccato illumination. Lily sees the figure of her husband at the edge of this situation. She smells wood smoke in the air. Skinner taps her roughly on the shoulder. "You go ahead, wish your man luck. Might be your last chance."

The old man's gummy snort of pleasure actually eases her mind. He's just having a little fun with the downstaters. Still, Lily understands that Skinner is a restless bloodhound. Despite his scattered eccentricities he is genuine and bred to track to the death. She and Duncan will have to rethink this eventuality. To make for the forest or the hills, to give the posse the slip, to leave the car and clothes—to reinvent themselves and disappear—is not an option. There is the wrench of Tinker. Lily has been trying to tell Duncan that she has a familial obligation to the nanny. That she cannot go back to the city, back to nothingness. How to make him understand the importance of the lovely white femur! And they've only just begun; fold now with such a miserly bone count and all of it will be a wash. They haven't pulled enough from the garden to form a woman. They haven't gotten far enough to constitute success.

She trips across the lawn toward Duncan with only this intention. To tell him that they can't give in, can't buckle just yet. They haven't even found her head. Maybe then. Once they've found Tinker's skull they can run, leave the small bones buried.

She goes to him. He hesitates in the darkness. While he does step forward, she can see that he's confused, maybe resigned. She has flown across the strip of grass and into his arms to share the foreseeable problems with conventional escape. Instead, his arms close around her, he braces her as if catching something that's fallen out of a window. Her mouth opens against his own, an incisor cuts a horizontal slice through lip. They come at each other this way, with optimism hammered thin as foil, still sentient of all that is hostile, muddled, and injured between them. The inescapable trace of farm manure in the air makes everything less desirable. The Osterhagen they have never discussed is the one they have just arrived in at this moment, with the singular task of deciding whether to leave together. The others—the boar and the nanny, the pervert, the artillerymen torn between this graceless kiss and blasting a charge through the trees—are the complications they have invited to avoid being alone with the truth.

———————————

Lily sits up in bed. The linens around her are too tight, sterile. Like she'd been tucked into bed by a nurse. She hears Duncan plucking around in the sunroom below and touches her lip. It had stopped bleeding almost immediately, the wet flesh repairing itself at a stunning rate. Duncan had scraped a few dry specks from her chin, then walked beside her to the truck. Sat himself in the middle while Skinner drove them home. It was possible that they were thinking the same thing, how pleasant it was not to talk, not to encourage familiarity.

Lily snaps the top sheet and watches it billow over her fresh-shaved legs. When she hears him take the stairs quietly she tries to level the velocity of her breath and fill the room with a quiet, welcoming consistency. She rubs left leg against right, remembering the pleasure of frictionless calves. The bedroom door is partially open. Lily has re-created herself under the sheets in the likeness of sand, a soft landing. Yet beyond this rolling topography—more satisfying than sand, she knows—are the hard ridges beneath. Tooth and toe and nail and the simple, painful angles at which their mouths may meet. He must feel this? Her buried lures? For what other reason does he return to her each weekend? Lily sucks the small nub formed over her cut lip. In piecing together a dead woman might they also resurrect another?

He comes down the hall. She closes her eyes. He walks past.

Lily sits up. Despite the bread knife in her gut she sits up. She can scarcely believe it, the sound of his sneakers retreating down the hall. For some reason, she was sure he would come to her. She's embarrassed— no, she's outraged. Why is it that he won't even try? At some point in the night the radiance had returned to her. Couldn't he feel it? The afternoon that they'd sat together in the closet, in the ease of darkness, hadn't he felt it then? Or does Duncan think he can just go on living in the spaces around her? If so, Lily thinks, he's got another thing coming. Tomorrow night, he's got another thing coming.

CHAPTER 14

Articulations of the Upper Extremities

In the morning she watches Duncan unload groceries and wonders why the silent rubbing of her smooth calves failed to draw him in. She scoops her plain oatmeal right from the pot and watches him stock the cupboard, trying to ignore his careless shelving (the cans should be arranged by content, not size). Duncan's hair, she notices, has grown an extra inch or so beyond the collar. As he moves Lily thinks, I have licked the split between those shoulder blades. Felt his weight on top of me. Now the thought makes her envious, as if she's read these details in another woman's journal but has been denied the pleasure herself. Something about the leanness of those places, the scull of rib beneath his arm, the groove of lower back; they are unrecognizable. What would Duncan do if she went to him now? Slipped her arms around his chest, pressed her body to his back?

She crosses her legs, looks away. The trick, she knows, is to allow him to initiate. A year ago, she wouldn't have thought twice about offering him her body. A year ago, she was sure he'd accept, gratefully. Last night he'd kissed her to appease the jeering cannoneers, but the action was lined with the mercury of bad temper and the shame of being ridiculed. He'd forgotten himself. And she was encouraged. Now with the morning burning on, and distance back between them, she finds herself petrified of rejection.

Duncan begins a low whistle, something unmelodic. She knows the tune, the one he uses to fill space.

"What do you think?" She will try. "What are we going to dig up tonight?"

He pauses midbar. Ties a grocery bag in half. "Actually, I'm going to have to take a break."

"Oh?"

"Yeah. I got a call from work this morning. You were still asleep." He scratches his head and looks at the cans. "It's this idea we're working on for Stand and Be Counted. The Vietnam War."

"Oh." Lily's word for all occasions. Comes out round and mealy to disguise the burn.

"You can dig if you want," he offers. "But I've got to go back and look at some old footage."

She feels the roots of her hair incinerating. "No, that's fine. I'm busy too. At the library." Lily curses herself for having made this ridiculous pact to dig together. She can't renege now, as if she has nothing else to do up here, like she's dependent on him. As though her life, when tacked up alongside his, lacks diesel and passion.

He turns from the shelf suddenly, holding a can of beans. "Garbanzo? Same as chickpeas, right?"

She scrapes the last rubber edges of her breakfast. "They don't exactly hand out doctorates, you know."

He puts the can down on the table. "I know that, Lily. I know you're busy."

She can't look up or she will cry. She's done with this heavy lifting, this pretending, the illusion of chatter and interest. And what does Duncan know about Vietnam? He took a booze cruise through the Bay of Tonkin once. How's that supposed to sell jeans? Lily can feel him look at her and so she folds the newspaper in half, her eyes circling the same paragraph.

"So we'll both get some work done this weekend, okay?"

She doesn't respond. There's a static crackle surrounding him and it annoys her that he holds his work up like something that must be carried across a swollen river. In Duncan's paranoid landscape he is forever on the verge of losing his job. And in its impermanence it becomes vital, tragic, and necessary. Blue jeans as vocation.

As if you're writing the next Pulitzer, she'd like to say to him.

He moves to the refrigerator. Opens a carton of eggs and inspects for cracks. "Just try to keep clear of those guys, all right? Skinner and the Clan."

Jesus, is that a drawl in his voice? She goes to the sink, nudges dishes around to make room for her saucepan.

"Although, I think we handled things pretty well last night. And they seem to like you at the library, right?"

Lily watches the bowls capsize in the suds. "I'm there to work," she says, "not socialize."

Duncan starts to say something, but she cranks the faucet over his response. It's horrible, this sudden and insincere interest in her well-being. If he truly cared he wouldn't be pulling a runner twelve hours into the weekend. As the dishwater begins to lap at the brim of the sink she turns around to face him. He's standing in the same position, still watching her.

"You know, Duncan," she says, looking him in the eye, "they *are* offering a reward for the pig. I'm thinking of turning you in."

"It's my day off."

"And?"

"Give me something to go on. I'm watching Bob Hope reruns."

"What about you get to keep your job for another week?" Duncan closes the kitchen door behind him, stands barefoot on the porch.

"Kooch is in Jersey." Leetower yawns violently into the phone, adenoids vibrating like a tuning fork. "He was a prick on stilts yesterday. I was looking forward to a day away from him."

"We'll do it ourselves," Duncan says quickly. He's pleased at the thought of evolving the campaign in Kooch's absence. "I think I've got a way to work in the other jeans."

"Fuck, you're fast."

"The American Grunt Girls wear the flare legs, right? So we put the Viet Cong girls in the skinny jeans. Whatever your preference, we've got it—we're sympathetic to both sides."

"Girl-on-girl engagement? Are you serious?"

"Dead."

"It'll never make it out the door."

"You need to start thinking one-eighty on this, LT. I guarantee, there will always be someone to bring you back to zero."

"You're an inspiration to the red-blooded."

"Go with God. I'll be in by noon."

Lloyd says he's trying to sort out what type of pervert he would like to be. Until now he's been a dabbler. Crossing forms with the freedom of a student not yet decided on acrylics or oils, poetry or fiction. Certainly there are no absolutes, no hard-and-fast rules dividing the flashers from the frotteurs from the Peeping Toms. "But as it stands," he says, "I'm just a dilettante skittering across the surface of true talent."

When Lily left the house this morning, Duncan was still packing up for the city. Bon voyage, she thought, letting the screen door crack back against its frame. Now she follows the pervert between parked cars in the lot behind the library and is cheered by the fact that there is someone who looks forward to her company. She says nothing about the encounter with the townsfolk last night, abides by some intuitive precaution to keep such scenes on a separate grid.

Still, she feels a sting of pity for Lloyd's pear-shaped frame. He taps the bonnet of a Lincoln while telling her there's purity in choosing a single perversion, devoting one's life to it. This only reminds her of the pointed arch that she has somewhat abandoned in the library.

"You're boring when you think too much," she says and follows him into a lane that runs the ten blocks of Osterhagen. Lloyd holds out a fresh cigarette.

"Fire, Lily. Fire!" He snaps his fingers.

She comes up alongside him, sparks the silver lighter while they walk in gravel tire ruts. "You should just make the jump," she says, reminding herself to focus on his problems for a change. "Exist in a realm of action— reach out and touch someone."

"I just don't know what I want to be when I grow up."

When Lily suggests he compile a short list, draw up pros and cons for each, his features pinch in toward the center of his face. "Draw one up yourself. You sure waste a lot of time with me."

It's true. She should be sorting out the various abandoned approaches to her dissertation, the tumble of papers, the small mountain of books she dragged from the city. But all she can muster is a casual and scattered inter-est, the same clinical detachment she had experienced years ago toward the end of her undergraduate study in Italy. It was a weariness, she thought back then, of a hot Italian summer and a rambling life of scholastic ambi-guities. She'd gone to Italy hoping the snug little boot would kick up a squall in her soul, but she was knotted down tight. What was the point of her work? Lily had succeeded on paper but that was just cheap ballpoint. She understood the technical phenomena of building a cathedral with only compass, string, and a straight edge. But she simply couldn't feel it. Her professor had pointed out Brunelleschi's Renaissance discovery of linear perspective construction; how for the first time in the fifteenth century the eye of the viewer could finally be brought into mathematical integration with a painting. *Yes,* she nodded. The Gothic was positively brilliant for all it just barely accomplished before it was handed over, before it ushered in the Renaissance.

Four blocks in and the lane gives way to yards strung with clothes-lines, the chewed lace of fencing. Lloyd ducks beneath a sugar maple, holds apart a bracket of chicken wire. She has to crouch on all fours to pass through the snag into the backyard. Lily thinks, the Pied Piper is leading me through the lanes of Osterhagen. *And I follow happily.* There's something compelling about this fat little man; he advocates deviancy with a brand of reasoning she can get behind.

"We're going to have to climb the roof of that garage." Lloyd points across the yard. "Get up there, darling, and you'll have earned your bum fluff."

Lily wipes her forehead, pushes her glasses up her nose. "That's at least nine feet." She hears complaint in her voice, the old worry returning. The lot is wild with shrubbery, the untrimmed arms of several bushy trees. But they might make it, she thinks. If they stick to the peripheries, skulk along the narrows between fence and maple trunk, they might reach the garage. Then climb the rain barrel to the corrugated-tin and tar-paper roof that leans in toward the second-story window of the house.

They wind through the clotheslines and bird calls, the grass and petrol-scented mysteries of garden sheds. While her heart is beating faster Lily is aware of the life around her. Somewhere the hum of morning television, the ratchet and whirl of sprinkler heads, a child or a cat mewing beyond a fence. There is a palatable pleasure in these things and she would like to stick out her tongue to gather them.

"You go first." He nods up at the roof.

"What?"

"Hurry up, Lily. The key is to not stand still."

Knowing her forehead must resemble crinkled foil wrap, she takes a few quick breaths and attempts to smooth it out. She hates that so many moments in her life seem to come down to this pressure—a chance to act or fail and no space in between.

"Okay," she says, ignoring the bleating of her heart. "But don't look up my skirt."

"You're wearing pants."

Lily allows him to boost her to the top of the rain barrel. From there she snatches at the lip of the eaves and pulls herself up. It's a messy scramble, craning each leg over onto the safety of the roof. When she gets both knees up and tucked under her, she begins to feel the metal structure bending under her weight. She has to shift and slot her legs between the ripples of the shingles to stop the buckling.

"Get under the gable," he calls up. She wonders how long he's been waiting to use that tremolo stage whisper. Lloyd is already climbing the barrel, his tongue thrust between his lips with the effort. Maybe she should look away. She can't bear to watch what can only be the sloppy acrobatics of ascent.

To her surprise, Lloyd scales the garage wall with ease. While she watches, he hoists his lumbersome body over the eaves as though maneuvering a lithe frame. He may as well have been trained on parallel bars. Lloyd executes a fluid tilt and swing and lands on the sheet metal without a sound. And then it strikes her. All this time she's been humoring him—his romantic notion of cross-genre perversion, his blundered attempts with the schoolgirls—when, in truth, he really is a professional. There's fear in Lily's heart suddenly; it clicks to life with the speed of fuel on fire. Could it be vertigo? The fear of uniformed officers? The understanding that Lloyd has done this many, many times? That's my problem, Lily thinks. I never take anyone seriously until it's too late.

Lloyd crawls between the ridges until he's beside her in the groove of the false gable window. She reminds herself that she's not trapped, that she can lower herself back down the other side of the garage, that she can drop to the grass and roll as though she'd been dumped from the sky. It's dogs and perverts that can smell fear from great distances, so she'd like to say something impertinent, show him she's not afraid. But Lloyd's not even looking at her. He runs the back of his hand over his mouth. She follows his gaze and realizes that by leaning forward they have a view into a window ten feet away.

Inside is the kind of bedroom shambles that's best kept behind closed doors: a fitted sheet scrolled off the corners of a mattress, an old vacuum-tube television with a coat hanger receiver, a carpet mottled by dropped cigarettes. Everywhere, clothing as drapery.

Lloyd settles on his knees. "Check it out, hey?"

She forgets her fear of him in this abstraction of a room. This is orchestrated chaos, Lily thinks. Someone has caught wind of their plans and sent a crew ahead to disarrange, to tease filmy underwear from a drawer, to knock a stack of paperbacks off the nightstand. To not only rummage through the closet but to slide the closet door off its track and lean it there against the wall.

Lily begins to suspect she's part of a live studio audience, that applause will be cued and laughter expected. That she is not, after all, the only disaster waiting to happen. And if there are secret lives to be lived and phone conversations to overhear and boxes in closets through which to snoop, then let these things be plotted and beautiful. Let the ugly truths be beautiful.

"It's perfect," she breathes.

"It gets better," he says.

The car makes its displeasure evident halfway down the curved drive. The sound of polymer grading against hard rubber, a synthetic competition that vibrates in each nail bed and ignites a pilot light of anxiety in his belly. This wasn't happening on Thursday. Then again, he hadn't put the car in reverse on Thursday.

Duncan brakes slowly, lets the complaint die away, then puts the vehicle in drive. He inches back up toward the lean-to without a single tick from the front end and considers the feasibility of driving without shifting into reverse. His own father, regardless of the season, would let vehicles idle for a minute or two before setting off; a quirk he called "letting the juices flow," or "letting the kinks sort out," but that Duncan suspected had more to do with a lifetime of Minnesota winters than combustion systems.

He opts to let the car idle for a minute, hoping the rumbles will whisper out on their own, all the while ignoring a suspicion that some sort of Masonic will is behind this latest hiccup. Either that or his own agnostic punishment for fleeing from his wife this morning. It is not the goal of his summer to race back to the city with unhealthy thoughts of Lily multiplying by the mile, but there is a dissonance between her and his work that he just can't reconcile.

Last year, he'd been surprised to discover his One Show Award Pencils in the linen closet—the linen closet where Lily had shelved them beside the box of vacuum filters. Looking back he'd say this was the beginning of their mutual resentment. The moment after which their actions toward one another felt perfunctory and insincere. He brought the trophies back to his office, as though returning them to an environment of respect. But Lily's action had scarred him and he began to think that displaying them again after five years was the mark of a floundering hack. He locked them in the desk instead. This way he could open the drawer and pretend to fish for a marker while really just teasing them out of their velvet sacks for a quick fondle.

Truth was, the damage was done. Hadn't Lily made her position clear? His chosen life lacked the heft and gravity she required. It was something to be borne, like termites or chronic disease. Lily had evolved as a species. While he remained terrestrial and not quite upright she had entered the order of new world monkeys, was afforded a superior position among the trees. They could no longer recognize each other from these two different vantage points. It was really always a matter of time; she had been abroad, received a classical education. He'd sold out to commercial enterprise. With that single closet discovery last year, his path lost its luster. The haste and immediacy of this change frightened him; that one action from Lily could create such a profound change frightened him. So he devoted his days to reasoning his way back into a sort of love for his work. And if not love, then at least interest. And when interest failed, tolerance. But tolerance went away too. He was left with only an incipient motivation in which he could find nothing honorable or worthy: fear.

Duncan punches down the clutch and wiggles the stick into reverse, taps in enough gas to ease into motion. As he negotiates the curved lip of the drive the grind starts up again, this time the sound of teaspoons caught in the garbage disposal. It's a sharp turn of the wheel to the right while in reverse that's doing it. Duncan gets out and crouches by the left wheel. He runs his hand along the top of the tire but stops short at a section of the fender skirt that's crushed inward and then folded over like a flipped eyelid. He switches to his other knee and eases his hand, palm up, under the lip of molded plastic, pulling gently to snap it back into place.

The fender resists, but then begins to bend for him. He draws a portion of it back over the tire and then makes to slide his hand out. Only thing, his hand won't move. He presses it down into the tire and shifts it sideways, but the damaged fender has no more give. It's locked his wrist down in a polymer cuff. Duncan feels a tick in his throat, swallows against it twice, and sweats through his shirt. He tries pulling his hand forward; there's an inch of release until the ridge of his knuckles blocks the way. A trail of blood then, and shavings of skin that look like curled mozzarella. As it becomes clear that he's trapped, his humiliation is gently underscored by panic. He's been so caught up in his campaign, could he have inadvertently conjured an eerie form of Southeast Asian torture? His body temperature fluctuates, he begins to shiver in his own sweat. While he keeps absolutely still, there is no pain. Duncan leans against the tire, counts the hidden bolts on the rim, and waits.

CHAPTER 15

Temporary or Milk Teeth

Lloyd is the Magellan of rooftops.

"I think you've found your calling," Lily says.

He taps his lips. "Focus the mind, Lily."

She's not sure how long they've been crouched waiting for something to happen. The sun has slid out of its aggressive position, and in their pocket under the gable window both Lily and the pervert vanish with their separate thoughts.

This Peeping Tom undertaking is tough, requires a combination of stamina and luck beyond the pure gymnastics of scoring a decent vantage point. Lloyd, she realizes, is the cartographer of Osterhagen. His geography is the rooftops and alleys of the small town. She imagines he possesses encyclopedic knowledge of windows, alcoves, and terraces, the shelter of overhangs, all things scalable, the cover of shrubs at ground level, the slats of space between fence boards, the location of notches in these boards, the few remaining unstuffed keyholes, the sag spots where drawn curtains refuse to join. She has softened toward Lloyd, like butter in the sun. Wants to offer him something in return, if only as a reward for this adventure, or to fill the space of waiting between them.

"I killed the wild boar, Lloyd."

He turns to her. "The what?"

"The pig. You know, the mascot." Saws an edge of tooth into bottom lip. "It ran out in the middle of the road."

He shuts his left eye. Absorbs her better, perhaps, under single focus.

"It didn't exactly die. I had to sort of beat it to death."

"The pig is dead?"

Lily nods.

"The Sovereign of the Deep Wood? At your hands?"

"With a tire iron." Scratches her mouth.

"Jesus Christ, you're not even lying." Lloyd leans back and looks at her. "They've been searching for that thing for weeks."

"It was dark. It charged from the bushes."

"They've sent out search parties—hogs are a bitch to trap, you know."

"We hit it with the car."

"But why?"

"It was an accident."

"I mean, why didn't you tell anyone?"

"I didn't know it belonged to someone," she says. "And then it was too late."

Lloyd waits for more.

"So we left it in the ditch."

His face breaks open then with a sudden appreciation. "Oh, sweetie." He knocks her thigh. "I get it—you're a little thug."

She feels her forehead bunch. "This isn't good. It's just rotting away."

"Come on now," he says. "You're acting like this is the first bad thing you've done. But let me tell you how it is."

"Cue the music."

"These are peccadilloes. Misdemeanors. They help shape the character." He taps the back of her hand. "What was it like, anyway?"

"It was making this sound, you can't even imagine."

"You're not the first Colonialist to like a good pigsticking. When in India, hey?"

"I just wanted it to stop."

"Would have been brilliant if you used a spear. Sharpens the savage instinct—let's see your teeth."

She turns, resists punching him in the shoulder. "I'm not a brute."

"Suit yourself." Lloyd shrugs. "Just don't flake out on me now." And he nods to the window below. There's a woman in the room.

Lily flattens herself behind the gable ledge. Her heart is in her mouth suddenly and she's careful to purse her lips in case it should slip out. She has missed the woman's entrance, has caught her in the middle of a sequence of events that just might lead to an undressing. Like modernist theater, she thinks. The disrobing has begun somewhere offstage, continues as the character crosses from stage left to right, will conclude as she moves off into the wings. Arrive late and leave early, force the audience to engage, to draw in the missing strokes.

She hears Lloyd swallow, from his throat the familiar smack of stuck oxygen bubbles. She sneaks a look at him and thinks his eyes have lost their shrewd perspective. They seem to slide an inch or so apart from their usual position at the foothills of his nose. He's enchanted.

The woman below is much older than Lily expected, maybe a senior. Her hair has grayed—it has the wiry determination of a second-growth forest—but is rinsed the color of stewed carrots. She was expecting younger. A young, careless woman to take ownership of the snow-shaker state of the room, the plastic jewelry, the tatty novels. The woman's caramel hose are rolled down the calves, housecoat unzipped to the belly. Her breasts are loose under there, and as she moves about the room they seem to take turns peering from between the flaps. When she sits on her bed to pull up her stockings Lily is struck by the portrait: the Degas poignancy of the subject's unawareness, the soft humiliation of the body. Just like Tinker. A woman made to give her body up to strangers, in death and now again in resurrection. The old woman below is covered in flesh that is only loosely tacked to the bone here and there, at the elbows and temple and knees. Elsewhere, on the planes and round surfaces, it has lost its grip. Lily notices that a gully has sunk between the split of her breasts, that her belly has risen like a hill. A tangle of veins decorates her thighs, blue tinsel wrapped indiscriminately around a tree.

Lloyd starts fishing around in his pocket. Lily finds the motion distracting and turns to look at him. His breathing seems to have changed, his face is a new, muddy pink. She stops, holds her own breath. *Oh my God.* She curses her simplicity. He's doing what perverts do when they climb rooftops to watch women undress. This Peeping Tom business does not exist in isolation! It's foreplay. A pearl on the string of continuum. Only she'd assumed he'd go offstage to handle the last part. There's no question: his tongue has slipped out a bit between his lips; he looks oddly healthy. How could she have overlooked the fact that this would culminate in a sexual act? This is what she does. Again and again she underestimates the intentions of those around her, adulterates real-life urges. She has taken Lloyd and made him into a Disney version of himself. Hadn't she realized that by accepting this mission she would witness not only the intimacy of a woman unfurled, but also that of a man taking pleasure in this privacy? She looks from the woman to the crouched pervert. He is fixed on the window, his hand continues to rummage. Nothing else exists.

Nevertheless, she can't just sit here. "Jesus Christ," she whispers at him. "What are you doing?"

Lloyd looks at her. He breaks from the woman and stockings to look at Lily. His eyes saddle back up against either side of his nose. Lloyd follows her eyes down to his pocket. He draws out an unwrapped stick of gum, tucks it in his mouth.

Humped up against the wheel well Duncan has fallen into a lull, similar to sleep, but lacking in restful properties. As a result, his dreams are not really dreams, but scrappy re-creations of syndicated television programming from his youth: exhortative, musically overwrought, and of questionable production values. Through it all Duncan has kept one eye on the sun, aware that its position might give him an indication of the time. But he's spent too many years in the shadows of skyscrapers, intuitive sense has left him, the tradition of the sundial has been corrupted. All light is artificial light; it is the good grace of a corporation to be dispensed and recalled at random.

Hadn't he first felt its addiction years ago? Riding the elevator down the shank of the Proctor & Gamble building. Trying hard to gnaw back smiles, but the glint of Hawke's large teeth refracted in the mirrored paneling was blinding. The Tide client had fallen hard and fast for their new concept, Laundry Elves. *That was tight work, Chief.* The older man's breath a sour knot of color between them. *You can keep your job for three more weeks.*

Duncan had no other desire then; didn't want to write a book, didn't want to direct film. He thought, if he knew anything after years of fretting, it was that life didn't leave you with much space in which to stuff dreams. You got a block the size of a glove compartment if you were lucky. He had chiseled his dream down to one.

How remote and unessential that all seems now, sprawled on his back and pinned to a car. In his previous incarnation he may have lived as a man, but there is no denying that he has returned as a beast. Reduced to animal instinct. Once he lost sensation in his fingers—how long ago? one hour, two?—he began to feel a detached pity for the hand, similar to the way he felt as Lily took up the bones of Tinker's scrolled pelvis. His hand is no longer a blood member, but an appendage. Paw. He could chew it off if necessary. But when will it be necessary? When will Lily come home? If she does, in fact, come home. She may not; the library could very well be a screen to shade some seedy liaison, an affair, a lover following her up from the city. Just his luck. To be trapped, forced to bite off his left hand, only to discover the unsavory details of an infidelity he had, until now, never considered. Why else was she so adamant about staying up here alone? And how did she really spend her time during the week? She has barely mentioned the dissertation. The thought makes him angry and exhausted. He looks at the caged hand, remembers how it reached out to slap Lily's ass. It was the hand that performed the action and he could do nothing but watch.

Lily chatters the entire walk back to the library, hides her embarrassment in bubbles and yips. Lloyd doesn't engage. Has no interest in holding back shorn fence wire or taking cover behind the maples. His silence is so complete eventually Lily is sucked dry of dialogue.

"That was a disappointment," he says finally.

She is about to apologize, explain the shriveled prude of her soul.

"She wasn't what you'd call a looker," he says with remorse. "She was a turnoff, in fact."

Lily stops walking. Is struck by this indignation.

"I mean, I had that window scouted out."

"Well, I enjoyed it," she says, brighter than sunshine. "I had fun. It was great."

"Yeah, right," he sneers, his face a swill of vinegar.

"Besides." Lily starts walking again, wants to clear out of the lane in case there were any witnesses to their gangly drop from the rooftop. "Doesn't the, uh, gratification reside in the act of watching?" She adjusts her glasses. "Not necessarily in the subject?"

"You're talking big words now, Lily." Lloyd walks ahead into the library parking lot, slaps his palms against the hood of two cars. He turns to her one last time before hunching away. "If I'm gonna pull a stunt that could land me in jail," he says, "the least I want is a decent set of tits to look at."

She knows something's wrong when she sees the car in the driveway. Lily is off her bike before coming to a full stop in front of the house, wedges the front tire into the shaggy skirt of a boxwood tree. While it does occur to her that Duncan may have changed his mind, that he stayed behind to excavate Tinker's remains, the thought is so brief she snuffs it between two fingers before it has a chance to illuminate.

How deceptive angle and perspective can be, Lily thinks as she approaches the rear of the vehicle. A handsome woman from behind who, in turning, reveals a ruined face. She looks through the passenger window: an overnight bag, keys in the ignition. Her watch shows she's been gone for hours, more than enough time for him to leave.

None of it hangs well in her belly. Spying on the old woman now seems a dark and dirty business, knowing Duncan was just a few miles away the entire time. She starts toward the front door. Then stops. There is a sound ranging over the scrape of her sneakers in the gravel. Lily moves back to the car. She walks around to the driver's side where her husband is flat on his back, eyes shut.

She has neither the time nor ability to string together a sequence of words before Duncan opens his eyes.

"Finally," he says.

She has to lie on the hood of the car for leverage, reach over and into the wheel well, and force back the cracked plastic before Duncan can pry himself loose. He pulls hard from a crouched position so that when the car gives, he stumbles backward and has to fight for balance. Lily slides off the hood, making a move to help him, but he catches himself in time.

"Can you feel it? Are you all right?"

He holds the injured hand at an awkward angle, as though it were a prosthetic he was just learning to use. "I dreamt that I was buried to my neck in the desert," he says, testing each swollen finger. "In every direction, Lily, a blanket of sand. My head—for some reason it was smeared with honey. The sky went dark then, and the wind kicked up a cloud of sand. Like a big storm coming. The honey dripped into my eyes. The cloud got closer and I realized it wasn't sand, but a scourge of locusts."

She looks at him. "That wasn't a dream. It was an episode of *Kung Fu*."

He nods, looks at his fist again. The knuckles are drizzled with dried blood. Lily touches his arm.

"Come inside. We need to clean this."

He reaches for her then. At first she thinks he's trying to steady himself with his good arm, but the reach is slow, and when his fingers come to rest, they are on her cheek.

"Your skin, Lily," he says, "is the most beautiful skin."

Her heart is in her throat again, so visible and obstructive these days. She has to lower her eyes. How can a moment be like this—both sudden and slow? When Duncan begins to stroke her cheek she bites her lip to keep from talking. To keep from asking questions. It seems to her that they have wasted an eternity holding each other at arm's length. And all she wants is to feel inseparable again. Without thinking, she reaches up and touches his fingers on her cheek. Thinks she might read his meaning this way. An answer through her own skin.

"You saved me."

Lily reaches for his injured hand then. He lets her turn the fingers gently for inspection. "That's what I do." She wants him to take her upstairs.

"Lucky it's not my writing hand."

"Yes," she says. "The literary world can sleep soundly tonight."

He stops stroking her. His fingers drop away. With his drowsy smile extinguished, Duncan pulls back as though she were a careless splash of iodine.

"I have to go."

"What?"

"Go. I have to."

Duncan moves to the car. Lily watches him negotiate the door handle with his left hand, then, once inside, the ignition. The damaged wing he keeps to his chest. She knocks on his window as the engine starts up.

"Duncan, I was kidding!" she says through the glass. But he's already backing away from her, the groan of cleaving plastic his only response.

CHAPTER 16

Optic Nerve

Girls dot the grassy downhill spur between the library doors and the sidewalk. With the *dolce far niente* of a Saturday, they cluster in pairs, parties of three. A group of six shares bits of food from cellophane bags. To the untrained observer there is no pattern to these aggregations: the groups and subgroups, the laggards, those shearing from the flock, the casual cluck from one pair to another. All these things, indiscriminate and random.

But to Lily, her behaviorist eye glancing over the top of a battered copy of Panofsky's *Gothic Architecture and Scholasticism,* there is nothing arbitrary or incidental about the formations of girls. Their patterns of separation, alignment, and cohesion mark a complex social arrangement developed over the long days of summer term. On the lawn she recognizes the earphoned girl who was the victim of Lloyd's botched lechery attempt. With her is a kitten-faced blonde, her eyes colored up, lashes webbed and frosted. A cosmetic project of the Fauves, Lily thinks.

A breeze snaps through Osterhagen like a shuttlecock and people dither over office locks and shop alarms before turning for home. Lily too, her helmet beside her on the library steps, lingers over the Gothic and prepares for her bike ride. It took her several hours after the driveway incident yesterday to realize Duncan was really not coming back. That his temper, in addition to the horseshit about being called into the office, had given him the green light to flee until next Thursday. Well, that and her big mouth.

Last night she went to the cellar and sat with Tinker's meager collection of bones. And while she had been turning the story of the burial around in her mind—it just didn't sit straight, the lack of corporal integrity, the random scatter of her remains—what she was hoping for really was sympathy in the nanny's presence. A dense humility for all that the woman had suffered and that she herself lacked. She was trying to craft an apology to Duncan for her thoughtless crack. She wanted to focus on the long moment when he stood stroking her cheek. But her mind kept returning to the idea that he'd only snared himself in the wheel trying to escape her. And the apology dissolved then, quick and bitter under the tongue.

Down on the lawn Kitten and Audiophile are winching the waistbands of their skirts, each revolution hoisting hemlines up thighs. There's a self-possession about these girls that Lily has never experienced. As if their young bodies are piloted not so much by the brain, but rather by nervous tissue, the deep lymphatics, by fluid running alongside the spine, a stone lodged in the epigastric region, thirty slick feet of the alimentary canal.

And here she is, yards away and a different species entirely. One with no intuition, no gut instinct. It seems that *all* she can do is think. Think of how it is still only Saturday. Still half the weekend to go until Monday. Then the weekday stretch until Thursday. Thursday if he comes. The idea has surfaced—of course it has, a thought coughed into a fist—that one day Thursday will turn into Friday without him. This pledge that she's enacted, that they only dig in the garden when both are present, is quite specious. She's a Scheherazade, she realizes. Conducting a serial exhumation to ensure her husband's return.

In the staff kitchen Duncan empties out a filter of used grinds from the coffee machine. It's Monday and his humiliation at being trapped in the wheel well of his own car and then rescued by his wife has eased somewhat. He's left with only a few scratches as a reminder. But the very best remedy, he knows, is work. Arriving early, digging in, leaving late.

He spent most of his weekend locked in the apartment, icing his hand and watching an old bootleg copy of *Apocalypse Now* (the last forty minutes of which had accidentally been taped over with *Super Bowl XXVIII*). He was full of dread and wonder at the thought that a contorting river might hold such power over a man and couldn't help but make the connection to his own travels along the Hudson each weekend, the push and pull of a body of water changing direction with the tides. Leetower eventually sent over a sketch for a magazine ad. The marker rendering was a simple cross section of the Cu Chi tunnel network, but in each of the underground chambers, LT had drawn a girl soldier in Stand and Be Counted jeans. The drawings were preliminary, but Duncan could pick out the Viet Cong girls for their wispy eyes and tight ankles. In some rooms they were depicted demonstrating the mysteries of the Orient: punches, kicks, lethal jabs at the jugular. In others they lounged in hammocks strung from one clay wall to the other, sucking the starch from bamboo shoots. In narrow, scorpion-infested passages, Leetower drew Grunt Girls crawling in their wide-cuffed denim. In the war rooms they rifled through vital documents by the light of a Zippo, or went M-16 to AK-47 with their commie counterparts. The tagline ran across the top of the ad, *History Repeating,* each letter cut from jungle leaf. Leetower had taken his advice and created a sexually charged ant farm of women. Duncan was pleased. *The idea has legs,* he told the young art director over the phone, and regained a measure of confidence in the campaign.

As the fresh coffee brews, he walks over to the intern's desk, the poorest real estate on the block, wedged on the landfill between toilet and photocopier. Maybe it's the dead morning hour, but he's only just noticed the startling parallels between the cubicle landscape surrounding him and the underground miles at Cu Chi. The lack of natural light and privacy, the totalitarian functionality of such spaces. The North Vietnamese Army carved surgical operatories from the earth, war rooms, mess halls, everything necessary for a comrade to be born, serve, and expire. He considers the sallow, subterranean faces around the department. Could it be when the Viet Cong died, they were reborn as his colleagues?

Duncan gives the intern's chair a kick that leaves the dusty imprint of his foot. He feels a sudden disdain for the time-honored tradition of climbing the rungs. It's been years since he'd scrambled his own way up from the slums, the cubicle ghetto, but the very same taste of anxiety persists in his mouth. What was it that Hawke once said to him? One of those occasional pearls that fell from his mouth among the turds. *Remember, you're only as good as your last campaign.* He must remain vigilant. Especially now as Stand and Be Counted sprouts wings. Isn't it true that throughout his career, a man will do well to stop occasionally and remind himself to regard those around him with a suspicious eye? During prosperous times, rather than relaxing this code, efforts should be redoubled, as passivity and comfort are, for a man, akin to the polyp preceding the cancer. Duncan moves on to the next desk, positions the chair and boots the backrest.

Yes, he thinks. Rivals become the enemies who'll massacre you while you sleep. Hasn't history demonstrated—hasn't literature chimed in—that to be truly valiant, one must earn his chops for action? Seek out and destroy the enemy? Or better, destroy and then seek? Hawke would have agreed to this in his salad years, no doubt. So would have Luis Oster, Senior, in the year 1902. There was a man willing to cut the governess to bits for wronging him. It's no wonder that today, his great-granddaughter considers her own husband so irresolute—she has the same strain of bloodlust coursing through her.

Now Duncan finishes putting the boot to one row of cubicles, and starts down along the east wall of the department. He knows better than anyone that all great ideas seem absurd at first—but only until pop culture absorbs them. After which they tend to outgrow their masters, become pervasive and household, sometimes financially lucrative enough to allow the discarded masters to move forward. He's been working on a voice-over for a television spot that has his Grunt Girl crawling through the understory of Vietnamese jungle. With ten confirmed kills under her belt, she's just returned from a special ops mission with the Long Range Recon Patrollers. Was actually shanghaied by the crazy motherfucker Lurps to help chase Charlie up the Mekong Delta and into the no-go zone of Cambodia. It was against protocol but put an M-16 in her hands and, hell, everyone's fighting the same war anyway. Duncan has been considering the imposition of a voice-over, but wonders if this information will simply telegraph through the visual of his Grunt Girl, bulletproof, pulling the gooks back by the cinched pant leg, tearing them to shreds like a starved dog on a joint of meat—

He stops in front of Hawke's glass office, its vacancy easily confused for minimalist design. The great engine Upstairs has yet to descend and announce which new wrist they'll be fitting into their fist of steel. Sunrise does make the position tempting, however. An arc of eastern light illuminates a film of dust over the man's desk. Duncan steps closer to the glass. Across the surface of the scored metal someone has written in finger script:

RUN, SAVE YOURSELF

He tries the door but finds it locked. Brass's little trick to keep the minions from poaching office furniture. Was this Hawke's final message to those still in the pen? An alert from the old ranger who had read the signs, seen the scalpers riding over the bluff?

Tuesday, Lily decides to skip the library and, instead, bows her legs up at the knees and slots herself into the narrow sarcophagus of the bathtub. She rests an old thermos lid of sherry on the ledge. In the window, two trapped yellow jackets serenade her with the most extraordinary, the most enormous unmusic. The buzz and thud of insect against glass creates the Foley effects of snapped power lines or the blue light death of obstinate golfers, three-irons raised to the electric sky. . . .

She should write that down. Lily picks up the cordless phone from the ledge beside the thermos lid. She clicks on the handset, listens to the drone of ring tone and then, changing her mind, turns it off. Drains the cup of sherry instead. Thinks how nice it is to be drunk in her own private body of water. She sticks her toe into the corroded spout, inviting death by tetanus. No clawfoot romance and milky water here, no sir. No grievous Ophelia floating an inch below Millais's oiled surface. One would have to scale brick to spy on her, only to be disappointed by a view of her knees cropping up through the water. She forgets the thermos lid is empty, and raises it in a toast to the Invisible Man. To Tinker. Why hadn't the nanny simply turned to drink instead of kidnapping? Crime required such effort. Lily herself used to steal lipsticks from the Rite Aid. But it was an act of impulse, only forming into a habit and sustained during junior high because of her relative success. To snatch a child, though. That required hours of premeditation. The nappies and milk and jointed teddy bears alone. Lily holds the thermos lid between her knees. It's because she doesn't want children, isn't it? That's why she can't understand the risking of life. Become a fugitive to wipe the snotty nose of someone else's child? Although, there was a case to be made for avoiding the messiness of childbirth. For retaining all forms of ownership over your body.

⋅But what kind of deal is that? A kid without the fun of making it?

Lily slowly lowers herself further down in the hot broth, watching as her nipples pucker and respond to the heat. In the window, the yellow jackets rattle away in appreciation of her naked self. She runs a sea sponge down the inside of her thigh, raking it timidly against the flesh until it sets off an electric response. She has either forgotten or ignored the simple pleasure of being alone with her body. Fortified wine and the smell of soap have softened her reflexes. When she no longer feels like someone is watching her, she slips her hand between her legs.

By day the Viet Cong Guerrilla leads a draft plow through the rice paddy muck of her family farm. The docile water buffalo she rides requires only the occasional switch across the rump to keep it from straying into the bamboo hedgerow. Years of southwestern monsoons have cured the animal's hide into the tough-wearing leather of an old armchair.

Or maybe, Duncan thinks, it's not the monsoon rains that have worn down the buffalo's hide. It's the rolling friction of the VC girl's thighs in her skinny-fit jeans.

He turns to the marker pad on his desk. Come to think of it, why show the girl at all? He sketches the rectangular lump of a Southeast Asian ungulate on four stick legs, grazing in a swamp. Why not remove the product from the shot entirely? Might work. Might be brilliant to show the water buffalo, alone on some yellow silt bank, with just the straddle pattern of denim clad legs worn down either side of its withers.

He likes the print potential and begins shading in the creature himself instead of waiting for Leetower. And when the phone rings, he's so caught up in detailing the greasy patina marks on the animal's side that he doesn't recognize the caller. "Valerie from the Historical Society," the woman repeats. "Of Osterhagen?"

Duncan stops middraft. "Right. Osterhagen." He flexes his left hand, the humiliating sequence in the driveway pecking its way back in.

"Duncan, a couple things." The woman clears her throat, a prefatory effect which assures him that she, in fact, has an entire laundry list to run through. His mind suddenly sweeps back to Tinker. To the bones in the cellar and the lazy open grave. He sits up very straight.

"We've had reports of cannon discharge over the weekend. Just following up to see if you heard any of that?"

This is not at all what he was expecting. "No," he tells her slowly. "I don't think I did."

"You *were* in Osterhagen this past weekend?" the woman says. "Isn't this your work number?"

Duncan takes up his marker again. Draws a shark fin rising up out of the same swamp that the water buffalo is lolling about in. "I go up Thursday nights. I don't have the entire summer off, I'm afraid."

"I tried your wife at the house but there was no answer."

Brilliant strategy, he thinks. Tell a man his wife's never home.

"Is there an active cannon in Osterhagen?" he asks.

"Some of the old homesteads below Market Road got a hold of one. The farmers there pitched in, brought it back from the foundry in Cold Spring."

"I wasn't aware."

"You must have met Skinner? He's quite the character."

Duncan taps his notepad, chews at a stray bit of cuticle. "I have met him," he says casually. "At the library."

Valerie sighs down the wire. "We had to pass an ordinance against him. A few years ago. Well, more of a cease-and-desist letter. He was just firing that thing off willy-nilly. Made the summer people nervous as anything."

"Did you hear the cannon?"

"God, no!" Valerie laughs. "I live in Scarsdale, I'm just on the committee. My late husband owned a house in town."

That's a good thing, Duncan thinks, crossing her off his list of guests most likely to drop by unannounced. "Well, I'll let you know if we hear anything."

"Look, Duncan. Can I ask you something?" She ignores his conclusive tone. "Is Laura up there alone all week?"

"Lily."

"That's right. Lily. By herself?"

"Yes, Lily is by herself. She's writing her dissertation."

"Isn't that marvelous!" But Valerie's trill is distracted. "Duncan, not that it's any of my business, but you might want to rethink that arrangement. I know you're not strictly summer people—there's family history with that house—but the town is, you know, somewhat eccentric."

Instead of responding, he leans on his desk and weighs the risks of this conversation. He can't grasp what the woman is angling for. How much does she already know? And Skinner, Duncan's still not sure what to make of him. Despite his threatening prologue that night at the farm, the cannon hadn't been loaded. He'd fired a blank charge at the river. While the sound was shit-inducing enough, there was no ten-pound lead projectile launched into the woods as they were led to believe. *Not yet,* Skinner had muttered on the drive home that night.

"They tend to do things their own way," Valerie continues. "Some people there don't really welcome change. When word got to me that Laura was living there alone for the summer, well, I thought, that's such a big house for one woman by herself! And you can imagine I feel somewhat responsible. I did help arrange the opening."

Duncan stands up, walks around his desk, stretching the phone cord until he can reach the office door and close it. He has a sense that her uncomfortable thesis statement is on the horizon. "Valerie, I drive up to Osterhagen every weekend."

"Oh, I understand, I don't mean to pry. I just want you to be aware. Some people in Osterhagen, once they get it in their head that they don't like you—"

"Who doesn't like us?"

"I wouldn't know that, Duncan. Like I told you, I never go up there. I just hear things."

"Have you heard someone doesn't like us?"

"Not yet."

Christ. The last thing he wants to do is try monitoring Lily's whereabouts. These days, she seems to suspect anything he does of an ulterior motive. "Lily's at the library most of the time and they seem to like her."

"Oh, yes! Those women are old darlings. But I'm talking about, you know, this undercurrent. They've recently lost the town mascot. I don't know if you've heard?" Valerie's voice drops an artful octave. Duncan pictures her on the other end, telephone cradled between neck and shoulder, brushing cat fur from her pantsuit. "It's a wild boar—the mascot. The high school parades him around at homecoming. Something silly like that."

"Lily mentioned it."

"Well, that was Skinner's pig. He thinks someone stole it. Maybe it's unrelated, but some dormitory windows at Bard were shot at. I mean with a BB gun—they didn't break, but the kids got a jolt."

"He thinks some of the kids from Bard are responsible?"

"Well, like I mentioned, the windows didn't break. Anyway, Duncan, what I'm saying is, if Laura's going to be up there, she should just be aware."

Duncan scratches at his scalp. "*Lily* has spent her entire adult life in Manhattan."

"Oh, for sure. She's got her street smarts. I just wanted to say my piece."

"Whatever problems they might have, we can't really change our summer plans. It's kind of petty, this issue."

"Yes, that's it exactly. Petty! It'll pass. The pig will come back and it'll all pass. Everything does, isn't that the way?"

But now Duncan isn't so sure. When he hangs up with Valerie he's lost his thrill for the Viet Cong guerrilla girl and her tapered pant legs. What the Historical Society Matriarch has reinforced here is a real sense of reckoning. The possibility of comeuppance for a single, stupid, and innocent mistake that simply lacked a decent follow-through. And he has left his wife to face it alone. He looks at his left hand. Fresh skin is already growing to cover the injury. Lily's tough, he must bear this in mind. She released him from a fender skirt with her bare hands. Sill, tough means squat when a ten-pound Parrott rifle is rolled onto your front lawn. No, what he needs to do is get those bones out of the garden. Lily's stuck on the find and he knows full well that she won't budge until it's done. If this turns out to be nothing less than his own special ops mission into the Mekong, then at least his orders are clear: get your bones, get your woman, and get the hell out.

When the concert's over Lily raises the rotting window sash hoping the musicians will fly off without having to trap them under a jam jar. She's waving a toilet paper streamer out the bathroom window, flagging the wasps away from the tacky resin of the outer casement, when her eye catches on a white bundle in the garden. Lily sticks her head out the window. She's mistaken. It's not a white bundle lolling around down there. It's a sheep.

No way. She takes another look, thinking it might have something to do with the cooking sherry she just polished off. No. It's still a sheep. And now with its head lowered in Tinker's grave. My God, she thinks. This has got to be the worst bit of Orwellian recompense conceivable. Even the animals are revolting.

"Hey!" Lily knocks at the top of the windowpane. "What are you doing down there?" The animal keeps its hindquarters angled in her direction, its head down and grazing around the site. It must have detected from the tremble in her cry that she's pure greenhorn when it comes to negotiating with livestock. Perhaps her precision with the tire iron was nothing more than a lucky strike after all.

The sheep's fleece, all spit curls and marcel waves, betrays the renegade lifestyle of the untended: the crimped underbelly wool dragging like trampled hems, the flanks snaggled with twigs and grass and seasoned brown from a long, rasping massage against the base of a creosote-soaked telephone pole. Dirty sheep. She sees it raise its shock-headed skull from the hummocky pile of Tinker's plot to scout left and right.

"Up here, lamb chop."

The animal lifts its head to observe treetops for voices, turning to her finally, the source of recrimination, and it's only then that she realizes she was wrong yet again. It's not a sheep. It's a poodle.

Lily leans on the windowsill, naked, swearing off cooking sherry and overcome with either hysteria or a sense of adversarial one-upmanship. If only Duncan could see they're up against much more than Skinner's crew. A dog's urgency! The innate compulsion to dig! The poodle raises its left paw at her, either an atavistic impulse or the forgotten gesture of puppyhood, the shake-a-paw gag that delighted someone once. But Lily is not kindhearted.

"Go on," she shouts. "Get out of there!"

The dog lowers its trick paw. Its good humor has vanished; Lily isn't going to play. They face each other: the poodle, a filthy meringue, and she, naked at the breast. Nothing regal in that face, she thinks. There's a twitch of snout muscle as the poodle's lip ruches over its fang, forming a sneer that is not of Lily's anthropomorphic creation.

Lily, furious, barks twice out the window. She's surprised by the harsh and authentic sound that she produces. The dog, however, ignores her, turns back to the hole, and noses around for the spot where it left off. She reaches down, picks one of her sneakers off the floor, and launches it through the window.

Topography of the Cerebral Cortex

"After witnessing the dismemberment of a field medic from Alabama and shaking the trees for dog tags, Grunt Girl realizes she isn't going to win this war. We see her, jeans and cammies, under a tree that's literally strung with dog tags."

"Dog tags in trees?"

"Yeah," Leetower turns to Kooch, "I should have mentioned that. Idea there is someone's been blown sky high from a land mine, okay? So, the various bits, they end up in the trees." The tail of his sentence bends upward, seeking affirmation.

"Then Grunt Girl says—and we put this in quotes in the print ad— she says, 'What's left of the field medic from Alabama could fit in a shoe box.'" Leetower spreads his drawings on Duncan's desk. "See how the, uh, the quote functions the same as the voice-over on the TV?"

For a minute no one speaks.

"Well." Duncan, relying on monosyllabic ambiguity to communicate his disinterest, shuffles the concepts around. Maybe if he changes their order.

"Stick to pictures, Leetits." Kooch puts his feet up on the desk. "Doesn't it say *Art Director* on your business card?"

The boy sits and crosses his legs at the thighs. His lips are the color of bone. "Right, in the same place where yours says *Asshole.*"

"I'm rounding out a script here where Grunt Girl realizes the frayed edges of her jeans have grown into a scabbing wound on her calf. Right into the scab so that skin and war and denim are inextricably laced." Kooch slaps his broad mitt down over his notes. His cuticles are immaculate, Duncan observes. Bred for the barn but raised in the manor house.

"The field medic is alive. He's bent over Grunt Girl's leg with a rusty straight-edge razor, slicing the jeans away from the scabbing wound. Transferring his cigarette to her mouth the way two scuba divers may be forced to share a single oxygen mask." Kooch doesn't look to either of them for a reaction. He flips the page.

"Next spot. We open on a wide shot of an opium den."

Duncan stands, acknowledging a certain didactic thrill. While he needs to take these two in hand before the entire concept bleeds away into the furniture, he's got to admit he's pleased they've followed his lead instead of putting up roadblocks.

"You guys ever hear that saying, 'Kill your darlings'?"

"Yeah. Bob Barrie."

"No, it was Helmut Krone."

"Actually it was Faulkner." Duncan walks around his desk. "You two are close, but I think we're getting stuck on genre films. Let's go more stylized. Forget reality altogether."

"But we've already been talking to a couple guys."

"What couple of guys?"

"Who do shakycam. Guys we know, DPs mostly." Kooch's flat voice speaks of lapped terrain.

"Really. When did this happen?"

Leetower rouses himself. "What Kooch means is, we like frenetic randomness. Remember the Omaha Beach scene in *Saving Private Ryan*? But instead of dead soldiers, a beach full of hot Grunt Girls."

"And we intercut with some retro Super 8."

Since when have these little shits been talking to cameramen? Duncan walks the length of his small office. "You're getting way ahead of yourselves," he says, making a heroic attempt at calm. Sure, Hawke was always more gracious when handling his fledgling ideas, his experiments. But Duncan just can't seem to extend the same courtesy to these punks. It's Kooch, something about his watchfulness. As though he's humoring him, as though he knows Duncan doesn't have a clue as to where to lead the troops next, let alone bring home another One Show Pencil. He thinks of Skinner's speech at the library, how he'd rallied his men to bear arms against the boar thief. Even Duncan, who was more than aware of the pig's fate, was taken up for a moment in the visible charisma. It wasn't simple manipulation that allowed men like Skinner—like Hawke—to lead uncompromising campaigns. It was unequaled conviction, certifiable egomania that allowed them to fly under nuclear radar.

"I need an idea before you give me the camera angle, okay?" Duncan rubs the back of his hand across his mouth. "And where's the Viet Cong? I want to see her being hosed down with orange liquid. Orange, you know, to symbolize Agent Orange. But she's wearing skinny-leg Stand and Be Counted jeans—they resist the spray. She might even be enjoying it."

"Like a wet T-shirt."

Anne appears in the doorway, a pack of cigarettes and a file folder up against her breasts. She glances over at the rough sketches on the desk. "Look at all the fresh spoils you've dragged back to the Village of the Boys."

"We've had to interdict a lot of sleeping civilians."

"Excellent. Body count?" Anne strips the cigarette pack of its plastic sheathing. "I hear you're going to use a Vietnamese girl in the skinny-leg jeans. Very smart, Duncan. Girl-on-girl action is very in."

"Girl-on-girl action can bring the world together." Kooch stands, spreads the points of his shoulders so that he seems to clear the room with the wide brisket of his chest. "In the last spot of the campaign we're going to have the hot Vietnamese girl and the hot American girl making peace in a suite at the Rex Hotel."

"Whose side are we supposed to be on?"

"That's the beauty of it, McPherson," he says. "Straight leg, wide leg, Asian, white—let proclivities fall where they may. We get to shoot this in Saigon, right?"

Duncan feels the ache of annoyance at the root of his teeth. He does not like the way Kooch injects himself into the production of the campaign. Does not like it one bit.

"No money for Vietnam." Anne lodges a cigarette in the corner of her mouth. "Think Everglades. Actually, I was talking the idea around Upstairs. They are very keen on *History Repeating,* Duncan. They are right with you on bringing home some awards for this. First comment in the room—which I personally thought astute—was that we can really capitalize on the current trouble in Iraq."

Leetower spreads out on the sofa. "Why Iraq?"

"It puts everything in perspective."

"Wait a minute." Duncan holds up his hand. "You took the idea Upstairs?"

"Well, in general terms only," she says, feeling through her jacket pocket for a lighter.

"It's not ready for an audience, Anne. We're still brainstorming."

"But you said you didn't want to consult with anyone from outside."

"To consult on what? We don't even have a script written."

"They wanted something, Duncan." She looks at him, tweezing the cigarette from her lips. Her face, which had been riding calm, is now tacking hard to the wind. "Excuse me for giving them a reason to deposit your next paycheck."

Kooch whistles his appreciation.

Duncan's hand moves.

This is how it happens, he thinks. This is what they mean by losing control. How the arm, hand, and fist become not only as involuntary as internal organs, but also much more powerful; what does the pancreas do anyway, besides produce its sugar-seeking squirt of insulin? As his hand moves, Duncan understands, this is how simple striated muscle (the lackey of the brain) gains the ability to calibrate itself. Once a man strips down to his pure, simian heart, he discovers that all muscle has memory. This explains it, how each day, men perform certain actions they never thought themselves capable of. The trigger is woman. How easy it is for a woman with an obstinate will to undermine a man's efforts. This explains how the founder of sawmills and forefather of a town tamped his child's governess into the soil. Some say it's weakness to strike at the small, but a woman can invite aggression as well as any man. Many will even change before your eyes, their chins spreading into a hollow for the fist.

Besides, the Age of Chivalry had climaxed with *Ivanhoe*.

This is it, he thinks, feeling his hand gearing up with backward torque. This is what happens when talk fails. When reason fails, and words die with it. Hadn't he made a living scrambling words? Rearranging them until they revealed their molecular structure? Watson and Crick were amateurs. What he himself has done with words! So many years and they have been the only pliant company he's kept. He has shoved them roughly to the floor just to see something—someone—look up to him.

His hand moves, the monkey heart moves it. And Anne sees it move. She steps back. Kooch's whistle is a disappearing train. The air-conditioning vent drops a register. Anne is not afraid. There are two spots of color on her cheeks, as though someone had pressed a thumb against either side of her face. She is nearly pretty in her awe. She backs to the door but he knows she doesn't want to leave. They're just getting started.

"Jesus." Anne laughs through fine nerves. "It's a madhouse around here without a creative director, yeah?"

Leetower closes his eyes on the sofa. He has female lashes. "Burn the hooches," he says. "Kill every chicken and pig in the ville."

She admires the inverted symmetry of the two blue veins under her tongue. The deep lingual vein, twisting under a layer of soft tissue, precise as its pencil-rendered twin in the copy of *Gray's Anatomy* that she brought home from the library. She tosses a freshly polished silver spoon on the coffee table and rests the open book on her chest like a weighty bird. Between these two wings is a catalog of an assembled Tinker, although the real woman is scattered under a packed layer of dirt. Lily has run out of things to do. The light ticks away now, reading is a strain, sharp edges of furniture are lost in the dusk, corners are just faded pockets where walls may or may not meet. The sofa holds her loneliness, the ancient wadding presses shapes of lost men into her spine. A genealogy of posterior impressions, she thinks. How many have come before her, scrimmaged with the darkness only to expire despite the effort? And were any of them involved in the nanny's demise? She wonders if Tinker ever sat here. When the family was out, did she move from room to room, learning the feel of each chair beneath her weight?

Lily stretches on her side and stares at the fireplace that they won't be using this summer. A pleated skirt of iron in front to keep embers off the tiled hearth. Funny, she has already decided that these are the bones of the woman from the photograph. And the more she glimpses up here of human nature, the more likely it seems that Tinker's death was an inside job. Although, she really has no way of knowing. She could call her mother, the self-professed keeper of family trivia. What else did she know about the boy? About the vanished governess? The great-grandfather's temper? But the business is a little too *Turn of the Screw* for her mother's taste and definitely lacking in spiritual expiation. The woman was a missionary, after all, and always in a haste to get to the point, or to the act of contrition. Lily knows her mother will have no interest in the violence of the nanny's death; the story will only hold water for her at the point where Oster repents. For Lily, the story burns where he sins.

Her mother understands everything and nothing and in her counsel there is little salient meaning. At Thanksgiving she might mourn Lily as a child bride, offering her a single train ticket home. At Christmas she can be found lighting votives in hope of grandchildren. Lily can never quite warm up to these gestures—and not only because of their confused intentions. The truth is, she's embarrassed to be among the woman's priorities, the subject of prayers, after an entire childhood of being an afterthought. Still, Lily never has the heart to stop her. She's allowed her mother to pull her aside, remind her that a man wants the kind of woman who knows how to ease apart the knot of his day. Lily's hands, it's clear, have yet to learn this palliative gesture.

Coming home from her parents' house, relief always meets her at the elevator, scoops her up in its great mitts and carries her through the door. It is the dampening effect of concrete. In the city Lily is free to ease apart the strands of her own husband in her own way. If she so chooses. And hasn't she chosen? Duncan was unaware, but there were a million things she'd done for him and kept in her heart. Not indulgences, more like stepping forward in the dark to shift scenery. Tucking an extra foot of sheeting in at his side of the bed and switching his sliced white to whole wheat and never, ever reminding him that the bills don't pay themselves. Early on she recognized he needed a tract of land around him and so didn't complain when he worked late and weekends, or reeked of beer and smoke. When he got the idea to travel to Southeast Asia during the thesis year of her master's program she had even supported his shitty timing. Encouraged him to go without her. *It'll be good for you to do your own thing.* Christ, they weren't even married then and already she'd developed a sleight of hand to guard him from her own disappointment.

The phone rings, startling her. *Gray's Anatomy* slides to the floor, chapters fan from the spine and strain against the tack of glue. "Topography of the Cerebral Cortex" folds into a permanent dog ear. The phone must be dug out from between sofa cushions; the uncomfortable expedition of hand into the gorge of crumbs and grain.

There are several long seconds before he speaks and when he does his voice is full of surprise.

"You're home."

"Duncan?"

"Expecting someone else?" A screen of television laughter connects his words, the consonance of audience whelps and cheers.

"What?" she says.

"Why did you put my trophies in the closet?"

She can hear the studio audience sing along to the intoxicating chant of the network. "Are you drunk?"

"I want an answer."

She holds the phone away from her face, looks at the handset as though it has, in some way, gimmeled the transmission of his voice. What sort of answer? Anything she can offer he will only peel down to an ugly objective. Duncan thinks he wants to know things, but he can't even bring himself to admit to even simple indignities. His own anxiety around her parents being at the top of the list. Last year she was the one who had to watch him fret before one of their overnight visits. Duncan had tensed up like something bound and volatile, spent hours on a stepladder testing every lightbulb in the place. He even vacuumed the area rugs in one direction so that the nap stood stiff.

So when she removed his One Show Pencils from the living room and put them in the linen closet, it was meant to be an invisible action. Duncan would not have even noticed if she hadn't forgotten to return them afterward.

What are these doing here? He'd stood by the closet holding them one afternoon.

How could she explain? The inscriptions on the Pencils read: *Best Television Campaign: Tide, Laundry Elves.*

How could she sit and allow Duncan to stumble through an explanation to her father? That an award show existed for television commercials? Her father, aside from being humorless, had spent much of his own youth squatting in a Rwandan village hut, rifle strapped to his chest to guard against an aggressive mountain faction while his coffee beans were harvested.

"Lily," his voice rattles up from the city like a shaking pan of frozen peas, "I asked you a question."

Anger begins to move through the dense packing of her organs. She touches her healed lip and thinks of that miserable night in the old shit's farmyard, of her husband's loveless bite. And then, of all the small and good things she has done for him. Duncan has slept right through them. It's just like him. Forget the years of predictability, he had chosen to wake for this.

"They were five years old." She hears herself, salt pouring into the great slice of him. "Just gathering dust out there."

Before he can reply, a walloping blast sounds out. The house reacts first; windows knock against their casements. Around Lily loose items vibrate in the sonic aftershock. She feels the jolt in her neck, in the lean strip of muscle that winches around her windpipe. It's unclear whether Duncan hears the insult that precedes the cannon blast or her cry of fear that follows. In any case, when she recovers enough to say his name, the phone is dead.

CHAPTER 18

Structure of the Heart

Until today she believed they were too young for divorce. They'd only just left their twenties. Could still afford the wait-and-see attitude of youth. The universe might still intervene and shake a few tricks down its sleeve. Things could happen, an enormous cannonball could crater out the house and leave them clutched in one another's arms.

Or nothing could happen. Nothing at all.

It's been weeks of waking to the chorus of country birds. Another Wednesday in June and the days surround Lily like an iron lung. The library is closed for maintenance, the old building shut down by stale breath and floorboard music. She slips, instead, into the acreage of barley out back, entering just beyond the edge of garden where Duncan first found the headstone. His shovel is staked in the soil like a signpost. The crop welcomes her, parts with ease, the bristle tickling at the breastbone. This is the best way to travel through barley, she thinks. With the same parting and spreading motion of hair, of legs, of waves. A half mile to the west the sky drops empty of trees and the neighboring stubble fields slope into the Hudson. With jeans tucked into socks, Lily moves slowly toward the river; there are still a dozen hours left in this day and behind her is only the empty house.

Until today she and Duncan had only blunt edges and slow motion to bump up against. But this morning she woke and forked her tongue through her name—*Lily*—with the same cold thrust she's heard him use. This morning she saw the truth cross overhead like a formation of honking, shitting geese outside the window: she is waiting for Duncan to leave her. She's waiting for him to do it.

The truth is she's afraid of large strokes and sudden movements. There are dire consequences whenever she makes one. The wild boar for instance. And if she's still remorseful over the handling of the pig, how would she ever endure the guilt of euthanizing her marriage? Where would she go besides? There's no way she'll return to her parents, a cracked egg on their doorstep. The misery of their house perhaps worse than the misery of remaining pressed between the glass and screen of this sliding door. Her mother and father never warmed to Duncan, never exhaled in his presence. And while they couldn't turn a blind eye to divorce, they would at least blink rapidly, suggest an annulment. The tidy dissolution of the past five years of her life.

This morning she opened her eyes and saw fact. If they separated she would be the bereft one. From the beginning Duncan had been surrounded. He built himself a nest of sound and paper and resided there. He would never quite realize he was alone. Then, little by little, he would not be alone. There would be people with whom he could talk out his failure until it was drained from him like yellow fluid from an abscess. He was only thirty-two; soon he'd be ready again. Friends would embrace him, throw arms around their recovered brother, be ready with the flip observation that he was better off as God had made him.

And why shouldn't they part? The thought of children had never interested them—it wasn't as though they'd be giving up on anything bigger than themselves. Besides, her rectilinear tastes didn't nuzzle up alongside his. The noisy guitar bands he follows, *the wheedling yet revealing dialogue of a generation with nothing to rally around* that he participates in, none of these things has found its way into her own flesh. Some women, she knows, unpetal like marigolds for the right man. And here she is with nothing to unfurl.

The last time he tried to undress her—how long ago was that?—she had felt his hand across her breast, so sudden and heavy she thought something had dropped from the ceiling of their bedroom. She turned to face him; there was only darkness between them.

A hundred years ago, in England, people would pay to watch the unwrapping of Egyptian mummies. Lily's breath had caught in the serif of the words. *What do you think happened? Inside the wraps they found pharaohs turned into driftwood. Queens of dry, brown matter.*

Where had this knowledge come from? Whose voice had spoken, telling Lily to turn him away before he did it to her first? Duncan removed his hand. Not with the sudden motion of scalding water, but something slow and deliberate.

In the barley she takes a head of grain and squeezes. At least a month or two, they'd been told, until it would be ready to harvest. There is no give from the young plant; the straw binds the six rows of kernels like a tight scrotal sac. And that's how she comes to understand. Sees it then with the precision of an acute triangle. Nothing turns on a dime. She will never really identify the moment the pointed arch changed the architectural world because the Arabic influence had just leached in from around the edges. This is the same reason she doesn't recognize anything about Duncan. They have picked at each other for so long that new tissue formed. New bone calcified over the existing structure.

Lily clears a round patch in the grain and sits down. Against her better judgment she has watched for signs of what will happen next. Birds striking the sunroom window, the pattern of flight of a plastic bag, the scattering of twigs in the grass. She knows there are techniques of divination that are beyond her: the study of bones, the interpretation of laughter. Sideromancy, the burning of straw on hot iron. But Lily prefers the observable, the empirical. Happy coincidences, common denominators, even numbers. Things that happen twice.

———

She had met him before. Before the time they began to date, she had met him briefly, they had bounced against the surface of each other with a pleasant thud. And then they parted. And then they met again.

The second time she had just returned from Italy. She was walking in the area of the university, circumnavigating it really, waiting for her thoughts to polarize. Lily was trying to find a path to take her from the last two years in Europe to what lay ahead. Was it academics? A return to the seminar rooms and libraries divided into floors of prattle or hush. Eventually she might apply to the Institute of Fine Art for a Ph.D.

She had just put the question out there, so that when she saw Duncan—she realizes this in hindsight—she couldn't help but think it was the universe responding. Bright, efficient, prompt for once, it had dropped a piano on her. Maybe that was her mistake. Taking Duncan as a sign rather than a coincidence. But from that point on, she was unable to divorce him from the shape of her future.

He was with a film crew that day, wearing gloves against the bite of early spring and ratcheting the lid off a cup of coffee. Around them the city was bald, waiting for either buds or one last snow to smudge the hard edges. Lily had stopped short, his name in her mouth. He was standing with a gang of men and she was too shy to approach. Waited instead for him to recognize her or something of what had passed between them two years before.

There were things about Duncan that had vanished: the blink and stumble of boyhood, the loose pouch of a boy's body. He was rough and tousled, a kind of beauty discovered only when youth begins to disappear. A man now, hair snipped like corded wheat, a fine imprint of lines around his eyes. But the eyes—there it was. Exactly the same Indiana sky. She felt her mouth line with mink and a light in her belly rousing not the butterflies felt by girls, but the thousand frantic moths that awaken women.

Duncan saw her, turned toward her. Around them and then rising above them, the piers of the Washington Memorial Arch, and in the impossible fraction of time she imagined it took for her visage to complete the transit between his eyes and brain, she said to herself, *The processional arch was historically used for triumphant returns to the city.* And if she was looking for a sign of her future, something more portent, more flesh and blood than the burning of straw on hot iron, the analysis of pebbles, well, here he was. Duncan. He opened his mouth and said to her, "You're blocking the shot."

Lily's cheeks turned the color of pickled ginger. She wanted to bury her head in the shoulders of the production assistant who'd nudged her back through the arch. Back with the rest of the pedestrian traffic. She saw a young woman in a thin cotton dress and a sack of groceries step to the curb. Is Duncan making movies? she wondered. Has this all really happened while I was gone? As Lily watched a motorcycle ripped through the gridlock, came to a halt at the curb where Fifth Avenue traffic split east and west. The rider was anonymous and leather-bound but there was something equine in the way he straddled the bike. While the girl stood with her groceries, he began to rev his engine at her, the pattern of it a sexually suggestive trimeter.

This must be a romance, Lily thought, fascinated.

The girl didn't hesitate. Before the shopping bag had time to hit the pavement she'd mounted the bike and hiked her skirt about a mile up her thigh.

"Cut," someone called and a blanket was tossed around the shoulders of the actress. "Can I get playback before we check the gate?"

Duncan had walked over to the huddle of men around a television monitor. Lily thought, Jesus Christ, it's been two years and he's already written a movie?

"What is it?" she asked the production assistant.

"Panty hose." His walkie-talkie sputtered to life, mixed clicks and static into his words.

"What?"

"Panty hose commercial," he said, releasing the flow of detained pedestrians into the park.

The group at the monitor broke apart and men threaded off in separate directions as though relieved to be liberated from one another. Duncan's route was linear; it took him past the marble statue *Washington at War* and directly toward her. She didn't have time to compose her face or glance away or feign disinterest. There he was. She thought, His face is the same, not so changed after all.

"Lily," he said. "You're back." As though days or weeks had passed instead of the two years since their parting. "I almost didn't recognize you."

"I thought you were going to be a writer," she said. Her tongue, always at the ready with the wrong words. It was nerves, an eager need to jump to the crux and then circle back slowly to review details. Something in his face collapsed with the sentence, like the upright knocked from the single slope of a lean-to. She hadn't meant it that way—she was impressed. More than impressed, she was awed by him. Owling her head around the square, she noticed the towers of lights, the reflective disks, the garbled dialogue of a dozen walkie-talkies.

"I am a writer," he recovered. "A copywriter. I'm in advertising."

She nodded. "Well, I like panty hose." Then felt bullish and obeisant once the words were out of her mouth. Duncan smiled, though. He understood she wasn't good with the small talk and switchbacks before hearty discussions. Besides, it was obvious that he'd made it. A couple short years and his career was already under way while she was as aimless as ever. The moths darted in her belly.

They had met once right before she'd left the country. It was at the library. Sharing a table had led to spending the day together. They introduced themselves in the morning and by nightfall were alone in the house she shared with two Australian flight attendants. Had they even kissed? She didn't think so. Their mouths moved only with talk of how life was going to scatter them like the radials of dandelion satellites. They were both young enough to be comfortably unremarkable. Hands had crossed and touched that night. She had a sense that he was carried in a bubble, that he'd thrown open the hatch. And although she felt snug there, the exit was also in his eye. A conviction that fate held something in safekeeping for him and that their destinies were to play out without mutual distraction. Regardless of this, or perhaps because of this, their day was shaped like a sine wave, the end of it dipping below the horizon. When she watched him disappear down her street she understood she had met him and lost him all at once.

"I've thought of you," Duncan said to her in front of the Memorial Arch. "I wondered if I'd ever see you again." *Washington at War* regarded them from under the brim of his cocked tricorn. She looked up at Duncan, her legs lost some stability. The moths left her belly, picked Lily up beneath the arms and there was nothing left to consider. She drew toward him.

"Well, here I am," she said. And there she was.

Lily can't breathe. She tries, mashes barley shafts to death in her struggle to get to her feet, slaps at her puckered cheeks trying to suck down oxygen. She feels she might drown despite solid ground. Who will find her? Will Duncan know where to look?

Lily stands a shoulder over the grain and presses fingers against her face. Breathe, godammit. Slowly she begins to feel the underlying structure, the familiar geography of cheek and bone, and she breathes, realizes she has been breathing the entire time. She focuses on what is observable, barn swallows diving across the surface of grain, her hair gummed against her neck with a malt residue. Lily waits. Her heart continues to be unreasonable. Maybe it's the effect of that cannon, the clean and pitiful stack of bones in the cellar, but she suddenly understands what simple business it is to make a woman disappear.

CHAPTER 19

The Circulatory System

He will go upstate tonight. He's made a promise to Valerie of the Historical Society. This means he still has a long drive ahead of him—although Lily, the bones in the garden, all of it feels distant and poorly imagined. At the moment, the tight love in his chest he holds out to his small fraternity.

Strap-hanging on the number 1 train, and at the terminal end of Thursday's cocktail hour, they are oblivious to the interstitial stops and heaping of passengers. Something is spun between them, a conviction hoisted by four pairs of hands and growing in diameter until large enough to hold them in its volute shell. No small feat. What they have done at this point in history, Duncan believes, is form a band of insurrectionists, each member of the group chosen for a particular subversive talent. And he at the head, mounted on horseback.

In this raining, cabless city, they have loved him enough to come underground, to board and to follow him home. In exchange for the meager stash of beer in his refrigerator, Leetower, Kooch, and Anne will even watch as he packs for the weekend.

"Even Pershing took care of his troops first," says Kooch, with good humor that suggests, for one night, he'll concede to being an enlisted officer under Duncan's command.

They have been into their cups since three-thirty this afternoon.

A couple hours knocked off the official clock and transferred to the back of a local bar (an unlikely Western pub called the Badge and Holster), Anne signing the sum on her corporate American Express. Who was going to stop them? Who would dare argue their ascendancy? News of their progress has spread equally now between Upstairs and Downstairs people, the two communicating by their usual Morse code tapped onto air-conditioning vents. The question everyone wants answered: What new beauty has sprung from the Kiss of Death account? While there is talk of denim and war on both floors, the actual Vietnam executions are secret intelligence, kept off the shared drive and stored exclusively on Duncan's laptop. Not a single marker rendering is left out overnight or tacked to cork. They operate with a cabalistic fervor, mad-eyed as dot-commers before the big mash, before having the lining fucked out of them.

—Hello, Wing, Duncan says to his team.

—Hello, General.

It could just be the witchcraft of this flotilla, but over the course of their short tenancy on this project, the very thought of Hawke seems to be erased from corporate memory. His bungled efforts with Stand and Be Counted purged, leaving Duncan, Anne, Leetower, and Kooch innocent, prelapsarian, cruising the office with neither fig leaf nor shame.

—You are, each of you, a little piece of me, Duncan thinks.

—Yes, sir.

"Ravi keeps mentioning this glut of directors moving up from music videos to film." Anne braces her liquored weight against a subway pole. "They seem to think the pause in this continuum is television commercials. But I told her, forget it. We have money, get us a name, for chrissakes."

"That's our girl," Leetower tells her, shifting forward to allow Kooch to pass behind. They have all noticed the pretty office girl seated across from them, but only Kooch takes initiative.

"Anne," Duncan says. "When I'm God, you'll be rewarded for your shrewd wrangling of freelance producers."

She smiles. "You're just sweet because you're soused as a kitty."

Duncan briefly touches his finger to the end of her nose. "Untrue."

"Don't worry, Duncs. We'll make sure you're back on the wagon for your drive to the woods."

Beside them, he sees Kooch reach down and shake the office girl's hand. Then, loud enough for the entire car to hear, "It's Kooch. Remember that, you'll be screaming it later."

Anne takes the pole with both hands. "Listen, Chief, this is so confidential, but they've been asking me about you."

Despite the envelope of booze, Duncan feels a swift punt to the gut.

"I said to them, 'Get that goddamn sod back on Tide before he leaves us for happier pastures!' They know your wife's rich, you don't have to work. And I think it's going to happen this time, Duncan. They've okayed the budget for a Ukrainian dwarf."

My rich wife, he thinks. Alone in East Deliverance, New York.

"Wait until they see his paratrooper shit." Leetower is looking at Duncan as shyly as one man may be permitted to look at another. Until now, he's been dithering at the edges, waiting for his moment of admiration to materialize. "In spring Duncan's going to remove the Grunt Girls from the hurry-up-and-wait of ground warfare, the snaking on all fours through the grass. Separate their fates from the Leathernecks—the Marines—by stuffing them in a plane, strapping chutes to their backs. Screw the bunkers, Anne! We refresh the campaign in Q-2 with the Airborne Brigade."

Leetower catches his breath and Duncan thinks, I have gained mastery over the animals. Why is Lily never around for these moments?

"La-di-da," Anne says. "Duncan. Anything else I can do for you besides get your goddamn superstar packaged-goods account back?"

"Strip, sugar." Kooch shoulders back into their huddle. Duncan turns in time to spot the office girl push her way to the back of the car. "Nothing sleazy, McPherson. Give us a tasteful pole dance."

Anne laughs, lurches around the pole. "It was the fan dance that put me through college, boys." She begins a disturbing bent-knee shimmy down the length of the pole. Kooch whistles despite his defeat, the smell of single-malt scotch venting through the car.

Although Duncan hasn't forgiven her, he's noticed Anne's attempt to regain his favor since her screwup with Upstairs. She hasn't left his side the entire evening. In the train, he finds her lurching toward him suddenly, reaching for his head. There's a rack focus shift from her face to her hands. Wary of losing an eye, Duncan tries to rear away from the manicured spades of her fingers, discovers a depth-of-field issue in the action due to that last greasy tumbler of scotch.

"My liege." Anne holds him up with one hand. With the other, she pulls a paper napkin off his head.

He had forgotten the napkin. At the Badge and Holster they had folded him a snug crown then toasted his coronation.

"Over the course of your career, what would you say was your biggest mistake?"

Lloyd takes a drag of his Slurpee. "Once I paid to watch two Labs fucking. It sat poorly with me for weeks."

It's Thursday night and Lily stands beside the pervert, peering between cedar pickets at the rear of the tidy bungalow. "You'd call a do-over on it?"

"Nah, just part of the curve, Lily Mae. Same as killing that boar was for you."

"A curve or a turning point?"

"Well, man has always been a hunter. Evolution—should you hold forth such a notion—has yet to obviate the frontal incisors." Lloyd bares his teeth; each appear vaguely capable of tearing flesh. "Anyway, who's the interlocutor in this relationship?"

"Just one more question."

"Quickly, quickly." He shifts over a few slats along the fence to check on the driveway. "You'll have about ninety seconds once he gets here."

"Would you say that the prerequisite for a crime of passion is, exclusively, passion?"

Lloyd considers, nibbles the end of his drink straw. "I'm not one for strict dictionary definitions, but I'd have to say passions are, at best, ephemeral things."

"Shape-shifters, as the aboriginals would say."

"To take from a page of my own life, Lily Beth, there's a certain pre-school in Poughkeepsie. I spent hours outside the place. Christ, I'm surprised I still don't have the chain-link print on my forehead. I was younger, I was unclear as to the direction of my talents. And they were so docile, a field of grazing lambs. I thought I might go that way for a while." His sentence ends in the midregister. "But then, I see that little brunette from the library. With the pimples and earphones?"

"Audiophile."

"I'm drawn to her despite her terrible skin. Correction, on account of her terrible skin. I keep imagining the gratitude—you see it quite often with fat girls—but I think she's got it in her. And the idea of having that gratitude bestowed on me, at the moment, that constitutes passion."

Lily turns back to the driveway. A car noses in and banks left until it disappears behind the carport. She feels a slight rash of annoyance at Lloyd's theoretical slip. Why is it so difficult to find consistency in human beings? "I thought you said nonconsensual was best."

"I'll concede, it often begins that way." He runs a hand along the top of the fence and unlatches the gate. "Anyway, you're really starting to pick at the lint here. You want to ask a lot of questions or you want to see some good shit?"

"I choose B."

"Okay." He slides open the gate enough to let her pass. "The porch sags, so stick to the left because *I am not* in the business of pulling feet out of floorboards. Your best view is beside the baby stroller there. But when you hear me whistle, you come running."

Lily puffs air in her cheeks to keep focused.

"Remember to stay low, Lily girl." He holds out his drink straw and she fills her mouth with red syrup and ice.

"Ready?"

She nods, performs a quick jog on the spot. He punches her kindly on the shoulder.

The stroller is really an enormous pram, as spring-loaded and spoked as a golf umbrella. The padded carriage could easily hold her. Lily positions herself between it and the metal trash bin. It's not quite dark out so she's careful to raise herself by inches until acquiring a sight line into the room. The paint on the windowsill here is fresh, malleable enough in this late-evening heat to take up the tracks of her fingerprints. *Good job,* she tells herself. *Leave some DNA while you're at it.* She sponges her knuckle into the prints, attempting to obscure them.

The kitchen, oak paneled and unremarkable, forecasts a home where cleanliness outpaces décor. Furniture carries the round edges of country corners, the simplicity of boiled potatoes. The only indulgence, perhaps, is the beveled glass face of a hutch that shields a tier of marmalade glazed crockery. Around the dining table, wooden chairs of varnished pine, seared knots studding their shins like cankers.

A man enters the kitchen on the back end of his own sentence. His words are muffled by the double-paned glass but Lily picks up the rearing lilt of a question mark. His mouth moves over the sentence with a kind of presumption used to deliver definite articles: dates and times and capital cities. A woman comes away from the refrigerator, several jars in her hand. Lily hadn't seen her tucked behind the door. She is saying *yes,* her mouth and lips a dainty chisel in her jaw. There's a sense of transaction in her sloped walk across the room—but real or imagined? Lily tries to peg the ritual between these two but she worries that in taking her eyes off one she might miss a vital gesture from the other. Why the kitchen? The man stands in front of the glass cabinet. He is the type of handsome found behind a news anchor desk. Lily can tell his corporate predilection by the angled haircut, golf shirt, the casual shamble reserved for weekends. From a sheltered position beside the hutch, he pulls out a wooden high chair.

Lily has a sudden vision of her old professor in Italy, explaining Brunelleschi's discovery of linear perspective, how the manipulation of proportion and placement could fool the eye into creating believable distance. As the man drags the high chair toward the table, she sees that Brunelleschi was wrong. According to theory, while man and chair approach the plane of the canvas, they should both increase in size, their proportions maintained. However, it seems to Lily that the ratio between them changes. Yes, something is changing, an incongruity as they draw closer. Though it's not a formula issue. The formula itself is not corrupt. It's one of the variables, the high chair. It's enormous. Large enough that, after placing it by the table, the man is able to climb in and seat himself comfortably.

This is Lloyd's surprise then. His homemade bouquet of cheer. Lily turns to acknowledge his superior punch line, but in the twilight his skin and clothes have blended into the weathered cedar pickets.

The woman unscrews the jars of baby food, one pea green pot and another apricot. She ties a bib around the man's neck. Lily admires the way her fingernails are pared straight across and unvarnished, as though color and shape may be considered an unacceptable eccentricity by the trade. She dips into the green jar and begins to feed him. The man opens his mouth to accept the spoon and then follows this with a puckering motion. Several times she toggles the handle to dislodge the utensil. Lily is thrilled and nauseated. She watches as the spoon is coaxed from his mouth with a murmur of coos and the guppy-mouthed persuasion of baby talk. So much time, she thinks, has been wasted on white-collar peculations. As bankers and doctors are investigated, casino swindlers led away in cuffs, all this televised evangelism rising, they have missed out on these realities. What sorts of beasts humans are; it's dizzying to realize how little or how much it takes to make one happy. As the woman turns to recharge the spoon, the green pea mouthful is regurgitated. A slick trail of creamed vegetable bubbles down the infant-man's shadowed chin. The woman tuts and frowns and, using the edge of the spoon to scrape the mess from his face, feeds it back to him.

With fingers once again stuck to the moist sill Lily begins to feel that she's really peering over her own brick wall. How close-minded of her to think that she knew it all. That she'd seen enough and could be surprised by nothing. What else has she missed out on? What has gone neglected under her own nose, in her own home, between herself and Duncan? Yes, especially between herself and Duncan. If not for the set of bones, if not for Lloyd, would she ever see beyond her own sense of probity?

By the time Lloyd starts whistling for Lily's return, darkness has settled in. The woman has untied the bib and taken a seat at the kitchen table. Her blouse is undone. The man leaves the high chair and climbs over her lap so that together they form an unwieldy pietà. His slick head is bent, his mouth sucking at her breast with an urgency that Lily recognizes. It's the need to recapture something that's been lost, that someone has denied or taken away. And it seems to her that Lloyd wasn't that far off after all, the peeps are privy to all hard and soft humiliations. The peeps are set to inherit the earth.

"Leave the dead," Duncan orders as they push into the plague-blackened swale of a village.

But Kooch has turned around. "He's my partner," he says of Lee-tower, who's on the ground, entangled in the vacuum cleaner. "I'm going back for him."

"On your shoulders then." Duncan shows no compassion for his Young Turks. He is clearing a path through the strewn contents of his life to the Sub-Zero refrigerator. Anne, although as formidable as a well-packed bratwurst, is in danger of losing her skirt as she follows down the hall on her hands and knees. Kooch brings up the rear with Leetower over his shoulder.

Duncan moves a laundry hamper away from the refrigerator and pries open the door. The bulb illuminates the room, burning brighter, it seems, without any soft perishables—bread, crumb-spotted butter, the hoary crowns of broccoli—to absorb it. A corked and gamy fug swells out at him despite the scant contents. He leaves the door open, passes out the rations.

Leetower is dumped on the Mexican tile in front of the dishwasher. Anne pulls herself up on the hamper and raises a can to the sour chill of refrigerator light for examination.

"Life without a woman, Duncan, does not become you." She folds the tab back on the beer.

He is still rankled by her. Even now, the way she sandwiches one leg under the other on the laundry hamper. It's her undeniable presumption—how she has, with her last sentence and gesture, estranged him from his wife. She needs to be taught a lesson once and for all. And that is: a good account person is an ally who provides muscle at the wrangling end of an account. End of story.

"So let's be straight, boys." She takes a fizzy mouthful of tinned draft. "When can I show some stuff to Upstairs?"

My God, Duncan thinks. I'm going to kill her.

Leetower opens his eyes. "What happened?" He touches his eyebrows as though to ensure they haven't been razored away in jest.

Duncan fishes his voice out of a place of deep disbelief. "Anne, are you out of your fucking mind?"

It's interesting, the voice that comes out is not exactly his; the entire sentence is compressed, as though spaces between characters have been kerned out. Do the boys hear the change too? Can they see him in the gloom? Duncan holds up his beer to draw their attention.

"This is the deal, all of you." He forces a pause here although his mouth wants to run on. "I don't want anyone touching this campaign. Especially Upstairs. If they get involved they will disfigure it. Then I will come and personally exterminate each one of you. Regardless of who the leak is." He swings his beer in the direction of the door, some of the cold slosh dripping over his fist. "This is how we ran Tide. So you're either in completely, or get the fuck out now."

"We had Hawke on Tide."

"I am Hawke."

Leetower sits up. "I am Spartacus."

"Shut up," Anne says, walking over to the sink.

"Have you even seen the new scripts, McPherson?" Kooch stands at the counter beside her, running a pizza slicer over his palm. "Check it out. We've got Paratrooper Girl huddled in a C-119 Flying Boxcar, zooming over the rice fields with orders to destroy four tiny hamlets—suspected strongholds of the Viet Cong. Our voice-over says, 'Boy, paratrooping sounded great back in fucking Arkansas. But waiting for the drop signal in the clouds of Quang Ngai province proves another experience entirely.'"

"Yeah, yeah," Anne says, leaning against the sink. "Did I tell you the client wants to do a line of T-shirts next year?"

Kooch smiles. "We'll use our little Viet Cong. Her breasts, each one barely filling the smallest of rice bowls."

Anne clicks her fingernails against the stack of crystallized pans and casserole dishes in the sink. "You need a housefrau in here." She turns to Duncan. "Where has your little Lily gone, huh?"

Duncan looks at Anne, who is standing in his kitchen, but he sees Lily the night they found the bone. A welt across her ass conjured by his own hand. She had become so much more pliant the next day; how could he ignore his place in this? For a brief moment she had flexed before him, acknowledging his power to destroy her. What is greater than this, a woman brought to genuflection?

"Let me guess," he says to Anne. "You'd like to apply for the position?"

With her skirt still askew from the hallway crawl, the zipper hitting her at midflank, she looks at him without responding. Kooch is laughing. The happiness of the sound—of someone's laughter in the house— persuades Duncan to continue.

"Problem is, I don't shit where I eat." He's astonished to hear the words come out of his mouth but eager to see if they take. Whether she'll bend as Lily had.

Anne has a skin of sheet metal, though. She glances around the kitchen. "You sure about that?"

Duncan looks at Kooch, at Leetower on the floor. The minions are suddenly silent. They're waiting for his defining moment. He understands this; they're waiting for proof of his hegemony.

She makes it home before the cannon fires. The sound of the blast is still startling and for a moment it distracts her from her own disappointment at finding the driveway empty. She had a feeling that Duncan wouldn't show.

Lily wheels her bike up to the side of the house and stands below the peeling casement of her own kitchen. How much is revealed through open windows? Tonight she was the voyeur. Lloyd's disciple. She was allowed— no, encouraged—to be un-Lilylike. The ritual feeding, the conflation of limbs and breast she witnessed in the bungalow, accompanied her home, leaving Lily to question what about her own life is made more visible in the darkness.

Backing up to the maple stump near the wall of hedges, Lily has a view into the kitchen of the historical Oster Haus where a hundred-watt bulb holds vigil over an open cereal cupboard. The room offers no salient angle or insight from down here. Either that or she lacks imagination; maybe she should just face the fact that people like her are made to look *at* windows, instead of into them. Isn't the structure of a trefoil arch easier to deconstruct than anything that could happen behind it? For years she'd told herself that the study of art required the same talent present in the creation of art. Just last year her dissertation adviser wrote, *With a little application, Lily, I'm confident you could become the world's foremost expert on the pointed arch.* It was an offering of knowledge, so eccentric, so niche, it made her sick with delight. It was like the theoretical stretch effect of black holes on the human physiognomy. Imagine, to lodge in your heart a theory that most people could hardly grasp by the tail feathers!

Lily sits down on the stump, anchoring her sneakers in its lichen bumper. So why has the desire slipped away? The idea was once so urgent it left thumbprints on her neck. When she first told Duncan she'd chosen the pointed arch as her dissertation topic, she watched his brow lift in the particular way of a man retreating from the whack of a ball-peen hammer. She knew by that slight contraction of muscle that she'd struck terror in his heart. He had understood. Only the gifted could afford to pursue such an obscure and extraordinary blip in the human arc of development. For days after the Declaration of the Pointed Arch, she could tell that Duncan had both admired and despised her. The way he first let her silverware clang to the table before carefully adjusting it alongside her plate. He was both terrified and bound to her. He could never leave, never leave her depths—he couldn't hold his breath long enough to rise to the surface. Who would Duncan find to replace everything that she was? Did he think those little marketing dolls could hold concept and theory so tight to the bone? Did he think office girls understood spatial relations and linear perspective construction? Could any one of those skirts describe the double-bay vaulting system in the nave of Canterbury Cathedral?

Duncan had been impressed. For a brief moment she knew he really had admired her. History offered such a beautiful backlight; he had to shield his eyes against the dazzle of her. Isn't that true? Although she grew reckless in his awe. She began to chase the mind long-distance, following it until she became a speck on the horizon. And he was soon weary of watching. Who could hold his hand up against the sun all that time?

A string of knuckle cracks from the backyard pulls Lily from her trough of self-pity. The single light from the kitchen cuts a feeble slit in the darkness, but by it she can see a patch of scorched hedges shudder at the rear of the house. Instinct kicks in, she slides off the tree trunk and lowers herself behind it, hoping to blend into the humped silhouette. Out back, the hedges quiver as stems of the old fencing snap apart. Someone is coming through the shrubs. For a second she considers running but knows her legs will refuse this challenge. They are disobedient, sluggish with fear. Lily squeezes her knees to her chest. Where would she run anyway? Across the road, the stand of maples might provide shelter. But it might just mean running into the arms of a waiting posse. For all she knows the men may have come to flush her out of the trees. Isn't this what every bird dog knows? A quick, clean chase always makes for good sport.

CHAPTER 20

The Liver

In the apartment, Duncan tosses a balled rubber dish glove at Anne and says, "Get to work."

Around him, Kooch and Leetower hold back their breath, willing to forego exhalation in case it means missing minor auditory details.

"Go ahead, get busy."

Anne turns away from them. Lifts her hand, looks at her nails for a moment, as if to ensure they're each still in place. Then she slowly reaches across the sink and turns on the faucet. Hot water jets over weeks of Duncan's impossible crusts. His lips twitch. He gives Leetower, who is still on the kitchen floor, a meaningful glance to say, *See how she obeys?* Anne picks up the rubber glove, begins stretching it over her fingers. How is it possible, he wonders, that she's become so compliant? Is it this voice? How could he not have known? Imagine, to have lived over three decades without knowing his own strength. The sound of water rushing into the sink is the musical score of his ascendancy and it fills Duncan's desert cactus of a heart until Kooch reaches over and shuts off the tap. He is smiling at Duncan, but there's nothing friendly or respectful in those bared teeth. Nothing but fangs. He tugs at the rubber glove on Anne's hand and she moves toward him, begins to dry herself on his shirt. He takes her wrist, pinching his fingers around it. "Come on, McPherson," he says, still looking at Duncan. "Let's go join our fortunes in the bedroom."

Leetower sits up against the dishwasher. He watches Anne follow Kooch from the kitchen. Then he rests his head back on the floor. "Duncan," he says into the tile. "You are our next Tin God."

But Duncan is reaching up the wall for the telephone mounted by the corkboard. He must call Lily. While he still has the voice. While he can still whistle and spit marbles at the same time. The line rings through. He's aware that he was due upstate an hour ago. He remembers his promise to Valerie from the Historical Society, his solemn pledge to protect Lily from the seedy undercurrent of Osterhagen. Somewhere in the apartment, a door shuts and a toilet flushes.

"Get me an order of lo mein with spring rolls," Leetower says, his eyes now shut. There is no answer at the house. Duncan hangs up before the machine kicks in. There's no reason for her not to be home. No reason to be out this time of night in Osterhagen. He counts to twenty and dials again.

At some point during this attempt, Anne comes into the kitchen on one foot, screwing a heeled shoe onto the other. "Fucking Kooch bit me!" She snatches her bag off the floor and leaves.

Lily watches the mound of dwarf shrub cut itself free from the thicket and trot across the backyard. She has to hold her breath for a confused moment but then she's on her feet and on the move like a woman approaching a low chopper blade. Lily runs to the back porch and ducks beside it, tracking the figure as it circles the site of Tinker's grave. It lowers itself in a divot between hummocks and begins rasping at the dirt, sending up a spray into the grass behind it. In the denuded flower bed beneath her, Lily finds a large, faceted rock. If only Duncan had kept his word and come home tonight. They could be digging and returning some of the tired bones to the cellar. Instead, she's left with the Battle of the Cowshed on her hands. She bounces lightly on bent knees and, with an accuracy that was absent in her previous attempt with the running shoe, lobs the rock at the poodle.

In return, a surprised yelp as the dog rolls off the plot and away from incoming fire. She pats the ground for another rock, cursing Duncan for making her defend the homestead alone. The dog, a barbellated mass of twill, quickly reassembles on all fours. Without looking around for the source of attack it lowers its shoulders and skull in the manner of a herder avoiding a cattle hoof to the head and—she can hardly believe it—circles back to the grave. Lily looks down at the pebbles in her hand. It's not enough. It will just return, keep returning until it's poached something satisfying from the plot. She gets to her feet, takes a full breath, and charges into the yard. With arms apish and raised, and evacuative shrieks percussing in the night, Lily embodies what she hopes to be complete animal terror. The dog looks up, stands frozen for a moment before it turns and bolts for the barley field.

She chases after it, watching as the animal dives into the safety of the grain stalks. Lily runs as far as the edge of the grave and slumps over, hands to knees, her breath coming noisily. She remains motionless for some time, listening for the animal's retreat. Instead hears only the putter of a diesel engine, a night train to Albany. She wonders if her airborne imprecations have reached Duncan yet? Wherever he is tonight, whatever he's doing, may he stop a moment to gnash his teeth against the sudden, eviscerating pain of her bad juju. How many bloody animals is she going to have to take on?

In the garden patch a few thick inches of grass-peppered soil have been gouged out. Maybe the dog was on to something. Maybe there's something to be said for the canine sense of smell. She kneels to the ground, licks sweat from her upper lip. Is it really an *excavation* if she picks up a small hand shovel and just lifts away grass, broadens the circumference of the hole? Continues what the poodle has begun?

She promised Duncan she'd wait for him. Duncan promised he'd be home Thursday night. Sounds about even.

Lily starts troweling through the dry earth, working carefully to clear a shallow area the size of a cookie sheet. If she doesn't recover anything, no harm done. She won't bother telling him. There's no need to provide him with a running commentary, a blow-by-blow account of her night. Most likely he won't even ask.

She considers her successful tyranny over the poodle without surprise. The aggression is in her blood and in her parents' blood, a Mendelian truth smeared between two glass slides. They share the same tender-footed skill of advancing on the downtrodden the way one might approach a nickering horse. How else could her mother have persuaded the natives to embrace a Homeric god? *Meanwhile, in another quadrant of jungle, her father supervises the efforts of the indigenous people, who express gratitude at the prospect of clear-cutting their fertile plateaus to sow his bean crop.*

The trowel scrapes against a hard surface. Lily stops. Lays the tool aside. With steady fingers she clears earth from a chipped yellow patch in the ground. The dirt here is sandy and she has to rake away several inches in order to expose the entire flat pan of bone. She runs her fingers under the edges, plying it gently from the earth. The bone is about the size of her hand but triangular, shaped like a wing, she thinks, as it comes free. The airfoil design and cambered surfaces suggest it was created for flight; it even grows into a crude hook along one edge, just where a wing might latch to the body. But it's much too dense for flight. Lily holds it on her outstretched palm. Dense and irregular. In some places it's scalloped out to the depth of a saucer. And where the bone is the thinnest, two large perforations have formed. She sticks her fingers through these cavities, runs a fingernail along the blunt edges. A hole in a wing compromises aerodynamics, she knows. Puts an end to the lift-to-drag ratio necessary for flight.

Where in Tinker's body was this piece lodged? Lily turns the triangle over in her hand, curious, certainly. But beyond this inquisitiveness, beyond the constant cloying heat, she can't ignore the nagging feeling of nothingness. A bone is a bone, she thinks. Organic fiber. A structure nature has repeated a billion times over. Here she is, alone in Osterhagen, might as well be pulling rocks out of the ground. Lily sits back in the grass, crosses her legs. Thinks, this is totally no fun by myself.

Her emotions are so fluid and changing; how could she ever have agreed to base her entire future on something as irrational as a *feeling*? How to be sure she won't think the opposite tomorrow? Hasn't it been months—maybe a year—of living with Duncan at the very periphery of her life? One step further and there he goes, tumbling off the edge of the earth. Has she been afraid to be without Duncan, or just afraid to be left alone?

What animals we are, she thinks, looking up at the evening sky through a hole in the wing bone. Feral opportunists who lek and mate and move with the migrating herds. The dawdlers must be culled. Is this what Oster knew? That the trick to successful predation is to wait for the semblance of calm, the coast to clear, the homeless dog to circle, circle, circle, before lying down, the nanny to shut her eyes for a moment of rest under a tree where she cowers with her charge. Until the moment her great-grandfather dropped from the branches to cudgel the nanny to death, he likely had no understanding of what it meant to enact harm. And here's Lily, innocuous but of the same blood. She too only lying in wait.

The next morning she waits in the doorway of her husband's bedroom. If the nearly indiscernible rise and fall of his chest are any indication, he might very well have received her short-wave malediction last night. Fully dressed and unconscious, his jaw sagging apart and exposing the mossy underside of his tongue, Duncan takes small huffs through the nose. Lily notices that his bed linens are still tucked, although twisted, as if he'd struggled to crawl between the sheets but found the tight corners as impossible to negotiate as the lost end on a roll of Scotch tape.

Lily takes note of all the things that are wrong with this situation, and then itemizes these things in ascending order of urgency.

1. The fact that he has his own bedroom.
2. That he agreed to her idea that he have his own bedroom.

3. That she has no clue when he got home. Or where he was
   before that.

4. That she doesn't recognize much about him anymore—
   like his T-shirt, *Union Cap-C Votes Yes,* depicting a fist
   clenching a wrench. Or maybe it's a hammer.

5. The impossible-to-ignore stench of liquor distilled down
   to wound-cauterizing astringent.

Without thinking, she gives the open door a single kick (feeling better already) and listens to the ugly thump of wood and brass. In the bed
Duncan's startled limbs bend in a semaphoric contortion. He sits upright,
the way television characters often rise from nightmares, and peers at her
through sleep.

"Welcome back." Spoken like two arms folded across the chest.

The face before her is glaucous and confused, a map that will no
longer fold along its original lines. She notes a rim of dried lather on his
new scruff of beard.

"I'm going to look at the pig," Lily says, unsure of her intentions.

Duncan's eyes move over her, but how insignificant they've become in that face! As if someone had applied two thumbs and some
pressure and popped them back into his head. When he finally speaks,
she can hear the labor of his tongue unsticking itself from the roof of
his mouth.

"I'll come with you," he says.

If this were Greek tragedy, the wild boar would have sealed the fate of
their marriage. If this scene had been conducted on the proscenium,
Lily's hand in the extermination of the beast would represent the final
blow she herself had dealt to the union of husband and wife. She would
have slaughtered it and the sky would have grown funereal and the
ground given way between them. Towns, peasants, cattle sucked down

along the fault line. But waking life, she's come to learn, is never so neatly divided, so clearly cause-and-effect.

"What did you do last night?" Duncan says once they're walking.

Lily stiffens, remembering Lloyd's gift of the breast-fed man and the banishment of the poodle. "I read."

The sad thing is, even Hercules was careful to bring the Eryman-thian boar back alive. No question he made his share of mistakes, but the one thing he got right was the handling of the swine. It's been three weeks since they left the pig in the ditch and Lily is haunted by the Sovereign of the Deep Wood for all of the callous, sulking, and reactionary facets of her personality that it has revealed. *I have inherited a real mean streak, Duncan. It's pathological and I can only monitor it for so long. Like eight minutes. Then you're fair game, friend.*

But she'd rather die than be so pithy.

"I was thinking about Oster," Lily says instead.

"What about?"

"I was thinking about servants at that time. The women were something like chattels." She gives a rounded musculature to her words. "It wasn't uncommon for these big landowners sometimes to, you know, rape them."

"So, you've come around?" He rips a leaf apart as he walks. "Pointing fingers at your own kin."

"People," she says, with an obfuscation that is self-implicating, "are capable of the most unimaginable things. Maybe Tinker abducted my grandfather in revenge."

"You could ask the Crusaders." Duncan yawns, cranks his jaw in circles as though letting out a couple yards of fishing line. " 'Course they'd deny it. Apple never falls far from the tree, right?"

She would like to bite him, leave the crenellated pattern of her teeth in his shoulder. But that would only have the effect of flourishing a checkmark at the end of his last sentence.

"Those old guys didn't come around, did they?" he asks, skipping right over the discussion of Tinker. It's as though he went to the city and lost interest in their project.

"Not yet."

"What do you mean, not yet?" Duncan's voice is apathetic at best. He maintains several extra inches of gait beyond her as though she's something he wants to keep in his past. "You expect them soon?"

"Nature is grisly and perverted, Duncan." She takes in a succulent huff of air. "There's a dog now—a standard poodle—that's been coming around, digging. Twice this week I had to chase it away."

"Whose is it?"

"Nobody's. A stray."

"Poodles don't go stray."

"It's untidy."

Duncan says nothing. They continue walking. Of course she's trying to engage him, to lure him into some semblance of ease so that when she lays in and condemns him for his absence, the surprise and force will bruise him that much deeper purple. It would be easy enough to linger on some simple observations: the sway of chestnut branches and quivering aspens around them, the parch-bottom ditches framing the sides of the road like the gutters of a bowling alley. But this benign wallpaper of chatter will come across as hectoring, circumlocutory, and will dampen the searing ring of her jab. Better just to deal the uppercut now.

"I'm assuming you were drunk when you drove here last night."

"Yes." It's his voice that shrugs, not his shoulders.

"Yes? That's it?"

"Call it a low point."

Wow. Lily feels the same rush of heat that overcame her in the field, a parching awareness that he's going to leave her. Without an arrhythmic step her husband has crossed from casual neglect to a place where he is no longer responsible to her.

Duncan stops when he reaches the crumbled beginnings of the blacktop. "It was around here," he says and looks at her as though handing something over, stepping back now that he's seen her to her destination. His face is so changed, he seems to hold guard behind the sprigs of beard. This is how we are with each other, she thinks. This is why we're doomed.

For a minute they stand in the middle of the road like that. Only later will she understand that she was studying his face for recognition, however small.

"I dug in the garden without you last night," she hears herself say. "I found a scapula. From Tinker's shoulder."

Without coming any closer, without responding, he reaches for her glasses. When he slides them off her face, the trees blur. Within her narrow focal range, only the edges of Duncan are crisp. Only Duncan is illuminated. Without her lenses all she can see is him puffing on each oval of glass and rubbing them clean with a corner of his shirt. He holds them up, squints against fingerprints, and hands them back. Doesn't try jabbing them behind her ear—the awkward motion of replacing eyeglasses—but hands them back at waist level.

Lily takes the glasses and wonders what she's to do with this gesture. Is she pleased with the reach of his hand? Yes, she's embarrassed by the upsurge of her blood, the granular attention she's paying to the stubble on his chin. But everything excitable within her is mitigated by his reluctant face, by his silence. The action is just Duncan's judgment on thumbprints, on her slipshod ways; she is chain grease and smudges and stray hairs.

It is easier to move apart on the road then. There is a natural moment that comes next and it seems right to break apart and search the canal for the spot where the beast is turning back to dirt.

"There." She points to a mound in the ditch, to the wide span of maple leaves. On top of the mound she recognizes the rack of branches that he twisted from a young spruce. The pile of pig is smaller than she expected. Ravaged by winged things and wolves, most likely. Duncan and Lily stand at the edge of the road and sniff; the animal should be mulch by now. Yet, the air is all balsam and bayberry leaves and she knows they're both thinking the same things but are loath to consult.

This is the mistake Lily has made. This is the job Duncan could not finish.

There is the purr of electrical wires that sag along the road at intervals and, above this, a layer of bird chirrups. Lily hears each distinctly as she starts down the leeside of the embankment, dry sand sliding ditch-wise ahead of her. She steps toward the mound and picks off the branches, kicks away the cover of broad maples that are spread like serviettes. She pushes the last of the leaves with her toe. The pig is gone.

CHAPTER 21

Organs of Voice

In the evening he joins Lily out back at Tinker's grave. It's a night of treasure hunting in the inert soil where, according to the copy of *Gray's*, they recover two arm bones but no hand; a marble sack of tarsal and metatarsal bones that comprise the foot, but no phalanges. Duncan's thinking's that the toes may have been too small to remain intact and nestled against the foot; perhaps they were ingested whole by a passing sweep of worms. Once he's in the soil, he remembers the pleasure of searching. He realizes he's digging to make up for his absence, choosing to go wide rather than deep. He tells Lily this way he can be most effective.

Duncan feels a tremendous need for an element of normalcy in the garden. Not only to camouflage their midnight industry, but also to return his sense of reality. First, the pig was gone from the ditch. Then, this afternoon, he found a sizable puddle of vomit on the rubber mat of the Saab. And running behind his eyelids all day, every day, is a Möbius strip of women in Stand and Be Counted jeans so tight he has to prod and twist just to get an index finger under a waistband.

Also, Lily's been digging without him. Although the confession is hardly thundering in his universe of daily exigencies there's no mistaking the intention of her well-placed kick to the balls.

Duncan turns on the sprinkler, adjusts the spray so that it arcs gently back and forth over the portion of lawn that is still untouched. He torches a cigarette and scratches his ass. At its apogee, the lashing arc of water forms a curtain, an illusory screen to shield the grave. Holy fuck, Duncan thinks, we really did carve it up. This initial midnight survey shows that what began as a small garden patch has advanced like alopecia across the grass. This might pose a problem. In the event that Valerie from the Historical Society sends an emissary to visit poor Laura, the butchered landscape will definitely become a town issue.

Lily comes out of the house and steps barefoot across the porch. She's been storing away Tinker bits in the basement and is quiet. He shouldn't blame her for digging without him. Three weeks in and no one understands the urgency of getting those bones out of the ground more than Lily. He's the one who's not holding up his end of the deal.

She comes over and takes the cigarette from between his fingers, puts it in her mouth and sucks back. For a minute they stand there, on the same northern line of latitude, looking into the barley and listening to the sprinkler patching against the grass, beading against the green. She sucks again and gives him back the cigarette.

As they pass this transgression from hand to hand, he would like to gather up her hair and yank hard. Just to see. Rub the stubble of his new beard into her cheek until he leaves abrasion marks. Failing that he maybe would like to say something to her. Or even speak in a general, undirected manner using *thou* and *thee*. Perhaps it would be easier to admit he's failing her if he did so using the subjective and objective forms of the singular second person. But the words are too far out there. So let her make the first move for once. While he's not surprised that she's excavated, he is hurt by the thought. If she would just take hold of his sleeve now, these words might come, fluent and concise. She could even weep. This would be helpful, if she wept and moored against his hip. Or pitched herself at his feet. Near his feet. If only she could make herself the vulnerable one. Then he could finally look into her face, take it between his palms like an injury, and figure out what he's been doing wrong.

They were synchronized once; they ticked with Swiss precision.

What happened to that? Her early-morning rustling of bedsheets was a signal for him to wrap his arm around her as she began her crawl toward consciousness. They learned how the other could speak without using the mouth. At parties, when he caught her twisting her rings he knew to go gather up their coats. When they visited her parents it was understood that she would come and perch on the arm of his chair. It made him feel at ease—she knew that. It made him feel like a husband.

He's about to lose it all now, he knows. This woman who once understood him without the aid of exhaustive explanation. This long-legged, ink-stained virgin he found like a gift in a library carrel. Standing beside him tonight, perhaps, but not for long. Will she move on to someone else? Could she have already?

Say something, you jackass, he urges himself. Lily rolls her toes in the grass. She looks up into the sky and scratches her neck. She's offering him all these seconds. But who is she? Not the woman with whom he created a private language of hands. This replacement Lily is an oralist, a lip-reader who stands opposed to the use of sign language.

The moments, each fractional component, clock on in silence. He counts them as they go. Lily leaves him and moves across the lawn toward the sprinkler. His time has expired. She moves along the hedges. As she walks, crickets begin a string of chirrups. So sudden and orchestral that Duncan believes her body kinetics have cued their motion, their startling rapture, the frantic scratch of back legs. It's too hot a night for this dry-legged rhythm, for two sticks rubbing. He looks at the shrubs; the cigarette drops from his fingers.

"Jesus, Lily," he says over all that hind-leg racket. "Fire!"

As Lily passes, swaying to the cacophony made in her honor, the crickets begin combusting in the hedge. Yes, the crickets are burning.

She stops and looks around.

It's you, he thinks. You've inspired the suicide of an entire orchestra of insects. Duncan is not the hallucinatory sort, and doesn't need to rub his eyes or pinch flesh. As he watches he can see sparks of ignition in the thicket marking the property line. With the frenzy of dervishes, they're chirping themselves into self-incineration.

"You set the crickets on fire."

She laughs. Why is she laughing?

"You are messed up, Duncan."

He can only point, with a blistered finger, to the tiny fires where the crickets pop and smolder in the hedge. Sudden death instigated by a set of Circean hips moving across the grass. She follows this path, the extension of finger across the lawn and into the hedge.

"It's fireflies," she says.

Duncan's breath flutters and hooks. He steps back from the shrubs. He looks at Lily expecting the dark powers of cloud seeders and shamans. But he sees she's right. That she is just grass-stained flesh, susceptible and unsure.

In the shower, the weak dribble of water (too often a shade of russet brown) clatters as it boils up through the original cast-iron piping, so that Lily doesn't hear the sopping thud when the bathroom ceiling collapses.

Under hot water that has been forced up two vertiginous floors of derelict plumbing, she lathers out the night's activity and feels satisfied with the rubble of bones they've collected. A cobbler's pile in just one go. Listening to the grunt and strum and tangy whine of the shower pipes, she realizes—suddenly and miraculously—that all these sounds are coming together to form the basic chords of a musical lament. *I still miss you but my aim's getting better.* She's pleased by the thought, tilts her neck to receive the sweet heartland ballad full in the face. It's then that she feels the first blast to the cheek.

Lily opens her eyes and finds a churning cloud in the curtained tub with her. Hovering overhead is a swarm of yellow jackets: hairy, thick-vested, impossible to count, and at this proximity, more black than yellow. Wasps the size of grapes, incongruously suspended one moment, then

skidding down at her face, her shoulders, undeterred by the slick runway
of her skin or her screams or swatting palms. The yellow jackets' answer
is to peck at these, anything that interrupts their dive-bomb formation.

Duncan rips away the remaining portion of shower curtain that hasn't been
tangled in her legs and already torn down. Then, by swatting a cluster from
her head with a bath towel—roughly, but who knows what kind of force to
apply to a swarm of wasps—and wrapping her with the terry-cloth ends,
he's able to lift Lily from the tub and carry her into the hall.

"Shut the door! The door!" She's screaming inside the towel. Duncan puts her on the floor (drops her in his haste) and shoves the solid oak
hard enough to produce a Richter reading in his molars. A house of lav-
ish appointments, he thinks. Doors that slam, a boneyard out back . . .

He's afraid to remove the towel. Call it the kernel of his failing but
this has never been his place. Duncan stands over his wife, one leg on
either side of her hips. Years ago, when they divided up all the super-
powers, established which heroic qualities belonged to whom, Lily drew
Strength. Duncan got Invisibility. He hasn't been much of a husband,
this is clear. But he wanted her to feel somewhat protected with him up
here. And now in this way too, he has failed.

Lily shrugs off the towel herself. He doesn't move. She lies naked,
under and between his legs. The moment doesn't pass without *this* thought.
Her left eye is inflated, as though a small tulip bulb has been planted just
under the skin, just above the lid, on the slope of bone leading to her forehead. These two planes join under the swollen buckle of eyebrow, giving
her face a new winking asymmetry. Lily's hands are pricked and mittenlike;
some more at the shoulder, a scarlet horse bite on the cheek.

She cries without sound, and it dawns on him that instead of suc-
cumbing to cowardice he needs to buck up. This is, after all, the exact
state of defenselessness he's been waiting for. Her mouth opens with the

thrust of her sobs. Duncan sees the pink honeycomb vault inside and, at the same time, feels his own spine drain of that anxious, stiffening fluid. He bends, gathers her wet and wronged limbs, and carries her to bed.

Once he's inspected her under a good light, he counts six stings. Her lips haven't fattened, her tongue moves freely enough to skip the trip to the emergency room. He'd have to take her by force, anyway. Duncan puts her in bed the way that he found her, naked and limp, and her bath towel he stuffs into the strip of light under the bathroom door.

Down in the kitchen he gathers the utensils of comfort, the entire time not only aware of but relieved by the changing metallurgy of his blood. It's that old black magic, the virile components smelting from the skunk, and he is painfully, pleasantly aware of being led by his dick. Minutes ago, carrying Lily into bed, Duncan was careful to keep his groin away from her, a regained instinct reminding him timing was everything. It wasn't just her nakedness—although, Christ! The sight of her on the floor, slight and peach between his legs, there was no way to negate the effect of her helpless agony. How simple to bend and lift his wife. Why did he fear her under the towel?

Ice and a washcloth and some bite ointment and he charges back up the stairs, taking a quick whiff of his armpits as he goes. Lily was right about one thing. This business of discovery is the most exciting thing that's ever happened to them.

In her bed she allows him to fold the compress over her eye and cheek. She makes the shallow sucking noise of an animal caught in a trap meant for much larger prey. Although he wouldn't have believed it possible, he's grown even harder now. A section of mattress sinks with his weight and he makes a sly inventory of the parts of her that roll toward him. To maintain pressure on the compress he's required to lean over her and brace an arm on the far side of the bed.

"I look like a monster."

"No," he says, brushing wet hair from her forehead. Her skin feels hot and tender beneath his fingers. "You're okay now."

She reaches for him, catches his fingers in her own. "Thank God you're here."

He swallows. "You were screaming. You scared the shit out of me."

She's squeezing each of his fingers in turn. "It really hurts, Duncan."

He considers his erection. "How bad?"

"Pretty bad."

"The ibuprofen will kick in."

"I opened my eyes and there they were." Tears and stings have turned Lily's face into a scarlet mess. She releases his hand and pats cautiously around her hairline.

"They probably infested the ceiling joists. The shower softened up the drywall just enough." He feathers a dire lilt into his sentence. "Here I thought it was the crickets coming back for revenge."

Lily looks at him with one eye. "I'll call someone in the morning."

Duncan applies the compress a bit too hard and she winces. Call in the morning? Get out of bed and call someone? He was picturing a lengthy convalescence, the flesh-hued calamine imprints of her body on the sheets. He was not expecting the rational mechanics of the pest-control men.

"It could take a while." Duncan sucks his cheek grimly, considers his pacing. "There could be a half dozen nests under the drywall."

She nods, pulls the sheets up to her chin. "I'll handle it tomorrow."

Okay, he definitely does not like the way her voice has reshaped itself so quickly. What sort of an ancillary ability is this, to heal herself on command? Duncan lifts the compress. Nope, the bite on her forehead has boiled up to the size of a quail egg.

"They got you pretty good, Lily," he tries again. But his voice sounds like a feeble spatter of buckshot as she takes over the cold cloth and applies it herself. Duncan begins to feel an emulsification in his shorts.

"Maybe I'm depressed," she says.

"Depression is just anger without enthusiasm."

"So I'm angry, then." Lily's sniffles put him in mind of a pug with a sinus cold. The comparison takes the starch out of him. He stands up and turns off the lamp so that the room is swabbed only by moonlight. Then he comes back, shifts her gently, and lays down next to her on the bed.

"Lily," he says in the dark. "Don't be angry."

She doesn't answer, stares up at the ceiling.

Duncan keeps to his side of the mattress though he wants to somehow remain just within her reach. Her bedridden shape reminds him of the other rare occasions when she's shown herself frail, defenseless. "Do you remember the summer I taught you to swim?" he says.

She nods, adjusts the washcloth over her eyes.

"You were so angry you couldn't do it yourself."

"I couldn't float."

"You let me teach you. Do you remember? You let me do it for you."

"Yes."

"Lily." He takes the compress, smooths her hair. "Let me do this for you."

CHAPTER 22

The Testes

"**Y**our husband punch you in the face?"

Lily touches the poached lump on her forehead. The swelling hasn't diminished as much as it has pooled south over her browbone into the soft pocket of eyelid. With the swelling has come a partial gloam drawn over her vision that she finds somehow comforting. As though her inside and outside perspectives are finally aligned.

"Piñata accident," Lily says, hoping that by ratifying the girl's suspicions she might escape the insolent teenage watchfulness.

With a slow hand, Kitten tucks the cigarettes back into the waistband of her school uniform and smirks. "Piñata, hey? That's a good one."

The posture of the girl's craned hip and bent knee in front of the fountain are straight from the pages of some controversial classic. A *Go Ask Alice* of our times. Lily holds up the silver Zippo that Lloyd gave her. Shakes it a few times either to help eke out a bit of flame or distract the girl's intense watch by reflecting sunlight in her eyes. Through the oily fingerprints on the metal case, Lily catches a glimpse of her own face, a sizable portion of it red and distended. She's rather grotesque.

But there was no staying indoors today.

She had spread a tarp over the holes in the backyard in case the exterminators happened to wander out back. Duncan had set up his computer in the sunroom and, with a Rachmaninoffian command of keyboard geography, began typing with a furious intensity. From every end of the house Lily could hear him pursue his campaign idea through paddy land and DMZ zones, hoarding the advertising campaign around himself as though it might be spoiled by contact with the world. Certainly by contact with her. Of course she's curious as hell. But Duncan's not telling and she's not going to ask.

Although last night he had been kind to her, boiling tweezers before they realized wasps don't leave barbs. He lay next to her until she fell asleep—well, until he thought she was asleep. In truth, she couldn't drift off with him so close. She feared his kindness was scraped together from the odds and ends of the guilt he felt at not feeling. It's been weeks since they shared a bed in the city, and she can't even remember the last time she was naked in front of him. Last night, his pity for her body was the organic fiber holding the kindness all together. And so waking up this morning to the distant gunfire of his typing, she realized that his nursing had, if not appeased his guilt, at least equalized the force of its pressure.

Lily makes her hand into a shield against the breeze and holds out the lighter to Kitten. The girl dips her face into the cup. In this proximity there are new things to notice about her: beyond the modeled cheekbones—as though wadding were quilted into the upper reaches—behind the violet smudges of her eyes, is a rather fetching and inescapable sense of ruin. She touches the end of her cigarette to the lighter.

"You ever play Uncle?" the girl asks, sliding away from the flame.

"I guess I have."

"Look at my lip." Kitten tilts her head back. There's a scrub of whiteheads along her hairline as precise as Braille. Lily could touch and read it. Instead she steps back.

"Relax," the girl says, enjoying her discomfort. "I'm not a lesbo or anything. You see the scar?" Points to a white dart through her lip that interrupts the circle of her mouth.

Lily looks down over the rim of her glasses.

"We had a bet, me and this guy last summer? Who could bite harder, you know? Take it longer."

"That must make it hard to say uncle."

"See how my top lip won't come together exactly? That's called a crimson line, under where I had the stitches."

The girl is nearly impossible to look away from. She is the lip-glossed, shit-talking embodiment of the word *taunt*. This has been Lloyd's argument the whole time, that the inherent brand of sexuality among the kilt-and-stocking set is that of overdeveloped, adolescent prey. And now Lily sees it, up close and head-on.

She thinks of Tinker, who by all estimations was put in the garden by her great-grandfather. How come she can sort out the logic behind the exploitation of someone like Kitten—indeed, could build a fairly solid defense for it—while a scant collection of hundred-year-old bones, with no flesh, no life attached, has already struck her deep sense of indignation?

Kitten, relaxed against the fountain and smug in her assessment of spousal abuse, has been making a careful study of Lily's own face. But as intense as the girl's attention has been, it slips away from her and shifts to the side doors of the library.

"Your friend is leaving."

Lily turns. She's just in time to see Lloyd, with his plodding cat walk, exit through the cloister arch to the street.

"That's the same guy from the Dunkin' Donuts last year. And the bus too." Words and smoke coming out of the broken circle of lips.

"He's not really my friend."

"Sure," the girl says with a cynicism that Lily, while liking the quality in herself, loathes in others. "He's the one who asks girls to blow him on the Crosstown. I know it, he sat right behind me once."

For one delicious moment she thinks of telling Kitten that Lloyd is much more interested in ravaging her acne-pocked pal, Audiophile.

"I doubt you're his type."

Kitten laughs with a shameless arpeggio that only a fifteen-year-old would dare inflict on a listener. "Don't worry, I'm not into charity."

Lily feels a reaction in her chest; is once again aware of how the juvenile uplift that tags the end of Kitten's sentences constantly belies the content.

"But tell him something, okay?" The girl's smile reveals the perfect humility of one crooked incisor. "Tell your buddy I'll do him for three hundred bucks."

Lily just looks at her for a moment.

"You shouldn't smoke."

Kitten doesn't answer. She takes a haul off the cigarette then snaps it into the fountain. It hits the water with sizzle and triumph.

———

On her way out that night, Lily finds Ginger and Persian, brows like cable-knit stitch, crowded behind the reference desk examining something there.

"Who would do this?"

"Savages."

"Skinheads."

Lily must have a peek. Gathering her shoulder bag, she comes at the desk from an oblique angle, preparing evening farewells with her usual disinterest. But she stops short when she sees the object of their attention. The thing is curved like a bugle horn and baked the color of buttered enamel. Lily shuts her pained eye to ensure this is not a result of her own skewed vision.

"What is it?" she says, only to occupy the tongue, to prevent it from asking, *How did you find it?* She is startled by the tusk, looks around to see if there's any more of it.

"It's the boar," Ginger says. "In part."

"They found him across the river." Persian's voice barely registers. "In a taxidermy shop in Kingston." Lily notices the root end of the fang is still raw, as though it had been torn by hand from the muzzle.

"Someone brought him in to get stuffed—imagine Skinner having to buy back his own boar." Ginger pokes at the tusk; it rattles against the desktop. "He wants us to keep this here, do up a display for posterity."

"Why would anyone kill the Sovereign of the Deep Wood?" Persian asks no one in particular.

"You know, those Chinese eat anything."

"I can see why Skinner is on a rampage." The old woman's mouth shirrs around the words. She picks up the yolky fang, looks directly at Lily. "Whoever did this, I hope they get what they deserve."

The exterminator stands in the front hall, a loping giant in the narrow space. "You know pigs, they decay at the same rate as humans?" he says to Duncan. "I saw it on television—that's why they use them in those crime labs. Can tell exactly how long a thing's been dead." Safety goggles have left an imprint on the man's face, a red, circular emphasis over the nose and around the eyes, reminding Duncan of the importance of establishing and maintaining neutral eye contact through this seemingly random delivery of news. Apparently the Sovereign of the Deep Wood's carcass, turgid and firm, has surfaced several miles downstream, expelled onto a bank in Ulster County below the Kingston Rhinebeck Bridge.

"So it drowned?"

"Or someone drowned it." The exterminator looks up the landing. "When did you say you came to town? Three weeks ago?"

Duncan resists scratching his head furiously. "Three or four. Why?"

"Your wasp infestation started way before that. Long time before you opened up the house."

"Right." He rakes his hair out from his collar.

"You got another bathroom down here, don't you?"

Duncan finds himself nodding, caught by those circular imprints. "Just down the hall." But as he says the words he remembers the main-floor bathroom also faces the backyard. Had Lily closed those blinds? "Hold on, my wife was getting ready in there. Let me check if it's decent."

The exterminator scribbles something on his clipboard, doesn't look up. "No, I'm saying to keep the upstairs one sealed for twenty-four hours. I fogged it again after getting out the nest."

"Oh," Duncan says, with transparent relief. He grabs the checkbook Lily's left on the hall table. "Sure, we can do that."

"Meanwhile I'm going to get the ladder. Where's the best spot to get on the roof?"

"The roof?"

The man looks up. His mouth, crooked as an accidental gash, expresses his growing impatience. "How'd you think wasps got in—by ringing the doorbell? Read your contract. Part of our service agreement is that we fix up the point of entry for you too."

Duncan nods unhappily; the complications are endless.

"Lots of the other guys just get out the nests and call it a day. We even do a follow-up check in a few weeks."

"Right, okay." He stares at the red welt on the hooked bridge of the man's nose. "Only now's not a good time. I'll have to get back to you when my wife's home."

"I tell you, the longer you wait, you're just inviting back whatever got away." He lifts his clipboard and uses it to scratch his chin. "But if you gotta consult with the pants, go for it."

"It's just the arrangement with the Historical Society," Duncan says. "They need to know anytime we, uh, do anything structural."

"Well, you folks don't have to be around for me to get up on the roof. You only here part-time, right? I can come back anytime."

"Actually, we're here pretty much the entire summer." He skims quickly around his own absence.

"Really?" The man rips an invoice off his pad, his business number printed with the crude and deliberate serifs of Middle English. "You been hearing that cannon at night?"

Duncan folds the invoice carefully. No point in feigning ignorance with the locals. "Yes, we've heard it." After all, a yard full of men saw him at Skinner's that night. "Guess it'll stop now that he found the pig."

"Well, that's damn unlikely." The exterminator laughs. "That crazy old bastard's not looking for a thief anymore. We've got a killer on our hands."

CHAPTER 23

Muscular Coat of the Stomach

It's been a long time since she's seen any of his work and she is curious. Duncan is a talker by nature, an opinion-seeker who freely solicits the views of cabdrivers and checkout girls, who is always deferential to the taste of the house sommelier. And yet, he hasn't once asked Lily for her opinion on his spots. She slithers into the sunroom. He has rarely been so tight-lipped or guarded about a project and she takes this as an indication of his growing confidence in the campaign.

> OPEN ON: Morning sky, South Vietnam. A battalion of paratroopers hang like poppies over a rice field. Once they've pulled their chute cord, all that's left is the silent acrobatics of drifting into battle. No soundtrack here, just the accelerated breathing of a first-time search-and-destroy.

Lily flips through the first of the overturned pages. It's natural, isn't it, to want insight into her husband's work? His achievements? As discordant as their relationship may be, she does know how fervently he wants to be a success.

> CUT TO: Rice paddies, jump boots touch down. What follows is a frenzy as soldiers disengage from parachute twine,

struggle to discard the canopies, to slosh across wet fields, leaving prints on the yellow silt. (Think: the first thirty minutes of Spielberg's *Saving Private Ryan*—minus the explicit carnage.) Across the road they spot the stronghold of the Viet Cong, a complex of villages they've been ordered to take out. The ground between them is littered with the conical shade hats of farmers, runners in flight. In the clover patches, sheep are bleating. Several jump cuts here as they storm the rice paper village. This segment's shot with a handheld camera to produce that stuttering shutter quality of a newsreel. Film is sapped of color.

The random camera action illustrates the thought: What does one soldier mean in the swarm that descends on the cluster of muck and straw peasant domes? Some GIs use firethrowers to ignite the grass-roofed huts. Others use historically accurate Zippos. (Anne—check if we require an OK from Zippo Manufacturing Company.) Throughout the village, any hole in the ground—whether it be full of vegetables or munitions or children—is treated to a grenade. (Note for set design: ideally, we want to re-create burning huts from the famous Morley Safer footage of the Burning of Cam Ne.) The actual detonation of the grenade is preceded by a shout, "Fire in the hole," a phrase that acts as a guarantee or a rabbit's foot. If I say it, it shall be. As though the mechanical energy of the grenade is just an extension of the young soldier's will. As though the young soldier's will is just an extension of the 173rd Airborne Brigade's will. This chain of command must exist; without it the 173rd becomes an illusion cloaked in the reek of blue cordite.

Jesus. Lily looks up from the script. When did Duncan start writing this? She walks between the sunroom and front hall, trying to move out of the pocket of odor surrounding this spot. She glances down the drive to make sure he's not coming. When did this happen, when had words acquired smell?

C U T   T O : Close-up shot of young paratrooper, removing helmet. As helmet comes off, long hair tumbles down, we realize the soldier is female! She is our American Paratrooper Girl in jump boots and flare-legged Stand and Be Counted jeans. The ville is ablaze now, all around, soldiers removing helmets—all of them female! Livestock run in all directions, adding to the confusion. A pig runs into frame and our girl raises her M-16 and shoots it. She's a crack shot. This to foreshadow next scene. She lifts a door flap with the butt of her gun.

C U T   T O : Interior hut. We see four women, shoulders draped with small children, squatting against the back wall. They begin screaming in the high pitch of the province. Why don't they surrender? The roof collapses on them. Paratrooper Girl staggers away.

S U P E R   U P   O V E R   P I C T U R E : All War is R-rated.

But Paratrooper Girls are following orders. The chain of command being the cornerstone of all military operations. Without it, young soldiers would be setting fires to a circle of huts, silently wondering if they've got the right town, wondering what the hell are they fighting for.

S U P E R   U P   O V E R   P I C T U R E : History Repeating.

Lily opens the front door in hopes of a breeze. She moves through the hall and back toward his desk, trying to fit this new direction into the groove of Duncan's original brief. He was supposed to be writing a commercial for women's jeans. So where did this stuff—the slaughter of farm women—come from? Even with her scant knowledge of war, she'd say the borrowing and cursory handling of the Vietnamese conflict is highly inappropriate for a denim campaign. And vulgar. It's obvious Duncan's portraying a war without bothering to develop the historical dimensions of the subject. His references lack solid materiality; it reads like pulp. Just an amalgamation of battle scenes stripped of context to allow more on-screen gore. And the use of women? Lily shakes her head. This isn't advertising, it's misogyny.

Which is why Stand and Be Counted will love it. She slides the script under the pile where she found it. It's sick, bordering on satirical, and just the sort of troubling and sensational Hollywood-studded television fodder that Duncan's client will eat with a spoon. Lily's never doubted his talent for work. For understanding the risks and offenses sometimes necessary to break through the clutter reel of trash out there. In fact, if she knows anything about ads from the years she's spent with him, she's willing to bet he'll take home an armload of awards for this. Perhaps another gold One Show Pencil. In terms of the moral scope of advertising, Lily herself has no battle to wage. She's known Duncan far too long to be troubled by industry details. If she wanted to whine about hypocrisy and lack of societal value, she'd start with her own career and the university. Lily touches the knoll on her forehead and remembers Kitten's loud and hopeful spousal abuse accusations. No, what worries her isn't the platform. It's the genesis of the creation, the source of his inspiration.

Duncan knows he's being watched. He's got the countenance of a criminal; the slouch, the eyes all viscous shift along aisles of hardware, his beard growing in at awkward angles. When he walked in, old Wakefield nodded from behind the counter. *I got my eye on you, buddy.*

He buries his hands in his pocket. Doesn't help that he's totally forgotten what he's come for. Something for the nanny, for digging out the nanny. He feels scattered today, but also strangely useful. Earlier he'd cracked open the upstairs bathroom to tape plastic over the crumbling ceiling plaster. Now he's taking a break from the TV scripts he's been pounding out. He's decided to present the scripts as monologues, starting with a ninety-second launch spot, describing the action first and then showing storyboards at the end. He thinks the Stand and Be Counted client needs more performance than presentation. After all, at first even *he* was surprised by his own outrageous manipulation of Vietnam. But if Duncan's learned anything from men like Hawke, it's how much you can get away with if you look like you know what you're doing. He's seen it work on Anne and Leetower. Even Kooch. They intuit the strength of his belief in the work, and with just that, they climb on board.

Duncan stops in front of a rack of shovels. It's hard to believe the garden was his project, initially. Lily had ordered him here to pick up something. A fine-point spade? For the smaller bones. Or a brush and pan to sift dirt. Duncan lifts a broad trowel, turns it over in his hands and then puts it back on the display rack. He's read that over half the bones in the human body are in the hands and feet. So it seems impossible that they haven't come across more of the small ones. He can't imagine Oster holding any back; who would risk that sort of link to a vanished nanny?

Duncan's been chewing over the lumber baron's culpability. If you want to call it culpability. After all, once Oster had set up a successful sawmill, the next logical step was to produce an heir to that mill. He wanted to replicate himself—a man of importance. Why not create a family to rival the Vanderbilts? The Astors, maybe. Thinking about it in those terms, Tinker really had brought about her own brutal fate by attempting to rob him of this lineage. Later, to ensure there was no evidence, she was disposed of in the one place where he could keep an eye on her. What man worth his salt wouldn't have done what Oster had? Yes, Duncan's quite certain that Tinker is all down there. They just haven't dug deep enough.

"Something I can help you with?"

The voice jars him, seems to come from an aisle over but Wakefield is actually standing shoulder to shoulder with him. Has puddled together in the periphery.

"You the guy at Skinner's the other night? Mr. and Mrs. up at Oster Haus?" The man wears a leather apron with bulging pockets. His nails are ground down to the quick, the thick fingers of one who sorts staples and drill bits for pleasure. "Doing some gardening up there?"

Duncan hasn't spoken in hours, has no clue what polyphonic and crazed sound he might make if he opens his mouth. But the old store owner is waiting for some reply.

"Thinking about it."

"Sure, saw you buying a shovel the other day." The guy frowns. "Looking for another one already?" He looks Duncan over as if drawing up details for the clan report.

"Can't have too many." Duncan shrugs. Does Wakefield have an idea of what's been going on in the backyard? He might. It's a small town; all it takes is someone out for a drive, stopping to take a look at the historical Oster Haus, the acres of Dutchess County barley surrounding it. Then Tinker will be taken away from them. Even if it was her own fault she ended up where she did, Duncan doesn't want anyone else poking around the bones of his nanny.

"Well, least we know you're not trying to bury the pig up there, hey?"

Duncan snorts, startling the both of them with this attempt at laughter. This is no way to deflect suspicion. The man takes a step back, picks a slipped coil of garden hose off the floor. "You hear Skinner's on a real tear now?"

"I think I heard something," Duncan says.

"That bloody pig." Wakefield shakes his head and winds the hose back on the shelf. "They fished it out of a dumpster. By the old sawmill—that restaurant. Imagine it's been rotting to hell in this heat."

"Dumpster?" Duncan fights for neutrality in his inflection.

"I do have it on good account that the boar's head was bashed in."

"You're kidding."

"No, sir. I am not."

"Who'd put it in a dumpster?"

"Well, ain't that the million-dollar question." Wakefield leans against a rack, raps his knuckles against the flat pan of a shovel blade. "Tell you what. I know Skinner now for a number a' years. And to him, nobody is above suspicion around here." He looks at Duncan as though inspecting the quarter-inch shank of a carbide router bit.

It's unclear whether there's an element of threat in this last section of speech. An informal notification that he and Lily have risen to the top of the perpetrator list? Dismissing the fact that he's technically guilty of the crime, Duncan finds himself skipping to the defense. *We have no motivation.* He's told Lily this a number of times to reassure her. But then, how relevant is motivation in these parts? Here, in the heartland of cow tipping, their motivation need be as simple as getting a kick from wrongful death.

"You'll excuse me." Wakefield moves down the aisle toward the back room.

To call the posse.

Duncan heads for the exit. He needs to get out of there. To move quickly, but not too quickly. He feigns composure, takes his time as he approaches the storefront. An odd unguent is collecting in each palm, making it tough to ease the door open without triggering bells. He stumbles out of the place. Cuts across the parking lot. Believes he could have executed a hammer and anvil tactic on an enemy camp with more grace.

Calm down, Chief, he tells himself, disoriented and blinking against the Sunday sky that has, since he's been in the shop, acquired the same gray, pixilated waver as his computer screen. The Osterhagen witch hunt is about as accurate as a game of Telephone. Both he and Lily had been amazed by yesterday's stories. How could two hundred pounds of pork make its way from a dry creekbed into both the downstream roll of the Hudson *and* a taxidermy shop in Kingston?

Still, knowing what is truth and what is outrageous gossip brings him little comfort. For each new kink in the narrative is maliciously wrought. He suspects the nature and scene of the crime are changing to suit Skinner's secret indictment plan.

The one good thing, Duncan thinks, the one saving grace in the latest incarnation of slaughter is that the modus operandi has actually evolved past his own capabilities. The deluded band of old farts can trick themselves into believing the hog was killed intentionally, but there's no way to accuse him of single-handedly hoisting that dead weight up and over the rim of a dumpster.

Instead Duncan tries to focus on what he came to town for. A half-hour walk for what reason? Maybe it's just a sign that work is going well. You forget things. He starts walking back up the hill toward the house, kicking the same stone all the way. Has to chase it out of the ditch a couple times. Duncan has just over a week until he presents to Stand and Be Counted. Until he easels up his sweat for those tasteless cloth merchants. As he turns onto the dirt road, the rain starts coming down. The drops are well spaced but large enough that it takes only a few to turn his green T-shirt the colors of variegated foliage. He realizes he's going home to Lily empty-handed. This wasn't the plan; he'd like to hide his hands behind something, however small. Duct tape or bolts or a double-headed hammer. But it hardly matters. Something tells him all they could possibly want is already there, under the soil.

Lily carefully squares up the stack of sheets so that her spying is less obvious. She goes back and stands in the open door. Duncan could be back at any time with the wheelbarrow. They've managed, in the course of their clumsy night maneuvers, to snap the wheel off their old one. Drove it into some pothole or other. The backyard had looked ravaged this morning. As though a Paratrooper Girl had launched several grenades from an upstairs window. Their intention was just to stretch the garden a bit, extend the perimeters and gather up the rest of Tinker without making too much of a fuss. Surely she wasn't scattered across the entire yard? But this perimeter extension had turned into nibbles that have now turned into great bites of lawn.

Maybe Duncan's found his game. Maybe hitting his stride means he's writing about things that he's never actually experienced. But even this thought isn't pleasing to her, as if his stride is a train he may or may not catch. Does he get off on this? No wonder he hasn't showed any interest in her—his tastes have evolved, or devolved—he's gone to the dark side, hardcore and militant. And she can't ask, can't bridge the divide from indifference to familiarity. There's still no spirit of ease between them to allow this. It would be as difficult as trying to explain her hours with Lloyd, his knowledge of rooftops and kitchens, her own abnormal curiosity. Or the fact that she has quietly shelved her dissertation—so quietly, she realizes, it's even news to her—believing that if the pointed arch really wants her, it'll come and get her.

She shifts her discomfort back and forth. Outside the air seems to hold its breath as the sky gathers up a turbulent mash of clouds. Of course, this isn't the first time she's suspected all writers of being megalomaniacs, sparking characters to life just so they can reach down and play them like the hand of God. *Dance, monkey, dance.* She just wonders why he's decided to sell jeans by burning women and babies to a crisp.

And what about that five-fingered smack to her ass? The painful cannon kiss? No. This is faulty logic, of course. An oversimplification of the thousand wishes and desires firing through his brain each hour. Arriving at a creative concept is not masonry; it doesn't adhere to a formula. She knows better than to take his work personally.

She takes it personally anyway.

Who can explain hidden aggression? The tickle of it can be kept down to a feather most days. Although, if she sometimes wants to kill Duncan, doesn't it follow that he wants to kill her too?

The truth—when you really come down to it—is that she doesn't need Duncan. Not in the traditional sense. Not for the mechanics of opening jars and carrying large boxes. Despite the heat, she shivers. Thinks of herself in the hated posture of the pigsticker; sprattle-legged over the wild boar with a tire iron in her raised fist. What sort of damage does a woman like this do to a man? If he has stopped loving her, isn't it because she's given her husband no soft spot to land? Not a single fissure to seep through? She was supposed to let him hold doors and reach high shelves.

She was supposed to let him kill the pig.

It was a wheelbarrow. Duncan remembers it only as he comes around the back of the house and finds Lily in a plastic windbreaker dragging the cracked tarp around the garden. While his wife's been toiling against the rain like a pioneer woman, here he is, empty-handed, having failed his one simple task of the afternoon.

"There were no wheelbarrows," he says.

Under the flimsy hood, Lily scrapes her hair back from her face, avoiding the swollen side of her brow. The rain has picked up enough to obscure her eyes behind her glasses.

"I swear I saw one outside the hardware store yesterday."

"Yeah, well. Not today." He picks up a side of the tarp and helps drag it over to the garden. "I did get the latest on the Sovereign of the Deep Wood, though."

"More?"

"Not more, just worse," he says. "A dumpster this time. Behind the Old Mill."

"Does that preclude us?"

"Wishful thinking."

The soil has turned viscous in places and tugs at his sandaled feet with a pleasant sucking action. Duncan considers standing in place, allowing the earth to take him if it so wishes. The mud doesn't seem to stop Lily. She skims across the surface as though she's been waist deep in the business her entire life. This familiarity with the land, her shine to the country and the elements quietly bothers him. Not once has she mentioned any need to return to the apartment, even for a day or two. Which leads him to wonder what she'll do once the summer is over. Does she have any intention of returning home? Or will she simply wait here to be run out of town?

"How's your face?"

She looks up from under the hood. "Slightly less disfigured. At least my cheek and hands are fine."

"I'm surprised you left the house like that yesterday. To go to the library."

"Why?"

"Your eye was nearly puffed shut. I thought you'd stay home."

"Well, you were busy working. I didn't want to disturb you." Lily's staring at the ground near the hedgerow, wiping her glasses on her wet skirt. She lifts a patch of grass that has been skinned from the soil in fine strips. "Come and look at this."

He slowly pries his feet from the mud, circles the scarp and crag to squat beside her near the hedge. Lily flips back the shredded lawn. Underneath are a series of holes, each the depth of a mixing bowl and still relatively dry under the grass lids. Her peasant skirt, meanwhile, has grown damp and sticks to her legs and ass so that he can see the high cut of her underwear.

"We didn't dig these," Lily says. "That dog was here."

"The poodle?" Some sort of lace underwear he's never seen before. When has she started wearing lace underthings? "I don't think poodles dig, Lily. They're water retrievers."

"Any dog will dig if there's something to unbury." She stands up quickly—could she tell he was looking at her ass? "Maybe that's why we're missing so many small bones."

"And here I thought it was because you've been digging alone."

She looks at him. "I *dug* alone. Once."

"Are you sure?"

Lily's moving back to her end of the tarp. "Why would you say that?"

He follows and takes up an opposite corner, stretching the heavy canvas over the south side of the plot. "There's not much to do here all week." Duncan tries to weed inflection and injury from his voice. "A cold case in your very own backyard. I'd be tempted."

"Well, that's you." She's avoiding his face. "I've been working."

"Right. How's the pointed arch going, by the way? The library, how are you finding it?"

"Why do you say it like that?"

"Say it like what?"

"The *library*. Like you can't imagine anyone taking pleasure in a pursuit that doesn't involve motion picture. You talk like it's a personal affront to you."

"Well, I've got to wonder why you haven't made it over to Bard. They've got a real library. At the level you're working at, I can't imagine the Osterhagen Lending Library is meeting your research needs." He works his way toward her, up along the side of the garden where the dog holes are. "I mean, wasn't that part of the reason for staying here? Bard is close by?"

"I just haven't made it over yet." When she looks away he knows he's caught her in some sort of lie. But the thought only fills him with the same sour happiness he felt while Anne was soaping his dirty dishes. It's the triumph of his hairy, sweat-stained will.

The garden has produced a sizable rock reserve. Lily uses her foot to roll a five-pounder over an edge of the tarp. "Besides, I don't need additional research at the moment. I'm structuring a bibliography and writing an outline." She moves away from him again. "And you know, Duncan, if I was really honest about it, I would be in Europe now, doing on-site research."

"If you were really honest?"

"Yeah. If I hadn't decided to stay here this summer instead."

A loose, horsey snort spurts from his sinus cavities. "What's holding you back, Lily? And don't say Tinker. Tinker didn't exist when we got here."

She's silent for a moment. "Does it matter?"

He waits. Waits for the words to elucidate her meaning.

Then turning her face up to him: "It's me doing all the heavy lifting here."

Her simple delivery, the flat and firm belief in herself, nearly sends him across the grave at her. "What, are you crazy? I drive up here every weekend—you don't think that's making an effort?"

"You're punching a clock."

"What are we talking about here? Us, or this bloody house, or what?" He throws down the tarp. "Are you seeing someone?"

She looks up, surprised. "Where did that come from?"

"I have no idea what you're doing up here, Lily." He talks with a sawed-off tongue, half his words lost in anger. "Or who you're doing it with."

She remains silent.

"You want to accomplish something? Come home."

"Accomplish something?" Her voice rises sharply in the rain. "You don't give a shit about my accomplishments."

He stops, tries to rein in his words. But he can feel the swift roll from his mouth, his shoulders rise and drop in defeat. "You're right," he says finally. "I don't know. I don't know if I do."

Lily turns the same shade as newsprint. She bends over suddenly. He thinks she has lurched in pain but a moment or so later she straightens up, her hand cupped and loaded with mud. Before feeling the cool ooze of it on his face, the heavy drip between shirt and chest, he sees Lily's swollen eye blossom as raw as purple onion. Duncan has to shut his own eyes to prevent the mud, which, against the cheek and nostril, carries the consistency and faint aroma of Turkish coffee dregs, from blinding him. He lifts the bottom of his shirt to his face and wipes. When he can open his eyes again, she is gone.

CHAPTER 24

Organs of Digestion

"Wake up," he says.

She recognizes his voice, his face, even as he grows out of her amorphous dream shape. He is moving away from her, a swift and dark form against the morning light.

"You need to get up, Lily. They're here."

She opens her eyes, sees Duncan in his boxers, moving to her bedroom window. And beyond the window, the spark of orange sunrise. She pushes herself to her elbows—it's strange to find him here, in her room. As if the waking Duncan is less probable than one conjured by her subconscious.

"Who's here?" She casts her first glance at the alarm clock. It too provides incongruous evidence: 3 a.m.? A chime sounds somewhere in the house, the percussive appeal of a doorbell, and with this she finally wakens to the lucid overlap of her surroundings.

At the window, Duncan's hair stands up from his head like a crown of palm fronds. Lily cringes; the details of last night are returning. That handful of mud. She slides out of bed, goes to his side, and looks down over the front yard. She was right on one account, it's nowhere near sunrise. Instead, the deceit of morning. A dozen torches burning across the lawn.

Duncan immediately regrets his cavalier attitude of the previous weeks. If only he had kept his eyes open, his ear to the ground like a good Indian brave, he may have foreseen how vigil could easily turn to riot.

Now they've come for recompense, the entire village descending on their front lawn. Thankfully he'd been too tired after the muddy conflict last night to drive back to the city. That would have left Lily here alone with this. In the hallway she tries to push out from behind him but he stops her with a contraction of biceps. He'll do the talking here. Duncan takes a deep breath, reminds himself that the defining feature of tragedy is always this insoluble conflict between hero and environment. And so when he throws open his front door, it's done with a great salting of fear and a nod to the inevitable.

"Lucky you answered." Skinner fingers the doorbell, which is hot and smoking, bells still pealing through the house. "We were gonna start shooting," he says and flashes the ashy black length of what appears to be an M4 rifle. Behind him, at the foot of the porch, Emmett, with the same goose-egg skull as his father, heaves up a lit torch in greeting.

Duncan feels Lily's breasts and hands pressed to his back, her stomach curving against the line he draws in the doorway. It's sick that he's happiest in these moments—when she's small and clinging to him in fright.

"We got a little business to take care of." Skinner rests the semiautomatic in the crook of his arm with the readiness of a folded umbrella. He looks Duncan up and down, the smeared white of his eye visible despite the darkness. "There's a killer on the loose."

Behind him, he hears Lily choke.

"What can we do for you?"

"Search party. Change out of your skivvies and let's go."

Duncan looks at the gun. "You planning on using that?"

"Sure I am." Skinner lifts the rifle again, but this time squares it against his shoulder. He aims at one of the front windows. Duncan feels Lily grab at his waist. The old man pulls the trigger. Together they brace against the destruction of glass and wood frame but instead hear the high-speed collision of water and window. A fine vapor follows, a bit of laughter from the front lawn.

"Don't know why, but the pig used to like it," Skinner says in a fond voice as he lowers the water gun. "Stupid animal."

Duncan knows his wife is going to lose it. Lily, who was raised in a house free of boys, has only conjectural knowledge of the formative role played by water pistols, firecrackers, shit talk. Instead of relief or amusement—which he finds himself overcome by—Lily is lit by anger. She shifts away from his body and draws up alongside him. Duncan spots Wakefield under the boxwoods, a couple others from the cannon firing. Most of the men are armed with flashlights. Contrary to his initial impression from the bedroom window, there are only three or four actual torches among the crowd, their wooden handles home-lathed and shifted uncomfortably from hand to hand. The smell of butane fills the air.

"Hey," Lily says to the men at the bottom of the steps. She's forgotten her glasses in her bedroom and squints furiously at the assembled. "This is not funny."

Duncan is suddenly aware of her nightgown, some white cotton scrap woven together from a roll of gauze. He steps in front of her, shields her from the torchlight.

"It's three a.m.," she continues over his shoulder. "We were asleep."

The men give her a long, unfriendly look, as if assessing the price she'd fetch in John Deere replacement parts.

Skinner clears his throat, makes a sound like bubbles blown in a glass of milk. "You two ever hear of a volunteer fire department?" He leans back against an unsteady porch rail. "I want you to guess: What is the key to a successful volunteer fire department, hey?"

The crowd is silent.

Skinner cups a hand to his ear.

"Volunteers?" Duncan says.

Lily punches him in the kidney.

"Correct!" The old man jumps up. "You think those firemen say,

'Well, I don't feel like volunteering'?" He turns to address his posse on the front lawn. "Let's say, what happens one night when Oster Haus catches fire and—look at that—no one wants to volunteer? Everybody's just standing around, watching the place burn to the ground?" Skinner looks back at them. "You two ever think like that, hey?"

"Christ," Lily says quietly.

Duncan wonders if she's as impressed as he is.

"You want to get a little in this life, folks, you got to give a little."

In his ear Lily says, "You think any of them have gone in the back?"

In considering their current level of vulnerability, Duncan factors in this near-naked wife of his, the smashed Saab in the lean-to, the bones in the cellar, and the garden itself, which is looking more grave than garden. "Lock the door," he says out of the corner of his mouth. "And don't come out."

Her crinkled forehead means she's not tracking his plan.

"I'm going with them. You stay put."

"Are you crazy?"

"No discussion, Lily. Just do it." Then he turns, steps onto the front porch.

"Okay," he says to Skinner and in doing so is aware of offering himself as either decoy or sacrifice or both. "How can I help?"

The turbid eye watches him for a moment. "Some Arab bought out the lumber mill a few years back," he says, "but I never yet paid my respects."

Although Duncan's objective is to move the men off the property, he's surprised by his sudden desire to carry one of the torches through the woods. The clan, however, considers him a potential liability. Beyond providing brute manpower he's a downstater unfamiliar with the dense ecosystem of a hardwood forest. This opinion becomes obvious when Emmett, the silent brigadier to his father's major, hands him a flashlight.

Skinner has divided them into groups of three and employs the mobile tactics of guerrilla warfare in approaching an unsuspecting target. Duncan admits a certain anxiety when the old man refuses to reveal the nature of their mission. His only words as they assume linear formation in the narrow band of trees, *You'll find out soon enough.*

The copse begins at the end of the driveway and meanders down to the back lots of Osterhagen. They keep to one side of it while Emmett is sent ahead as a scout to sweep south through the scrub. Duncan can follow the blaze of his torch for half a minute before the man's swallowed by the bush.

"Emmett don't talk a lot," Skinner says, falling into place beside Duncan. "He's retired now but worked maintenance on all the civil war cannons in Poughkeepsie." In the forested darkness and torchlight, Duncan thinks the old man could be mistaken for some sort of woodland elf. A midsummer guide causing benign mischief among lovers.

They continue in silence, Skinner leaving him now and then to survey the formation of his renegade band. The only indication of his position is the occasional snap of twigs in the periphery. Duncan estimates they're traveling about a mile east of the road where he and Lily hit the boar. And while the moon is a thick magnet tonight, drawing the bay of dogs in the distance, it fails to illuminate their path through the dense canopy of branches. The forest here has been recolonized by pioneer species, trees that have risen to cover what was once destroyed by both Oster's timber empire and the occasional eastern windthrow. The blindness keeps Duncan on edge. His eyes are impatient, slow to adjust and lacking the reflective properties of other beasts and men. He is grateful, however, for the forgiving spring of forest floor that muffles the sound of their advance.

Skinner again drops in alongside him. "What have you heard?"

Duncan stops, listens. "Nothing."

The old man motions for him to keep walking. "I'm talking about the Arabs." He pronounces the *A* and the *rab* as two hard and equally detestable entities. "You hear they killed my pig?" Despite the man's ornamental

stature among the towering growth, there's something specious and terrifying about his conclusions.

"You know for sure?" Duncan asks slowly.

"I'm telling you, ain't I? They brought him right to my doorstep."

"How do you mean?"

"You heard. Ground up into pork sausage—one hundred pounds of
pork sausage delivered to my door." The old man's breath comes in
rosemary-scented puffs. "That pig alive was over two hundred pounds.
This is what happens when you let those sorts into a town."

Duncan is careful to keep his beam tracking through the understory.
He's not surprised by this new and gruesome conjecturing on the old
man's part.

"Maybe it wasn't the same pig."

"What?"

"Maybe they sent you a different pig," Duncan says carefully. "Like
a gift. When they heard yours was gone."

Skinner stops dead in his tracks. He turns to Duncan. "It's people
like you," he says with a black look, "who turned this into a country of
spineless chickenshits."

There's a ruffle of foliage and Emmett emerges from behind, his face
dim and excited. Duncan recognizes the look, pure *Heart of Darkness*.

"Ready." The first, the only word out of his mouth.

Before positioning Duncan behind a stationary Chevy Nova, Skinner
tells him that knowledge of his target's disposition, weaponry, and morale
figure into this surprise attack. "To get the data we needed, some mem-
bers of this operation had to use deception."

Duncan takes this to mean some of the guys must have eaten a meal at
the restaurant. Clocked the dining room's hours of service, maybe. Noted
all exits. They have just emerged single file from the bush at the northern
edge of the Old Mill parking lot. Emmett, receiving his word of command,

positions the men around the exterior of the restaurant building: behind vehicles, a wheelchair ramp, a cement trough full of sleeping crocus.

Duncan crouches behind the car with Skinner. His motivation at the start of the night was to get these yokels off his property, away from the garden and the remains. But he must admit he's surprised at the coordinated effort; tucked by the rear wheel of the Nova, Duncan finds a paintball gun and cartridge waiting for him.

"This is gonna be real simple." Skinner peers around the back bumper, signaling across the parking lot to Emmett. "Your target's the window over the bicycle rack there. When I give the command, you shoot."

The lumber hall is separate from the hotel building and has been converted into a dining room with picture windows cut through broad timber planking. While the place is closed, a dim overhead lamp reveals an elegant dining room, its white table linen tacked down by thick water goblets.

"You know," Skinner says, leaning against the Chevy. "I'd like to know what the Sovereign of the Deep Wood ever did to them." He turns to Duncan then. Beneath the red liquid quiver of the old man's eye there is conviction that Duncan has no business denying. There is truth in there: that shit flows downhill, that a life of head butts against the world eventually comes down to one final moment. You've got to grab it when it comes, with one hand if it's all you got left. Skinner gets to his feet, his septuagenarian knees popping like whipper snappers.

"Fire on the target!"

Duncan does not expect a ride home. Having fled back into the jungle like any good guerrilla, he follows Emmett about a quarter mile up the river along the railroad tracks before coming to a gravel road lined with vehicles. Barely enough time to catch his breath before the boys are shaking hands, someone claps Duncan on the back. Wakefield gives him an appreciative nod before climbing into his F-150.

Skinner motions for him to dump his paint rifle in the bed of his pick-up. "We'll give you a lift." The old man works up a large wad of phlegm and horks it into the ditch. Duncan swings open the truck door, hears the hinges grind to rust powder. Emmett's already at the wheel. And sitting beside him, upright and occupying half the remaining vinyl bench, is a filthy white poodle.

When they pull into his driveway, the morning light is already greasing the windows. Duncan sits between Skinner and the door, the mess of a dog spread across their laps. With each of Emmett's unnecessarily forceful turns of the wheel, the animal rolls off their knees and lands at their feet. Duncan has very little sympathy. The poodle's breath smells like Chinatown in August. The entire ride, the animal has been watching him with undeceived eyes. The growl in the dog's throat broken only by the occasional yelp as he slides to the floor mat.

"He don't like you," Skinner says, pulling the poodle back up by the scruff. "Where's his goddamn collar, Em?"

Emmett doesn't even look over at the animal. "Dunno."

"I can get out here," Duncan says, realizing they're halfway up the drive. Emmett ignores him, continues until they reach the house. Skinner holds the dog back as Duncan opens the door. But as he slides out, the poodle breaks free of his master's grip. It leaps over Duncan and lands on the driveway with the grace of a high-kicking chorus girl.

"Jesus, Murphy." Skinner hops out of the truck behind Duncan. "I'm gonna lock that bastard in the shed." They watch the dog make like a bandit for the backyard. "Where the hell's he going?"

"I'll get him," Duncan says quickly.

He starts to run.

"He'll bite your goddamn hand off!" Skinner begins to lope along behind him.

As his knees crank Duncan thinks, I'll never get there in time. As he

circles the lean-to, he is suddenly aware of his own arms and legs in rela-
tion to the geographic coordinates of the yard and the grave. He can hear
the old man behind him, age and bagpipe lungs posing only a slight disad-
vantage. He imagines a satellite view of the grounds and locks down their
positions—the old man's versus his own—performs quick calculations of
distance and speed, factors in the poodle's quadruped pace. And Duncan
knows, through a combination of formula and intuition, that he has lost.

Then Lily comes around from behind the house. Lily, who is bent at
the waist, mouth set with grim effort. Lily, who has the poodle by the distended scruff of the neck and is using both hands to drag it alongside her.
Lily, his wife! Lily, for whom he has never before felt such joyous affection
and gratitude. He and Skinner have no choice but to wind down in a
dead heat, nearly tripping over one another in their efforts to decelerate.
The old man's lungs make known their displeasure at the sudden wind
sprints. The massive canine twists under Lily's grasp, tries to fix its mouth
on her slender wrist. She looks at Skinner, thrusts the animal toward him.
"Keep your damn dog out of my yard."

CHAPTER 25

Cartilage

"How was the retirement party?" Leetower lowers himself onto the sofa the way a camel sinks to the ground, with the gentle buckling of legs. "Did the vets enjoy your literary masterpiece?"

Kooch looks up from the paratrooper television scripts. Duncan can't help but notice the acute slope of his forehead in profile.

"I took home a couple waitresses."

"Love those Jersey girls." In his sketchbook, LT is penciling a drop shadow behind the doodle of a semiautomatic. "So Vietnam was a hit."

"Well, we got a campaign out of it and I got laid twice."

"I'm impressed, Kooch."

"I'd be impressed if you'd shut up and focus on the work." Duncan's irritable and exhausted. After last night's hunting expedition, he had just enough time to shower and start his drive into the city.

"Jesus, Duncan, you're turning Kurtz on us."

"Let's go back to the collateral," Duncan says. "I don't want to give Stand and Be Counted any reason to kill this shit." He takes out the rough marker renderings. "My gut tells me we need to go in with a totally fleshed-out campaign."

"But you said that would only overwhelm." Leetower turns to a blank sheet, holds his pencil over the page as though sensing a pedagogical moment.

Duncan presses his fingers together into a power tepee. He has left Lily in the path of potential lunatics. In an effort to avoid focusing on this reality he decides to lay some business acumen on his charges. "We've been living with the idea for a while now, but this Vietnam thing *is* risky. We can offset any trepidation by showing how it blows out in collateral."

"Where's the risk?" Kooch folds the television scripts in half and looks at him with that same fanged smile as last week. "We're not targeting vets. We're talking to the eighteen-year-old girls the vets want to fuck."

He's nearly had it with Kooch, the way he hurdles over authority to make every encounter confrontational. He's got a brick shithouse of a body and a mouth to match, leaving Duncan with the suppressed desire to frag his sorry ass.

"We work with Product Development, get a commitment from them for a new line of colored denim. I want to give them names like Blue Cordite, Yellow Phosphorous, Agent Orange."

"I've got the illustrator working out a few ways to present the line." Leetower taps his pencil nervously.

They both look at Kooch. "What do you got?" Duncan asks.

"What do I got?" He picks something out from his nail and wipes it on a mouse pad. "I already came up with the campaign. What else you want?"

Duncan's steepled fingers slide apart. A fine mist collects along his hairline. It must be delirium caused by his sleepless night, because he swears he just heard Kooch say the campaign was his idea.

"Duncs, you have some killer veins in your forehead."

Before he can speak, Anne walks in and slaps a file folder on his desk. Judging by the clenched lines of her jowls, by the sound and force of her entry, it's safe to say that she's still surly from Thursday night. She won't even look at the junior peons.

"So, you're getting Tide back, Duncan." Anne runs a tongue over her teeth. "Next week, after you've presented Stand and Be Counted, you get all the midgets you want. You should know, however, that I had to talk you up. I blew roses out of your ass. I'm sure they think we're fuck-ing. They're even giving you Hawke's leather sofa."

Next week. Why doesn't this elevate him?

"Also, Leetower and Shithead here are off Tide. Which I am *so* sorry about." She awards the boys with a terrifying smile. "But it was inevitable. Upstairs is concerned with the optics of a junior team alone on Tide. Someone's put the bug in their ear that P&G will want to see the team's reel."

"We're not junior. We're intermediate."

"And not just any reel," Anne says from her seat in the steamroller. "But one with some groundbreaking, anthemic, 'Why 1984 Won't Be Like *1984*' masterpieces on it. Not that dog-walker wank you two got into *Communication Arts*. I was in the meeting on Friday, so I'm reporting straight from the horse's mouth: 'If Duncan's off Tide, you better be replac-ing him with those Apple guys.' Incidentally, Duncan, you're cheaper. So congrats."

Duncan has forgotten all about the midgets, about the entire laundry world. Work has been just hooches and wallows for him. He's no longer the smooth-faced boy who had worked diligently at Hawke's feet to turn Chernobyl babies into elves. One Show Pencil or not, how to go back there, to the land of small men? When here, he has surrounded himself with snipers and Lurps, rear-hatch gunners, jump school graduates, the snaking Mekong River and Graves Registration. Honeydippers burn-ing the shitpots! His own client isn't even worthy to receive this work. How will he make it his ongoing priority if he also has Tide to contend with?

"So, Stand and Be Counted, next Tuesday morning." Anne looks at Leetower. "I want you there in case they have questions about the art direction. We're on at eleven in their boardroom."

"So what are we supposed to do after that?" he asks on behalf of the partnership. It seems Kooch has enough sense to keep quiet.

"Guess it's back to writing coupons for you boys." She smiles.

Once Anne takes leave, Leetower sighs and bows to Duncan. "Well, looks like you've been proclaimed Emperor of the Gibbons."

"Yes. I'll be living in trees and staining bark with my urine."

Kooch looks at him. "You wouldn't be there if I hadn't given you the idea."

Duncan snorts, feels the spray of it across the back of his hand. "You are a fucking piece of work," he says to the other writer.

"Really?" Kooch sits up. "Because I could hear crickets chirping before I started talking about Vietnam."

"I think you might have just ruined your career."

Kooch throws his head back, an imitation of laughter. "Don't count on it."

Lloyd approaches her study carrel with a shoe box under his arm. "My dancing shoes, sweetheart." He lifts the lid on a new pair of high tops.

Lily looks up from her copy of *Gray's Anatomy*. "You give sneakers a whole new meaning," she says.

"Enough about me, Lily." Lloyd settles into the desk beside her. "This morning I would like a complete description of your childhood bedroom, please."

She closes her book, looks at him. "And what has brought on this desire?"

"The shivers of your girlhood are always with me."

"What year are we talking?"

"Adolescence. The traumatic years."

Lily chews on the end of her pen. "A spring awakening."

"Don't skimp on the details."

"My childhood bedroom," she says, thinking of the house in Albany during the fallout of her mother's missionary years, "had a revolving door."

"Promising intro."

"I was ten. There was a nun in the house."

She's an ascetic, Lily remembers her mother saying later, while signaling to the paramedics to lift the stretcher over the rosewood floors. *We thought she was just in seclusion.*

When they had a particularly contemplative guest it was Lily's bedroom, tucked away over the garage and visited only by a drill of woodpeckers at the window sash, that was offered up first. Though her mother was partial to the tonsured Franciscans or the Poor Clares, the quiet room with the pink canopy bed had been given to a reclusive Eremite a week earlier.

Lily had skulked the corridors with the jealousy of the displaced, with a sudden nostalgia for dolls that she'd previously abandoned. For a few days she watched as meal trays were left in the hall. The housekeeper, used to the fickle eating habits of hermits, exchanged cold food for hot without a word. Lily, meanwhile, grew anxious waiting for the nun to emerge.

It took another day of fretting until she had an idea. Although she'd have to become invisible, crouch low, suck in her breath in order to execute it. How else to see those pink walls again, or to give those dolls—her dear children—their liberty?

She had never seen an expired body but imagined it might resemble the sick and ailing Ethiopians from her mother's church brochures. In her mind, the dying required constant vigilance, someone to swat flies from the mouth and swollen bellies. The woman in the bed, though, while rank, was too desiccated for flies. Death was nothing like sleep, Lily thought. And heavenly sleep was a lie. She had pushed open the heavy door and understood everything at once. It was there in the crinkled stillness, mouth gaping.

Later she stood in the hall with the group of Vietnamese boat people her parents were sheltering in the pool house. They watched the paramedics thumb around for the old woman's pulse. *It's these Eremites,* her mother said, wringing her hands at the foot of the bed. *They ask for solitude, and then—heart attack.*

You can smell it out here, Lily said.

Her mother turned, surprised to see her among the crew at the door. *You get to your room.*

This is my room.

Well, wait in the kitchen then.

Some of the Vietnamese children were hopping foot to foot, tugging at their mother's arms. *They get to stay.* Lily frowned.

That's because they're Vietnamese, Lily. They've been through worse.

————————

"Did the refugees touch you in your sleep?"

Lily stops packing her shoulder bag and looks at the pervert. "They were perfectly kind. You asshole."

It's odd, but she hasn't thought of the dead nun in years. So many fossils, she thinks. What sort of anthropology can account for these bones resurrecting together?

Lloyd sighs and finishes tying the laces of his sneakers. He stacks his feet on the library carrel. "Lily, Queen of the Wasps. You waste your idealism. Have you or have you not been watching me for the past ten minutes?"

She gathers up her satchel and looks at his new shoes. Each one is topped with a mirror the size and shape of a sand dollar.

"Your problem, darling, is that you see what you want to see, believe what you want to believe."

"True, I give you too much credit."

"Listen." He lowers his feet and leans across the desk toward her. "I've been thinking about your little situation. With the mascot."

"Please, no thinking."

"You know, at first I hoped you'd flourish in a life of crime. But I've got to be truthful, Lily, it doesn't do a thing for you."

"I'll get over it."

"Okay, you're not going to like this," he continues. "But I have a suggestion. You should confess."

Lily's shaking her head even before he finishes his sentence.

"If you'll allow me to quote you, 'Exist in a realm of action for once!' They're doing up a display in the lobby with the boar's tusk—whatever hasn't been ground into sausage." Lloyd stops to chuckle at the latest fabulist tale concerning the boar's remains. "How will you walk past that every day, Lily? In fact, at the risk of being pilloried, I say you need to take this one to the top—to old Farmer Brown himself." Lloyd sits back in his chair, pleased.

She wants to cuff him. "That's not going to happen." Thinks of their close call with the poodle the other night. She can't let their transgression with the wild boar jeopardize the possibility of exhumating the entire Tinker. Sunday, after literally flinging mud at her husband, Lily locked herself in her room (not that he was wanting in) and held the photograph of Oster Haus up to the light. Blocked out the sound of Duncan in the shower, and tried to see something new in the dark smudge of governess. But there was only the whip of dark hair, one arm around the child, the other held up against the sun. She can't tell Lloyd, but she has sworn a larger secrecy to the thigh bone.

"Just look at yourself, Lily." And he lifts one mirrored foot up on her carrel again so that she might catch her reflection. "Beyond the wasp stings—which are clearing up nicely. You're cranked to full volume. You have something to get off your chest." He turns in the direction of the reference desk. "You didn't really turn it into ground pork, did you?"

"Forget the pig," she hisses. Looks around to make sure they're still alone. The crowd on their front lawn, the tusk in Persian's hands, all of it a reminder of the wide swath she's cut through town. Would Skinner have had the ugly task of tearing the fang from the body? Three weeks in the ditch and it had already turned the color of old rope. The ease with which she knocked off the Sovereign of the Deep Wood actually does support Duncan's old idiom: *The apple doesn't fall far from the tree.* If she were to be cast in one of his TV spots, she would be the GI calmly setting fire to innocent villages of old men and women.

"Is something else wrong?" Lloyd's sunken eyes are on her. "Come on, cupcake, free yourself. Your dissertation is plagiarized? Is that why you so seldom work on it?"

"How cavalier, you giving me advice." She lifts a finger at the man. "Who's the impotent one here?"

"You'd better be talking metaphorically."

"Mirrors? Come on, coward. Is that the best you can do, look under skirts for the rest of your life?"

"Okay, Lily, I understand. Just sock it to me, I can take it, baby."

She stands up, pivots her head on her neck, listens to the pop of hollows and ball bearings. She's exhausted by men, the constant natter of them. "Shit or get off the pot, Lloyd."

"You've got a point." He taps his lip, contemplates. "Now that you're the scourge of the town, it sure takes the heat off me."

"What's that supposed to mean?"

Lloyd shrugs. "The Jews could have really used you during the pogroms." He stands and straightens his shoe mirrors. "If you will excuse me, sweetheart, I've got some skirts to chase."

Duncan is in the habit of checking his messages with his office telephone set on speaker. He has discovered there's a small but rewarding sense of accomplishment—a nod to the light industry of multitasking—when he's able to retrieve messages while moving around his office, hands free to sort through papers, tie laces, or adjust the window blinds.

After punching in the four-digit code (predictably, the month and year of his wedding) his voice mail clicks awake and releases its stored data. He is bent over a file cabinet near the door when the message is relayed, when the sound lifts from the suddenly crystal Samsung speaker, and fills his small office with the chirping madness of crickets.

Heads pop out of cubicles and doorways all along the corridor. Duncan stands for a moment, telescoping the file folders in his hands, amazed by the high-fidelity reproduction of insects. It is the sound of a great plague coming, the sound of his waking terrors, free from obfuscation, from treble and bass.

He makes his way down the corridor of the creative department. Kooch isn't in his cubicle. Duncan takes a seat at his desk, which is partially hidden behind a support beam. He doesn't bother scouting around the drawers or trash. He's not expecting jars of miked grasshoppers. The real evidence is intangible: Kooch is nothing but a hack writer with a flair for intellectual property theft and who holds a grudge against a man who will not let him rise.

Duncan leans back in the chair, props his feet on the desk, and waits.

CHAPTER 26

Nervous Tissue

It's a good thing he stopped shaving, as his beard helps to cover the keyboard imprint on his face; that universal ordering of tabs and bars, the grout between keys, numbers in the upper reaches with their ghostly and misunderstood *alt* functions. When Duncan lifts his head, the computer screen also emerges from stasis, just seconds behind him, displaying the time. Seven-ten. But which seven? Which day? He rolls his neck through 360 painful degrees of rotation. His neck and jaw have spent an entire night in an unfortunate angle on the keyboard. Kooch hadn't returned to his desk last night. Or if he did, Duncan had already fallen asleep while on watch. The office is empty, the east windows bright enough to indicate morning. He looks down at Kooch's wastebasket. It's been emptied; the cleaning staff has been in. How could he have slept through the vacuum cleaner?

Duncan limps down the hall toward his office, intent on routing out the small stash of prescription codeine he keeps somewhere in his cabinet. The phone on his desk is flashing. When he punches in his code, he hears Lily. Her call came last night. At first he can hardly make out the message, she's snorting back words in a loose-limbed struggle against tears.

. . . there were two wheelbarrows where I said I'd seen them. And then that Wakefield man tells me, he says that the dog dug up a human bone. Like a tibia? And that it was running through town with the bone in its mouth until Skinner brought it to the cops—he brought the bone to the cops, not the dog—because people

had seen it, you know? So he had gone to the police. And Duncan, that's Tinker's
tibia and now people are talking about the wild boar and the human bone like it's
all connected. So we need to get her out of the ground, because now they're trailing
the dog to see where it's going . . .

He saves the message. Something he rarely does unless it includes a
meeting time or a phone number he's apt to forget. But here, no date, no
meeting, no request, just the small and frayed voice of his wife.

"And now, for something completely different." Lloyd directs her off the
sidewalk and into the crack between two office buildings. She is not pleased
by the prospect of leaving the yard unguarded, but there's no way to forestall
this evening with Lloyd without a hefty explanation. And as careful as she
might try to craft a passable lie, Lily knows, he'd still smell right through it.

Lloyd motions her to keep quiet until they reach the broad alley that
stretches west through the remains of some scattered commercial buildings. "One thing, Lily," he says once they emerge into the alley, "you're
going to have to promise to abide by a rule here."

"*A* rule?"

"I mean, whatever happens, remember—*we watch but we do not touch.*"

"I'm not the frott here."

"No, I'm saying we are like the walking dead, okay?" Although Lloyd
is no more attractive at night than he is in daylight, there's a crepuscular ease
to his features, a pundit's sense of assurance that blooms in this darkness.

"I'm granting you permission to see the natural world, but not to in-
teract with it. No changing of circumstances."

"Your greatest prologue yet." Lily jumps a few steps ahead of him
along the alley, trying to forecast their target among the back doors and
stone-chipped windows. "Where we going anyway?"

Before she can get a yard away, he's at her side. He pins her arm with
surprising strength.

"Swear it." He's never touched her with any force before.

She knows enough to look Lloyd straight in the eyes, into those two, deep-set prunes. Only by opening her entire face to his can she convince him, and herself, that she's not frightened. Lily wants him to know that unlike his dim-witted teenage *gigs* she will not allow him the pleasure of a struggle.

"Okay. All right."

He lets go of her arm.

"So what's so different about tonight's field trip?" She forces herself to continue walking. Her voice sounds steady and unaffected, as polished as it was last night in the hardware store. *Probably a cow bone. I've seen Skinner's poodle—that dog is no retriever.*

"Excellent question!" Lloyd regains his smiling affability and continues along beside her. "Tonight's excursion is part entertainment, part test. While it's true that Adult Babyhood is fascinating, I'm worried that I've been giving you a unilateral view of the perv world, Lily."

"There's more?"

"Sure. I want you to know that it's a rich, multifaceted place where nearly everyone can find his niche—if nearly everyone was true to their guts."

"And morally skeptic."

"Amen." Lloyd stops, turns her in the direction of a white stucco building behind a grid of plank fencing. He walks slowly toward the edge of the property. "Like I said before, as a peep you see a lot of things before you get a nude. Well, I came across this little beauty a couple months ago. Took a while to figure out the timing, of course. But the thing that might strike you about this situation is that it's devoid of sexual perversity."

"Some of that rich tapestry of experience you just mentioned?"

"Yes. People are bewildering." He pushes her along a narrow path behind the fence. "Motivations are fluid and therefore often inscrutable."

Lily thinks of Luis Oster. She can't imagine any sort of fluid motivation that would have caused her great-grandfather to tear a helpless governess to bits. Madness, perhaps. Some sort of neurological problem.

She glances at Lloyd, who's squeezing behind her through the two-foot margin between building and fence, and wonders, not for the first time, if she might be touched by that same madness herself.

They move through an alternating host of parking lot smells: gasoline, banana skins, deep-fried wontons. She inches along, pressing close to the building in order to avoid the splintered planks of the fence behind her. Under her fingers the stucco wall feels like a landscape of flattop mesas in miniature, the moss sprouting in the chines of uneven plaster as prolific as chaparral bushes and scrub. About three feet ahead, a ground-level window is lit. Lloyd signals her and they nose up to the ledge, each claiming a bottom corner position.

Inside is a rustic, wood-paneled dental operatory with a floor-mounted spittoon and vinyl-trimmed chair. A Rockwellian throwback, Lily thinks, compared to slick city dental offices where modular seating and flat-screen TVs provide distraction from oral angst. Here, overhead lights throw murky yellow where surfaces should appear sterile.

The dentist—for who else would he be this time of night—is alone and stands drying his hands at the sink. He's a craggy-nosed man, salted gray and pleasantly avuncular, with a crisp surgical smock over a corduroy shirt and chinos. Lily is relieved to engage in nonlibidinous voyeurism tonight. Despite the Depression-era gloom and outdated dental equipment, there's something about the older man—perhaps the set of his chin—that she finds kindly and heartwarming.

The dentist putters with some instruments and Lily takes in the rest of the cramped surgical studio. On the wall facing the dental chair is an illustrated medical diagram of a bisected head. The color-coded squirm of soft tissue, hard bone, and cartilage puts her in mind of the finicky job of picking meat from a boiled crab. The echoing chambers of the nasal and oral cavities dominate, then the southbound connection of the nasopharynx, the oropharynx, the laryngopharynx. The maxilla bone on top and mandible below. The tongue—always, forever, mostly in the way. All these tunnels and passages. Some slick-walled and wet, others with a clever lining of cilia fluttering at each breath, busy sieving out foreign particles.

She exhales sharply, trying to clear her own nasal passages of the alley funk surrounding them. It's astounding, really. The human head is a labyrinthine construction that has virtually assembled itself, or at least has evolved itself, into a compact and self-cleaning unit. Such little upkeep required on the outside—a wash from time to time, run a little balm over the lips in cold weather—compared to the unparalleled self-regulating functions within.

Lloyd had to stand on his toes for a clear view. He comes down, performs a single squat, then flexes both hamstrings before returning to his watch. When Lily looks back in the window, the dentist has taken a seat in the chair and stretches his arms overhead. Might there be a visit from the succubus yet? There are canisters on a dolly behind the spittoon, laughing gas, two slender metal rockets, green and silver with blurred pressure gauges.

As Lily watches, the kindly dentist pulls a jelly face mask out from behind his headrest, untwists the pinched hose that connects it to the nitrous oxide, and straps it over his mouth and nose. He fiddles with the valves, combining and releasing his own personal nitrogen and oxygen cocktail.

Lloyd is watching her. But she keeps her eye on the dentist. He settles into his chair, unfolding a newspaper as though settling in for the *Times* and a nap.

"Don't forget," Lloyd whispers. "You swore."

Why had he used the word *test* tonight?

In the operatory the dentist begins to mutter, the paper spread on his lap rising and falling. His eyes are shut and he stretches out his hands and feet. Lily finds herself holding her breath for several long moments until the first giggles emerge, sputtering from the corners of his mouth. She turns her best pinched face on Lloyd. What she means to convey is, *So, fine, a nitrous oxide addict. There are worse things.* She wants to challenge his notions about her boundaries. It bothers Lily that he paced her through such elegant foreplay, swore her to oaths before turning her on to a dentist who uses hippie crack. Lloyd's studying her carefully, but doesn't seem to pick up on her jaded skepticism. She feels a tweak at the back of her neck. Her animal undercoat rising in response to something. But in response to what?

Lloyd's watchfulness *is* making her uneasy. At the same time, the force of the dentist's mirth grows as the minutes pass. The downthrust of each laughing spell is followed by a few moments of silence where he lies perfectly motionless. The newspaper slides to the floor. What happens with too much gas? Lily scrolls through her knowledge bank in vain. The answer to this question, she suspects, was not covered in any of her chemistry lessons at St. Agatha's.

Another rush of electricity at the back of her neck. Could it be the business of Lloyd's hand on her arm that's thrown her? There was real force in those five fingers.

She's troubled by the way the man in the chair has begun to wriggle out at either end. As though shaking off an infestation of the extremities. Also, his laughter is subsiding. She wishes Lloyd would quit staring. This is definitely not as fun as the breast-fed man. Inside the operatory, one of the dentist's loafers falls off. The pane of glass between them is thin and the sound of the shoe striking the floor startles Lily. She tries to laugh it off but the effort only serves to heighten her awareness of the dentist's laughter. No, his lack of laughter. The man is silent now, has grown flaccid. And, by the stillness of his chest—

"I think he's passed out."

Hips slide from vinyl seat. Arms splay to the sides as if the body's being prepped for a gutting.

Lloyd finally turns from her to look through the window. "Yeah, I'd say he has."

The gas mask is strapped at the back of his head. Because the jelly chamber is fogged, Lily guesses the seal between mask and mouth and nose is still intact. She moves back from the window.

"Why would he strap the mask on?"

"Silly him."

"He should've held it," she says. "It would have just fallen off."

Lloyd comes down off his toes. "It always has in the past. Do you think he's trying to off himself?" But his concern is baroque, gilded.

She tries reading the pervert's face in the meek operatory light. She knows this voice, of course, this method of rhetorical questioning. But does she believe it?

"Is this part of the thing?" she asks.

"It's a sleeping dog, little sister," he says with nothing in his eyes. "I'll bet they don't do this shit where you come from."

She turns, knocks on the glass. "I'm going to go look for a phone."

Lloyd puts his fingers on the window.

"I won't give my name," she adds.

Lloyd keeps his fingers on the pane, as though the glass is a conductor of ugly energy between the two men.

"You'll do no such thing."

The remaining codeine pills have slipped from their envelope and have come loose in his pocket with a handful of like-shaped breath mints. Duncan draws out five white tablets. His neck and shoulders are hounding him for relief and in the dim car interior he downs the handful.

He reaches Osterhagen with minty fresh breath and takes the country bypass west of the town, past the infamous site where they exterminated and abandoned the Sovereign of the Deep Wood. He drives slowly along the dirt road, not knowing what to expect here on a Wednesday night in the country. How far sounds might carry.

Duncan reaches the house and drives a couple hundred yards past the place, pulling into the first clearing he sees off the road. He gets out and throws on an old sweater to guard against burrs and branches and deer ticks. There's a clear moon overhead and with its assistance, he tackles the ditch and thickets with surprising ease. The split rail fence sags under his weight but holds, and it's a short climb beyond this into the narrow field of stubble. Here, Duncan can see across the flats to the start of the barley crops. He starts hiking back toward Lily.

The house stands over the grain, folded up for the night without a single candle burning to greet the surprise guest wading through the barley. When he pulls out alongside the house, the same moon that got him through the scrub now reveals that Lily's bike is gone, both ends of the chain lock hanging from the porch rail like empty shackles. At least, he thinks, it's a voluntary absence. He digs through his pockets for the house keys. Brings up instead a beer cap, a paper coaster, and a plastic cocktail sword. Fuck. Duncan watches his cool curl into wisps and float away. He's aware of what he's done wrong tonight: fleeing the office, leaving several campaign components primed to unspool in an air already rank with mutiny. But he wants to see Lily. Or, more accurately, he wants to see her when she least expects it.

Duncan turns to look down the driveway. He could return to the car and search for the keys. But neither the long walk down the road or through the field will be possible now that he's actually beginning to feel the drain of the meds. He knocks on the door instead. He knocks, knowing there won't be a response. He knocks because a man can only plan so far in advance and, quite frankly, he hasn't thought of what might happen beyond this front-step encounter.

What's he expecting to find anyway? Evidence of witchcraft? Tambourines and candle wax? The golden ram idol of forest nymphs? Or maybe he wants to find her in the garden, breaking her promise once again. Expose her in a small lie that'll allow him to extrapolate to a larger lie. Another man? Someone brazen and unafraid of nature. Someone whose attributes can be brought down to a concise set of bullet points, an index-card explanation as to why she should be set free.

Duncan walks around to the backyard, where the grass sighs, passing away strand by strand. He keeps within the shadow of this blight of a house, all the while wishing the Crusaders had never come into the piece of ill-managed property. At least in the city he could follow his wife if he had to, find out where she went at night.

The massacred lawn bears a strong resemblance to the topography of eastern seaboard sand dunes. The terrain is still tarped from their Sunday downpour. Lily has neglected to roll away the rock weights and fold up the canvas, which would allow the soil to dry. Here and there the tarp sags where rainwater has pooled. Duncan's shovel is still staked where he planted it in a mound of grass. He sits on the sweep of porch. The only differences he sees in the dig site are the changes brought about by precipitation. The small mountains of soil remain, their peaks chewed down by rainfall. Beyond the yard the barley heads dip and toss vigorously, but hold. They have another month to fight gravity.

What will he do when Lily gets home? If she gets home? Drag her into the woods and give her such a seeing-to? It's something he's never considered before. But maybe he should now. After all, the written, spoken word has failed. The structured sentence, vocalized intelligibly, restructured with plosives, both barked at her and sung, this has failed. All he's left with is articulate muscle.

Duncan sees the thing coming out of the barley before he hears it. He slides down the porch to the bottom step. Why isn't it a surprise? Out back, the grain whisks apart and he knows that all along he's been waiting for Lily's avatars to emerge. The obstinate governess, leading a man's pride off by the hand. The Viet Cong, setting miles of underground *punji*-staked labyrinths. The flare-legged Grunt Girl, waiting for the Zulu on the small-boned Latinos she'd sent down to spring those tunnel traps. Down on her hands and knees, her face pressed close to the forest floor, listening to the whisper of steam vents, the expiration of grass, the sighs of the frontline dead conducted up through roots. Those tunnel rat souls, all of them, small puffs of smoke.

He crawls from the porch, lowering himself in the soil as though the paleontological era of upright vertebrates is over. He spreads himself on the ground, drags nipples and nuts across the last few feet of earth until he's reached the two mounds of dirt nearest the staked shovel. Duncan jockeys between these two lookouts, following as the dog moves from the hedge to the garden, its white fur luminous among the foliage. The smell is familiar here, something he has eaten or watched burn. He eases forward a bit, the animal unaware of his presence. It's squatting at the edge of the tarp, urinating, the sound a sharp spray against canvas. Duncan gets to his knees, watching as the dog edges under a corner flap and starts to dig.

Too many of us want what's in the soil, he thinks, rising to his feet. He has to tell Lily this. He moves across the boneyard. Warn Lily that taking Tinker from her grave is just the beginning of an unexpected responsibility. Hereafter, they have no choice but to spend the rest of their lives together, fending off disruption, chaos, personal ambition, the charge of those who would bite them at the neck and leave them dry.

Let's start now, Lily. Duncan lifts his shovel, steps directly behind the dog, and clobbers it over the head.

CHAPTER 27

Of the Teeth

She can hardly bear to watch as the man slides out of the armless dental chair and strikes the checker-box linoleum.

"His mask snapped off." She sees the rubber tubing of his gas mask caught in the headrest. She begins pounding her fist against the glass. "Wake up!"

Lloyd's hand is on her, not exactly twisting, but bending her fist backward and then pushing her down the strip of grass between the fence and the office building.

"He could die."

"We're all going to die, Lily."

"Fuck your Jesuitry."

He smiles but doesn't let go until they reach the alley. He stands with his back to the fence as though ready to tackle if she tries anything. Lily holds both her arms against her chest.

"Sorry to manhandle you. But you did swear."

She feels short of breath. "I don't even know what to think here." Her voice is girlish and insulted.

"I'm sure you'll come up with something." He starts walking away from her into the shadows.

She has to hustle to catch up. "Why did you show me that?"

"Crossed the line, hey?" Lloyd smiles evasively. "You like to think you're tough. Really you're just a chump."

She stops. "You're calling me a chump?"

"As long as you can spin those wheels."

"Hold on," she says. "The pervert is calling *me* a chump?"

"Certain girls deserve what they've got coming, right?"

"Watching a man," she flares her hand in the direction of the office, "maybe take his life. That's crossing the line."

Lloyd begins to laugh. "You're the sophist, Lily. You probably think what? That you're a great liberal?" He shakes his head as if she is pitiful. "But you've never done anything wrong. That's why the little things bother you so much—smirches on your sterling record of close calls."

She can't believe this articulate ugliness, or more precisely, she can't believe how he's turned his ugliness on her. They move through the buildings now, and as much as she had it in her to help the dentist, she finds herself marching quickly away from the scene, if only to part ways with Lloyd.

Once they're out on the sidewalk he relaxes back down to his pear-shaped stroll. "Listen," he says, turning to her, congenial again under the streetlight. "I told you there'd be a quiz. In my books you pass on so many other levels. How can I hold one night against you?"

He stops walking and holds out his hand.

She looks at his fat palm but doesn't take it.

"Let's just agree to disagree, Lily."

She allows her mouth to gather into a rich smile. "I'm just here to provide you with an objective view of yourself."

"That is more kindness than I deserve." Each word saccharine-coated.

"It's clear to see how comfortable you are—how much you like it—on this side of the glass."

He nods. "Where the average folk are."

"See, I don't believe you're ever going to become the great frot-teurist you want to be. You are a Peeping Tom and nothing else."

"From one failure to another?" He looks at her. "Is that the idea?"

In the morning, Duncan finds himself in the front seat of the car, roasting in a sweater that's skewered here and there with twigs and stems. His forehead is slick, the trail of moisture less viscous than perspiration. When he rubs his face, his hands come away patterned with mud created by his own body fluids and the dirt of a hasty burial.

Never one for early morning, Duncan sits and looks out the window, trying to slow his recollection of the previous night into manageable increments. But outside, his shovel is leaning up against a tree and provides undeniable evidence. Also, he's sitting on a dog collar. He pulls the tongue of blue leather out from underneath him. A killer's memento, he thinks, buckling the strap at its loosest notch, twirling it around his finger.

He waits for the incriminating thought to come, but it seems that remorse and conscience are pretty concepts grown too short in the leg, too tight across the chest. Duncan had believed it was the double shot of codeine that had made him giddy, but this morning the feeling lingers. Had it been a dingo or some trailer trash rottie that he'd draped over his shoulders last night as though he were the Good Shepherd, he couldn't be more satisfied with himself. No, the fact that it was a rangy poodle does nothing to discourage his self-righteousness.

The only wrench in the whole business had been trying to find his way back to the house last night. How could he have gotten lost in a patch of forest the size of a handkerchief? Only explanation was that he'd been describing circles around base camp. Maybe the codeine did have some effect on his internal coordinates. It had taken an hour or so to make it out to the dirt road. Then he walked about a quarter mile, trailing the shovel, until realizing he was beyond the house and nearly at the river. Duncan spun around, undiscouraged, thinking he might walk up to the front porch, stretch out on those questionable floorboards, and wait for Lily to trip over him. She'd either be coming or going. And in the direction of her landing, he'd have his answer. But he came across the car in the clearing first. With the pills making it impossible to continue in an upright position he reclined the passenger seat and slept.

Despite the parcel of land between them this morning, he can hear the slam of the back door, followed by the rasp of the screen latching into place, then the leaves of the softwoods rushing to fill the space around the morning sounds of Lily's bicycle gears. Duncan turns the key partway in the ignition and checks the time.

He gives Lily a head start and then follows her, easing the crippled Saab out of the clearing and onto the gravel shoulder. The chestnut trees bordering the road have dropped early fruit and he drives over them, pleased with the crunch of the spiny husks under the wheel. In the sunlight Duncan can see the lip of crushed bonnet through the windshield. Instead of replaying the humiliation of the wild boar, he reminds himself of the silent and bloodless slump of the poodle.

In the second layer of his consciousness—that pink spongy layer resembling insulation fiber—he is aware of a huge lack of discretion here, taking the car into Osterhagen in daylight. However, this morning he's operating strictly at the first layer of consciousness, the one lined with billboards and FM radio waves, and it's telling him he doesn't care. Something is changing just beyond his sightline. He's got a wife to tail.

He catches up with Lily at the highway junction, trails her bicycle at an eighty-yard lag, keeping one eye on the surprising volume of Osterhagen morning traffic, and the other on the locomotion of her ass on the bicycle seat. It takes her ten minutes to reach the downtown district and another five until she stops at the library.

She actually does stop. Pulls up in front, locks her bike to a post with the ease and familiarity of daily routine.

He idles in front of some shops, slouched beneath the shady mercy of an alder branch, while she unclips her helmet and shakes out her hair. He is surprised to feel his heart beating in his mouth, as if relief volleyed the organ up there. She is still true. Despite the rift between them, she is still his wife.

She crosses the lawn and goes right into the library.

Duncan is alarmed by the pleasure he feels, tries to control it by starting angry fires. Circles back to the beginning when he was unable to kill a pig. Such a small failure and yet she insisted on pinning it to his chest.

He pulls up the hand brake and feels under his seat for a pen. *This thing with the pig, Lily—enough is enough,* he writes on an unpaid parking ticket. *Rewind to that night and believe me—not only would I finish the thing off, I'd fritter it on the spot. I'm obviously a simple guy and can't keep up with these mental Olympics you've got going on. It's like I'm up in the nosebleeds and you're down in the box, sipping gimlets. If you plan on remaining my wife, Lily, get your ass up here.*

Startled by a tap on his window. A thick finger, a cracked yellow nail whittled to the stub. He somehow recognizes it. Yes, Duncan knows the hand but takes a breath or two to move up to the face. It's Wakefield hunched toward the window. Of course. Duncan realizes he's parked directly in front of the shop.

"Hey," the old guy says, eyes not on Duncan but scouring the car interior. "What happened to your front end?" The voice is muffled through the sealed window as though it were traveling a great distance to reach him. For a second Duncan believes he's referring to his face, the streaks of sweat and dirt. Then he realizes the man's talking about the car.

There's a pause here where Duncan has an opportunity to act neighborly. In the moment or so it'd take to lower the window, he could concoct an explanation. A fence, a cyclist, a drunken bender in the city. But none of these things come. Panic takes him instead, stem to stern. He throws off the hand brake, knocks the car into first, and rips a streak down the road.

This morning she found the dentist's name in the slender phone book, called and asked whether the doctor was taking any new patients. Then she held her breath. The receptionist, she told herself in the pause between

question and response, seemed too blissfully pleasant to have found her em-
ployer dead in the operatory this morning.

He certainly is taking new patients. When would you like to come in?

Check your nitrous oxide levels, Lily said and hung up the phone.

So what if it was a cheat? The result is she's feeling much more disposed to seeing Lloyd after their argument last night. She can't wait to
present him with news of the dentist's survival. She will wave it in his
face like a flag captured from the tower of his pervy little kingdom. Lloyd
is just a mental pugilist lacking a sparring partner. She sees it now.

She folds her coil notebook open to a call number in the American
Fiction stacks and scans the cutter numbers on some spines. There's a book
she has in mind for Duncan, the Graham Greene novel, but she has turned
in three aisles short at the *D*'s. Even though it's late in the game, the book
might spark some thoughts for his campaign. Or at least create a square of
familiar ground between them, beyond the terror of the townsfolk, give
her footing from which to ask questions. She continues toward the back of
the building, glad to know that for once she's not in any way responsible for
a major Osterhagen tragedy. For once she and Duncan are not the hairpins
in the socket, the ones conducting skunk energy through the little town.

She'd told her husband that her grandfather's abduction was likely a
"rape and revenge" story. She admired Tinker's ingenuity in this version.
Instead of sticking old man Oster with a pair of sewing shears, she got
him where it would really hurt—by carting off the boy. But after last
night, Lily suspects that even this account is a bit clean-cut, somewhat
naive and small-minded.

She has to review her theory based on her new knowledge. Hold it
up against the mottled light of this new dimension the pervert's opened
up for her. *The Secret Life of People.* Isn't this the rubric of her new education, what Lloyd has been trying to tell her in his own magniloquent
way? That she's not meant to have a definitive answer, but rather to understand that there are infinite answers?

Lily steps between the corridor of shelves, into the heart of the *G*'s, having given up on the call numbers and now just skimming for *Greene*. She turns into the next set of shelves and glances down to the end of the aisle. At first she doesn't understand the arrangement of bodies slumped up against the wall. Because the positions of the figures are distorted, the picture strikes her as incomplete. There's the rigid truss of arms and legs, a hip's line of force—the mathematics of push and pull. Lily blinks. Repeats. The physics are impossible to register in one eyeful.

He has the girl raised up on her toes and pressed against a shelf. Parts of his body—arms and legs—are thrust toward her, as though he's leaning into the weight of a looping punch. From behind, Lily thinks his shoulders are strong enough to be yoked and made to pull a wagon through town. His knee is raised and cleaves the girl's thighs apart; one of his hands is lost there in the bunches of her skirt. The other is on her small face, on Audiophile's small face, his fingers like a muzzle on a beak. Lily can see that he's holding her head still with the simple threat of his pinky finger over her eye. The girl's lid is creased shut, fluttering below this finger. Her hands are clenched and pecking at his shoulder but the disproportionate scale of their bodies suggests her fight is without progress. There is some sound that carries over to Lily, some music from her small, songbird throat, but it's screened by the palm of Lloyd's hand. He has planned for this, that's for certain. He has set his trap too deep in the stacks for the girl's music to reach anyone that can save her.

Somewhere in Lily's belly the idea registers that she should do something. She is watching as his hand comes down out of the skirt, the girl's underwear coming with it. They're covered with orange flowers—daisies. She sees daisies. Try to think now; she could unlace the tangle of girl and man. Although this sort of knotwork requires skill. Where are her own hands? Somewhere at her sides, cramped and broken.

Lloyd has drawn the panties down the girl's calves and scuffles to get the stretchy fabric over each foot. Then he presses his elbow into her belly, bracing her against the wall with one arm while he raises the underwear to his face. Against his mouth and nose and sniffs deep. Audiophile's free eye follows him. Tracks his hand as he lowers the scrap of material and stuffs it in his pocket. Lily feels her mouth as a pouch of unwieldy stones, the weight of it drawing her empty head forward. She wants to help this creature. She wants to free her. But how? There's no one here to show her the technique, how to release a snared bird.

Lloyd's hand returns to the skirt, struggles with it as one might with a stubborn valance. Lily thinks, How long will this last? Hovering is the most expensive form of flight. How long until the muscles slump from fatigue? Lloyd's knee is between her small thighs. If only the girl could fly away, Lily thinks. She's aware that these long moments are illusory, that everything is happening at an alarming speed. That when the girl finally pries her leg loose, she's actually taking advantage of the sliver of a second required for Lloyd to shift his weight from one foot to the other. And though it seems a month of Sundays before Audiophile jams her knee between Lloyd's legs, the incoming thrust is so rapid that he actually looks at his crotch in surprise before curdling inward like a salted leech.

Lily looks up to the ceiling, considers all possible points of exit. A hummingbird would lift and dart. She, however, turns and runs.

CHAPTER 28

Metacarpal Bone of the Ring Finger

Duncan stands in the leaking chill of the open refrigerator, lips crimped around the orange juice spout, dazed about the dog and now also wincing at his bad judgment with Wakefield and the car this morning. Nothing you can do now, he thinks, lowering the juice carton, but put it out of your head.

He's listening to Lily through the ceiling. Dropped things: a shoe, a book, a belt buckle. Also, something round and important. Round because, when it falls, it rolls in the direction of warped flooring. Important because she chases it out into the hallway. A man should be made to live beneath a woman before he marries her, he thinks. Before he even makes himself known to her. There is incredible intimacy in the ceiling, the floor, the space in between.

This evening, with Lily moving around up there, stacked *on top* of him, he's got more checks in the Vague and Unstable column than anywhere else. He's got a theory about fiefdoms and another about barnacles, but neither fully explains his situation. What is this coupling tendency? A man chooses a woman, selects her above all others, and takes her away to live in a box. Then the man loses the ability to address her like a human being. For reasons he cannot explain. And the woman locks herself away in a smaller box within the larger box. That they are in the same box is essential, Duncan suspects, for the ease of sex. He remembers reading that barnacles, while cemented headfirst to rock, procreate by extending their organ over and into a neighboring barnacle. For the crustaceous it's necessary to live within a penis length of a neighbor. But remove the sexual (as he and Lily did so many months ago) and you're left with largely agricultural motivations. Duncan suspects the contemporary custom of joining fiefdoms has its roots in smart farming policy, is evolved from the feudal system. And so here they are today, acting like vassals, when really, he is a robber baron at heart.

Duncan shuts the refrigerator, composing his thoughts. There's a bit of swish left in the orange juice carton and he stands tipping his head back to catch it. Why is he unable to ask the simplest question? *Where were you last night?* What about her renders him an inarticulate ass?

Duncan holds the recalcitrant belief that, in love, one being must eventually consume the other. That two are superfluous; how long can two unhinged creatures rummage together in the wild? Duncan wishes for the companionship of an old geezer. Not a crazed vigilante like Skinner, but someone who has seen success with the opposite sex, who's chosen a wife for her deft hand with the plowshare and her knowledge of calving practices. A salty dog who's lived through a world war. Yes, an old man with rheumy eyes who'd punctuate his lessons with a quivering finger to illustrate where Duncan has veered from the path.

He looks out the kitchen door to the backyard and the barley beyond. The sun has lowered now, but still clings like a burr to the clouds. The garden is blistered into mounds of earth from which they've pulled the woman's bones and over which he dragged the dead poodle last night.

It's the perfect time of evening, he thinks, for Skinner's clan to douse their torches in petrol and come after them. Hasn't anyone noticed the correlation between their arrival in town and the number of missing animals? He's reminded again how he botched things this morning. Not only by trailing Lily directly through town, but by blasting the hell out of there with Wakefield practically latched to his window. What should he tell Lily?

What about that you killed a dog and slept in the car? a salty old-timer would have advised him. *Then you followed her. To make sure she actually goes where she says she goes.*

Old men, Duncan thinks, know how to handle women. They had universal perils to distract them. An abundance of commies and Nazis to threaten their daily existence. Maybe the threat of a posse wouldn't unnerve him so much if he were involved in large-scale issues. It was too bad they weren't alive in the shadowy antebellum years, poised between one epic battle and the next. We might do well in crisis, he thinks. But without the immediate threat of conscription or the rise of a dictatorship, Duncan can't see much to bind young man and wife together.

Doorbell's ringing, the old man says.

The cop is not a swallower of bullshit. Lily understands this the instant she opens the door and sees the straining collar. Maybe it's the way he's driven the cruiser partially onto the front lawn and left the red and blue lights flashing. Maybe it's the prairie flatness of his eyes or the puckered stretch of neck visible over the collar of his uniform, but Lily is already considering her escape options while he tells her his name.

Duncan walks out of the kitchen, comes and stands beside her so that their two bodies fill the entire door.

"What's this about?" he asks the cop as she knew he would. He thinks they've come for Tinker. Or the boar. Someone has finally put the pieces together. She feels Duncan's arm loop over her shoulder. It's intended to look protective, but feels inflexible there, rigid. She glances at it from the corner of her eye; instead of closing around the cap of her shoulder, his fingers and thumb are spread and neutral. Not the way a man grasps a woman, Lily knows.

On the other hand, he is close enough that she smells him, the quiet battle of his soap and sweat. What if she reaches for his hand? If she drags it down around her breast, forces his fingers to clamp down around her nipple?

And then what? Lily tells herself not to think too carefully on this one.

Out front, the synchronicity of cruiser lights in the yard—now red, now blue—is mesmerizing, a helix spiral in the eyes. She's susceptible, it seems, to these trances and flusters. Earlier she had fled the library and biked along the river, trying to keep an eye on the calm green of Ulster Landing a mile across. But her head was swimming in a milky broth and she surfaced from it only to pick small rocks from her sandals. What should she tell the cop? That the details were justifiable? That she was the one who had spurred the pervert to action. *We die by our lethargy, Lloyd!* A rally cry as tight as a good boat.

To see it, though—the girl pinned like a creature to cork—to see it was another matter. First thing her brain did was clear out of the room. The great cheerleader vanished, left only bits of string and paper in the corners. It was the gut that had to step in. The gut that finally transmitted the image of that word, *No No No.* What an ignoble creature, her brain. All along it had convinced her to shout down the rest of the body. What a double-dealing snake in the grass.

"We got a complaint about a guy's been harassing some young girls," the cop says to Duncan. "Guy's been seen at the library. Checking if you got some information on his whereabouts." He pulls a mug shot out of a notebook and holds it just above Lily's sight line.

"We're told you're doing some studying at the library? You might have any contact with him?" The cop's eyes graze over Lily for a second before retreating back up to the safety of her husband. "Lot of the ladies don't want to admit when they've been harassed." He starts clicking a ballpoint pen with his free hand.

Lily's mouth opens, she's struck by how young Lloyd is in the photo. His hair is ruffled, the jowl paunch extending from mouth to chin is barely an embryo.

"What did he do?" Duncan asks.

"Just like I said." The cop, as though recognizing in himself a nervous habit of repetitiveness, stuffs the pen into his breast pocket. "We got reports on him before: exposing himself, making lewd comments, that sort of thing. This time he got a girl right in the library." He coughs. "Touched her improperly."

Here then, Lily thinks, a chance to break from the bloodline. Here's the moment, let the peasant gut step forward. In overthrowing the head it will represent the body below the neck, all that lives coiled and stacked, sightless and overlooked. *Of course I knew the man in the photograph; we are on intimate footing. Together we have stalked the daughters of the village.*

Duncan's arm has sunk into the groove of her shoulder. Without thinking, she puts her hand up against his chest. Only realizes it because of the pleasant hardness of his body, the thump of heart beneath. How will she explain this to him? How far back will she have to go? He's just relieved that Tinker's safe, she knows. That the boar continues to be shrouded in mystery. Still, he wants the cop gone. Duncan takes the picture from the officer's hand, shows it to Lily. What he doesn't realize is that the mug shot captures a youthful face. Not just full of requisite hope, but of something better. Certainty.

"You know this guy?"

It is no easy task to take down an entire system. What has been set in place has guided her for years. She feels herself shaking her head. "No," she says. "Never seen him."

He has created a convection current using only a fan and an open window. What late-night genius, what craft, he thinks, shoving the mattress to the middle of the room. He pushes it like a barge through the reeds, into the radar zone, into the crosshairs of two conspiring machines. The window and the fan. Duncan believes his only hope for sleep is to locate the bed at the heart of this static crackle, where hot air is displaced by cold. His hands are blistered from the shovel. He presses them together and drops one knee on the mattress to test the orientation. There's a definite chill. A less handy man would have suffered, pacing the halls in boxers, sat up smoking in the kitchen, running wet cans of Coke across the fore-head. But not Duncan. He holds up his swelling hands to the current.

He looks at the flotsam and jetsam of sheets on the floor. He'd torn the linens from the mattress during his first phase of sleep, a failed attempt to drift under the wave of the fan alone. He spreads his body back on the bed. It would be good if his blisters released their warm fluid. The fan points up toward the window and if he lifts his hands, he can hold them in the stream.

Duncan studies the hump in the ceiling plaster and thinks, Where's this all going, anyhow? He lays in the air stream with this trinity of frayed ropes. His work, his marriage, and the skeleton in the garden. He is try-ing to connect them, sniff out a plot where the terrors of the first teach him patience for the second, which brings meaning to the third. But he's missing the bend and hitch that'll tie all three together.

"Duncan?" The door is open (necessary engineering for his air sys-tem), and he lifts his head. Lily in a nightgown and glasses, a book pressed against her stomach, tentative at the door. Duncan can almost hear the vi-bratory hum of her nightgown skirting the floor as she hovers. Waits to be invited. And it seems to him he has spent years coaxing her into rooms, guiding her in and out of doors, carrying her across thresholds—*I'll still love you in the morning, Lily.*

"You okay?" he asks.

She walks into the room and steps over the litter of bed linen with-out answering. Swims out to his barge, hands him the book. *The Quiet American.*

"Maybe it'll help you. With the campaign." She pushes her glasses up her nose. Duncan sits up, scratches a spot through his boxers with one hand, flips to the spine of the book with the other. This is an instinctive move, executed to assess the weight of her sincerity. It's not from the library. It doesn't bear the military spinal stamp of the Dewey decimal system. It's a real book, one she had to purchase. He's surprised by the gesture, the effort behind it.

What should he say? That the more he pulls from the ground of one woman, the less he understands of the other? Instead he holds up the book as if she might not know to what he was referring. "They published this in '55. You know that Greene was, uh, basically predicting the American war with Vietnam?"

Lily nods, flops down on the mattress, and he feels the coils sink away beneath him.

"I can't stop thinking about Tinker," she says. Lily wants to talk about the bones, cozies up for some discourse on their discovery. But he's not thinking about the nanny, can't put his mind there. Not with her body splayed out beside him, not with that red-herring paperback at his side. Why is she here? Why did she think he'd still be awake?

"And that dog, running through town with Tinker's shin in its mouth. They've got part of her leg in a police station somewhere."

"I think you need to let it go," he says, remembering how the shovel-on-dog impact vibrated to his elbows. "The dead are often spread around. Especially the important ones."

"Yes. All those saints, cut up into relics."

"When you're hot, everyone wants a piece of you."

Her smile is thankful but suspicious, as though he had told her she was beautiful. "I'm so tired, but I can't stop wondering what happened to her." She turns over on her side. "Do you wonder what happened?"

"No." He says it before considering all possible meaning.

She pushes her glasses back on her head, pulls herself up. They sit on the mattress regarding one another. "I probably haven't given enough credit, I don't think, to the complexity of the situation."

"Yes," he says.

"I mean, I didn't leave enough space for instinct."

"You've just evolved beyond it." He's determined to stay light on his feet until he figures out what the hell she's talking about. "Sort of like the appendix."

"I credit my family for underestimating impulse," Lily admits. "If an argument's well thought out it has a right to exist. And vice versa."

Duncan shrugs. "They *are* German."

"Well, how about this for a break in the bloodline?" Lily sucks at her cheeks in an enunciative way. "I think Tinker's death was a crime of passion."

He has to laugh at the hush in her voice. This coming from a woman who chronically defaults to the obvious explanation. "I don't know," he says. "I was thinking she got caught in the thresher after all, Lil."

As her truncated name leaves his mouth he flushes with embarrassment. They both look away, eyes hunt for shore in opposite corners of the room, two strangers acquainting over a soggy mattress. Yet there's a piquancy in Lily's voice that he has nearly forgotten, and to extinguish it would be either cruel or impossible. He plucks at the mattress pad.

"In each of the nine million retellings I've heard of your grandfather's abduction, they always find him the next day. But in the barn—and not rescued by his father."

Lily nods him on, as though welcoming his theory. Which, he realizes, will have to be made up as he goes.

"What if the reason no one talks about the father's involvement is because when he actually finds them making for the river, the boy refuses to return with him?"

"Because Tinker raised him, essentially."

"So he chooses her. The father has to drag them both back, but he sees the boy's choice as a betrayal, a dishonor to the family."

"Right. Like, what will the Astors say?"

"And Oster has no choice but to kill the kid too."

Lily sits back; the jut of her lip tells him he's overshot on intrigue.

"Think about it, Lily. What God giveth, God taketh away." He forces the baritone out of his voice. "The power of destruction—there's no greater achievement for a man."

"My grandfather was alive until I was eight."

"Technical detail."

"No, but listen," she says, bunching her nightgown under her knees. The fabric is stretched over her body like a fine tent.

"I'm listening." Duncan wonders if she's wearing anything underneath.

"I think Tinker was actually my great-grandmother."

"Are the Crusaders aware of this?"

"My grandfather—the boy in her charge—is actually her son. Luis Oster impregnates Tinker, right? Most likely his wife is unable to conceive. So they allow Tinker to stay on as the nanny, but they raise the child as their own." Lily shifts to her knees, her story requiring elevation for proper locution. Now the nightgown's twisted so that the side slit parts over a thigh.

"Everything's fine while the boy's just a baby. But as he grows up, Tinker can't be reconciled to the idea of her own son calling someone else Mother. Meanwhile she's just treated as hired help. And so, one day, she takes him and tries running away." Lily takes her eyeglasses off her head and bites on one of the arms. He can see her tongue, wet and preoccupied, prodding at the frame.

Duncan rubs his palms. "Tinker stays at the house because of her son," he says with considerable effort, "even though Oster continues to, uh, rape her?" A tick of the heart dovetailing the end of his sentence.

"Maybe." Lily folds the glasses. "Or maybe she liked it."

Okay. He's having trouble upholding his end of this plotted conversation. Even Lily, who has come to him under the guise of Tinker-talk, betrays a catch of the throat with her last words that suggests her intention is thumping away in a place her mouth can't quite reach. He looks at her body, the fan rumpling her hair like fresh laundry.

She catches his look. "It's cool in here." She swallows. "My room is hot."

A short while ago she made it clear that she couldn't tolerate touching bodies in the heat. Why the change of heart? He can't bring himself to ask, although there's nothing he'd like to know more. He looks down at his palms and is overtaken by sadness, the opaque bubbles like a pox across their interior. He can't even stretch them apart fully. Lily reaches over and slips her fingers into his palm. Her hand seems so small and submissive there. She begins to trace a circle around the blisters. Duncan's head nearly flies to pieces. She leans over, the mound of her palm resting on his wrist.

"I made you work hard," she says. "I'm sorry."

He chokes on something—what? Anger? Yes, that she has to cloak this touch with double meaning. Anger that she is never willing to lay herself bare. Duncan reaches out, puts both hands on the neck of her nightgown, and acts with a violence that no longer surprises him. He tears her gown apart at the buttons. It splits like a shucked cornhusk. For a few seconds there's just a rain of buttons against the hardwood, then the sudden exposure of her breasts. She pulls back, touches her chest as if he's plunged a stick through her. But she doesn't move to cover herself up.

Like the night in the kitchen, he thinks with horror. The slap zinging through the room with the trajectory of a rubber ball. Like the Grunts in the tunnel and the kids in the huts. The dog. Anne pouring dish soap over his filthy mess. The look on Lily's face. What kind of man does she see with those amazed eyes, that open mouth?

There is a stranger kneeling on his bed not making a sound, and to her he says with sudden truth, "I wanted to see you again."

Common Characters of the Ribs

Lily of the Rooftops,

Have you heard? Made the leap the other day and am now officially a Man of Action. Got the flower-print panties to prove it! Our little friend (you remember Audiophile?) won't be using the Dewey Decimal System again without thinking of Yrs. Truly . . . I'd say I took it a step or two beyond the frott, Lily. Got her up against the Great American Classics before she squared me in the nuts. Nearly hammered them flat, but that's an occupational hazard, right?

Anyway, you won't be seeing me around—gotta lay low since the heat is on, baby! I know you'll miss me, but where I'm going, you just can't follow. I don't usually say thanks. But the upshot is, I couldn't have done it without you and your spectacular intolerance of weakness, Lily. Hope that one day I can bring you the same measure of freedom. Repay the favor in kind.

Until then, keep your curtains open and a song in your heart, darling!

Frotteurly Yrs,
Lloyd

The note is written on the front of an envelope and carries over to the backside. Lily's found it stuffed under her bicycle seat, the unsealed flap poking out from the padding. Inside the envelope are three gently squashed cigarettes.

Lily sits on the grassy slope of library lawn. She has collected her books, cleaned out her carrel. Courage hadn't come; she did nothing to help the girl. She has associated with a felon, aided and abetted a crime, watched it happen. Perpetrated several punishable offenses herself. It all just sounded so right at the time. Now she wonders to what other dark places has she followed her head. With Duncan, in particular. Or rather, away from him.

Last night she had gathered the gown around herself and felt her way back to her room. She lay naked in the dank night, her head full of dissonance. Was this Duncan's final gesture toward her? If she's ever to think of his hands again, will they always be initiating this violence on her? Will they ever complete it? It seems to her that she had lain there last night welcoming it. Even his violence—anything that resembled a follow-through. What was it that had driven her to his room in the first place? The way he held her while the cop stood at the door? They *looked* so united, couldn't there be some truth behind it still? And she felt safe. Of course, this she didn't realize until later. There was something lit inside of her, a charge in her belly, binding each breast. She had gone to him, knelt on his bed in order to give herself over. Hadn't he understood? It was quite possible he just didn't want her. But she didn't believe in such decisive endings. Even after he'd torn the gown, she still thought he might come to her. Slide on top of her finally, a hand on her forehead, the other between her legs. Come to finish what he started.

He never came. She woke up alone, soggy, naked. She woke up rejected. The charge in her stomach was dim and distant.

Lily rolls one of the flat cigarettes between her fingers to plump it and pats down the corners of her bag. Her lighter is missing. She lies back in the grass. Reminds herself that at the very least she's made Lloyd happy. The pervert has cocked his ear to the sky so that his particular vocation might be whispered down. People are getting on with their lives. Seems she's the only one who can't pick her thread loose from the knot.

They keep low in the shallow tub of garden. Duncan would rather crouch and dig, but the shovel requires leverage and so he stands. Lily kneels and shifts soil from the plot into mounds along the lip of grass. The breeze tonight snaps the barley heads around, forcing him to listen through this for the sound of gravel crunching in the drive. Although they haven't talked about the cop's visit last night, Duncan believes there is a new, intuitive drill in place for the safe recovery of Tinker's unsheathed frame. In case of unexpected visitors, they will drop their tools, snake through the switchback territory that is now the backyard, knock out the porch light, and get down to the cellar through the basement door. Duncan will use an old chair back to buttress the door in addition to the lock. He imagines he might even be forced to rip off his T-shirt and use it as a mitt to knock out the hot lightbulb. An unnecessary action, but one he likes.

This reminds him that Lily hasn't said a word about the torn nightgown. He wishes she would because he has no clue how to approach the topic himself. Instead, here they are, digging a dead body out of the garden like it was any old Friday night. She's probably avoiding the topic for a reason. And while it irritates him, it strikes him as some sort of intuitive desire. The need to remain the injured party sends Lily scrambling into the upper story of the trees to suck her opposable thumb.

"This reminds me of those pictures you took in Vietnam," Lily says. "Of the Viet Cong tunnels."

Duncan grunts, doesn't tell her he's already worked this parallel. She sifts dirt with her fingers; they have created a system whereby he boxes out a chunk of dirt and she sorts through it for smaller bones.

Lily stops, looks up at the trees. "Did you see that?"

He wipes his forehead, sees nothing but branches.

"A bat," she says and then surveys the entire sky. "I hate bats."

"They eat insects."

"How's it coming anyway?"

"What?"

"The campaign, Duncan." There is a metallic pitch in her voice that he dislikes.

"Right now? It's heading into the jungle of the Tay Ninh province."

"Right." There it is again, shovel against rock.

"We present to the client on Tuesday," he says, trying to infuse a sense of conclusion here. It's times like these—when Lily's at her most metallic—that he's reminded of her Crusader lineage. She'd deny the heredity, but a thousand years of the jeweled and brilliant history of burning *masjids* and chasing heretics on horseback through desert wadis isn't just going to come to an end with one woman.

"If you want to run it by me, like a focus group or whatever, I'd be happy to listen."

He rubs the scruff of his chin. "Thanks. I don't want to talk about it now."

"Oh. That's all right."

"I mean, it's hard to explain without the visuals. You don't show that kind of thing until it's ready."

"That's okay," she says again, rising and stretching her legs. But it's clear he's hurt her feelings.

"Besides, it's your turn," he says to lighten the nick. "You want, I can read your dissertation."

Instead of declining him outright, she laughs, squats in another quadrant of the garden.

"I guess I wouldn't understand any of that, huh?"

"That's not it," she says.

Duncan starts nosing through some soil with the tip of the shovel. He wants to move away from these interior rooms of their life. Tries for something with greater exposure. "That's bad news about the girl at the library."

Lily shrugs.

"Listen. Maybe you should take a few days off from that place," he says.

She stops, picks up a spade, and looks at him. "Why?"

Because I don't want some pervert touching you inappropriately, for fuck's sake! But he's afraid of these words at this stage of their relationship, afraid of her derision; that he should express concern about this, but nothing else.

"Well, if you're here, we can dig during the day."

She looks away from him to make small cuts in the soil and he knows he's said the wrong thing. She keeps her jaw balled like a fist and her eyes on the ground but her head is nodding. Is this agreement or outrage? He plunges the shovel into the new northern soil and it stops against something. He taps the edge and knows it's the clink of bone.

They put their tools down. One thing they are coming to love with anguish—if not each other—is Tinker. They put down shovel and spade and bend over new bones.

These are the first that seem to have been buried with any logic. They unearth the grouping from the sides as if excavating along the perimeters of an ancient building. They dig around the cage of bones, leaving the structure intact in the ground. Tinker's chest appears in the soil. So narrow and white Duncan feels his own chest constrict. The ribs rise like a domed ceiling over some sacred place.

Lily kneels by the rib cage. "There is a reason why you can't read it," she says to him, then looks away over the field. "I haven't done anything."

He doesn't understand. "Haven't done what?"

"Work." She sits up suddenly, as though she might stop herself. As though she may still tip truth and logic to one side of her tongue. Duncan doesn't grasp her meaning but feels a tight binding under his arms. Lily's watching his face and an awareness falls over him. Before he understands her words, there is this awareness.

"There is no dissertation, Duncan."

Of course.

Lily, perhaps realizing it's too late to go back, goes forward. "Since we came up here. No, even before that—I haven't touched it." It's a series of streams she's jumping here, all with the same momentum, so that he sees she can't stop even if she wanted to. "Do you understand? Not a single page. And I don't care if I never write another word again."

He can feel the pulsing of his throat, blood circling through a cone. "You've been here an entire month, Lily. We've been living apart an entire month."

She looks down at the bones.

"What the fuck have you been doing then?"

Lily lifts her shoulders, says nothing.

"Is there someone else?"

"No."

"Are we separated? Is that it? Is that why you came up here in the first place?"

"I don't know," she whispers.

"You don't know! Jesus Christ, Lily. You don't know if we're separated?" Duncan is not surprised by his anger or by the swift current of his blood. He kicks over his staked shovel. Lily recoils against the sound. He wishes for nothing more but her words to come and cut him free. And still, he is conscious of even this—of having to persuade his wife to cut him free.

"Every weekend I follow you up here like an asshole. And the whole time you're trying to tell me we're separated."

"That's not true."

"What *is* true?"

She doesn't answer but sits for long minutes at his feet, her hands in the soil. They're waiting perhaps, both of them, for the blood to slow.

Lily presses each of her fingers gently between Tinker's ribs. "Do you realize," she says after several long minutes, "that this is where the heart goes?"

Duncan looks. The soil under the dome leaves no trace of the heart it used to shelter.

"The heart turned to mulch."

At first he thinks she's laughing at this observation, but when she turns her head he realizes she's gagging. Lily pushes to her feet and runs toward the barley. Then, bent at the waist, she vomits into the grain. Duncan comes up behind her, gathers up her hair until she's done. She sinks to the ground and cries after she vomits, or perhaps she cries partway through.

He kneels beside her and slides his hand down Lily's back, between the sharp angles of her shoulders. There is a new frailness there that frightens him. She is all brittle and spindle, mismatched chairs pulled up to the fire. He wants to pick her up and carry her through the grain. Hide her away somewhere safe.

"Lily, I want you to know—" He stops, tucks a wet strand of hair behind her ear. "My God."

She rubs her hand across her mouth, looks at him.

"I killed that dog."

For a moment she doesn't move. Not even a blink. Then something sparks in her face, a swift understanding passes between them. A distant language is recalled, each verb brilliant, chipped from stasis. She sits back, presses his hand. Lily is illuminated.

CHAPTER 30

Connective Tissue

There are two hundred and six bones in the human body. They are missing nearly one hundred of them. It rains all day Saturday and Lily worries about the grave they have opened and left exposed.

"Not much we can do," Duncan had said this morning, leaning against the porch rail under the cover of the eaves.

"We could tarp it again."

"Yeah." He tossed a cigarette into the soil. "But it's been coming down for hours." There had existed between them all day a vibrant solidarity that neither dared acknowledge for fear that it would vaporize. Last night's confessions may have seemed lurid and crude, but they were secrets exchanged as offerings—the dog was his offering. Not the muscle and guts of it, but the knowledge. He had eliminated that which he detested the most: a man standing impotent at the side of the road.

Now in the cellar it's the small bones after all that drive her to pieces. She has accumulated a gym sock full of what are either hand bones or foot bones or, quite possibly, both. Proximal, middle, and distal phalanges, she has poured them out on a sheet of cardboard and tries arranging them according to the illustrations in *Gray's Anatomy*. She holds a woman's fingers and toes, but all these bits feel foreign, without context. Trinkets. It's like imposing curatorial order on a collection of cupboard knobs, kitchen fuses, buttons, misshapen chocolate truffles.

She looks at long bones on the table. "What do you think?" she asks, holding a cylindrical phalange. "Hand or foot?"

Tinker is silent on this one. "How would you know? You have no head." Lily shifts the sole remaining tibia and the fibula (of what they believe is the right leg) and sits on the edge of the table. Until yesterday they had confused the narrow fibula with the radius bone of the forearm. But after finding its illustrated counterpart in the osteology section of *Gray's,* Duncan had moved it down to the leg.

"Don't worry," she says, picking up Tinker's femur by the knobby head and placing it over her own thigh. "We're going to get all of you out of the ground."

Tinker's femur is shorter than her own. Lily lies back so that the two women are side by side. She places the humerus over her upper arm, hooks a fifth rib around her own chest, the shallow pan of the scapula under her shoulder and the clavicle in front.

"You were just a little thing, weren't you?"

The official version of her grandfather's kidnapping did not begin, or end, or linger on the nanny since she would, early into the tale, disappear from the storyteller's lips and into the alternating flow of the Hudson. Instead, once Lily's mother had drawn an audience, she would start with the boy, Luis Junior, whose naughtiness at the dining room table prompted his abduction. By launching this narrative with conflict, the young protagonist was given a role in his own demise. The nanny was to take him to his room where he would finish his meal alone. Later, when mother and father went up to say good night, they found both his dinner tray and his bed empty. The nanny was gone as well.

Oster, to the requisite sound of female wailing and grief, made a quick search of the house and land. Those days, the Hudson was a main transportation artery and, on account of the sawmill, Osterhagen boasted a sizable landing. It was thought that the woman and child may have caught a steamer for the city. Oster took a couple of men with him and set out for the river, only to return a few hours later, empty-handed.

Here is where the official version skips to daylight: a stable hand discovers the child out by the barn, shaken, sticky with tears, flecked with hay and full of remorse for his behavior at dinner. It was decided that the nanny—lacking corporeal presence and still in need of punishment—had been washed away in the tidal flow.

Yes, her mother's version flattens the nanny to villainous dimensionality. She was an antagonist with neither name nor motivation beyond fulfilling her typecast. The crone who, unable to have her own child, settled on abducting one from the manor house.

Who really was this Tinker when she was clothed in muscle and skin? Why did she give the boy to the Osters if he belonged to her? Lily strokes the rib that has lodged between her own. And if he didn't belong to her, why would she stay, knowing what would come scratching at her door each night?

There is *one* motivation, but it is so visceral that Lily had nearly blinked it away until recently. She had been without desire herself for so long, she'd forgotten that it ever existed. Lily holds up the curved rib bone; all the while she's been waiting for the pointed arch to come and save her when she's had this round arch inside the whole time. Sure, the acute angle was superior for bearing loads, but the barrel vault crowned some of the strongest walls ever built. Wasn't there valor in this, that a simple curve could hold up stone and cast iron and the ceiling over a heart?

Maybe there is one final turn in this theory. Maybe Tinker was grateful to Luis Oster, lumber baron. Grateful for the touch, for the unlacing, the stripping of the corset. Down to the flesh and she could breathe, finally. Maybe he had placed his mouth over hers and blown. Done the kind thing and raised those flattened ribs. Why had it been so hard to believe this—what a woman would do for touch? Lily stares up at the beams that run across the ceiling, that keep the parlor and the sunroom, the kitchen, Duncan and the Viet Cong, from collapsing in on her.

Yes, this is how the story goes. Tinker was just a nanny, with nothing to recommend her. But he had come to her in the night. It was her wish. He touched her so that her skin fell away. Just here—his hand against the sternum, between the elastic arches of bone, he had bent his dark head and licked fat from the furrows of her heart.

Lily watches as the woman on the table beside her sits up, nudges each wedge of vertebrae into alignment. She begins to count the collected parts of her body. *The last part of this story is a sad one, all right? As you know, the .casting aside of bones always begins as the touch of love. That's how it is in the beginning. But the truth always shakes out in time: some of us are just too feeble to illuminate a face for long. We're left behind. A slow abandonment, but there it is. We're alone as we were before, only worse. The muscle has memory. Takes up space inside.*

Let me tell you what I did, the woman says. She has lost count of her bones and begins to arrange them in small piles instead. *I waited for harvest, for the fall. The man and the boy had left me by then. One morning I walked out into the field of barley. I walked out right into the path of a swather, then I crouched low and waited.*

She turns the fifth rib over, inspects it from each angle. *It's not pleasant to take inventory of yourself this way,* she says. *At times it's best to remember that the whole is always greater than the parts.*

CHAPTER 31

The Internal Oblique Muscle

"I'm positive this is against the Declaration of Human Rights," Leetower says.

"Fuck the declaration." Duncan pulls the art director's head out of the desk cabinet. Earlier this morning he'd come into the office to find that someone had jimmied the lock on his drawer. They'd left the velvet sacks of the One Show Pencils, but filled the rest of the space with HB number 2 pencils, their wooden skins chewed to hell. How frustrating, Duncan thinks, that at this stage of evolutionary development a man—considered perceptive, immune to flattery even—could lose the intuitive ability to recognize a quisling from his handshake or the degree to which he is able to meet the eye. How unfortunate that it's only by taking the quisling by the shirt collar—first with the threat of a good garroting and then by shoving his head into a desk—that he may be made to reveal his true character.

He lets Leetower sit upright. Then holds a pencil to the boy's mouth. "Open up." Betrayal might be expected of women, but cunning in a male—an underling—it's vile and sly. It's the death of heroes, the exit ramp from manhood.

Duncan himself never dreamt he was betraying Hawke when, a few weeks before the man's departure, Upstairs took him to lunch at the Mercer Hotel and, through circuitous discourse, asked him what exactly *was*

Hawke's ongoing input on the Tide account since their glory days of five years past? The fact that Hawke rarely came in before noon, that Fridays and Mondays were out-of-office days where he'd take his phone calls in Westchester, these things were common knowledge available to anyone with a watch and calendar who cared to stand in the office lobby and wait. So had Duncan fudged his boss out? Hardly. What he was doing there, third bourbon sour in hand (just keeping up), was trying to assert his own role on Tide. *Yes, yes, we know you created the Laundry Elves. But we can't rest on our laurels, can we? In any case, you might benefit from a break from packaged goods. We'll see if we can't get you to help on some other business. We need to create another showpiece account here, yes? But more on that later. Let's get back to Hawke. . . .*

"If you're innocent, Leetower, you have nothing to fear." Duncan can hear Skinner's soggy baritone tower from his lungs but he doesn't let go of his shirt collar.

"Duncan, man. This is a two-hundred-dollar Varvatos shirt you're stretching the hell out of."

"You want to do this the hard way?" He waves the pencil in front of Leetower's face.

"What about principle?"

"Are you kidding? This is advertising."

"I just want you to know, I swear I had nothing to do with this." Leetower closes his eyes and lets Duncan fit the pencil, lengthwise, between his teeth. He's never noticed it, but Leetower's incisors flare slightly from the arcade of teeth. He runs the pencil lengthwise through his mouth, searching for a point of contact. But the bite is all off. Leetower opens his eyes. Looks up at Duncan, but not in an *I told you so* manner. Not with triumph, but rather as if to double-check his liberty.

"It wasn't me."

He lets go of Leetower's collar. "Well, someone wants me out."

"It's probably a joke, Duncan. You know how this place twists people."

"Is Kooch saying Vietnam was his idea?"

"No," Leetower says, looking unsure. "I mean, I don't think so. First I heard was the other day in your office. When Anne told us about Tide."

Duncan grips the back of his chair. "I'm sorry, LT. I had to make sure." He's waiting to be overcome by a fear of his own actions, a remorse or disgust. He waits, but the feelings just don't come. In fact, there's something horribly pleasing about the way the boy stands up near the desk and waits, rubbing his neck.

Duncan moves around the chair and puts his hand on Leetower's shoulder. "Sit down, sit down." He points to the spot on the sofa next to the brown smirch they'd discovered a month ago. "Sit, sit, sit."

Leetower obeys. He folds his legs at the ankle the way Duncan's advised him to (the feminine thigh crossing had people in the department rolling dice and speculating). Duncan sets himself on the edge of the desk closest to the sofa. He runs a hand through his hair, rolls up one sleeve, and leans on his arm. "Listen, LT. I just want you to know, no matter what shit goes down here, I've got your back, buddy."

"Okay." The boy nods. "I'm with you."

"Are you here to kill the hired help, Duncan? Because I have a major presentation next week that could really use my attention." Anne picks the chewed yellow pencil off her desk and throws it back at him. It bounces off his chest and rolls under a chair.

"You hear Kooch has been telling people Stand and Be Counted was his idea?"

"Then why come to me?"

"So you have heard?" Duncan tugs the hair at the back of his head. "You let him slander me and you did nothing?"

"Why would I want to drive you out of here?" Anne slides a pair of reading glasses over her nose. "Without you there is no Stand and Be Counted. Without Stand and Be Counted there's no Christmas bonus, no free weekends at the Fire Island house. No coke parties. You're such a selfish asshole, Duncan." She turns back to her computer screen.

He shrugs down onto her sofa. "Well, somebody's filled my desk drawer with pencils."

"So take up sketching." Anne adjusts her glasses and looks at him over the frames. "And Jesus Christ, get some sleep. You look like one of those fucked-up heroin addicts from the old Calvin Klein ads."

"Yes, consciousness," he mumbles, eyelids slack. "That annoying time between naps."

"Listen." She glances into the corridor. "For the record, if you're going to point fingers, choose somebody known for his bite."

The trick to the CoffeePot Café is to overlook the homogenous exterior. Nestled alongside a UPS Store in Osterhagen's sole strip of franchised sellouts, the CoffeePot suffers unnecessarily from the uniform salmon plaster facade and the neon cast-off glare of the 7-Eleven next door.

Inside, someone has fought back with fervor. The pioneer spirit surfaces in the cleaved log paneling, the hewn pine tables, two rows of faux leather booths separated by a split rail fence. From her window seat Lily can hear the counter girls' uninterrupted chatter, their voices rising bravely over the horse-powered growl of the espresso machine. One tells the other her plans for skipping town come fall and starting a new life with an aunt in Staten Island. Attending a college for hospitality service. But earlier when she served Lily coffee, her pour sloshed out of the cup and flooded the saucer.

Lily's been at the window booth the past hour faced with a sliced but uneaten grilled cheese sandwich. Panofsky's cracked and tattered *Gothic Architecture* is with her as well, its pages loose and tucked back against the spine unsequentially. Nothing out of the ordinary, nothing to forecast the unease that falls over her when she spots Skinner's truck pulling into the parking lot. It rumbles on loose bolts, its tires trailing wet shit and hay. Lily sucks back her breath, watches the old junker narrowly skim her bicycle out in front of the café.

The old man slides out of the cab. She hasn't seen him since the night she caught his poodle, but his walk across to the CoffeePot is the same lurching swagger. Unpromising. One glance at his cambered approach and even the counter girls stop their dreaming, pour him straight black in a paper cup. Lily slides down in her seat, hoping for transparency. She wishes Duncan were here. Wants to tell him that she's learned a thing or two about isolative analysis. That it's never really been about that night on the dirt road itself—but about all the subsequent moments they have chosen to leave unrectified.

"Your husband's a good shot," Skinner says.

Lily straightens her shoulders. Draws her cold saucer of coffee toward her. "I hear they had to close the sawmill. For a major cleanup."

Skinner picks up the sugar bowl from her table. "Maybe we did the town a favor. You hear there's a body buried around here?"

Lily shakes her head, opens her eyes wide. "Is there a cemetery nearby?"

"I'm talking a killing's taken place. My own dog came around with the bone." Skinner bends and unleashes a turbulent cough over the table. "Where's your husband, anyhow?"

She rotates her cup. As much as she doesn't want to imagine Tinker's leg clenched in that filthy mutt's mouth, she knows she must engage in order to avoid disclosing Duncan's location. "What sort of bone did you find?"

"A human one." The old man looks at her with impatience. "We just cracked open something bigger concerning those Arabs. The same mighty son of a bitch killed my boar also killed a man."

Lily toys with her teaspoon. "How do you come to that?"

"I'm no genius, but that's how these psychos work, start small then work their way up."

"You don't know that."

"I got the bone. I'm more certain than most."

Lily can't help it, her laughter at his unforensic indictment is quick and bitter. "Why, was the bone in the same ditch as the boar?"

Skinner tips the sugar bowl into his cup. "This whole town's gone to hell." He picks up her sandwich knife to stir his coffee. "They got lids for these cups, or what?"

It's only minutes later, when Skinner pulls back out of the parking lot, bald tires rotating along their original track, that she realizes her mistake.

CHAPTER 32

Organs of Special Sense:
The Tympanum

Duncan sits in front of his jimmied drawer watching Leetower stack the layouts and scripts for tomorrow's presentation in a portfolio case. Earlier, he made the boy empty out the gnawed pencils from his desk. Now all that remains are the velvet satchels containing his One Show Pencils. He places each of them in his bag.

"You think getting pulled off Tide will hurt my career?" Leetower asks, tugging the zipper on the nylon case full of mounted storyboards.

It's Kooch who answers, his beefcake frame appearing at the door. "It can't hurt you, Leetits, because you're nobody to begin with."

LT looks up. "Spoken by the poster boy for social services."

"Today you're a dispensable piece of shit. Tomorrow, Stand and Be Counted will rebirth you to a better life."

"Christ." Leetower picks up the case. "Like *Cats, the Musical.*"

"Put that stuff in my car," Duncan tells him.

"You might want to hold off, little buddy." Kooch walks into the room, holding up his yellow notepad. "I think I got gold right here."

The art director looks between his boss and his partner. He fidgets with the portfolio handle.

"In the trunk, LT." Duncan tries to keep his voice steady, his eyes trained on the kid until he picks up the portfolio case and moves out into the hallway. Kooch is standing in the middle of the office, legs set apart like some hard-riding ranch hand.

"Listen to this," he says to Duncan, flipping through his notes. "We got a chopper lifting off the roof of the Presidential Palace during the fall of Saigon, right? But suspended from its skid is a human chain of Grunt Girls."

"I know it was you," Duncan says.

"Each girl's got on a different cut of Stand and Be Counted jeans. It can be print or we use it as a store banner, on the Web site, whatever."

"I know it was you with the pencils."

Kooch stops, earmarks his notes. "I heard. I wish I could take credit for that little prank, Duncs." He drops down on the sofa.

"You're off Stand and Be Counted."

"The hell I am." Kooch props his feet on the upholstered armrest. "You can't take me off my own idea."

"Jesus, that's getting old." Duncan stands up, walks around the room. Then, worried that he's betraying his anxiety, sits back down on the edge of his desk.

"I gotta tell you, Duncan, man-to-man. It's feeling like we're here to work out your personal problems." He leans back, folding his hands behind his head. "We're supposed to be selling jeans, remember?"

"Are you *trying* to jeopardize your writer slash on Stand and Be Counted?"

"Slash?" Kooch looks at him with surprise. "You better be shitting me."

Duncan holds up his palms as if to indicate he's fresh out of accolades. "I'll be going up to the podium, if that's what you mean. But I will mention you."

"I'm going to need more."

"There isn't any more."

"Creative director."

Duncan laughs. "I'm creative director."

"That's debatable," Kooch says quietly. He starts patting around the sofa under his ass.

Duncan feels a hum of unnatural scale in his left ear. He presses a palm against it, creates suction, and counts to three. Still, the bright, whistling strain continues.

Kooch's hand comes out from between the cushions. He holds up a chewed pencil, crafts a look of surprise that's worthy of community theater. "That is definitely the mouthwork of a maniac," he says, examining its crenellated patterns.

Duncan reaches over and slaps the pencil out of his fingers. It flies across the room like an arrow, then strikes the wall with the clatter of tossed furniture. "Get out of my office."

"Why is it so difficult for you to give credit where it's due?" Kooch leans back on the armrest, smiling dreamily. "Is it because you haven't done anything worthwhile in five years?"

The sound in his ear has evolved. From reedy whistle to jet stream to monkey howl. The echo of cannon fire replicated through the vacuum of space. And the last thing Duncan remembers before he attacks Kooch is, if this were the jungle, there'd be only the tremble of bamboo before his unexpected incarnation of Death from Above. As it is, Duncan descends onto the sofa from his desk—roughly table-top height—but he instantly gains purchase on the younger man's arms and legs and shag of wolf hair. Kooch is bewildered, his reflexes are slumberous in response to the overhead assault, and for a few blurred and glorious moments Duncan's got him pinned at the neck and knees.

They begin to grapple in earnest. For the first minute or so, Duncan employs superior clutch, demonstrates an understanding of choke, uses the structure of the other man's bone and fiber as leverage to get him off the sofa and to the ground. A folding chair tips over. Otherwise there's no sound, no articulated noise beyond the snorts and brays that score the struggle.

As Duncan tries to wrestle Kooch toward the trash can full of pencils, he begins to understand the sort of animals that their bodies comprise. The spring-loaded muscle packaged tight under sheets of skin. The sheets of skin dim and freckled under sparse fur. Claws studding both hands. Duncan wants to fit an HB number 2 between the beast's rack of teeth and close the book on this Cinderella story. But Kooch, at some primordial level, is conditioned for surprise raids and gains enough traction on the carpet to allow him to flip Duncan. He also lands the impressive first swing on the left side of his face.

The reed pipe blasts at his ear again, this time stuck on a single note, E. The sound is critical and shrill and helps raise Duncan to his feet. And though he's not fast enough to parry a right cross, he has time to get in two quick jabs that make Kooch's head snap like a tethered ball.

Duncan is suddenly aware of Leetower in the room, circling the peripheries like a man waiting his go in a dorm room gangbang. For a moment the boy's actions are unclear. Is he waiting to break the fray or to join in? But his hand is moving toward Kooch's arm, and as he locks down, he takes the drive out of his partner's punch. He's gonna break things up, Duncan thinks. He straightens his footwork, then notices that Leetower has *both* of Kooch's arms behind his back. This confuses him; he's opening his partner up to attack. Handing him over like a punching bag, in fact. The moment won't last. He knows it. Already Kooch is bending forward, trying to throw Leetower to the ground. Duncan rushes in, his right arm finally free of striated muscle command, and he feeds Kooch an uppercut that is, if not textbook, at least powerful enough to cause an explosion of tiny bones.

———————

Duncan's broken thumb is set at St. Vincent's, the same hospital where Kooch has been admitted, a stream of morphine pumped straight into his veins and his jaw to be wired shut. Although he hasn't asked for any intelligence on the matter, Duncan is told that after the triage is complete, Kooch will be taken upstairs to the surgical ward.

"One week," the nurse says and gives Duncan a small envelope of

Vicodin. "When your swelling goes down we have to replace this with a plaster cast." She has a concerned voice that he finds surprising in a city full of exasperation. He looks at the lump of gauze at the end of his arm; the metal bracket holding his thumb in place is partly visible through the wrapping.

"Is there someone to drive you home?"

"Yes," he says. Although he seems to remember Leetower dumping him and Kooch *and* the car at the emergency entrance and fleeing.

"Your friend's going to be here for a while. They'll probably encourage him to file a mugging report when he's conscious. You should do that too." The nurse moves the bed tray away from the examination table, giving Duncan room to put his shirt on while she prepares his sling. "Just be careful what you do when you're on those pills," she says.

CHAPTER 33

Blood

Some subtle noise from the lean-to has Lily walking out of the house to investigate. Much later she'll realize how the gravest confrontations are always precipitated by the inconsequential; the sound of a pickax chipping into packed dirt, the intermittent creak and snap from the hobblebush.

She finds Skinner in the lean-to, poking through a set of wooden shelves that her father had salvaged from a tack house and which Duncan had stacked with gardening supplies. Lily's outrage is only slightly miti- gated by fear.

"Excuse me?"

If the old man is surprised by her appearance, he gives no sign. He turns slowly to her, scratches the hollow of his throat. "You never answered me yesterday. Where's your husband?"

"What are you doing in my garage?"

"You call this a garage?" Skinner looks up to the sloped beams, the lines on his forehead cast in triplicate. "Where is your car is what I want to know?"

Lily folds her arms across her chest, remembers the night of the torches, how successful Duncan had been at leading the entire clan off their property and into the woods. "Duncan is in the city today," she says, with- out half the charm or ease he might be able to muster. "What can I help you with?"

"How did you know the boar was in the ditch?"

Lily shrugs, tries her best for casual though she had spent all of last night thinking about the slip. "That's the rumor. Among about a dozen others."

"Wakefield says he saw your husband in a car. Outside his shop. Says the front end was smashed in. Says that something was very wrong with him."

"I don't follow," she says, and truly doesn't.

"I'm thinking it was the two of you all along." Skinner waggles a crooked finger at her, at her invisible husband.

"The two of us what?" Lily reminds herself how dogs always smell fear. But to make matters worse, she finds herself eyeing the old shovel Duncan's left propped against a wooden stud. She's caught suddenly by a glint of light reflected in its metal fender.

Skinner turns, follows her eye to the tool in the corner. "You did the boar in. And Christ knows what else."

Lily forces herself to meet the old man's pouchy eyes. "That's ridiculous."

"Not at all. It's making good sense to me."

"What's next? You're going to blame us for your missing dog?"

"Who says my dog is missing?"

A pause then, the click at the end of a reel. Her voice is a faint projection on a white wall. "It's a joke."

Skinner lifts a blue dog collar from the top of the wooden shelf. "It's no joke," he says.

The ringing sound is just an alert, an audio charge to startle him from the sofa. What actually forces him out of sleep is the burning agony of his right hand and the search for the telephone in the squalor of the condo.

The receiver is under a chair cushion, which is under the kitchen table.

"Jesus Christ, tell me you've got the boards!" Anne's shriek paralyzes him.

Duncan rests his head on the chair cushion and looks up at the underside of the *wenge* table. "Yes."

"Thank fucking God," Anne yells. "What the hell happened last night?"

He decides that he liked the shriek better.

"Duncan, it's all over the agency—no, look, I just got an e-mail from Ravi. It's all over town. It's only ten a.m.!" There's a break in Anne's shouting voice and Duncan hears her hiss as she reads the e-mail to herself. He wonders if it's a bad sign that the underside of the table is rotating.

"Jesus, Duncan. You and I have to go present now. Where the fuck are you?"

"Under the kitchen table. You called me."

"What happened? Kooch is waiting for surgery—" Anne takes a breath. "Wait, you have *all* the scripts and boards? We have no copies here."

"Yes. I've got it."

"And Leetower was fired, so it's just you in front of the client."

"What?"

"They walked him out this morning."

"Why?" He tries to sit up, but the table looms too close to his head.

"He fucking put Kooch in the hospital!" Her voice peaks and flattens as though she's wary of someone listening outside her door.

Duncan rolls out from under the kitchen table, keeping to his knees in case he faints. "Who told you that?" he asks. His voice is just the tail end of a voice, hardly registering. "Did Leetower say he did it?"

"Listen, Duncan. You've got to get there now. I want these boards in front of them before they hear about this nightmare."

Could it be—did the kid really take the bullet for him? Duncan is surprised, touched. His right hand throbs with an unpleasant regularity.

"Leetower didn't hit him, Anne. I did."

"You did not."

"Kooch got in some good shots."

"Never mind! Don't tell me, Duncan. I don't want to know—I don't care." She takes a deep breath that rattles a bit. "You've got the boards, right?"

"Yeah."

"TAKE THE BOARDS TO THE CLIENT. NOW!"

Lily swallows, watches Skinner twirl the collar around his index finger.

"I don't know where that came from." She is genuinely surprised. Duncan had failed to mention the existence of this little trinket.

"I'll tell you where." He takes a step toward her. "Off the neck of my dog."

"I've got nothing to tell you," she says, turning from the lean-to. The front door is unlocked, a quick twenty yards, seconds away if she runs. She doesn't take a step before the old man's got her by the arm.

"I said, where is my dog?" His old claw is pincer-tight against the soft flesh of her inner elbow. He holds her arm up to his veined cheek as though it were a telephone receiver he was growling into.

Lily's mouth is parched, her tongue full of grit. "Let go of me," she manages, tugging to free herself.

Skinner laughs. "You thinking of calling the cops?" But he lets go with a shake. "Now don't make me ask twice, when's your husband get back?"

Lily backs away. She moves out of lunging distance but does not run. She refuses. The old man is not going to move her. She straightens her spine, roots herself to the gravel drive, then swallows deeply to unstick her mouth. "Get off my property," she tells him.

Skinner clears his throat, spits at her feet. "That's what I think about your property."

Lily looks down, surprised at the fine spray of saliva that has caught the toe of her sneaker. Same sneaker she once lobbed at his dog. When she looks up, Skinner is already hobbling down the drive.

"I'll be back when he's back, hey?" he calls to her. "Count on it."

She kicks gravel over the ball of phlegm. She is certain that he means it. Taking down a single woman is no great feat; he's waiting for the bigger billy goat to cross.

The Saab, with its leprous shedding of paint and trail dirt, looks hideous in the apartment's underground garage. Duncan notices how the cars on either side have been parked as far away as their yellow-trimmed stalls will allow.

In the trunk, the portfolio case is squeezed in between some of Lily's books and the accessories he had packed for this misguided summer: a small hibachi, two tennis rackets, and running shoes. Duncan digs out an old bottle of water he'd stashed in case of an overheated radiator and uses it now to wash down two Vicodin. He's going to need it, he thinks, as he eases into the driver's seat. Duncan takes the sling off his arm and pulls two fingers of his ruined hand out of the gauze in order to work the gearshift.

When the pain subsides a bit, he reaches over and turns the key, adjusting some controls so that the AC blows awake. A few dead leaves scatter off the dash, along with a maple bud. *Helicopters,* he remembers calling them in Minnesota, for the whirling pattern of their descent. He watches the bud, animated by the blast of air, as it strikes the sunroof and then choppers down to the passenger seat. It lands in the seam of the upholstery where a yellow pencil is neatly tucked.

It takes him a couple tries to dislodge it from the seat. Duncan's left hand won't quit shaking. When he holds it up, his fingers are vibrating so violently that the pencil turns to rubber; an illusory golden wand, chewed from pink nib to lead tip.

He places it between his teeth. It's a perfect fit.

When the Marines burned Cam Ne, they got it on film. The footage was sent home where, despite controversy, it aired on CBS. The attack on the complex of villages was documented. It existed, Cam Ne. If you wanted to, you could spool that film backward and watch, in monochrome relief, as flames in the grass-roof huts slip quietly back into upheld Zippo lighters. Watch a minute longer and you see soldiers lowering these lighters, taking the fire back. Only in the world of artifice can there be this dialogue between the before and after. A man can watch what he has done and rewind it so that the act is undone.

Duncan has watched this clip several times during the past month. Play it in reverse and the Marines suffer no consequences taking out Cam Ne. But Duncan will have to be prepared for consequences. At twelve-hundred hours, Tuesday afternoon, he should be on the twenty-third floor of the Stand and Be Counted offices in the Flatiron District, wrapping up the presentation that will secure his place as Head of the Ergophobes. Instead, he's already left the Taconic behind and has reached the municipal road, the familiar turf of dirt and blacktop.

He has finally ferreted out the dissenter: it's been himself all along. He has created enemies where there were none. Looked at Lily as though she'd pinned him to the mat, when it was his own shadow that had taken him down for the count. To have dominion over the animals, it means nothing without having gained mastery over himself, accepting the fact that he is as brokenly perfect as the day he was born.

There's a reduction that has to take place before Duncan can become the man he's wanted to be all along. To shed all his loose skin and pass not through the eye of a needle (that would be simple grade school physics) but rather, to gain the approval of his harshest self. The only way is to hold fast and let them burn the fort out from under him as he knows they will try to do.

Out on the dirt road, Duncan pops the trunk and, with his left hand, removes the boards from the portfolio case. He doesn't need to look at them anymore. He's realized that he's not alone in his lusty taste for violence; at some point every soldier, man, and monkey wants to see just what he's capable of doing. But the man—he's the only one who'll ever want to see what he's capable of undoing. Again with his left hand and the support of the inner elbow of his right arm, he piles the boards on the road, right around the spot where he was unable to euthanize the wild boar. Then he goes back to the trunk to fish the lighter fluid out from under the hibachi grill.

Here's where you kill your darlings, Duncan. Pledge loyalty to yourself. A sort of blind obedience that will not go unnoticed, will not leave a bad taste of decay and foolishness. He douses the pile of foam core boards and scripts with the fluid, then takes the lighter he stole from Lily out of his pocket. He knows this: he's following a natural trajectory, turning a graceful arc. Shredding the last paper bird of his starry-eyed innocence.

CHAPTER 34

Red Marrow

The ceiling in the bathroom is being held in place by a stretch of clear plastic and green painter tape. Cradled up in the tub, Lily finds the view as curiously satisfying as an anatomy model with a cutaway window into the abdominal cavity. As long as it holds it serves as a transparent zoological divide between her and any yellow jackets smart enough to pull up stakes and colonize further down the stretch of ceiling rafters. She has no clear plans to get the drywall replaced. In fact she has no clear plans at all. What *do* we do now? She must consider some form of escape. Take what she can carry and hop a bus to the city, or thumb a ride. How far will the old bicycle take her? Should she call Duncan or wait? At the moment she's out of her element, submerged in water, with nothing required from her other than dermal waterproofing and the usual oxygen intake.

Until she hears a vehicle pull up. Lily tenses, presses a sponge against her chest. Skinner? Or Skinner accompanied. Outside the engine cuts and a single door slams. It couldn't be Duncan—not in the middle of the week and not on the day of his presentation. As she listens, she thinks she can hear the slow drag of steps up the porch, through the front door. Yes, that's the front door opening and closing. A dilatory reminder that it has been left unlocked. Maybe it is Duncan. But what if it's not? She thinks of Lloyd for some reason. Lloyd who wrote to say he was laying low. But the Lloyd she knows is a master at biding his time. Hadn't he done that with Audiophile? Chose the isolated aisle of classics, set the snare, waited until the girl stepped in?

Although both her legs are stretched out of the tub, Lily is submerged to the neck. She tells herself she's safe underwater. The footsteps cross the foyer and start up the stairs. The Protection of Water functions along the same principles as the more commonly known Protection of Blankets.

When the shuffle of feet ends at the bathroom door, she turns to look. It's neither Lloyd nor Skinner. But is it Duncan? She sits up, her wet shoulders and breasts now exposed to someone she doesn't quite recognize. His neck and the front panels of his shirt are scorched brown, an air of smoke and something else—industrial carpeting?—carries into the bathroom ahead of him. It doesn't distract Lily from his hand, which is wrapped in a filthy cast. Both eyes are bloodshot and one boxed to a sickly plum, an injury visible despite the black streak of exhaust that runs up his face.

Lily gets out of the tub. "What happened?" She pulls on her old robe and goes to him.

"Fire. Fight. Not in that order."

She takes his undamaged hand and leads him to the edge of the tub to sit. She kneels in front of him, noticing the streaks down his face are just smudged cinders. There is a plug of dried blood in his nostril.

"Should we go to the hospital?"

He shakes his head. Further questions feel a bit useless at the moment. What would she do with a response? Instead of asking, speaking, she reaches for his shirt button. Thank God, she thinks. Thank God he's come.

Duncan is watching her. Lily's own breath strikes her with its timbre and velocity; she's embarrassed that her breathing should have these athletic qualities when all she's doing is helping him remove a burned shirt. She knows he's watching and she is terrified to meet his eyes. And these buttons. She forgets how to unfasten them. Her fingers have to relearn the motion as they work higher.

Why can't she even look at him? She has three buttons left and a
thousand things to say. But words are a tangle of bicycle locks in her
mouth. Lily pulls the shirt across Duncan's chest, eases the hand—it really
is set in a cast—through the cuff. She pretends to fuss with the shirt while
he stands and tries unzipping his jeans with the left hand. She pauses, not
like she hasn't done it before. He can't get the zipper down. So, what is
she waiting for? Lily helps him take off his jeans and boxers and all she
can see is the color of her hands pulling them away. He's unsteady on his
feet and takes the arm that she offers him for support. He gets into the
bath. Into the water that was her water. Duncan hunches into the same
position that she occupied just minutes ago. Lily is still kneeling. She puts
her hand in the tub, not to touch him, just to have this water in common.
Duncan raises his left hand, reaches for her, slips his fingers through the
hair at the nape of her neck and closes his eyes.

————————————

Later that night, the earth takes him. He's at the edge of the hole looking
down when the ground gives way under his feet. The moment is quick.
None of the slow-motion torpor of car accidents; he's licked right down.
Lily sees it all from the edge of the barley. She drops her shovel and runs
to him, her path sloppy through loose dirt.

"Duncan?" True, the trench is only three feet deep, but they have a
proclivity for laziness, forgetting trowels and spades at the bottom of the
pits. It's her fault, she should have forced him to stay in bed. Duncan had
washed and slept until evening and though he hadn't wanted to talk about
the arm in a sling, he did want to use the other one to sift through the
dirt. It was crucial—imperative—to get all they could out of the ground
before Skinner's inevitable return.

When she reaches him he's flat out on his back, the prongs of a garden rake scissoring up between his thighs.

"Jesus, did you land on it?" Lily drops to her knees.

Duncan touches his arm and winces, lifts his head. He spots the rake and looks between it and his crotch. Stunned or impressed, she can't tell which.

"Three fucking inches of grace." Lets his head fall back in the mud.

She reaches her arm down. "Here," she says. "Come up on this side."

But he doesn't move. He looks at her hand and then up at her face. She thinks the Vicodin must be slowing his reactions.

"Get in here," he says.

Lily takes her arm back slowly. Squints down the hole. "Did you hit your head?"

"Maybe." He pats the puddle beside him then extends the good arm toward her. "Join me."

She sits back on her heels. "There's slugs."

"There's no slugs."

"Leeches."

"Lily." Still looking at her.

But it's not so easy.

First of all—she'd like to tell him—*first off, I can barely hear you over all the racket going on up here.* She stares at him at the bottom of the pit. If she's learned anything this month and anything from her time with Lloyd, it's that there's never going to be a consensus among her vestigial urges and logic. So which should she listen to? When it comes to this muddy, bruised, and broken man reaching his hand out to her from the bottom of a grave, what should she do? Her mouth is dry, her tongue confused. Never has been an ace with the small words.

"Are you in trouble, Duncan?"

"I think so," he says. "Is that going to be a problem?"

Her cheek twitches. She tells it, *Shut up. Shut the hell up.*

When she kicks her feet out from underneath her, it's to slide down the same avalanched crest that took Duncan a few minutes ago. The smell of the loam is thick as old coffee. Duncan shifts the rake out from beneath and lets her squeeze in the gulch beside him. She can't help but settle into the side of his body, careful to avoid his arm. At first, the mud that seeps through her collar feels as uncomfortable as a hand that's been clutching a cold beer.

They stay like that, on their backs, looking up at their narrow slice of sky. A single bat flits past.

"It's echolocating," he says, his chest close enough to rest her head on. She could put her ear against it. Listen to the thoughts that never leave his lungs. She wants to reach her arm over him. Slide her hand into the curve of his elbow.

Lily turns her face toward his. Lips and teeth inches apart. Then she pushes up on one elbow, touches his shoulder through the muck. "Duncan?"

He turns, following her eyes behind him, and above. Lodged in the wall of slick roots and knobs, the familiar glint; a calabash of bone snared in roots and alluvium.

That night they unearth Tinker's magnificent skull. A solid amalgamation of bone marred only by a shallow fracture across the parietal bone.

Duncan gets to his knees and, with one hand, eases the globe from the dirt wall. A string of living snot escapes his nose in the effort. There's not enough room or light in the hole. Lily climbs to the rim to shine the flashlight down as he clears the root bundles from their treasure. They are both aware of the expectation, the ferocious desire to complete Tinker, to take ownership of her small body. He feels her slipping loose from the dirt, the ground finally giving up and delivering her into his hand. *Tinker, 1902.*

There's nothing left, of course, nothing to recognize of the dark woman at the edge of the photograph, holding back sunshine with one hand. Her eye cavities are enormous, silent.

We owe her this, Duncan thinks, passing the head up to Lily and crouching back down to pull away the lower jaw. He ignores the pain that's taking over his right hand. Above the earth, Lily puts the flashlight down and holds the skull up against the purple evening, rotating it in her hands, as if to give Tinker her first homecoming glance. Her first view of the grounds after a century of change.

"How did you end up in here?" she asks. "What happened to you?"

For the first time, Duncan is thankful for maggots, the sightless crawlers, thankful that they've left nothing on the bone. He's beginning to understand the importance of worms and the role they play in distancing humans from history. Not a single tooth is left in the mouth, he notes, brushing off the detached arc of jaw. This makes it easier to handle the pieces, to walk across the lawn holding a woman's mandible bone.

Lily follows him to the basement and unlocks the door. They trail mud inside. All that's left now is to place the skull at the head of the table, topping off their collection with the navigation system, the antique eyes and ears and mouth.

He can't seem to do it, though. Holding the two pieces, cradled in his sling, he turns to look at Lily. She is beautiful to him, covered in filth. When she wipes at her nose she leaves a trail of dirt across her cheek. He licks his good thumb and reaches out for her face. Just like that. As if he's been wetting his fingers and rubbing them against Lily all along. As if there has never been a gap or hesitation in this act: lick, reach, and touch.

"Hi, Wife." He just can't let it end.

"You've got grass on your forehead."

"Hi, Wife," he says again.

Lily moves toward him. He looks down at her hands. They take Tinker away from him; gingerly, they remove the two pieces from his crooked arm and carry them to the table. Place them at the apex of the clavicles. Lily's white arms are trembling too. And this he only notices when she moves back to him, reaches for him, connects their milky lengths around his shoulders. She's liquid hum against his chest.

They drop against the cellar steps and she closes her mouth around his, takes what air he has left so that she can breathe awhile underwater.

His hand moves between her spine and shirt, falls into the shallow groove of her hips. They work around the cast, their clothing comes away as if it's been loosely stitched. Foliage with no fasteners, no buttons or lace. Lily is in his mouth again, between his toes, across every hooked and hairy inch of him. There she is, licking the fresh skin behind his knees.

There they are, fucking like two maniacs on the cellar steps.

————————————

After, when they're good and splintered from the wooden staircase, when she's tethered to his lap with her legs curled around him, she says, "I still do. Love you too." Although he's unaware of having said it first. He is unaware of having said anything poetic in the last twenty minutes. In the close distance, a cannon fires. Duncan covers Lily with everything in him that isn't broken.

CHAPTER 35

Organs of Respiration

The digging commences soon after they rouse themselves from bed. It has to, it's their only advantage over other creatures waiting for nightfall. Duncan looks around the backyard. There is some definite destruction of property, willful acts of violence, going on here. The lawn is both humps and holes against a curtain of barley. Beside each pit stands the guts, a whipped mound of dirt and grass frosting.

"Do you think we'll stop? Once we find the weapon?" She stands beside him, faces the grave.

"I don't know," he says. "Let's not."

The search for the weapon (something blunt may have caused that parietal crack) has turned careless. It was bound to. After all the diligent occupation, the reverence required to handle a stranger's pieces—fiddling with her bits—sends them off the reservation. The pain in Duncan's hand is barely contained by drugs, and his small envelope is nearly empty. They become slipshod in their vehemence. There's a definite desensitization in pulling both rock and bone from the earth at random, not sure what they'll get with each overturning. Treat a rock with respect, toss a bone aside in distraction; it's bound to happen.

Lily lowers herself into a narrow trench. To loosen the dirt for his light sifting job, Duncan drills the spade into the ground and feels the ache of friction in his good palm. He's lanced and drained the first rash of blisters. But already in these farmed patches he can make out the next cycle of swell, their foamy custard filling. His blisters are generational, deliberate, vengeful.

He can't remember ever feeling so good.

He looks down at Lily, tunneling in an unexplored, southeasterly direction. Since she stopped wearing gloves, the alkaloids in the dirt have gnawed her nails down to the quick. Her hair's a nest. Her knees are notched and dented from the stones she's knelt on. What a method of resurrection, he thinks, watching her wriggle in the ditch.

And what of the splatter pattern he's left behind in the city? What of Anne, who has—no doubt—already braced her shoulder like a battering ram and taken down their apartment door? Or across town in a studio loft, how long will Leetower wear his bloodstained T-shirt of devotion?

There's also the man he's put in a hospital bed. When will Duncan begin to feel anything resembling remorse?

Even if he hadn't destroyed his campaign or Kooch's jaw, he wouldn't want to go back to the city, to the apartment, even back to last week. To that landscape of tissue and sponge. It's not sturdy enough to live on. He's afraid to leave and breathe that air again. Afraid to be left. When they find the weapon, what will they do? When will he know that he and Lily have gone deep enough? Will the hard surface make a sound underfoot, give them a solid place to start from?

There is no talk of what to do with Tinker. No ethical plan to share her with the universe or the town council. Duncan and Lily are it: sheriff, constable, and deputy. Because when you unearth your own private civilization, he thinks, you've got to do all the work yourself. You and your comrade, your lives undergoing the peculiar effects of phototropism together. Down there in that hole, scraping away, your ass, Lily, swinging with every lash of the rake.

Oh yes, this too. He has a desire for her that resembles the violence of adolescent lust. He considers jumping in the trench, kicking out a tree root for a toehold, and fucking her over a stone. Lily glances up at him during this thought, pauses, holds up her rake in prelude to a point she has yet to make.

"Don't stop, Duncan."

He knows, he feels it too.

In the cellar the woman reassembles. Spanning nearly five feet of table, she looks down through her hole-punched sacral bones, drawing legs together, arms akimbo, the graduated column of her spine missing several stories of vertebrae. The vault of her rib cage is collapsed, a frame flattened by the roof of one hundred years of dirt. At her side is a mound of bones too small to identify: various tips of fingers, delicacies of the inner ear, pivots and screws of the jaw, ankle charms.

Tinker props herself up on an elbow, fishes the small bones of her wrist from the unidentified pile, maybe a semilunar or a scaphoid. She flexes her hand, reaches up and touches the sore spot on her skull. Despite several missing fingers, she can slide and click her jaw into place. *What do we do now, Duncan?* she asks.

That night, under a rustler's moon, they finally come under siege. They have not been able to find the weapon; the day has brought only a series of irregular bones. Now they step around the parlor with the delicacy of thieves. The first round of poundings on the door has left Lily unsteady. She tries not to twitch while she peers out between the heavy paneled curtains.

There are men and there is fire and both elements come together on the front lawn with conviction. It's Skinner's anathematic return. This time he's come in the guise of peafowl flanked at the train feathers by a flock of torchbearers. They spread quickly through the yard, illuminating the shadows between boxwoods, between the house and the lean-to.

Once, Lily thought, if push came to shove, she could run for the trees. Into the woods to scale the largest pronged maple and roll its broad leaves up over her head. Now an entire clan stands between herself and the small forested patch out front. Duncan too must understand the impossible logistics of escape. He makes her come away from the window. Away from plate glass in slack casements, the double front doors that require only a well-angled kick to cave. He pulls her along the corridor, back into the belly of the house. Quickly now, through the kitchen to the cellar. Yes, the cellar, the buried warren that shelters the nanny. Lily is grateful at not having to make for the forest after all. She leans on Duncan's good arm to let him know how much better the earth is than life in the trees. They descend in tandem, the passage cramped and shabby, the familiar steps furred from hard use. How would she have survived it anyhow, a life up there in the canopy of leaves? How could she flourish when everything she desires is here below the ground?

If Duncan had counted on some tumble and yaw this summer he would never have imagined it involving the fury of townsfolk and the death of a wild boar. He looks out the small basement window to the back of the house and adjusts his sling. The path leading from the cellar door to the garden is clear but he knows they're not safe down here. That they can't hold out for long. That dry oak splinters under force and torches even easier. The doorbell's ringing. A continuous loop of "Windsor Chimes."

With his good hand wrapped in a T-shirt he's knocked out the cellar light, leaving only some quarter moon to open up shadows and spatter over the arrangement of bones on the table. He watches Lily at Tinker's side. The tragedy is this: once the nanny is discovered she'll be carted off, a loose jumble of pieces to assemble like a mobile. Later, at someone's leisure. This will be a disaster for Tinker. She's only just been reconnected, has only just begun to enjoy the touch of her rejoined limbs. If only they could hold their barricade a little while longer. A few more days of digging themselves out of stasis. At least until the pills run out.

Lily comes and pushes herself against his arm, watches him with eyes like walnuts. There's some kind of hope just past their luminous shells. Duncan leans against the cellar door, returning her touch, winding her hair around his fist. He was just beginning to remember so many things about her.

"What do we do now, Duncan?" she asks.

He doesn't know. He'd like to suggest that they just hold their breath and wait. Let the moment pass over the way time has designed it to, a slow, two-foot shuffle into history. But there's a crack of wood upstairs then. The thump of thigh and hip as ram. Brackets and hinges burst overhead, hardware is sent scurrying across floorboards with the propulsion of bullets. Then a stamp and rush. As Duncan's heart becomes the most raucous of all percussive instruments, the clabber of feet spreads up in the foyer, tracks through the house, over the well-worn grooves of their summer missteps. Just like that, the house is taken.

He unbolts the cellar door.

And then they are running, the grain slicing, a razor's nicking efficiency to all skin left visible, the underside of a chin, scored palms, inside each elbow. Sometimes he leads, sometimes they are side by side cutting a wide, ungroomed path through the crop.

They run across the fold of terrain, but no frontier awaits them. They are recusant, Duncan and Lily. Last thing he saw as they darted into the field was a rash of men boiling out of the house and into the backyard. Something followed. Something came after them through the field but now he doesn't dare look behind them—their trail of damage is easy enough to follow, the heads of barley lopped down, trammeled—but he keeps Lily's hand in his and does not look back.

What Duncan knows is that the land will provide. He tells himself, even the Cu Chi tunnels led somewhere. Into the steep embankment of the Saigon, where a comrade could be quietly washed to safety. And they're not the first to come this way. Hadn't Tinker set the course when she fled with her boy? The earth seems to remember the routing and helps to guide. They feel it tilting away from their feet; the running becomes easier, the sloping land giving momentum to their limbs.

Behind them, everything they've ever known. Ahead of them the grain breaks like a sudden relief and the threshing sound of their feet falls away and they cross into the flat slap of stubble before the river. They are cut and sore and there is the loss of Tinker's bones but behind them are fire and men.

He can hear Lily's breath, its stuttering delivery, and he goes ahead of her, tearing apart the curtain of saplings on the embankment. Tonight the river laps high, the rock table sucking up water as if quenching itself on the brackish offering. Duncan is mindful of illusion—the dark, humping hills of Ulster Landing appear to be within swimmable proximity and not the entire mile across he knows them to be. He steps on the shins of runtish trees, snapping down a path for Lily.

The sway of the current is impossible to measure in darkness. He loses the sling and enters the river, wading through the cattails and sleeping marsh wrens. The high level could mean an incoming tide and upstream flow. To the north, he knows, is Tivoli Bays, marshlands stocked with red-tailed hawks and kingfishers. The kayak routes he never got around to. Pastoral when observed from a fiberglass shell, gliding through the reeds in daylight. As the water sucks around his legs, he knows the river is conscious of him, his entrance. Is waiting to see what desperate plan he may have to swim across. Duncan steps up on a submerged rock ledge, then turns back for his wife.

Lily on the bank, sloughing off her shoes, toeing through the pokeweed and sumac. Looking for a place to start.

"Hurry, Lily." Duncan holds out his good hand to her. He sees her face quiver, but she comes to him, making a careful entry into the river that runs both ways. Her legs scissor through water until she reaches him and takes his arm.

"Here I am," she says. And there she is.

They stand to the waist in the unknown current and, in a language without words, make the decision. They agree to the one thing that is everything. Nothing else will exist after this—the house and the car and the bones—all of it gone. After tonight they will only have each other. The thought is enormous. But the warm grip of river and the smell of oily dirt calm him. Lily's hand in his, it calms him too.

The voices that rise up over the field are vaporous and distant at first, but swell as they drift down over the embankment toward them. Without speaking, they lower their bodies into the river, push off from the rocky shoals. Their quiet submersion wakes a community of waterfowl, sending it alight. Duncan and Lily paddle a clumsy ten feet from the shore, her left hand tucked under his injured arm so that they appear to move out of the reeds and into the moonlight with the pulsing locomotion of one swimming animal.

The fetch is unclear but he understands their best chance is to keep hold of one another. To stay close to the bank and go with the direction of the current, give up all thoughts of destination, of swimming with purpose. Hasn't enough time been wasted with the awkward motion of kick and stroke? The knowledge grows wide, breaks across his chest; in engineering this escape they've agreed to be carried together. As they skim out past the overhang of branches the sky is revealed, thickly seeded with stars. He signals to Lily to follow his example, to roll onto her back, as if enjoying a night dip. She flips over gently, buoys up against his left side the way he once taught her to and places her fingers in his grip.

It's possible that they'll be swept up to the mouth of the Sawkill Creek, arriving together on those estuarine banks. Or ferried downstream to the piers of the Kingston-Rhinebeck Bridge. Or beyond. All the downhill miles still to Manhattan, to the pulsing Atlantic, to the edge of the continental shelf and the vast Hudson Canyon.

But all of this comes later, he thinks. Right now they'll do well not to worry themselves with direction. Tonight their only concern is to stay afloat together, with hands joined and bones connected. Let the nautical miles bear them out. Let the river decide.

ACKNOWLEDGMENTS

This book came to be with the help of several gifted people and many safe harbors: My agent, Jamie Brenner, at Artists & Artisans for her sharp pencil and unflagging enthusiasm. My editor, Sarah Knight, at Shaye Areheart Books for her perfect pitch and craftsmanship. The long hours and tireless reads by the talented Annabel Lyon. An excellent suggestion by Tony Swofford which helped sway the course of this story. The space and confidence given to me by the MFA program at the University of British Columbia, and there, in particular, Andreas Schroeder. The Canada Council for the Arts and the Ontario Arts Council, both of which helped this book to flourish. And most of all, my family. Your enthusiasm and embrace is with me always.

Nancy Mauro lives in New York City. She has worked as a creative director and copywriter in both Canada and the United States and is a recent fellow and graduate of the prestigious MFA program at the University of British Columbia. Nancy's fiction and nonfiction have appeared in several literary magazines, newspapers, and anthologies, and her work has been recognized by the Canada Council for the Arts. She is at work on her second novel.

A   NOTE   ON   THE   TYPE

Bembo is an oldstyle serif font based on a typeface cut by Francesco Griffo for Aldus Manutius' printing of De Aetna in 1495. Today's version of Bembo was designed by Stanley Morison for the Monotype Corporation in 1929. Bembo is noted for its classic, well-proportioned letterforms and is widely used because of its readabilty.